新制多益 第二版
全真測驗通關
NEW TOEIC
TEST PRACTICE BOOK

Andrew Brown、莊耿忠 著
Rebecca Lee 英文校訂

新制多益 第二版
全真測驗通關

NEW TOEIC
TEST PRACTICE BOOK

國家圖書館出版品預行編目資料

新制多益全真測驗通關 = New TOEIC Test Practice Book / Andrew Brown, 莊耿忠著. — 二版. —
台北市 : 書林出版有限公司, 2025.05
面 ; 公分
ISBN 978-626-7605-11-0（平裝）

1. CST: 多益測驗

805.1895　　　　　　　　　　　　　　　114002133

應試高手 47
新制多益全真測驗通關 第二版
NEW TOEIC Test Practice Book, 2nd Edition

作　　　　者	Andrew Brown、莊耿忠
編　　　　輯	劉純瑀
英 文 校 訂	Rebecca Lee
校　　　　對	王建文、紀榮崧、李笑儀
出　 版　 者	書林出版有限公司
	100 台北市羅斯福路四段 60 號 3 樓
	Tel (02) 2368-4938・2365-8617　Fax (02) 2368-8929・2363-6630
台北書林書店	106 台北市新生南路三段 88 號 2 樓之 5　Tel (02) 2365-8617
學 校 業 務 部	Tel (02) 2368-7226・(04) 2376-3799・(07) 229-0300
經 銷 業 務 部	Tel (02) 2368-4938
發　 行　 人	蘇正隆
郵 政 劃 撥	15743873・書林出版有限公司
網　　　　址	http://www.bookman.com.tw
經 銷 代 理	紅螞蟻圖書有限公司
	台北市內湖區舊宗路二段 121 巷 19 號
	電話 02-2795-3656 (代表號)　傳真 02-2795-4100
登 記 證	局版臺業字第一八三一號
出 版 日 期	2025年5月二版初刷
定　　　　價	450元
I　S　B　N	978-626-7605-11-0

欲利用本書全部或部分內容者，須徵得書林出版有限公司同意或書面授權。
請洽書林出版部，Tel (02) 2368-4938。

目 錄

序 ii

關於多益測驗 iv

題型更新說明 vi

TEST 01 1

TEST 02 53

TEST 01 中譯・單字 105

TEST 02 中譯・單字 213

TEST 01 解答表 325

TEST 02 解答表 326

分數預測表 327

TEST 01 答案卡 329

TEST 02 答案卡 331

序

Simon Guey 桂慶中

市面上已經有很多有關 NEW TOEIC 的參考書，為何要推薦這一本？

第一，這本書的作者莊耿忠及 Andrew Brown 皆為 TOEIC 方面的專家，從事有關 TOEIC 的研究與教學超過十年。在成書的過程中，針對每一道題的內容及選項安排都經過深思熟慮，去蕪存菁，最後呈現出來的考題兼具高的信度與效度。

第二，Andrew Brown 是英語母語人士，具有高階的英檢學養，並因為具有英語文化的深層底氣，選擇考題內容時的仿真及精準度更高，更接近美國 ETS 測驗機構所出的全真考題。

第三，莊耿忠老師從事 TOEIC 研究教學及學生輔導超過十年，深諳 TOEIC 考生在解題過程中（不管是聽力或閱讀部分）可能碰到的難點與盲點，對症下藥，實質上幫助了成千上萬的莘莘學子。憑藉這種能力與經驗，在本書的編寫過程中，能非常深入地提供讀者必要的解說，大大減少讀者的認知負荷。

例如下面這一道題：

The iPhone 17 is expected -------- alongside the iPhone 17 Pro and Pro Max in September.

(A) to launch
(B) launching
(C) to have launched
(D) having launched

中譯 iPhone 17 預計在 9 月份與 iPhone 17 Pro 和 Pro Max 一起推出。

解析 is expected（預計）後面 + to + V~（不定詞），而 (C) to have launched 為完成式，表示發生在 is expected 之前，這與事實矛盾，故 (C) 錯誤。

讀者可以發現上面的解說淺顯易懂，這與一般類似的 TOEIC 參考書有很大的不同。相信讀者在讀完本書後，定能四兩撥千斤，以最少的努力拿到最高的分數。

　　助人為樂，與人為善，好書與大家分享，故樂之為序。

於高雄觀音山

桂慶中畢業於 Ed.D School of Education, University of New South Wales, Sydney, Australia。專攻英語教學、心理測驗、英文能力檢定、TOEIC 題型分析，並在大學及文教機構教授 TOEIC 多年。

關於多益測驗

什麼是多益測驗？

　　TOEIC 代表 Test of English for International Communication（國際溝通英語測驗）。多益測驗乃針對英語非母語人士所設計之英語能力測驗，測驗分數反映受測者在國際職場環境中與他人以英語溝通的熟稔程度。參加本測驗毋需具備專業的知識或字彙，因為測驗內容以日常使用之英語為主。多益測驗是以職場為基準點的英語能力測驗中，世界最頂級的考試。2012 年在全球有超過七百萬人報考多益測驗，並在 150 個國家中有超過 14,000 家的企業、學校或政府機構使用多益測驗，同時在全球超過 165 個國家施測，是最被廣泛接受且最方便報考的英語測驗之一。

研發單位

　　教育測驗服務社（ETS®）專精教學評量以及測驗心理學、教育政策之研究。1979 年該機構在日本企業領袖的要求下，發展出多益測驗。多年來，多益測驗已經在許多國家施行，並很快地成為職場英語能力檢定的國際標準。

測驗方式

　　多益測驗屬於紙筆測驗，時間為兩小時，總共有 200 題，全部為單選題，分作兩大部分：聽力與閱讀，兩者分開計時。

第一大類：聽力

　　總共有 100 題，共有四大題。考生會聽到各種各類英語的直述句、問句、短對話以及短獨白，然後根據所聽到的內容回答問題。聽力的考試時間大約為 45 分鐘。

　　　　PART 1：照片描述 6 題（四選一）
　　　　PART 2：應答問題 25 題（三選一）
　　　　PART 3：簡短對話 39 題（四選一）
　　　　PART 4：簡短獨白 30 題（四選一）

第二大類：閱讀

總共有 100 題，題目及選項都印在題本上。考生須閱讀多種題材的文章，然後回答相關問題。考試時間為 75 分鐘，考生可在時限內依自己能力調配閱讀及答題速度。

PART 5：句子填空 30 題（四選一）
PART 6：段落填空 16 題（四選一）
PART 7：單篇閱讀 29 題（四選一）
　　　　多篇閱讀 25 題（四選一）

考生選好答案後，要在與題目卷分開的答案卷上畫卡。雖然答題時間約為兩小時，但考試時考生尚須在答案卷上填寫個人資料，並簡短的回答關於教育與工作經歷的問卷，因此真正待在考場內時間會較長。

如何計分？

考生用鉛筆在電腦答案卷上作答。考試分數由答對題數決定，再將每一大類（聽力類、閱讀類）答對題數轉換成分數，範圍在 5 到 495 分之間。兩大類加起來即為總分，範圍在 10 到 990 分之間。答錯不倒扣。

資料來源：ETS 台灣區總代理 忠欣股份有限公司網站 http://www.toeic.com.tw/

題型更新說明

為何要更新多益英語測驗題型？

由於英語的使用現況有所進化及改變，ETS 的測驗及試題內容也必須跟進。ETS 想要確保多益英語測驗能反映出時下語言之使用情形，並檢驗受試者目前或未來在真實生活情境中所需的語言技巧。本次多益英語測驗之題型更新將包含近 10 年來使用頻率更高的溝通方法和技巧。

多益英語測驗將會有什麼改變？

為確保測驗符合考生及成績使用單位之需求，ETS 會定期重新檢驗所有測驗試題。本次多益英語測驗題型更新，反映了全球現有日常生活中社交及職場之英語使用情況。測驗本身將維持其在評量日常生活情境或職場情境英語的公平性及信效度。其中一些測驗形式將改變，然而，測驗的難易度、測驗時間或測驗分數所代表的意義將不會有所變動。

聽力測驗（Listening Comprehension）：時間 45 分鐘

\\	舊制題型說明		
PART	內容		題數
1	Photographs	照片描述	10
2	Question-Response	應答問題	30
3	Conversations - 10 conversations - 3 questions per conversation	簡短對話	30 (3×10)
4	Talks - 10 talks - 3 questions per talk	簡短獨白	30 (3×10)
	Total		100

更新後題型說明			
PART	內容		題數
1	Photographs	照片描述	6
2	Question-Response	應答問題	25
3	Conversations - 13 conversations - 3 questions per conversation	簡短對話	39 (3×13)
4	Talks - 10 talks - 3 questions per talk	簡短獨白	30 (3×10)
	Total		100

閱讀測驗（Reading Comprehension）：時間 75 分鐘

舊制題型說明			
PART	內容		題數
5	Incomplete Sentences	句子填空	40
6	Text Completion	段落填空	12 (3×4)
7	Single Passages - 9 single passages - 2-5 questions per passage	單篇閱讀	28
7	Double Passages - 4 double passages - 5 questions per text	雙篇閱讀	20
	Total		100

更新後題型說明			
PART	內容		題數
5	Incomplete Sentences	句子填空	30
6	Text Completion	段落填空	16 (4×4)
7	Single Passages - 10 single passages - 2-4 questions per passage	單篇閱讀	29
7	Multiple Passages - 2 Set-Based double passages - 3 Set-Based triple passages - 5 questions per set	多篇閱讀	25
	Total		100

聽力測驗的更新

1. PART 1 照片描述（Photographs）和 PART 2 應答問題（Question-Response）的題數減少。
2. PART 3 簡短對話（Conversations）的題數增加。
3. 對話中將會有較少的轉折，但來回交談較為頻繁。
4. 部分對話題型將會出現 2 名以上的對話者。
5. 對話中將包含母音省略（elision，如：going to→gonna）和不完整的句子（fragment，如：Yes, in a minute; Down the hall; Could you? 等省去主詞或動詞的句子）。
6. 新的題型將會測驗考生在對話中聽到什麼，以及在圖表中看到什麼。
7. 新的題型將會測驗考生談話背景或對話中所隱含的意思。

　　大部分的聽力測驗部分維持不變。測驗的總題數以及整體難易程度不變；測驗時間也不變，第一部分聽力測驗一樣需 45 分鐘的時間完成答題。

閱讀測驗的更新

1. PART 5 句子填空（Incomplete Sentences）題數減少。
2. 加入兩種題型，用以測驗考生是否理解通篇的段落結構。
   a. PART 6 段落填空（Text Completion）選項類別除原有之片語、單字、子句之外，另新增完整句子的選項。
   b. PART 7 單篇閱讀（Single Passages）題組內加入篇章結構題型，測驗考生能否理解整體文章結構，並將一個句子歸置於正確的段落。
3. 文字簡訊、即時通訊，或多人互動的線上聊天訊息內容。
4. 新增三篇閱讀題組，測驗考生是否理解內容關連性。
5. 微幅增加閱讀測驗中的單篇閱讀及多篇閱讀題數。
6. 新增引述文章部分內容，測驗考生是否理解作者希望表達之意思。

　　大部分的閱讀測驗部分將維持不變，測驗的總題數以及整體難易程度不變；測驗時間也不變，第二部分閱讀測驗一樣需 75 分鐘的時間完成答題。

TEST 01

LISTENING TEST 🎧 01

In the Listening test, you will be asked to demonstrate how well you understand spoken English. The entire Listening test will last approximately 45 minutes. There are four parts, and directions are given for each part. You must mark your answers on the separate answer sheet. Do not write your answers in your test book.

PART 1

Directions: For each question in this part, you will hear four statements about a picture in your test book. When you hear the statements, you must select the one statement that best describes what you see in the picture. Then find the number of the question on your answer sheet and mark your answer. The statements will not be printed in your test book and will be spoken only one time.

Statement (C), "He is looking at some documents." is the best description of the picture, so you should select answer(C) and mark it on your answer sheet.

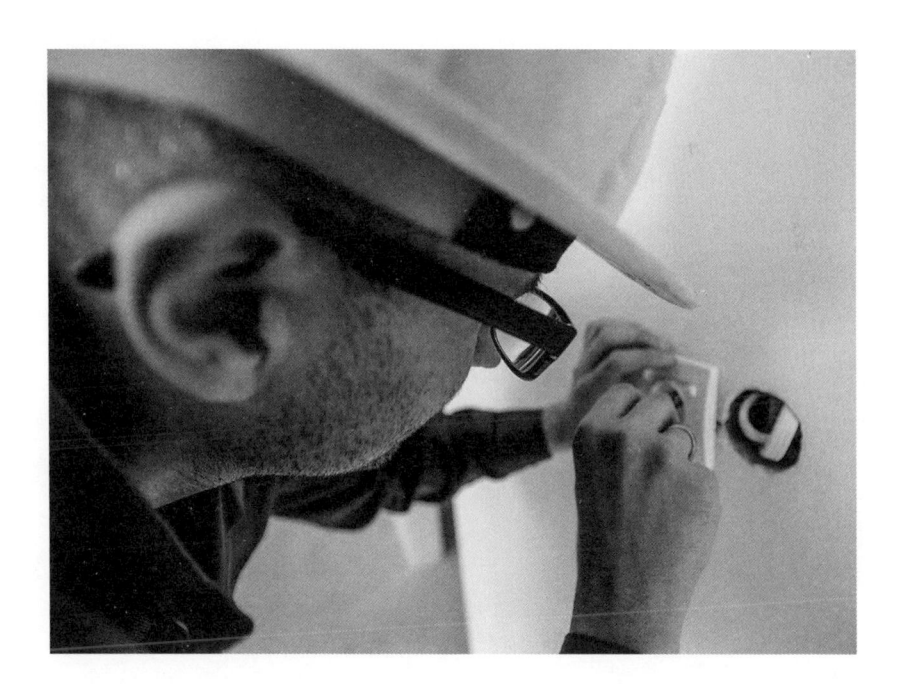

1.

2.

Go on to the next page.

3.

4.

5.

6.

PART 2 (02)

Directions: You will hear a question or statement and three responses spoken in English. They will not be printed in your test book and will be spoken only one time. Select the best response to the question or statement and mark the letter (A), (B), or (C) on your answer sheet.

7. Mark your answer on your answer sheet.

8. Mark your answer on your answer sheet.

9. Mark your answer on your answer sheet.

10. Mark your answer on your answer sheet.

11. Mark your answer on your answer sheet.

12. Mark your answer on your answer sheet.

13. Mark your answer on your answer sheet.

14. Mark your answer on your answer sheet.

15. Mark your answer on your answer sheet.

16. Mark your answer on your answer sheet.

17. Mark your answer on your answer sheet.

18. Mark your answer on your answer sheet.

19. Mark your answer on your answer sheet.

20. Mark your answer on your answer sheet.

21. Mark your answer on your answer sheet.

22. Mark your answer on your answer sheet.

23. Mark your answer on your answer sheet.

24. Mark your answer on your answer sheet.

25. Mark your answer on your answer sheet.

26. Mark your answer on your answer sheet.

27. Mark your answer on your answer sheet.

28. Mark your answer on your answer sheet.

29. Mark your answer on your answer sheet.

30. Mark your answer on your answer sheet.

31. Mark your answer on your answer sheet.

PART 3

Directions: You will hear some conversations between two or more people. You will be asked to answer three questions about what the speakers say in each conversation. Select the best response to each question and mark the letter (A), (B), (C) or (D) on your answer sheet. The conversations will not be printed in your test book and will be spoken only one time.

32. What are the speakers planning to do?
    (A) Hire secretaries.
    (B) Search for a part-time worker to sort out their files.
    (C) Train staff members how to discipline themselves.
    (D) Teach staff members how to interact with clients.

33. What is mentioned about management in the office?
    (A) Recruited workers should manage files well.
    (B) It is good to give orders to subordinates.
    (C) Managers should have authority in the workplace.
    (D) It takes a lot of effort to discipline oneself.

34. What does the man say in regards to customer service?
    (A) The new workers will need passion when talking with clients.
    (B) File management will enhance their customer service.
    (C) Keeping their office in order will increase their work quality.
    (D) Teamwork is the key to good customer service.

35. What is the conversation about?
    (A) How to avoid getting caught in a traffic jam
    (B) Why there is so much traffic at rush hour
    (C) The best way to travel around Brisbane City
    (D) How to get to Sunnybank by bus

36. Why is the 8:30 bus late?
    (A) Traffic is too heavy.
    (B) It broke down.
    (C) It left the bus station late.
    (D) The bus driver stopped for a 10-minute rest.

37. Why is it better to take bus 300?
    (A) Because bus 325 is crowded with people.
    (B) Because the earlier bus had an accident.
    (C) Because it can arrive in less than 10 minutes.
    (D) Because it can arrive faster than bus 325.

Go on to the next page.

38. What kind of people will want to buy their product?

    (A) Elderly people
    (B) Middle-aged people with an average income
    (C) Young people with little money to spend
    (D) Middle aged people who are well-off

39. What are the speakers discussing?

    (A) How to enhance their customer service in America
    (B) How domestic after-sales service should be done
    (C) What kind of people will buy scooters in Canada
    (D) The woman's findings on Canadian market research

40. What is true about the best way to enhance customer service?

    (A) Start a shop that can deal with customers' questions
    (B) Set up a repair shop in America.
    (C) Carry out a survey on customer's needs.
    (D) Hire staff who excel in handling customer enquiries

---

41. Where is the man bound for?

    (A) Hawaii
    (B) Penghu
    (C) Japan
    (D) Okinawa

42. Why isn't the ferry on time?

    (A) It was leaking.
    (B) It ran into a fierce storm.
    (C) It departed the last harbor 10 minutes late.
    (D) They are experiencing technical difficulties.

43. How did the station master make compensation to the passengers?

    (A) Give them free tickets
    (B) Give them free vouchers
    (C) Give them a refund
    (D) Give them a discount on their tickets

---

44. What are the speakers discussing?

    (A) How to save their own business from going bankrupt.
    (B) Practical ways to save a company from financial problems.
    (C) The downsides of making workers redundant.
    (D) Why they should spend money on outsourcing.

45. How did the woman say the problem should be solved?

    (A) Lay off a quarter of the workers.
    (B) Hire financial experts to help.
    (C) Keep all assets that they feel are dispensable.
    (D) Not rely on outsourcers.

46. What was said about downsizing the company?

    (A) It isn't a good idea.
    (B) It will possibly solve their problem.
    (C) It's the only way to cut costs.
    (D) It's harmful for workers' families.

---

47. What are the speakers discussing?

    (A) What they should do at the end of a fiscal year
    (B) How much money was spent last year
    (C) When to visit the tax bureau
    (D) When they will set up a joint venture

48. According to the conversation, what is a good way to know how much their business has grown?

    (A) Hand in tax returns to the government
    (B) Write a profit-and-loss statement
    (C) Count how many products have been sold this year
    (D) Ask their shareholders

49. What do they have to report to their shareholders?

    (A) The amount of tax they submitted last year
    (B) How much they are growing financially
    (C) How many products they have in stock
    (D) Their budget for the previous year

50. Where is this conversation most likely taking place?

    (A) In a business office
    (B) In a real estate company
    (C) In a telemarketing company
    (D) In a household registration office

51. What does the man ask the woman to do?

    (A) Appraise the value of a house
    (B) Sublease his apartment to her friend
    (C) Visit the exotic villa tomorrow
    (D) Persuade a customer not to buy an apartment

52. According to the man, what will get a person imprisoned?

    (A) Buying property in a red-light district
    (B) Subleasing an apartment to another person
    (C) Living in a house that was subleased
    (D) Vandalizing someone's property

53. According to the man, where are they going to set up their subsidiary?

    (A) In Singapore
    (B) In Japan
    (C) In Taiwan
    (D) In Hong Kong

54. Why is the company planning to buy a building instead of renting one?

    (A) The real estate agent will give them a discount.
    (B) They don't have to pay a large down payment.
    (C) They plan to stay in the area for a long time.
    (D) They don't want to keep changing buildings.

55. According to the woman, why is establishing a logistics company highly profitable?

    (A) It substantially increased the local employment rate in 2016.
    (B) Logistics companies make over a million a month.
    (C) It is the strongest industry in the country.
    (D) It is a niche market in Japan.

56. Where most likely is this conversation taking place?

    (A) In an overseas factory
    (B) In a business office
    (C) In a law firm
    (D) In the HR department

57. Why will Mr. Frankston get a promotion?

    (A) He led the marketing department to make more profit.
    (B) He is a very independent leader.
    (C) He holds a master's degree in management.
    (D) The president of the company elected him.

58. What problem was mentioned?

    (A) Their logistics system isn't big enough.
    (B) They spent too much money at the fundraiser.
    (C) The company's delivery speed is slow.
    (D) Why their marketing campaign wasn't successful.

59. Where most likely is the conversation taking place?

    (A) The human resources management
    (B) The procurement department
    (C) The research and development department
    (D) The IT department

60. What is true about Derek?

    (A) He lacks leadership skills.
    (B) His work ethic isn't up to scratch.
    (C) He is a pro-active worker.
    (D) He needs to work on his negotiation skills.

61. What does the woman suggest they do?

    (A) Give Derek time to prove he is a suitable candidate.
    (B) Send Derek an email.
    (C) Attend an on-the-job training course.
    (D) Phone Derek tomorrow.

Go on to the next page.

62. What are the speakers discussing?

   (A) The details of an activity
   (B) What was covered in a business meeting
   (C) How to upgrade their machinery
   (D) How much to invest in sales campaigns

63. According to the woman, how should they solve the problem of expanding to China?

   (A) Look at the problem from a different angle
   (B) Apply for a business license
   (C) Make their business more dynamic
   (D) Collaborate with the Chinese government in business

64. Who was given the role of supervising the activity in July?

   (A) Mr. Brown
   (B) The assistant manager of the sales department
   (C) Hilary Penn
   (D) The leader of the marketing department

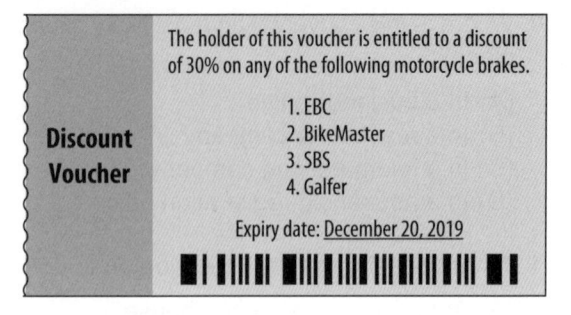

Discount Voucher

The holder of this voucher is entitled to a discount of 30% on any of the following motorcycle brakes.

1. EBC
2. BikeMaster
3. SBS
4. Galfer

Expiry date: December 20, 2019

65. Where were the brakes moved to?

   (A) Aisle 3
   (B) Aisle 4
   (C) Aisle 6
   (D) Aisle 7

66. Look at the graphic. Which brand of brakes will the man purchase today?

   (A) Galfer
   (B) BikeMaster
   (C) SBS
   (D) EBC

67. Where does the woman most likely work?

   (A) At an auto parts shop
   (B) At a paint store
   (C) At a sports store
   (D) At a restaurant

Albert's vehicle spare parts price list	
Alternator	$30
Generator	$25
Radiator	$20
Bumper	$27
Front and back door handles	$16.50

68. Where is the woman calling?

    (A) A motorbike repair store
    (B) A second-hand auto parts store
    (C) A car retailer
    (D) A mechanic shop

69. What is the man waiting for?

    (A) Spare parts for the woman's car
    (B) The products that the manager ordered
    (C) Tools to fix the car
    (D) A coupon

70. Look at the graphic. How much does the woman have to pay?

    (A) $30
    (B) $25
    (C) $16.50
    (D) $55

Go on to the next page.

PART 4 🔊04

Directions: You will hear some talks given by a single speaker. You will be asked to answer three questions about what the speaker says in each talk. Select the best response to each question and mark the letter (A), (B), (C), or (D) on your answer sheet. The talks will not be printed in your test book and will be spoken only one time.

71. What is the purpose of this announcement?

    (A) To cure breast cancer
    (B) To solicit donations
    (C) To obtain a free gift
    (D) To assist friends or family members

72. Who is the announcement for?

    (A) Those who live in Taipei
    (B) People living in Kaohsiung
    (C) People residing in Taichung City
    (D) Those who are suffering from an illness

73. When is the best time for the listeners to call the IAF?

    (A) Between 7 a.m. and 5 p.m. Central Time
    (B) Between 8 a.m. and 9 p.m. Western Time
    (C) Between 8 a.m. and 8 p.m. Pacific Time
    (D) Between 8 a.m. and 5 p.m. Pacific Time

74. Which direction is the storm front moving?

    (A) Eastern coast of USA
    (B) Southeast coast of USA
    (C) Mexico's west coastline
    (D) Mexico's north coastline

75. What does the speaker advise the audience to do?

    (A) Look at a satellite photo
    (B) Don't go out in the sun this afternoon
    (C) Put on suntan lotion tomorrow
    (D) Prepare for warmer weather

76. What will happen from Monday to Friday?

    (A) Temperatures will hit 38 degrees.
    (B) It will drizzle.
    (C) It will gradually get colder.
    (D) It will rain heavily for several days in the eastern part of America.

77. Who most likely are the listeners of the broadcast?

    (A) Bus passengers
    (B) Business executives
    (C) Vehicle drivers
    (D) Subway passengers

78. What does the speaker say about traffic?

    (A) Only one part of the city is having traffic congestion.
    (B) An accident is obstructing the traffic downtown.
    (C) It is clear on State Route 50.
    (D) It is fast only on north-south roads.

79. What is scheduled to happen at 5:30 p.m.?

    (A) The roads will be cleared.
    (B) A weather report will be broadcasted.
    (C) A baseball game will be played.
    (D) A traffic update will be aired.

80. What is the purpose of this announcement?

    (A) To notify listeners of a surfing activity
    (B) To invite people to attend a party at the town hall
    (C) To warn people of bad traffic conditions
    (D) To inform people of a parade activity

81. What did the speaker mention about lunch?

    (A) Only apple pies and strawberries will be served.
    (B) Lunch will be served prior to the activity.
    (C) People are invited to lunch at the Lifeguard Hall.
    (D) Lunch will be followed by a documentary.

82. When will cars have access to River Esplanade?

    (A) At 12 noon
    (B) At 3 p.m.
    (C) At 2:30 p.m.
    (D) At 2 p.m.

83. Where mostly likely would you hear this advertisement?

    (A) In a supermarket
    (B) On TV
    (C) On the radio
    (D) At a jewelry store

84. Who most likely is the speaker?

    (A) An office manager
    (B) A sales person
    (C) A business owner
    (D) A client

85. Which offer was NOT mentioned that would make purchasing appealing?

    (A) 10% discount
    (B) A lifetime warranty
    (C) Money-back guarantee within one year
    (D) A no-interest option for 8 months

86. What is the broadcast about?

    (A) A promotion for Apron JetStream Cafe
    (B) Gate numbers for a departing flight
    (C) Changing departure times
    (D) The boarding time for a flight to Los Angeles

87. What problem was mentioned?

    (A) The New York flight won't depart on time.
    (B) Passengers flying to Chicago will board after 3:15.
    (C) All flights for the day are cancelled.
    (D) The airport cafe will be closing early.

88. What was offered to the passengers?

    (A) A discount on flights this year
    (B) A voucher for an upgrade to business class
    (C) A refund at the counter
    (D) A ticket for free food and a drink

89. Who most likely is the speaker?

    (A) An auto parts salesman
    (B) An automobile sales manager
    (C) A government official
    (D) A mechanic

90. Why would customers be interested in going to this business?

    (A) Car buyers can get over 10% off.
    (B) It is the best auto parts shop in town.
    (C) Customers can continuously buy cars at low prices.
    (D) They repair customers' cars for free.

91. What free service does the company offer?

    (A) A free first oil change
    (B) Three years aftersales service
    (C) Free replacement of used parts
    (D) An engine stability test

Go on to the next page.

June 28th Short Speech Agenda		
Speaker	**Time**	**Topic**
Johnnie Harrison	5 minutes	The importance of finding a mentor
George Thompson	10 minutes	How my professor changed my life
Annie Johnson	3 minutes	Persevering towards success
Riana Zuckerburg	10 minutes	The best jobs to do after 2020

Brisbane Tour List of Destinations August 15, 2020	
Scenic spot name	**Time spent looking around**
City Botanic Gardens	1 hour
Catholic cathedral	20 minutes
Kangaroo Point Cliffs Park	20 minutes
Southbank	40 minutes
Queensland Art Gallery	40 minutes

92. Who is delivering this talk?

    (A) A prominent scholar
    (B) A famous athlete
    (C) A college professor
    (D) A graduating student

93. Look at the graphic. Which speaker is delivering a talk now?

    (A) Johnnie Harrison
    (B) Annie Johnson
    (C) Riana Zuckerburg
    (D) George Thompson

94. Where would you mostly likely hear this kind of talk?

    (A) At a graduation ceremony
    (B) At a presidential inauguration
    (C) In a college lecture
    (D) At a high school orientation activity

95. What is the purpose of the talk?

    (A) To educate tourists about the location of Brisbane
    (B) To survey the terrain of the Botanic Gardens
    (C) To familiarize travelers with the city's scenic spots
    (D) To convince students to attend the university

96. Look at the graphic. Which place might the tour group NOT have enough time to see today?

    (A) The Catholic cathedral
    (B) Kangaroo Point Cliffs Park
    (C) Queensland Art Gallery
    (D) Southbank

97. What will the people most likely do when the tour is finished?

    (A) Eat lunch at a restaurant near the river
    (B) Go abseiling
    (C) Go back to their hotel rooms
    (D) Take a relaxing walk around the City Botanic Gardens

Name of award	Awarded to which kind of company
Digital Technology Award	Companies with strong application of digital technologies
Best Growth Strategy of the Year Award	Companies with strong international expansion and market creation
Award for Innovation	Highly profitable and innovative companies
Global Investment Award	Companies that manage subsidiary businesses outside of their original market

98. What was the main purpose of establishing the company?

   (A) To become a highly-profitable and innovative company
   (B) To use advanced technology in their business
   (C) To compete with other biotechnology companies
   (D) To expand their business to all parts of the world

99. Look at the graphic. Which award is being conferred to Fareast Biomarine?

   (A) Digital Technology Award
   (B) Best Growth Strategy of the Year Award
   (C) Award for Innovation
   (D) Global Investment Award

100. What does the business focus on doing?

   (A) Developing nutritional products to fight cancer
   (B) Growing and harvesting a kind of small sea animal
   (C) Researching digital cellphone applications
   (D) Expanding to all parts of their domestic market

This is the end of the Listening test. Turn to Part 5 in your test book.

Go on to the next page.

READING TEST

In the Reading test, you will read a variety of texts and answer several different types of reading comprehension questions. The entire Reading test will last 75 minutes. There are three parts, and directions are given for each part. You are encouraged to answer as many questions as possible within the time allowed.

You must mark your answers on the separate answer sheet. Do not write your answers in your test book.

PART 5

Directions: A word or phrase is missing in each of the sentences below. Four answer choices are given below each sentence. Select the best answer to complete the sentence. Then mark the letter (A), (B), (C), or (D) on your answer sheet.

101. Our company is one of the most -------- and well-established travel agencies in this country.

    (A) repute
    (B) reputed
    (C) reputably
    (D) reputation

102. If you -------- for vacancies, services, or businesses in Taiwan, you have come to the right place.

    (A) are looking
    (B) were looking
    (C) have been looked
    (D) looked

103. You may also sign in if you would like to edit your -------- in the future.

    (A) advertised
    (B) advertising
    (C) advertisements
    (D) advertise

104. The iPhone 17 is expected -------- alongside the iPhone 17 Pro and Pro Max in September.

    (A) to launch
    (B) launching
    (C) to have launched
    (D) having launched

105. The General Manager has noticed that many staff members are currently not -------- to the dress code guidelines that were laid out in our firm's employee manual.

    (A) adhering
    (B) identifying
    (C) knowing
    (D) complying

106. You will no longer have to suffer -------- eye fatigue when looking at screens.

    (A) by
    (B) on
    (C) in
    (D) from

16

107. The new software, -------- was developed by our in-house team, has significantly improved our data processing speed.
    (A) that
    (B) which
    (C) they
    (D) it

108. -------- our online programs are not popular with prospective employees, they provide practical on-the-job knowledge.
    (A) Consequently
    (B) As
    (C) Instead
    (D) Although

109. The store is giving an -------- discount on this product this week! Get 25% off when you check out with the designated payment company.
    (A) addition
    (B) additional
    (C) additionally
    (D) additions

110. We have over 15 years of experience -------- with energy and power.
    (A) deals
    (B) dealing
    (C) to deal
    (D) dealt

111. Initially designed to be power saving, the new power generating device is now -------- to be high-speed spinning with zero attrition.
    (A) encoded
    (B) examined
    (C) improved
    (D) included

112. Taichung is filled with a -------- of great food from all corners of the globe.
    (A) variety
    (B) various
    (C) variously
    (D) vary

113. One of the premier -------- to enjoy both exotic and local cuisine is the Art Museum Parkway.
    (A) stations
    (B) senses
    (C) sources
    (D) spots

114. Take a look -------- the recommendations inside the folding pages of the brochure, or listen to what the wait staff has to say.
    (A) for
    (B) into
    (C) at
    (D) through

115. The university is 25 miles south of central Sydney and -------- reached by car or public transport.
    (A) greatly
    (B) shortly
    (C) rarely
    (D) easily

116. The on-the-job training offered by this teaching center is the skills, knowledge, and -------- needed to foster creative thinking.
    (A) compliments
    (B) complements
    (C) competencies
    (D) commodities

Go on to the next page.

117. Employees learn in an environment -------- they will need to practice the knowledge and skills taught in the program.

    (A) where
    (B) which
    (C) that
    (D) what

118. Our safety -------- and accident rate have been improved. As a result, all drivers in our company are now certified to drive Hi-Los.

    (A) positions
    (B) standards
    (C) requirements
    (D) concerns

119. The best employee to -------- a phone interview is the hiring manager.

    (A) conduct
    (B) consult
    (C) console
    (D) concern

120. For over 25 years, Axiomtek -------- among the major manufacturing companies in the field of industrial computers and embedded systems.

    (A) was
    (B) had been
    (C) has been
    (D) is

121. Since its establishment, the company has -------- gained worldwide recognition for its innovative designs.

    (A) incredibly
    (B) successfully
    (C) probably
    (D) fortunately

122. As a valuable and reliable industrial manufacturer, this corporation is devoted to producing -------- solutions that support users in achieving success.

    (A) on-the-job
    (B) versus
    (C) state-of-the-art
    (D) diplomatic

123. Our consulting company takes pride in what we do through our -------- to excellence.

    (A) component
    (B) composite
    (C) condition
    (D) commitment

124. Our focus is on developing new products -------- the most advanced technologies and customer-based experiences.

    (A) using
    (B) to use
    (C) uses
    (D) used

125. The company provides an extensive line of industrial computers, -------- embedded eBOX & tBOX systems.

    (A) includes
    (B) including
    (C) to include
    (D) included

126. Our goal is to develop high-quality and cost- -------- server appliance hardware platforms.

    (A) effective
    (B) deductive
    (C) creative
    (D) submissive

127. The free association techniques used in psychoanalysis empower the analyst with chances of knowing -------- is happening in the patients' unconsciousness.

    (A) what
    (B) it
    (C) that
    (D) which

128. The theory initiated by Jean Piaget is a -------- view on human cognitive development.

    (A) contemporary
    (B) revolutionary
    (C) necessary
    (D) compulsory

129. For the deaf or hard-of-hearing, complete -------- to Microsoft products and customer services is available.

    (A) process
    (B) access
    (C) recess
    (D) excess

130. For those majoring in psychology, the position of personality assessment is -------- in the personnel department.

    (A) appreciable
    (B) considerable
    (C) predictable
    (D) available

Go on to the next page.

PART 6

Directions: Read the texts that follow. A word, phrase, or sentence is missing in parts of each text. Four answer choices for each question are given below the text. Select the best answer to complete the text. Then mark the letter (A), (B), (C), or (D) on your answer sheet.

Questions 131-134 refer to the following advertisement.

Join us for a spectacular trip to see waterfalls and cascades along the Kashez River. The first few miles are ---------- flat, and the Kashez River is mostly out of sight. ----------, there
                                     131   132
will be views of the surrounding mountains. After about 2 miles, the trail will begin to run alongside the Kashez River. ----------. But then it will begin its 500-foot descent to Black Cascade.
                                                   133
Along the descent, there are numerous waterfalls and cascades ---------- the river makes its
                                                                        134
way to lower elevation.

131. (A) surprisingly
     (B) frequently
     (C) presumably
     (D) relatively

132. (A) Besides
     (B) However
     (C) Or else
     (D) Accordingly

133. (A) At first, the river is relatively calm.
     (B) People used to come here.
     (C) Most visitors like to be here.
     (D) It is a pleasant experience.

134. (A) so
     (B) thus
     (C) as
     (D) but

Questions 135-138 refer to the following letter.

May 5
Blake Wood, General Manager
Linden Appliances
30 Botany Road

Dear Mrs. Wood,

I am here to draw your attention to an issue we have had with a recent order from yourselves (ref no.46MA38RT). Not only was the ---------- **135** a week later than agreed, but when we tried to use the spare parts, we found that 50% of them were ---------- **136** and basically useless. I spoke to your customer service manager, Jane Brown, about this matter. I hoped that you would replace the damaged spare parts, but she informed me that the spare parts were intact when delivered to us. ---------- **137** .

I believe that I am entitled to an explanation as to why Jane Brown has not answered my email. ---------- **138** this issue is dealt with promptly, then unfortunately, we will be forced to take further action. Please inform me how you are going to resolve this issue with the least possible delay.

Sincerely,
Gary White
Sigma Production Director

---

135. (A) delivered
(B) delivering
(C) delivery
(D) deliver

136. (A) damaged
(B) devastated
(C) destroyed
(D) detained

137. (A) I was pretty upset.
(B) I talked back to her to vent my anger.
(C) I felt angry and decided not to talk to her again.
(D) I emailed her last week, but still received no response.

138. (A) Otherwise
(B) Nevertheless
(C) Unless
(D) Therefore

Questions 139-142 refer to the following letter.

Dear Mr. Sage,

After our ----------- on Monday, my business partners and I talked about the situation, and we
           139
concluded that we intend to buy your business, Twice Over. We are willing to pay your

----------- purchase price of $75,000, which includes both the business and all the equipment
  140
necessary to operate it, as per our discussion.

-----------. We will ----------- all the necessary paperwork. These documents will be signed and
  141   142
completed, and we will tender payment, as agreed.

Sincerely,
James Brown

139. (A) negotiation
     (B) conversation
     (C) promotion
     (D) discussion

140. (A) request
     (B) requesting
     (C) requested
     (D) requests

141. (A) We would like to meet with you next Monday, October 5, to finalize the sale.
     (B) We would like to call you next Monday, October 5, to inform you of the sale.
     (C) Both parties will have to hire a lawyer.
     (D) Both parties will have to resolve the conflict through legal procedures.

142. (A) fetch
     (B) carry
     (C) make
     (D) switch

Questions 143-146 refer to the following letter.

Mr. Peter Frantz
108 Oxford Street
Glen Cove, MA 39452

Dear Mr. Frantz,

Thank you for your letter ---------- April 4, 2020. In response to your request for more information about our company, I am ---------- with this letter a brochure about our company. ----------.
I will be available to meet with you next week. Please call my secretary anytime to set up an appointment. ----------, if you have any questions, please feel free to call me at 482-9278.

Sincerely,
Sophia Smith
Executive Manager

143. (A) dates
 (B) dated
 (C) dating
 (D) date

144. (A) enclosing
 (B) enclosure
 (C) enclosed
 (D) enclose

145. (A) You are expected to know more.
 (B) I hope you find it helpful.
 (C) It is assumed that you are knowledgeable.
 (D) You will be well-informed.

146. (A) Above all
 (B) Up to the present
 (C) After a while
 (D) In the meantime

PART 7

Directions: In this part you will read a selection of texts, such as magazine and newspaper articles, emails, and instant messages. Each text or set of texts is followed by several questions. Select the best answer for each question and mark the letter (A), (B), (C), or (D) on your answer sheet.

Questions 147-148 refer to the following letter.

Date: July 1, 2019

Petra Hamilton
48 Montague Rd, Sunnybank Hills,
Brisbane, QLD 4101

Notice of Intent to Vacate

Dear Petra Hamilton,

This letter comprises my written 30-day notice that I will be moving out of the flat that I am renting from you on July 31, 2019.

I am leaving because I got a new job in another part of the city. If you find any serious problems with the flat, please contact me as soon as possible.

Please be sure to advise me on when you will return my security deposit of $300, and also if you will be deducting any money for damages other than normal wear and tear.

You can reach me at 0979-055022 and 25 Shell Road, Morningside, Brisbane, QLD 4170 after July 15, 2019.

Sincerely,
Jesse Hilton

18 Dorchester St.,
Coopers Plains, Brisbane, QLD 4101

147. Why is Jesse Hilton moving?
(A) The location of the flat is too inconvenient.
(B) He found a new job.
(C) The rent is too expensive.
(D) The flat lacks basic amenities.

148. Where will Jesse Hilton be after July 15?
(A) In Sydney
(B) In America on a business trip
(C) In a different suburb of Brisbane
(D) In Coopers Plains

Questions 149-150 refer to the following online chat discussion.

Oliver [15:33]:	Hi, Lily! I want to know how to make an international call to Jamaica. Is the country code 2?
Lily [15:34]:	Are you residing in the USA?
Oliver [15:35]:	Yes, in Indiana.
Lily [15:36]:	Well, the country code is actually 1. Next, you need to dial the area code 876.
Oliver [15:37]:	Ok. Got it. Then I just dial the person's local phone number, right?
Lily [15:39]:	Yes. Then you should be able to reach them.
Oliver [15:40]:	What if the line is blocked? Last time my friend called a country near Jamaica, they couldn't get through.
Lily [15:43]:	That is because most telephone service providers give people the option to block all international calls. That is why the call couldn't be made.

149. What information is Oliver asking Lily for?

   (A) The contact details of a Jamaican enterprise
   (B) The best time to ring their overseas buyer
   (C) How to make a phone call to a different country
   (D) A way to block international calls

150. What is indicated about telephone service providers?

   (A) They provide poor phone reception.
   (B) They allow people to block calls from overseas.
   (C) Their customer service quality is poor.
   (D) They limit customers to making domestic calls.

Go on to the next page.

Questions 151-152 refer to the following advertisement.

Bobco Plumbers

A well-established company is seeking 4 energetic and experienced plumbers.

Hours: Monday to Friday, 8:30 a.m. to 6:00 p.m. plus overtime (evenings and weekends)

Contract: On-going

Pay: Negotiable

Job description: Bobco Plumbers is Melbourne's largest independent plumbing company. Due to expansion and an increase of Spanish speaking clients, we have vacancies for fully-qualified plumbers who are proficient in Spanish or at least can communicate at a conversational level.

Duties: Doing interpretation of blueprints and building specifications to completely map the positions of pipes, drainage systems etc. Also, installation of fixtures, fix water supply lines and systems for waste disposal. All applicants must be proactive and be able to provide excellent customer service.

151. What is true about the nature of the work advertised?
    (A) Workers will have to repair broken windows.
    (B) Workers will spend most time in the office.
    (C) Workers will be required to install pipes.
    (D) Workers will have to interpret statistical graphs.

152. What special skills do applicants need to possess?
    (A) Ability to construct buildings
    (B) A good command of the Spanish language
    (C) Be able to draw up blueprints for city buildings
    (D) Be able to answer customer inquiries

Questions 153-154 refer to the following memorandum.

To:	All Staff <stafflist@freeway.com>
From:	supervisor@freeway.com
Date:	March 4
Subject:	March 12 closure

I have recently been advised that the electricity in this building will be cut off next Tuesday due to the fact that repairs will be conducted on the electrical system. This will make it very hard for us to get anything done, so everyone will be allowed to take a day off work. I hope that everyone can find a way to continue your responsibilities from home.

The team leaders who are in charge of doing South American market research need to email me any of their findings. I will need them Wednesday morning before the annual conference.

Regards,
Sally Willington

153. Why will the office NOT be open on Tuesday?

(A) The general manager will be away on a business trip.
(B) All employees will attend the conference.
(C) There will be no electricity in the building.
(D) No one needs to work on market research.

154. What does Mrs. Willington tell the team leaders to do?

(A) Send her an email
(B) Have a meeting about conducting market research
(C) Avoid using electricity
(D) Contact an electrician

Go on to the next page.

Questions 155-157 refer to the following news article.

Publix Restaurant Chain Ownership up for Sale

On Friday, Forever International, a large organic health care chain store based in Utah, announced its plans to acquire the Publix restaurant chain. Henry Miller, the owner of the chain, had been considering holding a large auction so he could pass on ownership of the chain. As stated by people with inside information, Publix has officially decided to not change the restaurant's name as part of the deal. Mr. Miller built his business from the ground up 35 years ago subsequent to graduating from business school. It was only a matter of time before the business started to become highly profitable. After 4 years' time, he had already started restaurants in Saint George, Logan and Cedar City. Now it has expanded to over 40 locations nationwide.

155. In the news article, the word "acquire" in line 2, is closest in meaning to

(A) obtain
(B) surrender
(C) release
(D) accept

156. What is suggested about Mr. Miller?

(A) Publix has expanded to many parts of America.
(B) He started Publix over 40 years ago.
(C) He is skilled at negotiating.
(D) He majored in finance.

157. What kind of a company is Forever International?

(A) A restaurant chain store
(B) A large organic chain store
(C) An international trade company
(D) A sole proprietorship

Questions 158-160 refer to the following email.

To:	f.andrews@chinatravel.net
From:	zhangwu@gmail.com
Date:	June 16
Subject:	India travel

Dear Mr. Andrews,

My name is Zhang-wu Yang, I'm an avid traveler and cyclist who is residing in Beijing City, China. While flipping through a local travel magazine, I came across chinatravel.net. Your site seems to be an all-inclusive resource for travel-themed articles and related news about China.

I'd like to bring your attention to an electronic guidebook that my company recently published. It introduces all of my best-loved traveling routes in Chengdu and contains a complete collection of maps, mile markers, and precise descriptions of scenic spots. I also noticed that you included a specific page which is devoted to cycling around China; could you please mention my travel guide on this website?

The title of my book is *Around China in Two Months*, and can be bought through www.aroundchinaintwomonths.com/BS4KX. I would be extremely grateful if you could share this with those who subscribe to your website and weekly emails.

Thanks so much,
Zhang-wu

158. What is indicated about Mr. Yang?

(A) He lives in Chengdu City.
(B) He is a tour guide in China.
(C) He is passionate about traveling.
(D) He is in charge of a travel website.

159. Why is Mr. Yang writing to Mr. Andrews?

(A) To recommend his own travel guide
(B) To do appraisal of a business article
(C) To recommend a tour of China
(D) To confirm the publication of his new story

160. In the email, the word "all-inclusive" in paragraph 1, line 3, is closest in meaning to

(A) comprehensive
(B) absolute
(C) accurate
(D) finished

Go on to the next page.

Questions 161-163 refer to the following article.

Sharp Communication Skills Make Outstanding Business Leaders

Richard Branson, a highly successful billionaire and founder of the Virgin Group, attaches great value to developing strong communication skills. He once stated that "Being an adept communicator is the most important skill any entrepreneur or business leader can possess."

Mastering the art of communication is the key to having an advantage over your competition and to influencing others. One of the most important communication skills to cultivate is the ability to give a powerful presentation. Here are several ways to help you deliver an exceptional presentation so that you stand out from the crowd.

Research: The first step in preparing for a speech is to conduct in-depth research on your topic. When that is done, one should structure an outline and jot down the key facts to support the key message of your speech. Next, revise the content you will cover, rehearse your speech by repeating your content aloud more than three times. Doing strict preparation, as well as learning from each presentation, can help to not only improve your presentation skills, but also gain more confidence in your public speaking ability.

Focus: A speech that rambles isn't going to impress the audience because it will make the speaker seem to be unorganized and egotistic. Before writing the outline of your speech, make sure that you write down the key point of your speech in one sentence and then expand and develop the speech's structure and content from that key sentence. Only by aiming to satisfy the interests and needs of your listeners will you be able to keep them engaged while you are speaking.

Passion: Having a deep passion for the subject is contagious and helps you engage your audience while you are speaking. Leaders who show passion when delivering presentations come across as more charismatic and authentic. Studies have shown that those who convey information with sincerity are more persuasive and can exert a stronger influence over their audience.

To sum up, honing your communication skills by regularly practicing public speaking is the best way for you to transform into a powerful and influential leader in your company.

161. According to the article, why is it important for businessmen to enhance their communication skills?

    (A) They will have a better public image.
    (B) It can help them to have the upper hand over their competitors.
    (C) It can turn them into passionate people.
    (D) They can become sincere people.

162. The word "egotistic" in paragraph 4, line 2, is closest in meaning to

    (A) self-centered
    (B) modest
    (C) reserved
    (D) passionate

163. What is indicated about the way to appealing to one's audience?

    (A) Delete filler words from your speech
    (B) Digress from the subject you are covering
    (C) Continuously revise the content you write
    (D) Be enthusiastic about the topic they talk about

Go on to the next page.

Questions 164-167 refer to the following online chat discussion.

Tommy: [4:13 p.m.]	Two weeks ago, we signed a contract with AVAPowerPC and they agreed to finish complete construction of our website by the 19th of September, 2019. However, on the 20th I gave them a call and was told that only one-third of the website was finished.
Stanley: [4:14 p.m.]	What does the contract stipulate in regards to what they have to finish for us?
Franklin: [4:16 p.m.]	It says that the visual design, site development, site-mapping and wireframing should be done. What about the content design?
Tommy: [4:18 p.m.]	We agreed to do half of the content design, because there are some complicated parts of content that only people with expertise can complete.
Stanley: [4:19 p.m.]	There is something else that you may have overlooked. In the prior written agreement, it states that Tommy has to give them our part of the information for them to type into the website's structure by the 15th of September, 2019.
Tommy: [4:21 p.m.]	Oh no. It completely slipped my mind. I was so tied up with other work in the office.
Stanley: [4:25 p.m.]	Well, I guess we know the reason now. Tommy failed to fulfill his obligation, which constitutes a breach of contract, so we can't really terminate the contract or seek monetary damages.
Franklin: [4:28 p.m.]	How long did they say it will take them to finish setting up the website and have it launched?
Tommy: [4:29 p.m.]	About another 10 days. We can extend the deadline for the company so they can finish what they agreed to do. But I will need to negotiate this with the team leader of this project, and see if we can reach a consensus on how to handle this problem.

164. What was Tommy supposed to give the website developing company?

(A) A copy of the contract
(B) A copy of the prior written agreement
(C) A detailed explanation of how to complete the website
(D) His company's complex information

165. What is indicated about the work AVAPowerPC agreed to do?

(A) Build a website by the 20th of September, 2019
(B) Finish designing all of the content
(C) Do website development and visual design
(D) Type up the company's difficult content

166. What will Tommy most likely do next?

(A) Negotiate the price of building a website
(B) Visit AVAPowerPC Company
(C) Finish the rest of the website himself
(D) Try to reach an agreement about the project's new deadline

167. At 4:21 p.m., what does Tommy mean when he writes "It completely slipped my mind"?

(A) He didn't take a clear look at the prior written agreement.
(B) He forgot to sign the contract.
(C) He forgot to give the website developers his company's information.
(D) He didn't finish typing up the information on time.

Go on to the next page.

Questions 168-171 refer to the following news article.

At a press conference on May 22, Donald Alberta, president of National Association of Investors Corporation, announced that the construction of a massive LEGO World Theme Park in Okinawa, Japan will commence in one month's time. Mr. Alberta expressed his desire for this large-scale case to improve the regional economy and tourism industry by attracting many investors from Taiwan and Japan. -[1]-

With many getting wind of this project, there have been growing concerns from tourist guides and local people that constructing such an attraction will encroach on the surrounding areas. -[2]-

According to a survey, most citizens and business owners in the neighbouring areas view this as a positive sign. "The new theme park will be highly appealing to tourists. It will be beneficial for this area in the long term," said Lucas Smith, an Okinawa resident and hotel owner. -[3]-

This theme park will not only capture people's interest, but it will also be a great place for the masses to enjoy outdoor entertainment. -[4]- The research conducted by experts in tourism shows that the revenue generated by tourists who visit will not only be beneficial to the theme park founder, it will also greatly invigorate the local tourist industry.

The theme park will include an adventure submarine ride where people can search for treasure in a sunken LEGO shipwreck. There will be more than 1,500 real animals, including fish, stingrays and sharks that will swim around the tank while riders are exploring.

---

168. What does the article discuss?

(A) An investment project
(B) Why Japan's tourism industry needs to be boosted
(C) A rapid growth in the entertainment industry
(D) Tourist attractions promoted by local magazines

169. In which of the positions marked [1], [2], [3] and [4] does the following sentence best belong?
"Nonetheless, the theme park will undoubtedly breathe life into the economy in neighboring areas."

(A) [1]
(B) [2]
(C) [3]
(D) [4]

170. What is true about the theme park?

(A) It will be based in mainland Japan.
(B) It will have over 2,000 kinds of animals.
(C) You can take a submarine ride and hunt for treasure.
(D) Construction will start in the middle of August.

171. What is suggested about the influence of the theme park?

(A) It will stimulate Okinawa's economic growth.
(B) It will have a negative influence on surrounding hotels.
(C) Many Chinese people will invest in the island's tourism industry.
(D) People will gain more interest in LEGO.

Questions 172-175 refer to the following announcement.

Company Budget Surplus

I'm pleased to announce that, for the first time in three years, our company has a modest budget surplus. -[1]- This was only made possible by each department's prudent spending throughout the last three quarters. Owing to the fact that our accountant has confirmed that this surplus is a sign of an increase in profits, we are planning to reinvest 30% of this money into our business to increase our productivity and lower the amount of taxes we have to pay. -[2]- These monies will be set aside for two purposes. Firstly, money from the budget surplus will be used to upgrade our office machines and invest in machinery that will bring in greater profit. Secondly, we will expand our production capacity by spending more money on employee training, opening another factory in Tanzi Industrial Zone, and increasing the use of marketing in our expansion.

-[3]- Department managers and division chiefs, please send me a memo and specify which items in your offices or department are taking a lot of wear and tear, and should be our first priority to upgrade or replace. Also include a detailed explanation of the particular products that absolutely need to be bought and how they will benefit you in your future work. It is important to note that we will lose any funds that aren't used up by the end of July this year.

-[4]- Further information on our plans for expansion and dates for employee training will be announced in one month from now.

General Manager
Taylor Wittham

172. In which of the positions marked [1], [2], [3] and [4] does the following sentence best belong?

    "Within a month's time, department managers and division chiefs will be notified of the precise amount that will be at their disposal."

    (A) [1]
    (B) [2]
    (C) [3]
    (D) [4]

173. The word "capacity" in paragraph 1, line 9, is closest in meaning to

    (A) size
    (B) facility
    (C) stability
    (D) competency

174. What will the company do in the near future?

    (A) Increase training sessions for employees
    (B) Open up a subsidiary in Nantun District
    (C) Expand their business to Europe
    (D) Establish a logistics company

175. Why do the department managers and division chiefs have to send the general manager a memo?

    (A) They have to state which items in their office need to be replaced.
    (B) They need to explain how cooperating with other departments is beneficial to their work.
    (C) They have to notify their manager how to pay less tax.
    (D) They have to inform their CEO how their budget surplus was spent.

Questions 176-180 refer to the following form and letter.

Hotel One, Noosa, Sunshine Coast

Thank you for choosing to stay at Hotel One. In a concerted effort to enhance the quality of customer service and make all guests feel a greater sense of belonging in our hotel, we are kindly asking your honest opinion on your experience during your stay. Please spend some time to fill out the survey and return it to the receptionist when you check out.

Date: July 15
Customer Name: Jacob Morrison
Phone number: (07) 5447 5440

The purpose of your visit at our hotel was   ☐ Business   ☐ Pleasure   ☑ Both

	Excellent	Good	Average	Below Average	Poor
Friendliness of front desk staff	✓				
Room and bathroom cleanliness				✓	
Comfortable bed and furniture		✓			
Reasonable price of room		✓			
Heating and cooling within the room		✓			
Décor			✓		
Overall, how would you rate our staff's hospitality, courtesy, kindness and ability to handle all problems?			✓		
Your OVERALL EXPERIENCE as a guest			✓		

How likely would you choose to stay at this hotel again if you were to return to this area? __50:50__
Would you recommend this hotel to someone else, if they needed to find a hotel in this area? __No__

■ Comments:

I stayed in Hotel One for 3 nights. My first impression of this place was the customer service was super friendly. Not only were all three receptionists at the front desk competent, but they were also able to answer all of my questions and went out of their way to have my bags delivered to my room on the second floor. However, I experienced some problems on the second and third nights of my stay. At night time, I tried to turn on the hot water but after two minutes it was still cold, so I called room service workers to have someone fix it. Later on, a room service staff called and told me that my room wouldn't have hot water for the next two nights. Even though I was allowed to take a shower in another room, I felt this inconvenience made my stay a little uncomfortable. On the third evening, I expected to have my room cleaned up after I returned from sightseeing. However, when I got back, the beds weren't made and the floor was still a little dirty. Aren't the housemaids supposed to clean up the guests' rooms in the daytime while the guests aren't present? I need someone to explain why both of these things happened ASAP. Overall, I suggest that you upgrade the quality of your hotel's amenities and learn to handle emergencies in a way that won't have a negative influence on guests during their stay.

Go on to the next page.

Jacob Morrison
55 Mackay St, Moore 4606
QLD, Australia

Dear Jacob,

I'm the head manager of Noosa's Hotel One. It has been brought to my attention that your recent visit to our hotel was not up to par. As you are aware, providing the highest level of hospitality and making our guests feel at home here is our number one priority. Hearing that some aspects of our hotel's service have fallen below that standard is certainly something we will address promptly.

Even though there is no excuse for what happened those two nights, I'd like to explain the reason behind those problems. There was a pipe break in the same section of the building that you were staying and we couldn't find a plumber until the third day of your stay. The problem was more serious than we thought and repairing the pipe took a lot longer than we anticipated. On top of that, what made matters worse is two of the housemaids who are in charge of cleaning called in sick on the morning of the third day of your stay and we couldn't find anyone to do their work.

I truly hope that you can forgive us for the inconvenience and trouble this may have caused you. As a gesture of good will, we request you to kindly accept a free stay of two nights at our hotel the next time you come here as compensation for what you experienced.

Sincerely,
Marvin Smith
30 Sunset Dr., Noosa, 4567
QLD, Australia

176. What was the result of the housemaids calling in sick on Mr. Morrison's last day at the hotel?

(A) Mr. Morrison's room wasn't cleaned up before he came back.
(B) No one could fix the pipes when there was no hot water.
(C) The manager had to take a long time looking for someone to do the work.
(D) The halls weren't cleaned up after Mr. Morrison returned.

177. What does Mr. Morrison indicate about his stay at the hotel?

(A) The housemaid's cleaning skills are not up to scratch.
(B) He is dissatisfied with the interior decoration.
(C) The receptionists need to work on enhancing their customer service.
(D) He feels the staff workers don't know how to deal with emergencies properly.

178. In the letter, the word "gesture" in paragraph 3, line 2, is closest in meaning to

(A) command
(B) expression
(C) bid
(D) motion

179. What was mentioned about the problems that occurred during the second and third night of Mr. Morrison's stay?

(A) Mr. Morrison couldn't use any water because of an electricity problem.
(B) Mr. Morrison's room was left untidy because the housemaids forgot to clean it up.
(C) It took a long time to find a plumber and have the pipes fixed.
(D) The housemaids did a lousy job of making his bed.

180. How did Mr. Smith choose to compensate Mr. Morrison for the problems that he experienced?

(A) Give him a voucher to use at a nearby hotel
(B) Allow him to stay in Hotel One for two nights
(C) Give him a refund on the last two nights of his stay
(D) Give him a 3-night stay for free

Go on to the next page.

Questions 181-185 refer to the following receipt and letter.

Natman Hardware
Door Hardware Price List

568 Widget Street, Kingaroy, 4608
QLD, Australia

Email: jacobm.natman@gmail.com

Phone: 305-714-6120

👍 Top quality! Top Service!

Customer Order No. 568-479-280

Date: December 5, 2019

Client Name: Jacob Morrison

Client Address: 55 Mackay St, Moore 4606 QLD, Australia

Quantity	Description	Price per unit	Total cost of products
44	Door hinges	$6.30	$277.20
24	Door knobs	$8.50	$204.00
60	Door knockers	$5.00	$300.00
10	Mail slots	$4.50	$45.00
		Sales Tax (5%)	$41.31
		Total	$877.51

Note: Delivery fee is $10.

Jacob Morrison
55 Mackay St, Moore, 4606 QLD
Australia

December 6, 2019

Dear Mr. Morrison,

Not long after we sent out your order and receipt for the goods ordered on the 5th of December, you sent us an email and made the following complaint: "The items that we purchased last week were just delivered to my shop. After carefully looking everything over, I feel that there has been a real big screw-up. Firstly, there were 6 missing from the box and we received 5 hinges that were different from what we paid for. Also, there are 10 mail slots that seem to be broken. Finally, when the delivery man showed us the receipt, the total price of all 4 products was $10 more expensive than what we agreed on last week. If there has been a change in the price of products, shouldn't we be informed about it before you sent out the products?"

We examined the cause of your receiving the wrong amount of products and now understand why this happened. The person who was in charge of packing the boxes accidentally confused your order with another order. However, we are unsure who is responsible for the broken items. In two days, I'll send a worker to your company to retrieve the 5 door hinges and the broken parts. As I will be visiting a customer in close vicinity of your shop around 10 a.m. next Thursday, I'll deliver all the replacement items, including the items missing from your last order. In regards to the change of price, last time I mentioned that we will be charging $10 extra for the delivery fee. I hope that you accept our heartfelt apology for what happened. To make it up to you, we will give you free delivery for all items you order from us in the next two months as well as a 10% discount on the total price of the mail slots. I'll do everything in my power to ensure this doesn't happen again.

If you have any other enquiries, please don't hesitate to contact me.

Sincerely,
Jason Spears
General Manager, Natman Hardware

181. What is indicated about the door hinges?

(A) Over ten of them were broken.
(B) Some were damaged by the delivery man.
(C) The worker who packed the boxes sent Mr. Morrison the wrong order.
(D) Seven of the door hinges delivered were different from what Mr. Morrison ordered.

182. In the letter, the word "retrieve" in paragraph 2, line 5, is closest in meaning to

(A) repair
(B) get back
(C) save
(D) find

183. How much will Mr. Morrison have to pay for the mail slots?

(A) $45.00
(B) $40.00
(C) $44.50
(D) $40.50

184. How many door hinges did Mr. Morrison receive on December 5?

(A) 50
(B) 44
(C) 40
(D) 38

185. How did Mr. Spears promise to compensate Mr. Morrison?

(A) Give him a 5% discount on all items for the next month
(B) Cover the cost of product delivery until March 2019
(C) Not charge him delivery fees for the next two months.
(D) Have the door hinges and mail slots delivered for only $5

Questions 186-190 refer to the following schedule, email, and message.

Sygnio Inc.
Weekly Shift Schedule with Pay

Date Name	Mon 12/5	Tue 12/6	Wed 12/7	Thu 12/8	Fri 12/9	Sat 12/10	Sun 12/11	Hrs	Pay
Sarah Brighton	10 hrs	12 hrs	10 hrs	12 hrs	12 hrs	OFF	OFF	56	$1288
James Mitchell	10 hrs	12 hrs	10 hrs	8 hrs	10 hrs	OFF	OFF	50	$1150
Douglas Witton	OFF	OFF	12 hrs	12 hrs	10 hrs	12 hrs	11 hrs	57	$1172
Andrew Fitzgerald	12 hrs	OFF	12 hrs	OFF	9 hrs	OFF	OFF	33	$759

To:	masterchief.sygnio@gmail.com
From:	magnificent.sygnio@gmail.com
Subject:	Mistake in Shift Payment

Dear Mr. Harrison,

I just took a look at the schedule that was given to us. I think you made a mistake in calculating the amount of money I will be paid for last week's work. Let me explain and you can judge for yourself.

Firstly, last Tuesday morning I substituted for Douglas, because he took sick leave during the first two days of the week. That day, I worked a total of 10 hours. Secondly, I was originally going to take my personal leave on Tuesday. But when I was asked to come into work last Tuesday morning, I asked you if I could take Thursday off instead. Could you please adjust these details on the schedule and clarify the exact amount of money that I will be paid?

Thirdly, Sarah claims to have worked for 12 hours on Wednesday. If that is the case, and we get paid $23 dollars per hour during weekdays, she should be paid an extra $46 dollars for last week's work. Please confirm this.

Sincerely,
Andrew Fitzgerald

Dear Andrew,

Thanks for your email. I checked out the number of hours that you and Sarah worked last week. My answer is as follows:

1. You were right about everything you said about your pay. You can rest assured we will pay you for the work done on Tuesday.

2. I recall what happened last Wednesday. I asked Sarah to stay in the factory and work a total of 13 hours. That means she'll get another 23 dollars on top of what you said in your last email.

If there are any more issues regarding the payment you feel you deserve and your reason is valid, I'm open to negotiation.

Mr. Harrison

---

186. In the email, the word "clarify" in paragraph 2, line 5, is closest in meaning to

    (A) make clear
    (B) complicate
    (C) adjust
    (D) systematize

187. How many extra hours does the boss need to pay Andrew for his work?

    (A) 8 hours
    (B) 9 hours
    (C) 10 hours
    (D) 12 hours

188. For what day of work will Sarah get paid an extra $69?

    (A) Sunday
    (B) Monday
    (C) Tuesday
    (D) Wednesday

189. Why did Andrew have to work on Tuesday?

    (A) Douglas had to visit a wholesaler.
    (B) James had to re-install the multi-media software in the IT department.
    (C) Douglas came down with an illness.
    (D) Sarah had to take personal leave on Tuesday.

190. What is indicated about the hourly wages?

    (A) All workers make $30 on weekends.
    (B) Workers get paid on the 10th of every month.
    (C) All workers are paid $23 per hour.
    (D) Those who work overtime are compensated $30 per hour.

Questions 191-195 refer to the following job advertisement, online chat discussion and text message.

Balthazar French Cuisine

WE ARE HIRING!

Position: Restaurant manager

Job responsibilities:

- Demonstrate accountability for all budgets
- Order supplies
- Ensure that the restaurant complies with licensing, hygiene and health, and safety legislation/guidelines
- Seasonally update and change the key dishes on menus
- Conduct staff recruitment, training and supervision
- Increase company sales and forecasting future company performance

Qualifications and Skills

- More than 4 years of QSR experience
- A thorough understanding of how restaurants are operated
- Ability to work efficiently in a stressful environment
- Ability to coach and motivate staff members
- Ability to effectively advertise a restaurant through the media
- Experience in handling company budgets
- Experience in increasing company performance based on future financial forecasts
- Experience in innovatively promoting restaurants at trade and community events
- No criminal record and a satisfactory health checkup

How to apply:

Send your resume to George Finley, HR manager: gfinleymobilerestaurant@gmail.com.
For any inquiries about the job's details, please call George Hillster on 0956 476 367, or add my LINE: toronto777.

Go on to the next page.

Terry Hudson: (10:30 a.m.)	Hello, Mr. Hillster. How are you? My name is Terry Hudson. I just emailed you my resume. I hope you have had time to look it over.
George Hillster: (10:32 a.m.)	Yes, I'm taking a look right now. So far, most of your previous experience as a restaurant manager shows that you are the person we are hoping to hire. However, owing to the fact that you didn't mention anything about how you facilitate restaurant promotion activities at local events, I need you to explain how you went about increasing your customer base with the application of correct advertisement strategies while you were the manager at Cookston Country Club.
Terry Hudson: (10:37 a.m.)	During my time at the restaurant, I looked at events that were happening in my local area, and tried my best to get involved. For example, at the end of the year our community held a semi-marathon. I sent some staff to the venue and distributed pamphlets that said we would offer a discount for people who provided evidence that they finished or participated in the race. This brought in about 30 people, most of whom have become regular customers.
George Hillster: (10:42 a.m.)	That sounds great.
Terry Hudson: (10:43 a.m.)	I wish to clarify one aspect of my experience. I have only worked in one restaurant that served Eastern cuisine. Will I still be qualified for the position without 4 years of QSR experience?
George Hillster: (10:46 a.m.)	This will depend on how good you are at training new employees, as this will help to upgrade customer service and decrease the staff turnover rate. Our head chef has one last question to ask you before we consider whether or not to take you on board. Please reply as promptly as possible. Her question is, "If you were hired as our manager, how would you go about staff training?"
Terry Hudson: (10:50 a.m.)	Could I reply in twenty minutes from now? I have to handle some personal matters that just came up.

Hi, Mr. Hillster,

My answer to your last question is as follows.

I would first give them an orientation so they understand our restaurant's culture, regulations and way of cooking. Second, I would assign supervisory roles to my experienced employees so that they can lead and train new and current staff in different departments. Next, I would hire external trainers to teach employees additional work skills so that the employees feel motivated and appreciated by the company. Finally, I would recognize two of the top employees of the month by giving them an award so that I can boost overall staff morale and improve their work productivity.

Terry Hudson: (11:12 a.m.)

191. In the text message, the word "morale" in the second line from bottom, is closest in meaning to

   (A) reputation
   (B) appearance
   (C) personality
   (D) confidence

192. Why would Mr. Hudson mostly likely be hired?

   (A) He used to be a manager at a fast food restaurant.
   (B) He is adept at training staff.
   (C) His advertising methods are effective.
   (D) He has the ability to handle stress.

193. How did Mr. Hudson demonstrate competence in advertising his restaurant?

   (A) He took advantage of local events to bring in new customers.
   (B) His new employee training included getting involved in restaurant marketing.
   (C) He gave discounts to frequent customers.
   (D) He gave awards to employees for bringing new guests to the restaurant.

194. What is true about the methods Mr. Hudson mentioned about employee training?

   (A) He would have new employees learn how to cook from a manual.
   (B) He would motivate staff members by awarding the most diligent workers.
   (C) He would teach all employees how to run a restaurant.
   (D) He would teach staff members how to handle stress.

195. Which of the following qualifications in Mr. Hudson's resume does he need to include more information to show that he is qualified for the position?

   (A) Experience of innovatively promoting restaurants at trade and community events
   (B) Ability to effectively advertise restaurant through the media
   (C) Ability to work efficiently in a stressful environment
   (D) Experience handling company budgets and increasing company performance based on future financial forecasts

Questions 196-200 refer to the following form, letter, and email.

Name	Background and Expertise	
Dr. Fredrick Arkens	**Division:** Mental illnesses **Current job:** Chief of the Psychiatry Department at Jen-Ai Hospital, Taichung.	**Specializes in:** • Addiction treatment • Child and adolescent health issues • Pain management
Dr. Benjamin Brown	**Division:** Children's health **Current job:** Attending Pediatric Physician at Taichung Chengqing Hospital	**Specializes in:** • Children's cardiology • Children's infectious diseases • Cardiac rhythm disorders
Dr. Bob Taylor	**Division:** Woman's health and pregnancy **Current job:** Doctor at National Taiwan University, Faculty of Medicine, Affiliated Hospital	**Specializes in:** • Infertility • Maternal-Fetal Medicine • Nurse Midwifery
Dr. Robert Perks	**Division:** Orthopedics **Current job:** Chief of Orthopedic Surgery Department at China Medical University Hospital in Taichung City	**Specializes in:** • Shoulder and knee surgery • Foot and ankle surgery • Sports injuries
Dr. George Malcom	**Division:** Plastic and Reconstructive Surgery **Current job:** Attending Plastic and Reconstructive Surgeon at Taichung Lin Xin Hospital	**Specializes in:** • Breast surgery • Laser surgery • Skin cancer surgery

Gillard,

Thanks for offering to take my friends and I to see different doctors next week. Before we set out, I need to explain what health problems we are experiencing.

Three days ago, I injured myself while I was playing an intense game of volleyball with my friends and the tendons in the back of my left hamstring started to hurt. I am in dire need of finding the right doctor to help me recover.

Second, Isabella and her husband have made an appointment with a doctor in Taipei for next Tuesday because they need to ask some questions about how to use natural medicine and herbs to boost her fertility.

Next, Abigail has been suffering from trauma since last year and needs to get some drugs to help her fall asleep at night. She has been thinking of seeing Dr. Arkens, but she would like to know more about his background as a doctor before she makes her final choice.

Finally, Elijah's son was diagnosed with heart disease and was advised to return to see his doctor before the end of this month.

Thanks so much for your help.

Olivia Gilbert

To:	o.gilbert@yahoo.net
From:	gillard@gmail.com
Date:	July 26
Cc:	egrey@yahoo.net; abigail555@hotmail.com; isabella1988.fredricks@hotmail.com
Subject:	Next week's doctors visit

Dear Mrs. Gilbert,

I just got in touch with the Orthopedic Surgery at China Medical University, and found out some news which you will find surprising. As of last month, Dr. Perks relocated to Hong Kong and started practicing medicine in his own clinic there. I've found a more suitable doctor for you whose name is Nancy Sioux. She graduated from Stanford Medical School and completed her orthopedic residency at Lutheran St. John's Medical Center in Boston. She is a leading expert in the field of sports medicine in Taiwan and is highly proficient in healing sports-related injuries. I'll take you to her clinic near Taichung Veterans Hospital next Thursday.

Second, I did a thorough check into Dr. Arkens' medical background and found him to be a competent and experienced doctor. Not only does he prescribe natural medicine that can help alleviate the effects of anxiety and insomnia, but he also spends extra time counseling patients so that they gradually mentally recover and return to a normal life.

Please inform your three friends that I'll be going to Taipei next Tuesday, and the next day I'll have time to go to the hospitals in Taichung City.

Yours,
Gillard Allerton

196. What is true about the Dr. Robert Perks?

(A) He specializes in spine and shoulder surgery.
(B) He recently moved to Hong Kong to start up a new clinic.
(C) He will help Olivia with her tendon injury.
(D) He is experienced when it comes to elbow surgery.

197. Why is Dr. Arkens a suitable doctor for Abigail?

(A) He is able to reduce the effects of depression.
(B) He can help her overcome her addiction.
(C) He has experience helping young people with sleeping problems.
(D) He is able to counsel her so she can get over her trauma.

198. What is suggested about Dr. Sioux?

(A) She can help Olivia with her tendon injury.
(B) She graduated from Harvard Medical School.
(C) She did her internship at St. Luke's Medical Center in Seattle.
(D) She is adept at skull reconstruction.

199. In the email, the word "alleviate" in paragraph 2, line 3, is closest in meaning to

(A) ease
(B) agitate
(C) sustain
(D) assist

200. Which of the four people will be taken to hospitals in Taichung?

(A) Isabella, Elijah's son, and Abigail
(B) Isabella and Olivia
(C) Olivia and Elijah's son
(D) Abigail, Elijah's son, and Olivia

Stop! This is the end of the test. If you finish before time is called, you may go back to Parts 5, 6, and 7 and check your work.

TEST 02

LISTENING TEST 05

In the Listening test, you will be asked to demonstrate how well you understand spoken English. The entire Listening test will last approximately 45 minutes. There are four parts, and directions are given for each part. You must mark your answers on the separate answer sheet. Do not write your answers in your test book.

PART 1

Directions: For each question in this part, you will hear four statements about a picture in your test book. When you hear the statements, you must select the one statement that best describes what you see in the picture. Then find the number of the question on your answer sheet and mark your answer. The statements will not be printed in your test book and will be spoken only one time.

Statement (C), "He is looking at some documents." is the best description of the picture, so you should select answer(C) and mark it on your answer sheet.

1.

2.

Go on to the next page.

3.

4.

5.

6.

PART 2 (06)

Directions: You will hear a question or statement and three responses spoken in English. They will not be printed in your test book and will be spoken only one time. Select the best response to the question or statement and mark the letter (A), (B), or (C) on your answer sheet.

7. Mark your answer on your answer sheet.
8. Mark your answer on your answer sheet.
9. Mark your answer on your answer sheet.
10. Mark your answer on your answer sheet.
11. Mark your answer on your answer sheet.
12. Mark your answer on your answer sheet.
13. Mark your answer on your answer sheet.
14. Mark your answer on your answer sheet.
15. Mark your answer on your answer sheet.
16. Mark your answer on your answer sheet.
17. Mark your answer on your answer sheet.
18. Mark your answer on your answer sheet.
19. Mark your answer on your answer sheet.
20. Mark your answer on your answer sheet.
21. Mark your answer on your answer sheet.
22. Mark your answer on your answer sheet.
23. Mark your answer on your answer sheet.
24. Mark your answer on your answer sheet.
25. Mark your answer on your answer sheet.
26. Mark your answer on your answer sheet.
27. Mark your answer on your answer sheet.
28. Mark your answer on your answer sheet.
29. Mark your answer on your answer sheet.
30. Mark your answer on your answer sheet.
31. Mark your answer on your answer sheet.

PART 3 🎧 07

Directions: You will hear some conversations between two or more people. You will be asked to answer three questions about what the speakers say in each conversation. Select the best response to each question and mark the letter (A), (B), (C) or (D) on your answer sheet. The conversations will not be printed in your test book and will be spoken only one time.

32. What kind of car does the man want to rent?

    (A) Compact
    (B) Economy
    (C) Standard
    (D) Minivan

33. According to the woman, how much does the man have to pay for the damage waiver per day?

    (A) $11
    (B) $12
    (C) $13
    (D) $14

34. What fee did the man pay today?

    (A) Damage waiver
    (B) Personal accident insurance
    (C) Supplemental liability insurance
    (D) A deposit

35. What is the conversation about?

    (A) Ways to introduce a person's company.
    (B) The amount of salary managers should be paid.
    (C) How to help employees gain compensation.
    (D) How to decrease the turnover rate.

36. What do the speakers say about things to do in an interview?

    (A) Only focus on finding competent workers
    (B) Tell candidates about specific workplace culture
    (C) Offer high wages to attract skilled workers
    (D) Give the candidate a lot of praise

37. According to the man, how should their company show appreciation for workers?

    (A) Reward them for their hard work
    (B) Give them an award
    (C) Give them longer holidays
    (D) Give them more compensation leave

Go on to the next page.

38. What problem was mentioned?
    (A) Their production line is producing faulty products.
    (B) Their quality control manager wants to resign.
    (C) One of their customers is buying from another factory.
    (D) A client said they didn't receive products they ordered.

39. How will the problem influence the company?
    (A) They won't be able to mass-produce products again.
    (B) They will make less profit.
    (C) Their logistics department will lose money.
    (D) They will lose customers in Spain.

40. What products were sent last month?
    (A) Some radiators
    (B) 40 motors
    (C) 50 air conditioners
    (D) 20 car fans

41. What are the speakers mainly discussing?
    (A) Ways to exercise effectively
    (B) What to do after an operation
    (C) The best dentist to visit
    (D) Dental health and eye surgery

42. What problem did the woman say her father had?
    (A) He sprained his ankle.
    (B) He felt nauseous.
    (C) He suffered from periodontal disease.
    (D) Ten of his teeth fell out.

43. Where did the woman go last week?
    (A) To an operating room
    (B) To the gym
    (C) To a rehabilitation center
    (D) To her company's headquarters

44. Why didn't the man receive the goods he ordered?
    (A) The airplane carrying his goods departed too late.
    (B) He didn't pay the shipping fees.
    (C) The freight plane had an accident.
    (D) The woman forgot to dispatch the goods.

45. Who did the woman contact?
    (A) A law firm
    (B) An advertising company
    (C) A logistics company
    (D) A technology repair shop

46. When will the man receive his order of semiconductors?
    (A) In 3 days' time
    (B) In one week's time
    (C) 2 days later
    (D) Tomorrow

47. What is the conversation about?
    (A) How to get ready for a press release
    (B) The best way to test their prototype
    (C) The specifications of their product
    (D) How they should handle the reporter's interview

48. What will be sent to the news reporter?
    (A) Their press release and a cover letter
    (B) A staff member's resume
    (C) An article about how the product was tested
    (D) Specific details about how the product was manufactured

49. What product is going to be launched?
    (A) A new sports car
    (B) A smartphone
    (C) A truck
    (D) A four-wheel drive jeep

50. What problem does the woman mention?

    (A) She is under a lot of pressure at work.
    (B) She has a cavity.
    (C) She was diagnosed with cancer.
    (D) She had a nervous breakdown.

51. How does the man suggest the woman solve the problem?

    (A) Go on a holiday
    (B) Brush your teeth more than once a day
    (C) Visit a clinic
    (D) Decrease the stress in her life

52. What does the man say about exercise?

    (A) Working out can reduce stress levels.
    (B) He lifts weights 4 times a week.
    (C) Doing intense exercise is harmful.
    (D) Jogging makes one's heart stronger.

53. What was mentioned about the book that was published in 2019?

    (A) It was written on logistics administration.
    (B) The title of the book was *Stockholders*.
    (C) Over 100,000 copies were sold.
    (D) The price of one book is US $10.

54. What is true about the next book they will write?

    (A) It will be sold in Japan.
    (B) It will be a colorful book about vintage cars.
    (C) It will be a book for children.
    (D) The title will be *Colors of the Rainbow*.

55. When was the book *The Rich Mentality* published?

    (A) Last month
    (B) In January
    (C) In July
    (D) Four months ago

56. What was mentioned about the people who had an accident?

    (A) They hit a tree.
    (B) Their car was fixable after the accident.
    (C) They haven't fully recovered.
    (D) They paid around about $34,000 for their car.

57. What happened to the woman's car?

    (A) It was damaged by vandals.
    (B) It got hit by a falling tree.
    (C) It was destroyed in an earthquake.
    (D) It was hit by a truck.

58. Why won't the woman be compensated for her car's damage?

    (A) Her car was stolen.
    (B) She hasn't paid her premium for the past two months.
    (C) She didn't buy insurance.
    (D) The damages were a result of a natural disaster.

59. How much was the Ford Model A bought for?

    (A) About $555,000
    (B) Around $600,000
    (C) Roughly half a million dollars
    (D) Under $400,000

60. Where did the man purchase the painting?

    (A) At an art store in Paris
    (B) At an auction in France
    (C) At a shop in Germany
    (D) At a sale in Vienna

61. According to the man, what should bidders NOT do?

    (A) Start serious bidding in the morning
    (B) Tell others the exact items you plan to buy
    (C) Spend all of your energy before noon
    (D) Spend most of your money after lunchtime

Go on to the next page.

| Beastland Cinema |||||
| Weekly Showtimes: Sunday, July 21st to Saturday, July 27th |||||
Title	Genre	Evening Show	Night Show
The Calling	Crime/ Thriller	7:00	9:40
Interstellar	Adventure	7:10	9:15
Edge of Tomorrow	Action	7:20	9:25
The Equalizer	Action	7:15	9:30

62. Why doesn't the man want to watch the thriller movie?

    (A) Its movie trailer seems boring.
    (B) It has too much violence.
    (C) He just wants to read the novel.
    (D) He only is interested in comedy movies.

63. Look at the graphic. What is the name of the movie that the man wants to watch?

    (A) *The Calling*
    (B) *Interstellar*
    (C) *Edge of Tomorrow*
    (D) *The Equalizer*

64. What is the 7:15 movie about?

    (A) A man who stands up for innocent people
    (B) A movie about crime
    (C) A dramatic movie that was based on a novel
    (D) A crime movie with lots of killing

| Market Australia Website, Wordpress Inc. ||
Website construction fees	
1. Design & Building	$200
2. Content Creation	$280
3. Training	$20
4. Future Maintenance	$50

65. What is said about the Wordpress Inc.?

    (A) They are getting behind on their work.
    (B) They have just completed a website.
    (C) They provide customers with user friendly platforms.
    (D) They don't know how to fix their company's computers.

66. What is being tested now?

    (A) The company's website
    (B) The company's laptops
    (C) The iPads used by the company staff
    (D) The company's telephone system

67. Look at the graphic. How much does the company have to pay Wordpress Inc. for their services?

    (A) $280
    (B) $200
    (C) $50
    (D) $20

Name	Problem mentioned
Rita Williams	Dirty floor
Britney Spears	The company app isn't working
Carol Duncan	Didn't arrive at destination on time
Vanessa Aiko	Didn't receive a discount

68. Where do the speakers most likely work?

(A) At a taxi company
(B) At a train station
(C) At a law firm
(D) At a trade company

69. Look at the graphic. Which customer are the speakers talking about?

(A) Rita Williams
(B) Britney Spears
(C) Carol Duncan
(D) Vanessa Aiko

70. What will the speakers do next?

(A) Review their list of customer complaints
(B) Fill up on petrol
(C) Rearrange their staff schedules
(D) Organize a program to train drivers

Go on to the next page.

PART 4 (08)

Directions: You will hear some talks given by a single speaker. You will be asked to answer three questions about what the speaker says in each talk. Select the best response to each question and mark the letter (A), (B), (C), or (D) on your answer sheet. The talks will not be printed in your test book and will be spoken only one time.

71. What problem did Rudy mention?
    (A) He can't contact Alex.
    (B) Alex ordered the wrong amount of auto parts.
    (C) He will be late for the conference.
    (D) The deal with Gerber fell through.

72. What is Joy most likely to do next?
    (A) Check if Alex's number is correct
    (B) Meet with Rudy to discuss the Gerber project
    (C) Visit Rudy's office
    (D) Go to the conference

73. What did the speaker mention about Mr. Vaughn?
    (A) He'll be ordering some auto parts.
    (B) He is charging Rudy's company with plagiarism.
    (C) He's too busy to attend the annual conference.
    (D) He is the manager of a subsidiary company.

74. What kind of parents would be eager to buy this book?
    (A) Parents with disobedient children and teenagers
    (B) Parents with newborn babies
    (C) Parents with children who perform poorly on tests
    (D) Elderly parents

75. What have other people mentioned about this book?
    (A) It is helpful for understanding how to reward children.
    (B) They wish they had bought it before they had children.
    (C) It offers effective advice.
    (D) It was relatively easy to understand.

76. What kind of book is being advertised?
    (A) A history book
    (B) A fitness book
    (C) A biography
    (D) A parenting guide

77. What is the broadcast about?
    (A) Donald Trump signing a deal with India
    (B) American entrepreneurs investing in Indian restaurants
    (C) How India has become so prosperous
    (D) Why Donald Trump plans to buy Indian property

78. What is suggested about India's economic situation?
    (A) The current president is helping India to flourish.
    (B) India's stock market is getting stronger.
    (C) Growing real estate prices are not appealing to investors.
    (D) India is thriving mainly because of American investment.

79. According to the broadcast, why is investment in Delhi attractive to Donald Trump?
    (A) The price of property is lower compared to America.
    (B) Investment in the city's apartments is quite cheap.
    (C) He wants to buy a tower in Mumbai.
    (D) The president promised to give him a discount on Delhi property.

---

80. What is this news report about?
    (A) Mr. Philidor being charged for defaming an online critic.
    (B) Aaron Philidor filing a lawsuit against people for slandering his stepbrother.
    (C) The story of a financial advisor winning a lawsuit.
    (D) How to avoid getting into trouble with the law.

81. What is suggested about Ray Butowsky's conduct?
    (A) His business practices are unethical.
    (B) He is a man of great integrity.
    (C) He said things to ruin a journalist's reputation.
    (D) The comments he makes on live TV are too objective.

82. What charges were made against the *Toronto Times*?
    (A) They spread theories on the media about nature of Seth Dickson's death.
    (B) They offered Aaron Philidor a platform to lie about others.
    (C) They called Dyllan Velvet a criminal.
    (D) They made a dishonest deal with NBS News.

---

83. What kind of work does Loupe-Chaufourier specialize in?
    (A) Art collection and preservation
    (B) Leading art enthusiasts through art museums
    (C) International business
    (D) Tours of Austria

84. Why does the ad suggest customers make appointments in advance?
    (A) Denis Loupe and Claude Chaufourier's business schedule is hard to predict.
    (B) Denis Loupe and Claude Chaufourier are usually out of Austria.
    (C) They are often called away on business trips to France.
    (D) It is difficult to make an appointment with them for the weekends.

85. What kind of items are mostly likely displayed in Denis Loupe and Claude Chaufourier's business?
    (A) Books that describe the history of France.
    (B) Maps of Germany
    (C) A wide variety of art from many parts of Europe
    (D) Antiques from South America

---

86. Why will the speaker visit Ryan at 10 p.m.?
    (A) To give her documents she forgot to bring
    (B) They have to discuss an important project
    (C) They need to pack their luggage into the car
    (D) To show her a business proposal

87. Why does the speaker want Ryan to leave at an earlier time?
    (A) She has to attend a conference meeting at 8 a.m.
    (B) She has to collect her motorbike from the mechanic shop.
    (C) She was informed that the airport changed the departure time.
    (D) She hopes that Ryan doesn't arrive at the airport too late.

88. Where most likely will the speaker take Ryan?
    (A) To a repair shop
    (B) To a cafeteria
    (C) To an airport
    (D) To a bus stop

Go on to the next page.

89. Why isn't the Harriston Law Firm open today?

    (A) Its office is being refurbished.
    (B) It is relocating to another building.
    (C) The business went bankrupt.
    (D) It is vacation time.

90. What does the speaker mention will happen tomorrow?

    (A) They will take on a new receptionist.
    (B) They will offer some legal services on different floors.
    (C) The organization will shorten its business hours.
    (D) All attorneys will help with moving.

91. According to the speaker, how long do clients have to wait before the business starts operating again?

    (A) 2 days
    (B) 1 day
    (C) 1 week
    (D) 3 days

92. What is the purpose of the 2019 meeting?

    (A) To learn more about their subsidiary's growth
    (B) To gain insights into investment opportunities
    (C) To broaden their knowledge of accounting
    (D) To understand how much their mother company has grown

93. What was Mary asked to do?

    (A) Order another ticket for a shareholder
    (B) Cancel the secretary's ticket
    (C) Write the meeting minutes
    (D) Hold a meeting with the treasurer

94. What is TRUE about the upcoming conference?

    (A) Many shareholders from the company will attend the event.
    (B) Board members will be in charge of electing a new vice manager.
    (C) The vice president of the company will not attend.
    (D) The treasurer won't be able to come.

Meeting Agenda (updated on 1st of May)	
Presenter	Topic
Jackie Klein	Delay in delivery of products
Zhang Wu-Qin	Expansion of subsidiaries into China
Jessie Mollick	Printing of new brochure
Jimmy Stratham	New office location

95. Where most likely does the speaker work?

    (A) At a thermal power plant
    (B) At a department store
    (C) At a trading company
    (D) At an appliance retailer

96. What problem was mentioned?

    (A) There was a delay in the delivery of some goods.
    (B) Two dates on the schedule aren't correct.
    (C) Expansion to China is not possible.
    (D) They can't obtain a permit to do business overseas.

97. Look at the graphic. Which presenter might NOT have a chance to present during the meeting?

    (A) Zhang Wu-Qin
    (B) Jimmy Stratham
    (C) Jackie Klein
    (D) Jessie Mollick

Product order form Date: Friday, December 8		
Name of product	**Product price**	**Delivery Date**
Large royal sofa	$300	December 12
King-sized bed	$370	December 12
Queen-sized bed	$230	December 22
Pantry	$55	December 24
Stacking cabinet	$50	December 25

98. What is the telephone message about?

    (A) Changing a delivery date
    (B) Adjusting the date of a convention
    (C) Why Mr. Parker should get a promotion
    (D) The arrangement of a staff recruitment program

99. Look at the graphic. When will the mentioned items be delivered to Mr. Hilston's home?

    (A) December 12
    (B) December 22
    (C) December 19
    (D) December 14

100. What did Mr. Hilston say he will do today?

    (A) Pay the store a short visit
    (B) Call the furniture store back
    (C) Transfer money to the furniture store's account
    (D) Pick up the items he ordered

This is the end of the Listening test. Turn to Part 5 in your test book.

Go on to the next page.

READING TEST

In the Reading test, you will read a variety of texts and answer several different types of reading comprehension questions. The entire Reading test will last 75 minutes. There are three parts, and directions are given for each part. You are encouraged to answer as many questions as possible within the time allowed.

You must mark your answers on the separate answer sheet. Do not write your answers in your test book.

PART 5

Directions: A word or phrase is missing in each of the sentences below. Four answer choices are given below each sentence. Select the best answer to complete the sentence. Then mark the letter (A), (B), (C), or (D) on your answer sheet.

101. The annual Conference on International Cooperation -------- next month.

    (A) will hold
    (B) are held
    (C) is held
    (D) will be held

102. If you have any questions or concerns, please do not hesitate to -------- us at 380-9048 and ask for Jane Lee.

    (A) touch
    (B) debrief
    (C) welcome
    (D) contact

103. Due to the recent floods, all public parks will be closed -------- further notice.

    (A) until
    (B) during
    (C) before
    (D) unless

104. Come and see our new apartment -------- from 2 to 5 bedrooms.

    (A) ranged
    (B) ranges
    (C) range
    (D) ranging

105. All our flats have -------- carpeting, modern kitchen appliances, and spacious bedrooms.

    (A) face-to-face
    (B) room-to-room
    (C) wall-to-wall
    (D) door-to-door

106. Mr. Jacob -------- a great asset to our company over the years and we will miss him.

    (A) was
    (B) has been
    (C) used to be
    (D) will be

107. It is my pleasure to -------- you with information about Kent University's business management program.
    (A) inform
    (B) offer
    (C) support
    (D) provide

108. The sixteen courses required for the business management -------- take two years to complete.
    (A) diploma
    (B) certificate
    (C) degree
    (D) level

109. Please feel free to contact me with any questions -------- the business management program.
    (A) concerning
    (B) concernment
    (C) concerned
    (D) concerns

110. Cruise Direct is a leading online cruise travel company dedicated to -------- its customers with access to great deals on cruise vacations.
    (A) providing
    (B) provide
    (C) provided
    (D) provision

111. We work with the industry's leading suppliers, and that gives us -------- to special rates.
    (A) access
    (B) exit
    (C) pavement
    (D) road

112. Our company is so confident -------- we're willing to back up all the deals on our site with a price guarantee!
    (A) as
    (B) that
    (C) when
    (D) but

113. When it's time to make your reservation, our cutting- -------- booking engine gives you live pricing and availability.
    (A) piece
    (B) section
    (C) margin
    (D) edge

114. -------- you ever need the advice of an expert, our service staff are available via phone and LiveChat.
    (A) Would
    (B) Could
    (C) Should
    (D) Must

115. It would be helpful if you would -------- this authorization so the vendors will recognize me as your agent.
    (A) confirm
    (B) console
    (C) concern
    (D) conduct

116. If you would, please sign this document, save a copy, and return the -------- to me at your convenience.
    (A) draft
    (B) copy
    (C) original
    (D) replicate

Go on to the next page.

117. As an attorney and a long-time friend of your parents, I am -------- that you would turn to me for legal counsel.
    (A) pleasing
    (B) pleased
    (C) pleasant
    (D) pleasure

118. I -------- such rude treatment for several weeks from one of your tellers that I refuse to tolerate it any longer.
    (A) have experienced
    (B) experienced
    (C) had experienced
    (D) am experiencing

119. I am writing a letter in the hope of -------- a position as a laboratory assistant during next year's field-work in International Valley.
    (A) securing
    (B) requiring
    (C) demanding
    (D) struggling

120. I am sorry that I will be unable to -------- a time to meet with you next Thursday to discuss your career plans.
    (A) estimate
    (B) predict
    (C) schedule
    (D) obtain

121. During our last meeting, we came to some -------- decisions about working together.
    (A) primary
    (B) preliminary
    (C) preparatory
    (D) perfunctory

122. As --------, I have enclosed a copy of our most recent catalog, complete with price guides.
    (A) promising
    (B) promise
    (C) promised
    (D) promises

123. -------- I understand the need to restructure our department, I disagree with the plan to lay off nearly half of my staff.
    (A) Whether
    (B) While
    (C) When
    (D) Where

124. We have read your -------- plans to improve our tax deductible investment procedures and are very interested in your proposal.
    (A) innovate
    (B) innovative
    (C) innovation
    (D) innovating

125. If you can comply -------- our work requirements, please call me to discuss the legal implications of your proposal.
    (A) by
    (B) to
    (C) with
    (D) for

126. Those who pay within 30 days receive a 3% discount. We encourage you to take -------- of this money-saving opportunity.
    (A) advance
    (B) advantage
    (C) advice
    (D) advent

127. Customers -------- pay the $21 monthly service fee before the first-of-the-month due date pay only $20!

(A) who
(B) whoever
(C) what
(D) whatever

128. The reason I'm making you this offer is -------- you into the habit of ordering your computer supplies from us.

(A) getting
(B) gets
(C) to get
(D) got

129. We hope they are as satisfying to you to operate as they were for us to manufacture. They are second to -------- in dependability.

(A) all
(B) none
(C) both
(D) neither

130. With much reluctance, I wish to inform you of my -------- as personnel director, effective as soon as arrangements can be made to hire a new director.

(A) responsibility
(B) reduction
(C) resignation
(D) replacement

Go on to the next page.

PART 6

Directions: Read the texts that follow. A word, phrase, or sentence is missing in parts of each text. Four answer choices for each question are given below the text. Select the best answer to complete the text. Then mark the letter (A), (B), (C), or (D) on your answer sheet.

Questions 131-134 refer to the following email.

From: Gary <gary@oxfordu.edu>
To: Andrew@erols.com
Subject: Hotel Reservations for Conference
Date: Sunday, July 27, 2019, 21:38:01
MAIL-Priority: High

Dear Mr. Andrew Rice,

I just received your letter today and have tried to fax the hotel ---------- form down to you at 515-418-7749, but that number does not answer. ----------. I presumed the 27th was your deadline but not the hotel's. Please do sign me up for the meeting on the 28th and 29th. I shall be flying with Eastern Air (flight #2333), ---------- Dallas at 8:00 p.m. and arriving at DC National at 9:35 p.m. I can arrange ---------- a doctoral student at the City University to pick me up and take me to the hotel.

Looking forward to seeing you.

Prof. Gary Johnson
Texas Tech University

131. (A) conservation
 (B) reservation
 (C) preservation
 (D) subservience

132. (A) I felt exhausted after the whole thing.
 (B) It happened sometimes in similar cases.
 (C) It is a matter of time and effort.
 (D) I'll try later tonight and tomorrow morning.

133. (A) to leave
 (B) left
 (C) leaving
 (D) and left

134. (A) for
 (B) by
 (C) with
 (D) to

Questions 135-138 refer to the following business letter.

Dodge White
Customer Service Manager
Sage Digital Camera Corp.
300 Park Avenue, LA, California

Dear Mr. White,

On December 4, I bought a digital camera, with the product number RT-0756 from one of your shops ---------- Botany Road. Unfortunately, your product has not performed well, which is quite disappointing. To ---------- the problem, I would appreciate if I can have an exchange for a new one. ----------. I look forward to your reply, and will wait ---------- December 14 before I seek help from the consumer protection agency. Please contact me at the below address or by telephone at 0938-388388.

Sincerely,
Peter Johnson
56 Disgruntled Street,
LA, California

135. (A) for
 (B) at
 (C) on
 (D) in

136. (A) resolve
 (B) demand
 (C) conceive
 (D) exile

137. (A) We don't have to get this over with ASAP.
 (B) I may have mishandled the product.
 (C) Enclosed is a letter of complaint.
 (D) Enclosed are copies of my purchase receipt.

138. (A) while
 (B) until
 (C) despite
 (D) during

Questions 139-142 refer to the following business letter.

Paul Snider
R & D Department
Prime Human Resource Organization
200 Oxford Road
Atlanta, Georgia, USA

Dear Mr. Snider,

I am writing to ask you to ---------- an addition to your marketing team. Your organization has been in the news as a leader in the industry. I am an ---------- of new ideas, an excellent communicator with buyers, and have a demonstrated history of marketing success. ----------.

---------- is my resume for your review and consideration. I would like to use my talents to market your quality line of technical products. If you prefer, you may reach me in the evenings at (777) 666-3333.

Thank you for your time. I look forward to meeting you.

Sincerely,
John Linden

139. (A) consider
 (B) recommend
 (C) decide
 (D) promote

140. (A) creator
 (B) negotiator
 (C) producer
 (D) innovator

141. (A) I know it is high time that I applied for the position.
 (B) I have confidence that I can be a good leader.
 (C) I believe I would be a good fit in your organization.
 (D) I strongly recommend myself to be one of the members.

142. (A) Enclosed
 (B) Enclosing
 (C) Encloses
 (D) Enclose

Questions 143-146 refer to the following business letter.

July 10, 2019
Frank Zatinski
656 Gilmour St., Apt. 908
Chicago, IL 60611

Dear Frank,

We regret to inform you that your employment at Epson Systems Inc. will be ---------- as of
___143___
Tuesday July 31, 2019.

I would like to make it absolutely clear that in no way does your termination reflect that the company is in any way unhappy with your work performance over the past 18 months. ----------.
___144___
The company will give you one week's extra pay for each month you worked beyond 12 months. In your case, this will amount to 6 weeks of severance pay.

I am confident that you will be able to find another position in the ---------- near future. If you
___145___
would like, I would be pleased to write a ---------- letter for you.
___146___

Sincerely,
Ted Bohr
Unit Manager

143. (A) termination
     (B) terminated
     (C) terminates
     (D) terminate

144. (A) However, we are experiencing serious financial difficulties.
     (B) In fact, you have been one of our most productive employees.
     (C) No doubt, other employees will feel at a loss.
     (D) In any event, we are going to miss you.

145. (A) relatively
     (B) shortly
     (C) urgently
     (D) absolutely

146. (A) recommended
     (B) recommending
     (C) recommendation
     (D) recommend

Go on to the next page.

PART 7

Directions: In this part you will read a selection of texts, such as magazine and newspaper articles, emails, and instant messages. Each text or set of texts is followed by several questions. Select the best answer for each question and mark the letter (A), (B), (C), or (D) on your answer sheet.

Questions 147-148 refer to the following online chat discussion.

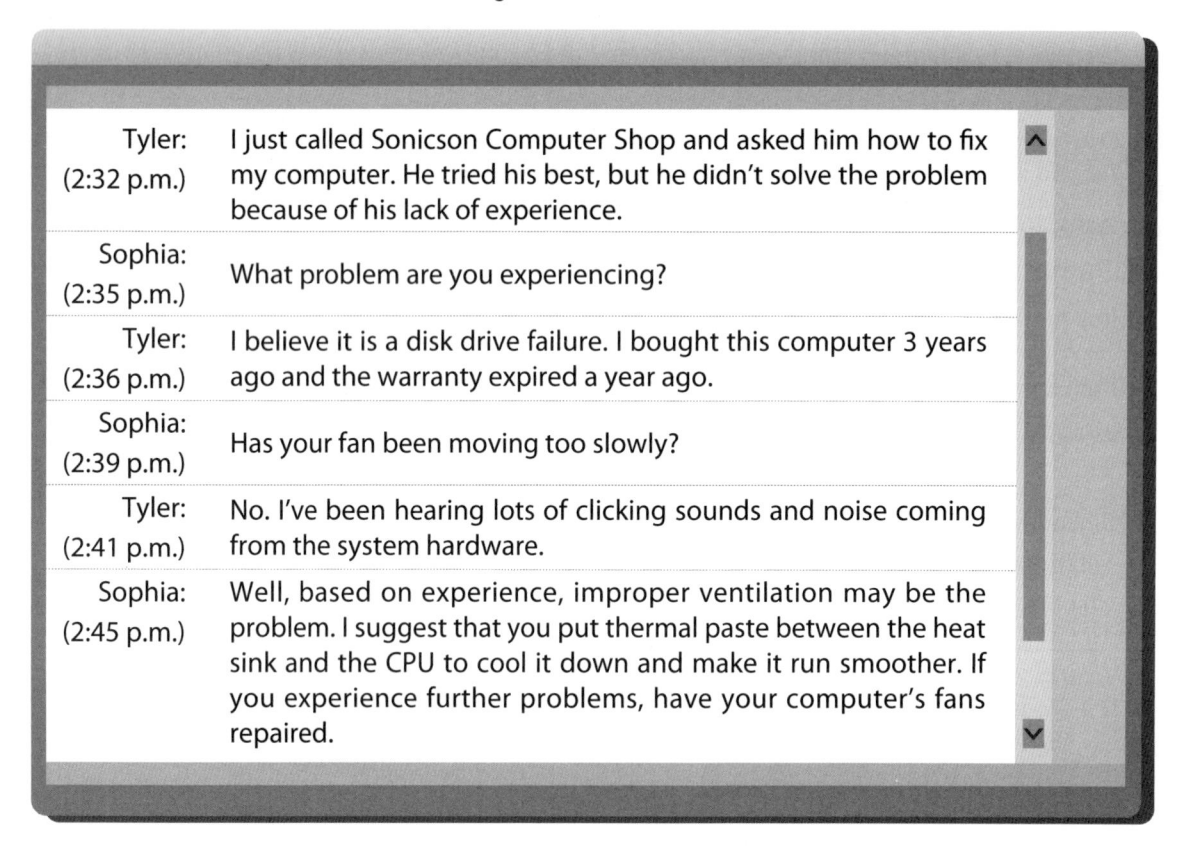

Tyler: (2:32 p.m.)	I just called Sonicson Computer Shop and asked him how to fix my computer. He tried his best, but he didn't solve the problem because of his lack of experience.
Sophia: (2:35 p.m.)	What problem are you experiencing?
Tyler: (2:36 p.m.)	I believe it is a disk drive failure. I bought this computer 3 years ago and the warranty expired a year ago.
Sophia: (2:39 p.m.)	Has your fan been moving too slowly?
Tyler: (2:41 p.m.)	No. I've been hearing lots of clicking sounds and noise coming from the system hardware.
Sophia: (2:45 p.m.)	Well, based on experience, improper ventilation may be the problem. I suggest that you put thermal paste between the heat sink and the CPU to cool it down and make it run smoother. If you experience further problems, have your computer's fans repaired.

147. What problem has Tyler been having with his computer?

    (A) His computer was infected with a virus.
    (B) His computer freezes sometimes.
    (C) His computer has been making clicking sounds.
    (D) His computer can't be turned on.

148. What did Sophia advise Tyler to do?

    (A) Take his computer to Sonicson
    (B) Shut the computer down when it makes sounds
    (C) Run the latest version of an anti-virus program
    (D) Use thermal paste to help the computer cool down

Questions 149-150 refer to the following invitation.

Dear Mr. Charles Brown,

In recognition of your longstanding contribution to the marketing profession and the care you have demonstrated in your charity work done in our community, the city of Trenton is proud to invite you to attend our 36th annual humanitarian ball & entrepreneur dinner. We are also honored to bestow the Hartman Johnston Memorial Plaque upon you to show recognition for your exceptional achievement as a businessman and commitment to the welfare of those in society.

April 22, 2020
Lord Gibson Hall
973 Drummond Street, Trenton

4:30 p.m.-10 p.m.
(Dinner time: 6-8 p.m. Award ceremony: 8 p.m.)

149. Why is Mr. Brown being invited to attend this event?

(A) He is a member of the city council.
(B) He is the manager of a charity organization.
(C) He is delivering a speech.
(D) He is receiving an award.

150. What is indicated about the kind of work Mr. Brown does?

(A) He does charity work.
(B) He owns a large international enterprise.
(C) He works at a job agency.
(D) He is a public speaker.

Go on to the next page.

Questions 151-152 refer to the following form.

Name: George Freeman
Department: Sales
Period: From Nov. 4 to Nov. 6, and from Dec. 16 to Dec. 19
Per Mile Reimbursement: 0.32
Total Reimbursement Due: $1198.00

Date	Description of events	Airfare	Lodging	Ground Transportation
Nov. 4	Traveling from New York to Boston for Sales 3.0 conference	$350.00	$150.00	$45.00
Dec. 16	Flying from New York to Tokyo for 10x Growth Conference	$434.00	$165.00	$54.00

Note: Due to financial problems our company is having, we won't be able to reimburse you until the beginning of March 2020. Sorry for the inconvenience.

151. What is implied in the form?
    (A) Mr. Freeman works in the HR department.
    (B) Mr. Freeman will be reimbursed in December 2020.
    (C) Mr. Freeman has to travel a lot for his job.
    (D) Mr. Freeman is a sales manager.

152. Why can't Mr. Freeman receive his reimbursement straight away?
    (A) The accountant made a mistake when calculating the money.
    (B) The company is struggling financially.
    (C) He won't be back at the company until next year.
    (D) He didn't submit his air tickets to the accountant.

Questions 153-154 refer to the following notice.

Apartment for Rent

This small luxury flat is on a quaint street and situated in the heart of downtown Taichung city, close to the art museum. The landlord has spent thousands of dollars finely furnishing it. It has a large and bright bedroom with a queen-sized bed, and a side kitchen that's equipped with all necessary amenities. The apartment comes with a Wi-Fi internet connection. What makes this place special is the 10 square meter terrace where tenants can relax and admire the peaceful surrounding scenery. This home is within walking distance to public transportation.

Apartment Features:

Bedroom: 1
Area: 45 m^2
Monthly price of rent: $10,000
Includes: 1 double bed, 1 table, 2 chairs, washing machine, refrigerator, Wi-Fi connection
Security deposit: 2 months rent

153. What is indicated about the apartment?

   (A) It doesn't come with a chair.
   (B) Tenants are able to relax on the terrace.
   (C) It is far from a bus stop.
   (D) It is situated on the outskirts of Taichung.

154. Which kind of people would want to rent this apartment?

   (A) Couples with 3 children
   (B) Young couples that have no children
   (C) People who usually drive to work
   (D) Those who like going shopping

Go on to the next page.

Questions 155-157 refer to the following advertisement.

Join us for our 30th Anniversary Party!
Sunday, November 11, 4 p.m. to 11 p.m.

Featuring: Live Entertainment, Food & Drink, Specials & Giveaways
Meet old Friends and Make new ones!
8896 Burmingham Ave
www.scottishpub.com

Note: Those who attend will receive a voucher (as below). If you bring a friend who is on a first visit, we will give both you and your friend two vouchers.

~Voucher~

Buy one of the following beers and get the second one for half price:
Sheepshaggers Gold, Santa's Swallie, Simmer Dim, Double Espresso, Ladeout, Kilt Lifter IPA, Seven Giraffes, Skull Splitter, Dead Pony Club

Present this voucher when you visit us.

Expiration date: 26th of November, 2019

• This voucher is only for two drinks, then it will become invalid.

---

155. What activity is being advertised?

(A) A restaurant opening party
(B) An anniversary party
(C) A clearance sale
(D) A beer drinking competition

156. What will people be able to do at the activity?

(A) Watch pole dancing
(B) Eat Irish food
(C) Enjoy entertainment
(D) Join in a dancing competition

157. What is true about the voucher?

(A) It will be given to those who come to the activity.
(B) Those who bring a friend will only receive one.
(C) It expires three weeks after the activity.
(D) It can be used to get more than two drinks for free.

Questions 158-160 refer to the following letter.

Craig Hilston
147 Brady Road,
Grantville, PA, 19973.

Optigma Enterprises Ltd.
Date: April 25
Subject: General Manager Resignation Letter

Dear Mr. Hilston,

Throughout my 7 years of employment at this esteemed organization, I've mastered the skills of managing, team leading and conflict management. After contributing much to the growth of this company, I've earned great appreciation, enjoyed a fine reputation, and developed my potential as a business manager to the fullest.

It is with mixed feelings that I'm announcing my resignation as I'm searching for a better position at Royal Kingdom Enterprises Ltd. During my tenure, I've not only strived to direct, manage and oversee the functioning of all employees and staff to the best of my ability, but I've also developed a special friendship with all members and I'll always miss their presence.

With this resignation, I wish Optigma Enterprises Ltd. a bright and profitable future in all their business endeavors. I kindly request that you approve my resignation and contact me at 5793-3682 to confirm my successful application.

Sincerely,
Jacob Turner
General Manager
Optigma Enterprises Limited

Go on to the next page.

158. What is implied about what he gained during his time at the organization?

 (A) Stronger team management skills
 (B) Ability to supervise and manage staff in the HR department
 (C) Stronger negotiation skills
 (D) Ability to resolve conflicts between enterprises

159. Why is Jacob resigning from his position at Optigma Enterprises Limited?

 (A) They won't give him a promotion.
 (B) There are too many disputes between staff members.
 (C) He wants to find a more suitable position at another company.
 (D) He doesn't feel competent enough to handle the work.

160. The word "tenure" in paragraph 2, line 2, is closest in meaning to

 (A) reign
 (B) ownership
 (C) time in office
 (D) residence

Questions 161-163 refer to the following invitation.

Dear esteemed staff and colleagues,

As we approach the end of the fiscal year, I would like to take this opportunity to show my appreciation for all the effort you have put into increasing our annual turnover during the last fiscal year. -[1]-

I would like to extend an invitation to all of you to attend our special event our general manager has arranged to reward you for your hard work. It will be held on Saturday, the 15th of June. -[2]- We have arranged a special trip to a winery in Cleveland, where we will enjoy a long, extravagant lunch in a restaurant overlooking a picturesque scenic spot. After enjoying lunch, we will have the chance to taste fruity red wine fresh from the vineyard, and then take a tour of the local scenic spots. I can guarantee it will be an unforgettable day. -[3]-

Activity details are as follows:

Activity Venue: Versailles Valley Vineyards
Meeting place prior to the activity: The front of our company's office
Meeting time prior to the activity: 7:30 a.m.
Time to return to the office: 6 p.m.

Would all who are interested in joining us on this special occasion please send an email to me at winston.brighton@gmail.com? -[4]- The last day to confirm your attendance is the 5th of June, 2019.

Yours truly,

Winston Brighton
Vice General Manager
Sequel Enterprises

161. In which of the position marked [1], [2], [3], and [4] does the following sentence best belong?

"We have had our share of ups and downs, and despite the great amount of pressure, you all performed extremely well."

(A) [1]
(B) [2]
(C) [3]
(D) [4]

162. The word "extravagant" in paragraph 2, line 4, is closest in meaning to

(A) normal
(B) moderate
(C) costly
(D) ridiculous

163. What is true about the trip the workers will go on?

(A) They will pay a lot of money for the bus ride.
(B) They will enjoy white wine.
(C) They will be able to take in impressive scenery.
(D) All workers were invited by the secretary.

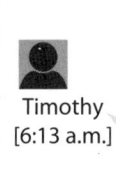

Questions 164-167 refer to the following text message chain.

Timothy [6:13 a.m.]: In the last five weeks, I've been experiencing lots of problems with my landlord. My apartment is old and I asked the landlord to inspect which things need to be repaired. He refused to do so. Also, last week I tripped over a crack in my front pathway and fractured my wrist.

Bradley [6:14 p.m.]: That's terrible. Did you let him know what happened?

Timothy [6:16 p.m.]: Yes, I did. I talked this over with my landlord, and he didn't seem to care. He even said that since I was paying so little rent, I should repair the house and pathway myself.

Bradley [6:18 p.m.]: That's ridiculous. I think you should seek arbitration and file a personal injury claim so you can be compensated.

Timothy [6:19 p.m.]: I'm planning on doing that. But with my landlord's strong personality, it'll be a waste of time trying to reconcile our differences.

Bradley [6:21 p.m.]: I guess you could consider litigation, even though it will be a lengthy and costly process.

Timothy [6:25 p.m.]: Litigating can cost a person a lot of money, and I don't want to spend so much right now. However, I'm certain this is serious and I doubt arbitrators can make sure that justice is done.

Bradley [6:28 p.m.]: I understand. I have been through something similar to you a while ago. After my company's landlord negligently caused a workplace accident, I hired a lawyer who was an expert in commercial and civil law to handle this situation. With his expertise, he helped my company to win the case.

Timothy [6:31 p.m.]: Well, you must know what you are talking about.

164. What was suggested about the landlord?

    (A) He takes good care of his property.
    (B) He wants to take his tenant to court.
    (C) He likes to spend money on repairs.
    (D) He was negligent and doesn't want to compensate his tenant.

165. What is Bradley's opinion of litigation?

    (A) It is costly and ineffective.
    (B) Lawyers won't be able to solve his problem.
    (C) It will save him more time than arbitration.
    (D) It can ensure that justice is done for Timothy.

166. What did Bradley mention about the incident in his workplace?

    (A) His landlord refused to fix the leaking ceiling.
    (B) An accident happened.
    (C) A death at his workplace led to litigation.
    (D) His landlord can't be reasoned with.

167. At 6:31 p.m., what does Timothy mean when he writes "Well, you must know what you are talking about."?

    (A) He decided to take the case to a lawyer.
    (B) Bradley is adamant that only arbitration will not work.
    (C) Bradley knows lots about civil law.
    (D) Bradley has a good knowledge of commercial leases.

Questions 168-171 refer to the following autobiography.

Autobiography

My name is Lucas Trump. I was born in Australia and raised in America, so I have dual citizenship. When I was in the second year of university, I successfully applied for a scholarship and was an exchange student in National Tokyo University for one year. During this year, I spent my spare time teaching English as a tutor on a part-time basis. After I graduated with a master's degree in English Language Instruction, I decided to stay in Japan and teach children and adults English.

I have a deep passion for teaching English, and it's this passion that drives me to continuously find ways to upgrade my teaching skills and excel as a language teacher. Currently, I am an English teacher at Amami Senior High School. I have wide experience in speaking, reading, writing and listening instruction, as well as helping students prepare for exams like TOEFL and IELTS. I have taught in high schools for more than one year, in university for one year as a part-time teacher, and in adult English cram schools for over 4 years. I have also taught junior high school students and young children English.

My father is an entrepreneur who runs a mechanic business, my mother is a housewife, my older brother is a general practitioner and a part-time lecturer in university. My older sister is an accountant and lives with her husband in North America, my younger brother is still pursuing his studies, my wife is Japanese who is very frugal and works hard to make our domestic life happy. My future goal is to further upgrade my language teaching skills and knowledge of well-rounded education so that I can help other Japanese students greatly improve their English. At the same time, I hope that I can strive towards becoming a high-level manager and educator, and give full play to my professional skills while working and growing in my career.

I sincerely hope that I will have an opportunity to work in cooperation with your company. It would be a great honor to use my teaching skills and methods to help English learners in your school, and be an example of excellence in English teaching.

Go on to the next page.

168. What is Mr. Trump's main goal as an English teacher?

(A) To teach children's English in the future
(B) To teach students how to pass the TOEFL exam
(C) To work in high-level management
(D) To do teacher training

169. The word "excel" in paragraph 2, line 2, is closest in meaning to

(A) to conquer
(B) to be inferior
(C) to be proficient
(D) to overcome

170. What kind of teaching experience does Mr. Trump have?

(A) He has experience teaching junior high school students.
(B) He has worked in adult language instruction for over 6 years.
(C) He has taught as a full-time English lecturer.
(D) He was a full-time English tutor.

171. What is true about Mr. Trump's family?

(A) All of his family members are in Australia.
(B) His father works as a family doctor.
(C) His older brother is an accountant.
(D) His spouse is from Japan.

Questions 172-175 refer to the following letter.

**Bidbest Inc.
13 Whicter Road,
Gillman QLD, Australia
www.bidbest.co.au**

March 24
Michael Murray
Teys F & B Corporation
1420 Alice Boulevard
Tokyo, Japan

Dear Mr. Murray,

I would like to take this opportunity to introduce my company to you. Bidbest Inc. has been recognized as one of the most prominent and pioneering food and beverage distributors in Queensland, Australia. -[1]- We have developed over 60 business units and we specialize in wholesaling food service, fresh produce, beer, and meat. We offer customers an extensive range of fresh produce, which is from 400-600 lines depending on the season. We have a splendid array of all prime, sub-prime and portion control cuts such as pork, veal, beef, lamb, game and poultry. -[2]- In addition, our company is also a market leader when it comes to distributing frozen seafood, cleaning products, and packaging materials. -[3]-

Our comprehensive product range, exceptional service, and user-friendly order facilities enable us to service a wide variety of customers. Some of our customers include pubs and clubs, hotels, restaurants, pizza shops, hospitals, offices, retirement villages, and prisons.

I became aware of your expertise in exportation and business expansion overseas from a brochure that was mailed to my office. -[4]- Please find enclosed this letter a detailed explanation of how my company plans to export to Japan. When I am not tied up with work, which will be in the next week or two, I'll take some time to visit you so we can discuss this in detail. Please advise me of a suitable time to visit you and take a look at my business plan.

I look forward to hearing from you.

Best regards,
Beckham White,
President, Bidbest Inc.

172. What is the purpose of this letter?

    (A) To introduce the way Bidbest does international business
    (B) To propose a joint venture with an exportation company
    (C) To introduce the correct ways to choose meat
    (D) To make an inquiry about how to expand their business overseas

173. The word "array" in paragraph 1, line 5, is closest in meaning to

    (A) display
    (B) adornment
    (C) package
    (D) settlement

174. In which of the position marked [1], [2], [3], and [4] does the following sentence best belong?
    "As we are seeking to expand to Japan, I'm hoping to know the steps that I should take to develop the Japanese market."

    (A) [1]
    (B) [2]
    (C) [3]
    (D) [4]

175. What does Mr. White plan to do in the near future?

    (A) Write up a business proposal for Mr. Murray
    (B) Start distributing products to retirement villages
    (C) Talk about his plan to export with Mr. Murray
    (D) Send an email to a business consultation company

Questions 176-180 refer to the following message and announcement.

Hi Fred,

Recently, I have been thinking that we need to implement some strategies that will both motivate all employees to work to their full potential and also recognize their contributions to the company. The best way to do this is to start an employee reward program so we can overtly reward four of the most earnest and productive workers each month of the year. This will not only encourage all employees to engage in healthy competition, it will certainly increase workers' performance. We can consider using cash prizes, but the rewards shouldn't be only confined to monetary compensation. We could also use other forms of incentives, such as free company parking for a month, a day off work, or coupon to a local spa.

Please write up a list of the most efficient and diligent workers in your department, and give them awards according to the following categories:

Name of Award	Achievement of Employee
Most Innovative Employee	Contribution and execution of creative ideas to enhance product development.
Outstanding Salesman of the Month	Increasing number of loyal clients and reaching or surpassing a sales target set by the sales department manager.
Excellence in Customer Service	Offering clients top-notch service that leads to clients' referral of other customers to our company and a dramatic increase in sales.
Best Team Player	Showing integrity in one's work ethics, being a cooperative and hardworking team player, and promptly fulfilling the tasks assigned by one's team leader.

I have already announced to all department heads that this program will start at the beginning of next month. You'll be in charge of organizing the awards from now on.

Yours,
Jimmy Abbot
CEO of Hummingbird International

Employee of the Month
Oliver Addington
1st of February, 2019

On behalf of Hummingbird International, I would like to extend our warmest congratulations to Oliver Addington, who has been the most efficient and productive worker in November. A recent graduate from the Weber State University, Utah, Oliver joined us in 2016 and immediately mastered the skills of leading a sales team and handling customer inquiries and complaints. During the course of the last five months, he has spent many hours of his personal time sharpening his sales skills by attending self-development seminars.

Oliver went through many months of arduous effort in order to complete the tasks that were assigned him. In the month of January this year, he single-handedly managed to generate in excess of $25,000 from selling vacuum cleaners, which surpasses the record that Kyle Dylan set at the end of last quarter by $7,000. He always shows a passion for excellence in customer service and this increased our frequent customer base by 10%. Most of these customers stated that they came to our store because our products were recommended by their friends. This accomplishment is not only quite exceptional, it also proves that anything is possible with persistence and hard work.

To show our appreciation for his dedication to our company's goals, our company is paying for Oliver's 6-day trip to the Bahamas for Christmas this year. This young man is an example to all of what dedication and passion for your work can do. All employees here have the potential to achieve exactly what Mr. Addington has done by earnestly completing the assigned tasks.

We congratulate Oliver for his great achievements and sincerely hope he keeps up the good work.

Fred Gardner
Sales Manager

176. According to the two passages, which awards will Mr. Addington receive?

(A) Most Innovative Employee; Best Team Player
(B) Outstanding Salesman of the Month; Excellence in Customer Service
(C) Excellence in Customer Service; Most Innovative Employee
(D) Most Innovative Employee; Outstanding Salesman of the Month

177. What is indicated about Mr. Addington's performance at work?

(A) He demonstrates integrity and completes tasks best by cooperating with others.
(B) He greatly increased the company's customer base.
(C) His passion for manufacturing increased his sales amount.
(D) He exceeded the highest sales record by $5000.

178. What is true about the company's employee reward program?

(A) The best employees are only rewarded with money.
(B) Staff members are encouraged after they come up with creative ways to enhance customer service.
(C) Rewarding employees' hard work encourages friendly competition.
(D) Those who are adept at customer service usually get the best reward.

179. In the message, the word "overtly" in paragraph 1, line 4, is closest in meaning to

(A) sharply
(B) undoubtedly
(C) publicly
(D) precisely

180. What is true about the way that Mr. Addington was recognized?

(A) His company paid for his trip to Hawaii.
(B) The company wrote a letter of appreciation to him for his hard work.
(C) His company gave him 5 days off work.
(D) His department manager publicly recognized him for his diligence in completing his work.

Go on to the next page.

Questions 181-185 refer to the following advertisement and letter.

Hiring: Highly competent manager assistant.
Job description: Woolworths is searching for a talented worker to take on the position of manager assistant.
Job requirements: The person must have good interpersonal communication skills, as well as be very efficient in dealing with very stressful situations. It is essential that applicants hold a bachelor's degree in business management or marketing, as they will be more qualified to hold this position.
Job description: The person's responsibilities will include assisting the general manager of Woolworths with paperwork as well as advertising and marketing Woolworths in the local district.
Salary: Negotiable. Based on the person's experience in business.
Starting date: Within the next 30 to 50 days.

January 13, 2019

Dear Brett Scoffield,

I am writing to apply for the position of manager assistant that was published in the *Greenwich Newspaper* last Monday. I have attached my resume to this letter and hope that you consider me for this position.

To summarize my resume, I would have to say that I fit most of the characteristics needed to apply for this job. I worked as the assistant for the chief operating officer in a computer company during the past five years. I am proficient in processing information with Word, Office and handling complicated tasks at the same time. I am a conscientious worker and have carried out many tasks that involve interpersonal communication in my last job. I also have lots of experience in business planning and coordination. I believe that this experience in business gives me a competitive advantage over other applicants and makes me more qualified to hold the position of manager assistant.

I have a question regarding my qualification for this job. I don't hold a bachelor's degree in business management or have lots of experience in marketing. However, I do have a business certification. Do you still see me as qualified to take on this position? I am willing to put the effort into getting a higher degree and learning the skills required to do this job well.

Thanks,
Andrew Lackley

181. What is the purpose of the advertisement?
    (A) To hire a suitable marketing expert for their company
    (B) To find a manager assistant
    (C) To find a suitable sales assistant
    (D) To hire a clerk

182. According to the advertisement, what type of work will the successful applicant do?
    (A) Give presentations on the business he works at
    (B) Represent the company at large events
    (C) Plan business trips for the general manager
    (D) Do lots of marketing and advertisement for Woolworths

183. What makes Mr. Lackley qualified for this position?
    (A) He is a good communicator and very diligent.
    (B) He holds a bachelor's degree in business administration.
    (C) He's experienced in marketing and advertising.
    (D) He's a good public speaker.

184. According to the letter, what is true about Andrew's work experience?
    (A) He was in charge of designing advertisements.
    (B) He worked as a C-level executive.
    (C) He is skillful when it comes to using computers.
    (D) He worked hard at marketing his manager's products.

185. In the letter, the word "coordination" in paragraph 2, line 6, is closest in meaning to
    (A) grouping
    (B) sorting
    (C) organization
    (D) sizing

Go on to the next page.

Questions 186-190 refer to the following autobiography and emails.

Dear Mr. Stratsfield,

My name is Andrew Johnson. In reference to your job advertisement in the *China Times*, I'm writing to apply for the position of HR manager in your company. I have attached my resume. Below is a copy of my autobiography for your reference. Please contact me in regard to my application as soon as possible.

Andrew Johnson

Autobiography

I was born in America and grew up in Australia. My major in university was human resource management. When I was in the third year of university, I worked as the assistant of a human resource coordinator and learnt the skills of workforce planning and supervision. After I graduated with my bachelor's degree in international business, I decided to continue working in the same company, and was eventually promoted to manager at the HR department. I am very experienced in both managing and supervising staff, and inspiring workers to perform their best in the company.

I am a responsible and earnest worker and have a deep passion for excellence in business. I make sure that I complete each task with particular attention to detail. I always find ways to upgrade my work skills and deepen my knowledge of how to run a business successfully. At the beginning of next year, I will obtain a dual master's degree in human resources and business management. Upon graduation, I hope to use my professional knowledge to help other people reach their potential in the workplace.

It would be a great honor to use my management skills and methods to contribute to your company and be a great example in workplace management.

To:	ajohnson.highmanagement@gmail.com
From:	stratsfieldnumber1@gmail.com
Subject:	Job application
Date:	June 25, 2019

Dear Mr. Johnson,

Thank you for your application and autobiography. My boss and I looked over your resume, and have to clarify some details about the nature of the job we are advertising. If you fit the requirements, then you will most likely be hired.

Firstly, my boss requires applicants to have 5 years of experience managing large teams of more than 40 staff members. Do you have this kind of experience? Secondly, we need applicants to have effective negotiation skills and experience handling conflict between staff. How much experience do you have in negotiation?

Please answer these questions and I will get back to you on the result of your application.

Sincerely,
John Stratsfield

To:	stratsfieldnumber1@gmail.com
From:	johnson.highmanagement@gmail.com
Subject:	Re: Job application
Date:	June 26, 2019

Dear Mr. Stratsfield,

Thank you for your letter. To answer your first question, I was the manager of a company with over 55 staff for a period of 6 years. During my time there, I resolved lots of disputes. I also evaluated staff performance, and offered training and consultations to improve the efficiency of staff work habits. With the support and guidance of my general manager, I handled issues related to salary, work benefits, and managed conflict between staff members.

Hope to hear from you soon.

Andrew Johnson

186. What is the purpose of the email written by John Stratsfield?
    (A) To inform Andrew that they can't hire him
    (B) To clear up some issues regarding Andrew's work experience
    (C) To inform Andrew that he is qualified for the position
    (D) To arrange a time for an interview

187. In the second email, the word "dispute" in line 3 is closest in meaning to
    (A) conflict
    (B) trouble
    (C) problem
    (D) confusion

188. What is said about Andrew's communication skills?
    (A) He is good at negotiating with other workers.
    (B) He isn't a good communicator.
    (C) He is experienced at negotiating the price of products.
    (D) He lacks the skills to deal with disputes in the workplace.

189. What skills does Andrew have that shows he's qualified for the position?
    (A) He excels in handling conflict, negotiating and inspiring workers to perform their best.
    (B) He has experience training workers from different organizations.
    (C) He has good time management skills.
    (D) He's a highly efficient worker.

190. What is stated about Andrew's knowledge of team management?
    (A) He is still learning the basics of managing staff.
    (B) He knows nothing about how to manage staff.
    (C) He already holds a degree in business management.
    (D) He has experience in leading large teams of workers, and was the manager of the HR department.

Questions 191-195 refer to the following online advertisement and emails.

Star Artefacts Galore

The finest collection of superstar collection items in USA!

Our store has a vast collection of highly sought-after items that were previously owned by American superstars. They are available for avid collectors and buyers to purchase.

Some of the items we have collected include many of Elvis Presley's belongings, such as his pink Cadillac, jumpsuit, bongos, the very Aloha shirt that he wore in his Hawaiian concerts, and a total of two hundred artefacts that have been moved from Graceland, Tennessee for preservation and sale. We also have items such as Michael Jackson's vest, as well as the white gloves and shoes that he wore at his Beat It concerts in the 1980s, and many more.

Our manager is also willing to pay 120% of the retail price to anyone who is in possession of collectable items once owned by a famous American superstar.

For more information, please visit us and decide what you'd like to purchase.

Price List for Products On Sale
Please click on the links below to view some of the artefacts that we are currently selling.

- ➤ Cars: Open for negotiation
- ➤ Instruments: $400
- ➤ Records, Tapes: $20
- ➤ Apparel: $50
- ➤ Music and songbooks that were signed by superstars: $70 to $90
- ➤ Accessories (rings, earrings, bracelets, etc): $25 to $35

For further information, please contact the store manager, Bob Stallard, at bstallard@sagalore.com.

Date:	January 21
From:	Sophia Calverta <scalverta@kmail.com>
To:	Star Artefacts Galore <sagalore@sagalore.com>
Subject:	Elvis Presley Guitar

Dear Mr. Stallard,

My father owns a beautiful Gibson J200 acoustic guitar that was owned by Elvis in the 1960s. I recently came across your website and thought that your shop might be interested in purchasing it.

The guitar was bought by Elvis in the early 1960s and was used for about half a decade in many of his concerts. My father purchased the guitar from an auction in Memphis for US$200 several years after Elvis passed away, and my father would like to sell it to a shop that cherishes such a valuable and historical item.

Please inform me of your purchasing procedures and how you would like to pay for the guitar.

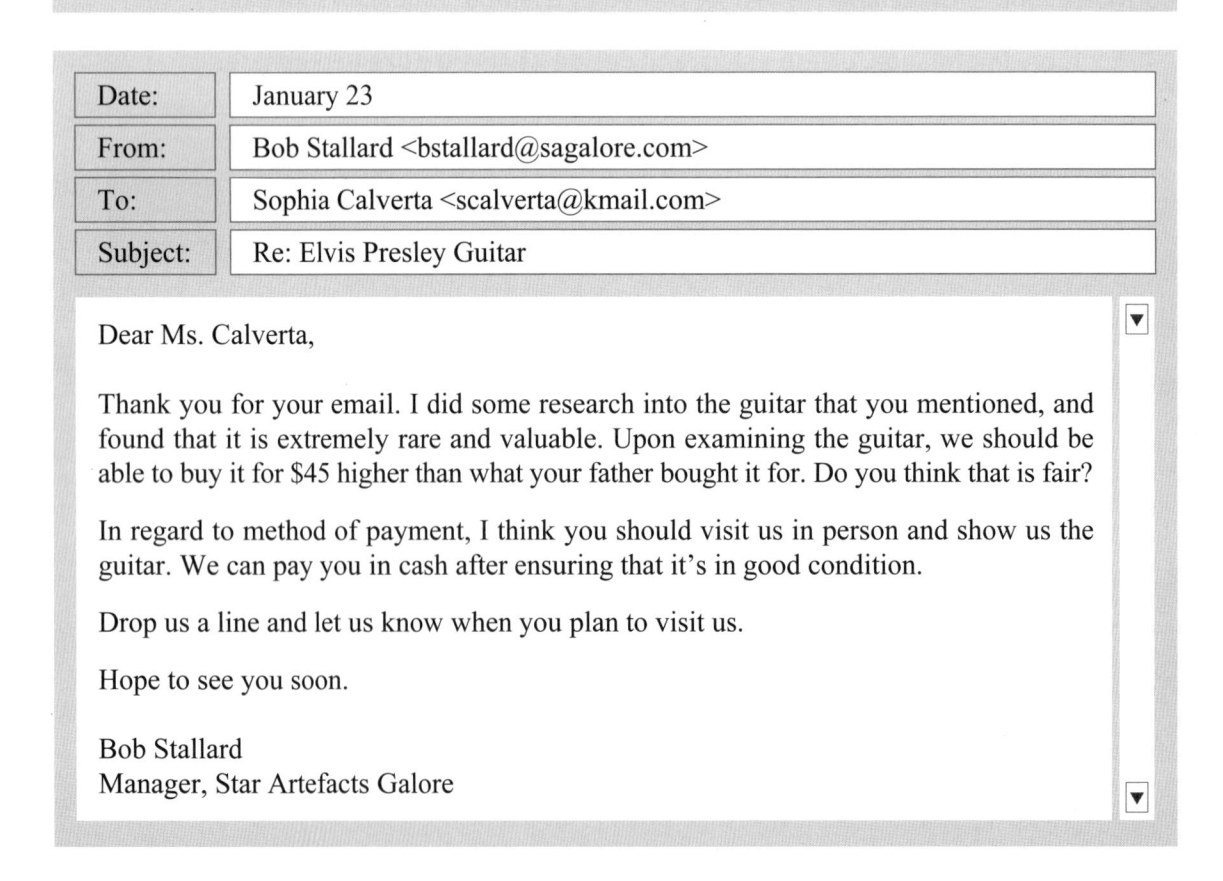

Thank you,
Sophia Calverta

Date:	January 23
From:	Bob Stallard <bstallard@sagalore.com>
To:	Sophia Calverta <scalverta@kmail.com>
Subject:	Re: Elvis Presley Guitar

Dear Ms. Calverta,

Thank you for your email. I did some research into the guitar that you mentioned, and found that it is extremely rare and valuable. Upon examining the guitar, we should be able to buy it for $45 higher than what your father bought it for. Do you think that is fair?

In regard to method of payment, I think you should visit us in person and show us the guitar. We can pay you in cash after ensuring that it's in good condition.

Drop us a line and let us know when you plan to visit us.

Hope to see you soon.

Bob Stallard
Manager, Star Artefacts Galore

191. What is NOT true about Star Artefacts Galore?

(A) It has a large variety of American superstars' previously owned valuables.
(B) The shop is seeking to expand the range of items it sells.
(C) It only has two highly sought-after items that belonged to Michael Jackson.
(D) The store sells songbooks with superstars' signatures for a very high price.

192. How much will Ms. Calverta sell her item to Mr. Stallard for?

(A) $250
(B) $245
(C) $240
(D) $230

193. What is suggested about Ms. Calverta?

(A) Her father attended Elvis' concert in Hawaii.
(B) She owned an electric guitar used by Elvis.
(C) She has an acoustic guitar that Elvis played for several years.
(D) She bought Elvis' Cadillac at an auction in Memphis.

194. What is indicated about Star Artefacts Galore?

(A) It sells clothes that were worn by superstars.
(B) Most of the items they sell used to belong to Elvis Presley.
(C) The store buys any valuable items despite the quality.
(D) They pay for valuable items by wiring money to the customers.

195. What is the purpose of Ms. Calverta's email?

(A) To enquire about the price of a CD being sold by the store
(B) To understand how she can cooperate with the store in selling artefacts
(C) To make an inquiry into the quality of Michael Jackson's vest
(D) To see if the store is willing to buy a rare acoustic guitar

Go on to the next page.

Questions 196-200 refer to the following notice, email, and article.

Attention Everyone!
Journalist Interview This Monday Afternoon

We have exciting news for all staff—*The Courier-Mail* will be doing a special report on our restaurant in an article that discusses the best restaurants to visit in Central Brisbane! The manager of the company has already contacted me and arranged for the reporters to come and interview the staff on Monday, 12th of December, at 12 p.m. Subsequent to the interview, photographers will also be there to take photos of our restaurant. The session will be between 40 minutes and 1 hour.

As this will be a great chance to increase our profits and exposure to the local community, I hope that all staff can place value on this meeting. All employees in our restaurant will be included.

Since we opened in July last year, the amount of frequent customers has almost doubled, so we all should be proud of being recognized by the media.

To:	Joseph Bates <jbates@trang.net>
From:	Jessica Robertson <jrobertson@couriermail.com>
Date:	Wednesday, 7th December
Subject:	Monday Interview Appointment

Dear Mr. Bates,

Last week we arranged to have an interview and photography session next Monday at 12:00 p.m. Owing to the fact that our work schedule will be busy that day, could we possibly change the time to 12:20 p.m.? Please make sure to confirm this time with your staff and let me know by tomorrow morning. As discussed last time, the interview and photo shoot will be at your restaurant, and we will ask you questions about the cuisine and beverages you sell, the history of your restaurant and how you have grown since the restaurant was established. Following this, we will take some photos of your waiters working and interacting with the customers.

Please contact me if you have any questions. Looking forward to seeing you all on Monday!

The Courier-Mail Photography Group

Stylish Aussie Restaurant

by Darren Allaway

When you dine out at Trang's Restaurant on any day of the week for lunch or dinner, you'll receive not only a warm welcome, and experience warm customer service, but also be able to enjoy exquisite local Australian food that will bring water to your mouth.

Established more than one year ago, the restaurant has grown into one of the most bustling and profitable restaurants on the West End. The menu features scrumptious kangaroo pie, organic salads, one-of-a-kind cranberry ice cream, and other delicious local Aussie food. The head chef, Andy Watson, comments, "We only choose native ingredients that can transform average Australian food into gourmet cuisine. We use the freshest ingredients from the countryside, including native herbs, berries, and spices to produce a truly Australian taste. We also offer a wide variety of wines to drink with your meals."

On a recent Monday afternoon, James Peters, a visitor from Ireland, was enjoying the food there. He stated, "This is truly the freshest and most unique tasting food I have ever tried in Australia. They sure put their heart into making fine gourmet dishes."

Trang's Restaurant is located on 143 Eagle Street, Eagle Street Pier, Brisbane, and is open seven days a week, from 11:00 a.m. – 9:00 p.m. The interior is decorated with Australian aboriginal art, and pictures of local scenery and wildlife. The staff are super hospitable and the delicious food can be bought at a reasonable price. Reservations are only needed for big events like parties.

196. In the article, the word "exquisite" in paragraph 1, line 3, is closest in meaning to

(A) delicate
(B) meticulous
(C) flawed
(D) unrefined

197. What is indicated about the interview?

(A) The chefs will be asked secrets about how they make the food so delicious.
(B) Mr. Bates will be asked questions about what food and drinks he sells.
(C) The manager will talk about the history of Australian cuisine in Brisbane.
(D) Photographs will be taken of the chefs interacting with diners.

198. What time will the photo shoot finish?

(A) Around 12:00 p.m.
(B) About 10:20 a.m.
(C) Before 1:30 p.m.
(D) About 12:50 a.m.

199. What is NOT true about Trang's Restaurant?

(A) It is open from 11:00 a.m. to 9:00 p.m.
(B) Its interior decoration includes native American paintings and local scenery.
(C) It's located on Eagle Street in Brisbane.
(D) It serves a large variety of wines to enjoy while eating.

200. What does James Peters mention about the restaurant's cuisine?

(A) It is impressive how fresh and unique the food tastes.
(B) He read an introduction to the food in a magazine.
(C) He thought the price of food wasn't reasonable.
(D) He wants to visit the restaurant again.

Stop! This is the end of the test. If you finish before time is called, you may go back to Parts 5, 6, and 7 and check your work.

TEST 01

中譯・單字

TEST 01
PART 1 🎧 01

1.

(A) The parents are accompanying the kid.
(B) Family members are lounging in the hammock.
(C) The child is holding his father's hand.
(D) The father is showing his watch to the child.

(A) 父母正陪著孩子。
(B) 家人正在吊床上休息。
(C) 孩子正牽著他爸爸的手。
(D) 爸爸向孩子展示他的手錶。

| 單字 | accompany 陪伴 | hammock 吊床 |

2.

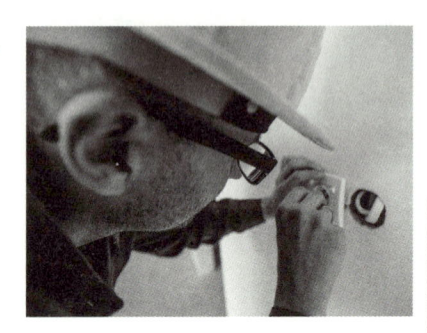

(A) The man is checking the wall.
(B) A man is changing a cable.
(C) The electrician is installing a switch.
(D) The man is switching the light.

(A) 男子在檢查牆。
(B) 一名男子在換電纜線。
(C) 電工正在安裝開關。
(D) 男子正在切換燈光。

| 單字 | cable 纜線；繩索；電纜 | switch 開關；切換 |

3.

(A) Friends are enjoying mountain climbing.
(B) Each hiker is carrying his own backpack.
(C) People are jogging on the road.
(D) Hikers are walking on the path.

(A) 朋友們正在享受登山。
(B) 每位健行者都背著自己的背包。
(C) 人們正在馬路上慢跑。
(D) 健行者正走在路上。

| 單字 | climb 攀登 | hammock 吊床 |

106

4.

(A) Hockey players are racing on the rink.
(B) Hockey sticks are crossing over each other.
(C) Athletes are kicking the ball.
(D) Hockey players are trying to maneuver a puck.

(A) 曲棍球運動員在場上快跑。
(B) 曲棍球球棍正交叉在一起。
(C) 運動員正在踢球。
(D) 曲棍球運動員正試圖操縱球。

單字	hockey 曲棍球	race 競賽	rink 溜冰場
	maneuver 操縱		

5.

(A) The musicians are watching each other.
(B) The girl is looking at the sheet music.
(C) The violin player is holding the music stand.
(D) The boy is playing the flute.

(A) 音樂家們正相互望著。
(B) 女孩正在看樂譜。
(C) 提琴手正拿著譜架。
(D) 男孩正吹著長笛。

單字	sheet music 樂譜	music stand 譜架

6.

(A) The books are being stacked beside the glasses.
(B) The glasses are behind the books.
(C) Books are lying on the carpet.
(D) The books are all sold out.

(A) 書堆在眼鏡旁邊。
(B) 眼鏡在書後面。
(C) 書正放在地毯上。
(D) 圖書全部賣完了。

TEST 01
PART 2

7. When did Bob resign from his position?

   (A) He quit on Tuesday.
   (B) I'll sign the contract.
   (C) He resigned himself to his boss.

鮑勃何時辭職？

   (A) 他星期二辭職。
   (B) 我會簽約。
   (C) 他聽從老闆的命令。

> **單字**   resign 辭職   resign oneself to 順從   position 職位

8. Which consensus did we come to on how to promote our products?

   (A) Johnson agreed to help us.
   (B) This project will promote our revenue growth.
   (C) Our products are defective.

我們推廣產品的共識已經到哪裡了？

   (A) 強生同意幫助我們。
   (B) 這個專案會促進我們營收的成長。
   (C) 我們的產品有瑕疵。

> **單字**   consensus 共識   promote 推廣；宣傳

9. Who is going to kick off the meeting?

   (A) We kicked off the meeting with a summary of finances.
   (B) Jill will start us off.
   (C) It's time to start.

誰來起始會議？

   (A) 我們由財務摘要起始了會議。
   (B) 吉爾會來開頭。
   (C) 現在該是開始的時候了。

> **單字**   summary 摘要

10. Can I upgrade to business class?

   (A) Let's start to improve it next week.
   (B) It's already too late to do so.
   (C) Business class is for long distance trips.

我可以升級到商務艙嗎？

   (A) 我們下週開始改善。
   (B) 已經太晚了，無法升級。
   (C) 商務艙是供長途旅行的。

> **單字**   improve 改善   distance 距離

11. May I have a money order?

   (A) I have cashed the money order already.
   (B) Sure, just wait a moment please.
   (C) I ordered her to withdraw some money.

我可以要一張匯款單嗎？

   (A) 我已經兌了匯票。
   (B) 當然，請稍等一下。
   (C) 我吩咐她去提領些錢。

> **單字**　withdraw（從銀行）提領　　money order 匯款單

12. Is your target market in China or Taiwan?

    (A) Actually, it's in Brazil.
    (B) We are a target for criticism.
    (C) We missed our sales target.

    你的目標市場是中國或台灣？

    (A) 實際上是在巴西。
    (B) 我們是被批評的對象。
    (C) 我們沒達成我們的銷售目標。

> **單字**　target 目標；對象　　criticism 批評；批判

13. Would you please give me some constructive criticism on my performance?

    (A) You need to work faster.
    (B) He criticized my work.
    (C) What he said wasn't useful.

    請對我的表現給一些建設性的批評？

    (A) 你得做快一點。
    (B) 他批評我的工作。
    (C) 他說的話沒有用。

14. Shall we have a closed-door meeting?

    (A) That's a bright idea.
    (B) The meeting is tomorrow night.
    (C) Close the doors, please.

    我們能開一個秘密會議嗎？

    (A) 好點子。
    (B) 明天晚上開會。
    (C) 請關上門。

15. Would you be able to apply for utilities for this building?

    (A) The utility of this building is certain.
    (B) Do you need gas or electricity?
    (C) I'm applying for a replacement.

    你可以幫這個建築物申請供應水電瓦斯嗎？

    (A) 這個建築物的實用性是確定的。
    (B) 你是要瓦斯還是電？
    (C) 我正在申請一個替代品。

> **單字**　utilities（水電、瓦斯等）公用事業；水電費　　certain 確定的
> replacement 替代；替代者／品

16. We should break even next month, shouldn't we?

    (A) No, we are actually far from making a profit.
    (B) My phone is broken.
    (C) We just started building the company.

    下個月我們應該可以損益兩平，對吧？

    (A) 不，我們實際上離賺錢還很遠。
    (B) 我的手機壞了。
    (C) 我們剛剛開始建立這個公司。

TEST 01
PART 2

17. Didn't you buy the toner?

   (A) Sorry, I forgot about it.
   (B) Jane wants to buy some ink.
   (C) I went shopping yesterday.

你沒買碳粉嗎？

   (A) 抱歉，我忘了。
   (B) 珍想要買一些墨水。
   (C) 我昨天去購物。

> **單字** toner 碳粉　　ink 墨水

18. Isn't Taiwan Union Bank a multinational bank?

   (A) George worked for an international bank.
   (B) No, they are only limited to Taiwan.
   (C) They've been to Taiwan before.

台聯銀行不是一家跨國銀行嗎？

   (A) 喬治為一家國際銀行工作。
   (B) 不，他們只限於台灣。
   (C) 他們以前去過台灣。

19. I'm calling to enquire about the job vacancy at your company.

   (A) The hotel is completely booked out now.
   (B) What would you want to know?
   (C) There is a vacancy at that school.

我打電話詢問貴公司的職缺。

   (A) 旅館已經完全被訂光了。
   (B) 你想知道什麼？
   (C) 那所學校有職缺。

> **單字** vacancy 空缺；職缺　　vacant 空著的

20. The newly bought machinery has a serious structural flaw.

   (A) Why not get it repaired?
   (B) The structure collapsed.
   (C) We bought some machines yesterday.

新買的機器有個嚴重的結構缺陷。

   (A) 為什麼不修理？
   (B) 結構倒塌了。
   (C) 我們昨天買了一些機器。

> **單字** serious 嚴重的　　structural 結構上的　　flaw 缺陷；瑕疵

21. What are we doing in collaboration with this business?

   (A) We're working on developing new technologies.
   (B) We're collaborating with a small business.
   (C) This will not work out.

我們正與這間企業合作些什麼？

   (A) 我們正在開發新技術。
   (B) 我們正與一間小企業合作。
   (C) 這不會有結果。

> **單字** collaboration 合作

22. When did our supervisor decide to take on new employees?

(A) We are employing two new salesmen.
(B) The supervisor was hired on Wednesday.
(C) They were employed on Tuesday.

我們的主管什麼時候決定聘用新員工？

(A) 我們將僱用兩名新的業務員。
(B) 這位主管在星期三受僱了。
(C) 他們在星期二受僱了。

> 單字　take on 聘用

23. When can I meet the personnel officer in person?

(A) He's not available to meet with anyone.
(B) We're in charge of personnel.
(C) He looks after our personal welfare.

我什麼時候可以見到人事部主任本人？

(A) 他沒空見任何人。
(B) 我們負責人事。
(C) 他照顧我們的個人福利。

> 單字　welfare 福利　　　personnel officer 人事部主任

24. Which co-worker took the minutes at our last meeting?

(A) I'm sure it was Jerry.
(B) I don't like to take the minutes at all.
(C) Our co-workers are very cooperative.

上次會議的會議紀錄是哪位同事做的？

(A) 我確定是傑瑞。
(B) 我不喜歡做會議紀錄。
(C) 我們的同事很合作。

> 單字　take the minutes 做會議記錄

25. Which department is in charge of cold calls?

(A) The telemarketing department.
(B) He seemed to be so cold.
(C) I called yesterday.

哪個部門負責電訪？

(A) 電話行銷部門。
(B) 他似乎覺得很冷。
(C) 我昨天打電話。

> 單字　cold call 陌生電訪

26. Why did you scrutinize the contract?

(A) I wanted to be sure of the fine details.
(B) Every aspect was placed under scrutiny.
(C) We are examining the contractor's proposal.

為什麼你要仔細審查合約？

(A) 我想確定更具體的細節。
(B) 每個方面都受到審查。
(C) 我們正在審查承包商的建議。

> 單字　scrutinize 仔細檢查

TEST 01 PART 2

27. Who would like to sum up the key points we discussed today?

(A) Jack did a summary of the agenda.
(B) Bill will give it a try.
(C) Britney's summarization was good.

誰會總結我們今天討論的要點？

(A) 傑克做了一個議程的總結。
(B) 比爾將會做看看。
(C) 布蘭妮之前的總結很好。

| 單字 | sum up 總結 | agenda 議程 |

---

28. Who marked up the price of this property by 7%?

(A) We want to know more about real estate and local property.
(B) The price rose a lot.
(C) Jason increased the price.

誰把這間房地產的價格漲了 7%？

(A) 我們想更加了解房地產和當地房產。
(B) 價格漲了很多。
(C) 傑森提高了價格。

| 單字 | mark up 提高價格 | property 財產；房地產 |

---

29. Where will I see the insurance broker?

(A) We should buy commercial insurance.
(B) He's a stockbroker.
(C) At the brokerage company.

哪裡可以見到保險經紀人？

(A) 我們應該買商業保險。
(B) 他是一名股票經紀人。
(C) 在經紀公司。

| 單字 | broker 經紀人 | commercial 商業的 | brokerage 經紀事業 |

---

30. Where can I find our company's law firm?

(A) It's next to the bank.
(B) You need to be firm with your subsidiary manager.
(C) We are studying corporate law.

我在哪裡可以找到我們公司的法律事務所？

(A) 它在銀行旁邊。
(B) 你必須嚴格要求你的子公司經理。
(C) 我們正在學習公司法。

| 單字 | firm 公司，事務所 | be firm with 嚴格要求 | subsidiary 子公司 |

---

31. What are our chances of winning the contract?

(A) It is a good contract for us.
(B) I'd say they are pretty good.
(C) We could get the prize for best actor.

我們有什麼機會簽到合約？

(A) 這對我們來說是一份很好的合約。
(B) 我覺得很有機會。
(C) 我們應該可以獲得最佳演員獎。

TEST 01
PART 3

Questions 32 through 34 refer to the following conversation.

M: Hi fellow colleagues, let's discuss the qualities we base our staff recruitment on. What do you think we should write in the advertisement?

W 1: Well, since we are looking for two females who will hold the position of full-time office secretary, I think that they must have exceptional interpersonal and communication skills.

M: Yes, I couldn't agree more. They must have a deep passion for delivering high quality customer service, and be cordial when interacting with our clients.

W 2: Also, they should demonstrate a thorough understanding of file management and also be self-disciplined and orderly in their office work.

W 1: And lastly, they must be team-oriented and work in a way that won't hinder other's work.

32-34 題參考下列對話。

男： 嗨，同事們，讓我們討論一下我們招聘員工時要求的特點。您認為我們應該在廣告中寫什麼？

女1：嗯，既然我們正在尋找兩位擔任全職辦公室秘書的女性，我認為她們必須具備出色的人際關係和溝通技巧。

男： 是的，我完全同意。她們必須對提供高品質的客服充滿熱情，並在與客戶互動時保持親切。

女2：此外，她們應該對檔案管理有透徹理解，並在辦公室工作中自律和有序。

女1：最後，她們必須以團隊為導向，並以不會妨礙他人工作的方式進行。

---

32. What are the speakers planning to do?

(A) Hire secretaries.
(B) Search for a part-time worker to sort out their files.
(C) Train staff members how to discipline themselves.
(D) Teach staff members how to interact with clients.

這三個人打算做什麼？

(A) 聘請秘書。
(B) 尋找兼職工作人員來整理他們的文件。
(C) 訓練員工如何自律。
(D) 教導員工如何與客戶互動。

---

33. What is mentioned about management in the office?

(A) Recruited workers should manage files well.
(B) It is good to give orders to subordinates.
(C) Managers should have authority in the workplace.
(D) It takes a lot of effort to discipline oneself.

有關辦公室管理方面提到了什麼？

(A) 新員工應該善於管理文件。
(B) 命令下屬是件好事。
(C) 經理在工作場所應該有權力。
(D) 自律需要付出很多努力。

TEST 01 PART 3

34. What does the man say in regards to customer service?

(A) The new workers will need passion when talking with clients.
(B) File management will enhance their customer service.
(C) Keeping their office in order will increase their work quality.
(D) Teamwork is the key to good customer service.

客服方面男子提到什麼？

(A) 新員工與客戶交談要有熱情。
(B) 檔案管理將可增進其客戶服務。
(C) 辦公室有條理將提升他們的工作品質。
(D) 團隊合作是良好客戶服務的關鍵。

單字			
	recruitment 招聘	position 職位	secretary 秘書
	interpersonal 人際的	cordial 熱誠的，誠懇的；親切的	interact 交流；互動
	demonstrate 展示；證實	self-disciplined 自律的	team-oriented 團隊導向的
	hinder 阻礙；妨礙	subordinate 下屬	authority 權力；權威
	enhance 增進；提升		

Questions 35 through 37 refer to the following conversation.

M: Excuse me, madam. Can you please tell me why the 8:30 bus to Sunnybank hasn't arrived yet?

W: The bus driver just called me and said that there has been severe rush hour traffic for the past hour. It should die down in about 30 minutes.

M: About what time will my bus arrive?

W: Well, it should arrive in about 20 minutes' time.

M: What other buses can take me to Sunnybank shopping mall?

W: I suggest you take bus number 300 because the earlier bus, number 325, will be crammed with people.

35-37 題參考以下對話。

男：不好意思，女士，可以告訴我為什麼開往 Sunnybank 的 8:30 這班巴士還沒到？

女：公車司機剛打電話給我，說一小時前有嚴重的尖峰時段塞車。應該會再塞約 30 分鐘。

男：我的公車什麼時候到？

女：嗯，大概再二十分鐘吧。

男：我還可以搭哪些巴士去 Sunnybank 購物中心？

女：我建議你坐 300 號公車，因為早一點往那裡的 325 號公車會擠滿人。

---

35. What is the conversation about?

(A) How to avoid getting caught in a traffic jam
(B) Why there is so much traffic at rush hour
(C) The best way to travel around Brisbane City
(D) How to get to Sunnybank by bus

這段對話在講什麼？

(A) 如何避免陷入交通壅塞
(B) 為什麼尖峰時段有這麼多的車
(C) 在布里斯本市旅行的最佳方式
(D) 如何搭公車前往 Sunnybank

---

36. Why is the 8:30 bus late?

(A) Traffic is too heavy.
(B) It broke down.
(C) It left the bus station late.
(D) The bus driver stopped for a 10-minute rest.

為什麼 8:30 這班公車遲到了？

(A) 交通太壅塞了。
(B) 公車故障了。
(C) 公車從公車站開出來時晚了。
(D) 公車司機停下來休息了 10 分鐘。

---

37. Why is it better to take bus 300?

(A) Because bus 325 is crowded with people.
(B) Because the earlier bus had an accident.
(C) Because it can arrive in less than 10 minutes.
(D) Because it can arrive faster than bus 325.

為何搭 300 號公車比較好？

(A) 因為 325 號公車擠滿了人。
(B) 因為早一點的公車發生了意外。
(C) 因為它可以在 10 分鐘內抵達。
(D) 因為它可以比 325 號公車更快抵達。

單字 rush hour 尖峰時段　　crammed 擠滿的　　crowded 擁擠的

TEST 01
PART 3

Questions 38 through 40 refer to the following conversation.

M: Jennifer, since you have carried out all the research on the Canadian market, I have some pertinent questions to ask. Who will be our target customers for our 125cc Yamaha motorcycle?

W: Mostly young and middle aged people belonging to the middle income bracket will be willing to buy one.

M: What strategies will we use to optimize our after-sales service in the country?

W: It is necessary to set up a shop that can handle customer enquiries and complaints. We'll also establish a local repair shop that can work on motorbikes that play up.

38-40 題參考以下對話。

男：珍妮佛，因為你已經對加拿大市場進行了所有的研究，我有一些相關的問題要問。誰是我們125cc 山葉機車的目標客戶？

女：主要是中等收入階層的年輕人和中年人願意買。

男：我們將採取哪些策略來提昇我們在該國的售後服務？

女：有必要建立一個可以處理客戶諮詢和投訴的店面。我們還將設立一個當地維修店，可以修理機車。

---

38. What kind of people will want to buy their product?

(A) Elderly people
(B) Middle-aged people with an average income
(C) Young people with little money to spend
(D) Middle aged people who are well-off

什麼樣的人會想要購買他們的產品？

(A) 老年人
(B) 一般收入的中年人
(C) 沒有多少錢可花的年輕人
(D) 富裕的中年人

---

39. What are the speakers discussing?

(A) How to enhance their customer service in America
(B) How domestic after-sales service should be done
(C) What kind of people will buy scooters in Canada
(D) The woman's findings on Canadian market research

說話者在討論什麼？

(A) 如何在美國增強客戶服務
(B) 如何進行國內的售後服務
(C) 加拿大有哪些人會買速克達機車
(D) 該女性研究加拿大市場的調查結果

---

40. What is true about the best way to enhance customer service?

(A) Start a shop that can deal with customers' questions
(B) Set up a repair shop in America.
(C) Carry out a survey on customer's needs.
(D) Hire staff who excel in handling customer enquiries

關於加強客戶服務的最佳方式何者為真？

(A) 開設一間可以處理客戶問題的店面
(B) 在美國設立維修店
(C) 對客戶的需求進行調查
(D) 聘請擅長處理客戶諮詢的員工

單字

carry out 進行，執行	pertinent 有關的；中肯的	bracket 等級
optimize 優化；提升	necessary 必要的	establish 建立，設立
repair 修理，維修	elderly 年老的	well-off 富裕的

Questions 41 through 43 refer to the following conversation.

M: I booked a ticket for the 8 a.m. ferry to Penghu Island. Why haven't the passengers started to board yet?

W: The repairmen just found out the ferry started to leak. We are moving it out of the harbor. A new one is on its way and will be here in 5 minutes.

M: Ok, thank God they found this problem early! Won't that mean that the time we embark will be delayed?

W: Yes. But to compensate for the passengers' lost time, we have prepared several complimentary food vouchers. They can be used at the Harbor Cafe over there. Here you are, sir.

41-43 題參考以下對話。

男：我預定了早上八點到澎湖的渡輪票。為什麼沒有乘客開始登船？

女：修理工剛剛發現渡輪在漏水。我們正把它移出港口。一艘新的就在來的路上，五分鐘內就會到達。

男：好的，幸好他們提早發現了這個問題！這不就意味著我們上船的時間會延後嗎？

女：是的。但為了彌補乘客損失的時間，我們準備了幾張免費的餐券，可以在港灣咖啡館使用。給您。

---

41. Where is the man bound for?

(A) Hawaii
(B) Penghu
(C) Japan
(D) Okinawa

該名男子要去哪兒？

(A) 夏威夷
(B) 澎湖
(C) 日本
(D) 沖繩

---

42. Why isn't the ferry on time?

(A) It was leaking.
(B) It ran into a fierce storm.
(C) It departed the last harbor 10 minutes late.
(D) They are experiencing technical difficulties.

為什麼不準時開船？

(A) 渡輪漏水了。
(B) 它遇到了強烈的暴風雨。
(C) 它晚了十分鐘開離上一個港口。
(D) 他們遇到技術困難。

---

43. How did the station master make compensation to the passengers?

(A) Give them free tickets
(B) Give them free vouchers
(C) Give them a refund
(D) Give them a discount on their tickets

站長如何補償乘客？

(A) 給他們免費門票
(B) 給他們免費的優惠券
(C) 給他們退款
(D) 給他們門票打折

單字

ferry 渡輪
embark 上船；登機
experience 經歷
leak 漏水；洩漏
complimentary 免費的
harbor 港口
fierce 兇猛的；強烈的

TEST 01
PART 3

Questions 44 through 46 refer to the following conversation.

M: Hi Jessica, how are you? I just heard that my friends' business has been running into trouble. Can we discuss some ways to help them get free from their financial problem?

W: Sure. What exactly happened to the company? Are they running up a budget deficit?

M: I guess they overspent on outsourcing and investing in markets they previously thought would be profitable.

W: That's not good. Well, firstly they should stop spending money on unprofitable markets, and finish business tasks on their own instead of relying on outside help.

M: Now that their company is in the red, they have been considering downsizing to cut down on costs.

W: I don't think that laying off workers is going to solve the problem. Instead, they should try to sell any assets that are not crucial to running their business.

44-46 題參考以下對話。

男：嗨，潔西卡，妳好嗎？我剛聽說我朋友的公司遇上麻煩了。我們可以討論一些方法來幫助他們解決財務困難嗎？

女：好的。這家公司到底怎麼了？他們出現預算赤字了嗎？

男：我猜他們在以前認為有利潤的市場的外包和投資這兩方面過頭了。

女：這樣不好。嗯，首先，他們應該停止在無利可圖的市場上花錢，並且自己完成業務任務，而不是依賴外部幫助。

男：現在他們的公司處於虧損狀態，他們一直在考慮縮減規模以降低成本。

女：我不認為裁員可以解決問題。相反的，他們應該嘗試出售對業務營運並非至關重要的任何資產。

---

44. What are the speakers discussing?

(A) How to save their own business from going bankrupt.
(B) Practical ways to save a company from financial problems.
(C) The downsides of making workers redundant.
(D) Why they should spend money on outsourcing.

說話者在討論什麼？

(A) 如何拯救自己的企業免於破產。
(B) 挽救一間公司脫離財務問題的實際辦法。
(C) 裁員的缺點。
(D) 為什麼他們應該花錢外包。

---

45. How did the woman say the problem should be solved?

(A) Lay off a quarter of the workers.
(B) Hire financial experts to help.
(C) Keep all assets that they feel are dispensable.
(D) Not rely on outsourcers.

該女子說應該怎麼解決這個問題？

(A) 解僱四分之一的員工。
(B) 聘請金融專家幫忙。
(C) 保留他們認為可有可無的資產。
(D) 不要依賴外包商。

46. What was said about downsizing the company?

(A) It isn't a good idea.
(B) It will possibly solve their problem.
(C) It's the only way to cut costs.
(D) It's harmful for workers' families.

關於縮編公司的說法如何？

(A) 這不是一個好主意。
(B) 這可能可以解決他們的問題。
(C) 這是縮減成本的唯一方法。
(D) 這對員工的家庭有害。

單字			
	deficit 赤字	overspent 花過頭，超支	outsourcing 外包
	previously 以前	instead of 取而代之；而不是	solve 解決
	assets 資產	crucial 關鍵性的；至關重要的	bankrupt 破產的
	redundant 多餘的；被裁員的	dispensable 可省去的，不必要的	harmful 有害的

TEST 01 PART 3

Questions 47 through 49 refer to the following conversation.

W 1: There are several things that we need to complete before the end of this fiscal year. Firstly, we need to do an inventory of all the products in our store.

M: We will also need to make a summary of our company's income and expenses by writing up a profit-and-loss statement. That way we can keep track of our business growth and company expenditure.

W 2: Hmm. We need to complete and lodge our income tax returns to the tax bureau by the end of next week.

M: It is also crucial that we plan ahead by reviewing our financial statements for this year and make a budget for the next business year. That way, we will better understand how to manage our money next year.

W 1: When all this is done, we need to report our business financial situation to our shareholders so they will have confidence in our future growth potential.

47-49 題參考以下對話。

女1：在這個財政年度結束前，我們需要完成幾件事。首先，我們需要對商店中的所有產品進行盤點。

男：我們還需要撰寫損益表來概述我們公司的收入和支出，這樣我們就可以追蹤業務成長和公司支出。

女2：嗯。我們需要在下週末之前填寫並向國稅局提出所得稅申報。

男：透過審查今年的財務報表並為下一個業務年度訂定預算，我們提前計劃也是至關重要的。這樣我們就能更加了解明年如何管理我們的資金。

女1：完成所有這些後，我們需要向股東報告我們業務的財務狀況，好讓他們對未來的成長潛力充滿信心。

---

47. What are the speakers discussing?

(A) What they should do at the end of a fiscal year
(B) How much money was spent last year
(C) When to visit the tax bureau
(D) When they will set up a joint venture

說話者在討論什麼？

(A) 他們應該在財政年度結束時做什麼
(B) 去年花了多少錢
(C) 何時去拜訪國稅局
(D) 他們何時成立合資企業

---

48. According to the conversation, what is a good way to know how much their business has grown?

(A) Hand in tax returns to the government
(B) Write a profit-and-loss statement
(C) Count how many products have been sold this year
(D) Ask their shareholders

根據對話，了解業務成長情況的好方法是什麼？

(A) 向政府提交納稅申報表
(B) 撰寫損益表
(C) 計算今年銷售的產品數量
(D) 詢問他們的股東

120

49. What do they have to report to their shareholders?

(A) The amount of tax they submitted last year
(B) How much they are growing financially
(C) How many products they have in stock
(D) Their budget for the previous year

他們需要向股東報告什麼？

(A) 他們去年報了多少稅金。
(B) 他們在財務上成長多少
(C) 他們有多少產品庫存
(D) 他們去年的預算

單字

fiscal year 財政年度；會計年度　　profit-and-loss statement 損益表　　expenditure 支出，開銷
crucial 至關重要的；關鍵的　　confidence 信心　　potential 潛力
venture 風險事業

TEST 01
PART 3

Questions 50 through 52 refer to the following conversation.

W: This week I will be visiting the exotic villa located on 4471 River Road in Colorado Springs. One of the tenants there wants to invest in property on the West End.

M: Ok. I suggest that they invest in the Fort Morgan estate. They only require a down payment of $15,000. Sounds good.

W: Also, my customers want to sublease their apartment so that they can make more money on it. Do you think that is a good idea?

M: Obviously not. Doing so could cause a person to receive up to six months in prison or a fine. In some cases, a person will be sentenced to five years in jail.

W: Ok, thanks for letting me know. I'll try to talk the customer out of doing this.

M: And another thing. Can you please come with me and do an appraisal of a two-bedroom house's value this afternoon? I'll need your expertise in this area.

50-52 問題參考以下對話。

女：這禮拜我會去參觀位於科羅拉多泉市里佛路 4471 號的異國風情別墅。其中一位租戶想在西區投資房地產。

男：好的。我建議他們投資摩根堡莊園，那只需要 15,000 美元的頭期款。聽起來不錯。

女：此外，我的客戶希望轉租他們的公寓，以便可以賺更多的錢。你覺得這是個好主意嗎？

男：顯然不是。這樣做可能會遭致最高六個月的監禁或罰款。在某些情況下，甚至將被判入獄五年。

女：好的，謝謝你讓我知道。我會跟客戶談談別這樣做。

男：還有一件事。你今天下午能和我一起去嗎？有棟有兩間房的房子需要估價。我需要你在這方面的專業知識。

---

50. Where is this conversation most likely taking place?

(A) In a business office
(B) In a real estate company
(C) In a telemarketing company
(D) In a household registration office

這段對話最有可能發生在哪裡？

(A) 企業辦公室
(B) 房地產公司
(C) 電話行銷公司
(D) 戶籍登記處

---

51. What does the man ask the woman to do?

(A) Appraise the value of a house
(B) Sublease his apartment to her friend
(C) Visit the exotic villa tomorrow
(D) Persuade a customer not to buy an apartment

男子要女子做什麼？

(A) 評估房屋的價值
(B) 將他的公寓轉租給她的朋友
(C) 明天參觀那棟異國風情的別墅
(D) 說服客戶不要購買公寓

52. According to the man, what will get a person imprisoned?

(A) Buying property in a red-light district
(B) Subleasing an apartment to another person
(C) Living in a house that was subleased
(D) Vandalizing someone's property

根據該男子，什麼會讓一個人被監禁？

(A) 在紅燈區購買房產
(B) 將公寓轉租給另一個人
(C) 住在轉租的房子裡
(D) 破壞某人的財產

單字			
	exotic 外來的，異國的	located 位於	tenant 房客，承租戶
	invest 投資	estate 不動產；莊園	sublease 將⋯轉租
	receive 收到	sentence 判決，宣判	appraisal 評價；估價
	district 區	vandalize 肆意破壞	

TEST 01
PART 3

Questions 53 through 55 refer to the following conversation.

M: Have you found a suitable location for our new subsidiary company in Hong Kong yet?

W: I have one in mind. It is located near the harbor. The current lease on the location will expire at the end of next month. I phoned them and was told that they will vacate the building by the 27th of next month.

M: Cool. But I think it would be better for us to just buy the place because we will be staying in the area for the long haul.

W: Ok. I agree. You definitely made the right choice. I believe that Hong Kong has a lucrative market in the area of logistics. This has been evident since the beginning of 2016, when it provided over 70,000 jobs to local people.

M: Hmm. It's true that local delivery businesses have been the driving force for the market, so if we develop our business to target this niche market, our annual profit will go through the roof.

53-55 題參考以下對話。

男：我們在香港的新子公司有沒有找到合適的地點？

女：我有想到一個。它靠近海港。該地點目前的租約將於下月底到期。我打電話給他們，他們說將在下個月 27 日之前離開大樓。

男：很棒喔。但我覺得我們最好用買的，因為我們將長期留在該地區。

女：好的。我同意。你的確做了正確的抉擇。我相信香港在物流方面是一個利潤豐厚的市場。自 2016 年初以來，這一點已經很明顯，當時它為當地人民提供了超過 70,000 個就業機會。

男：嗯。的確如此，當地的運送業務一直是市場的推動力，因此，如果我們發展業務來瞄準這個利基市場，我們的年度利潤將會達到頂峰。

---

53. According to the man, where are they going to set up their subsidiary?

(A) In Singapore
(B) In Japan
(C) In Taiwan
(D) In Hong Kong

根據該男子，他們要在哪裡設立子公司？

(A) 在新加坡
(B) 在日本
(C) 在台灣
(D) 在香港

---

54. Why is the company planning to buy a building instead of renting one?

(A) The real estate agent will give them a discount.
(B) They don't have to pay a large down payment.
(C) They plan to stay in the area for a long time.
(D) They don't want to keep changing buildings.

為什麼該公司打算購買建築物而不是租用？

(A) 房地產經紀人會給他們一個折扣。
(B) 他們不需要支付大筆頭期款。
(C) 他們打算長期留在該地區。
(D) 他們不想繼續改變建築物。

55. According to the woman, why is establishing a logistics company highly profitable?

(A) It substantially increased the local employment rate in 2016.
(B) Logistics companies make over a million a month.
(C) It is the strongest industry in the country.
(D) It is a niche market in Japan.

據該女子所說，為什麼設立物流公司的利潤很高？

(A) 2016 年大幅提高了當地就業率。
(B) 物流公司每月生產超過一百萬。
(C) 這是該國最強大的產業。
(D) 它是日本的利基市場。

單字			
	suitable 合適的	subsidiary 子公司	expire 期滿，到期
	vacate 空出；離開	long haul 長期	lucrative 獲利多的
	logistics 物流	evident 明顯的	target 對準，瞄準
	niche market 利基市場	establish 建立；創立	industry 產業

TEST 01
PART 3

Questions 56 through 58 refer to the following conversation.

M: Fellow colleagues, I have an important announcement to make. Our associate manager, Mr. Frankston, will be promoted to vice president as of next month. Throughout the past five years in this enterprise, he has shown strong initiative in his work, and with his guidance, the marketing department has increased their profit margin by over 10%.

W: I'm thrilled to announce that we made a profit of $30,000 with our fundraiser as of last week. How has the development of the supply chain been?

M: Well, we are still struggling to make our logistics delivery speed faster. I will send my colleague, Dean, to monitor and make sure it is managed better.

56-58 題參考以下對話。

男：同事們，我有一件重要的事要宣布，我們的副經理，弗蘭克斯頓先生將在下個月晉升為副總經理。在過去五年中，他在本企業中表現出很強的主動性，在他的指導下，行銷部門的利潤率提高了10%以上。

女：我很高興地宣布，截至上週，我們透過募款活動賺取了30,000美元的利潤。供應鏈的發展如何？

男：嗯，我們仍然在努力提升物流配送速度。我會派我的同事狄恩去監督，並確保它得到更好的管理。

---

56. Where most likely is this conversation taking place?

(A) In an overseas factory
(B) In a business office
(C) In a law firm
(D) In the HR department

這段對話最可能在哪裡進行？

(A) 在海外工廠
(B) 在企業辦公室
(C) 在律師事務所
(D) 在人力資源部門

---

57. Why will Mr. Frankston get a promotion?

(A) He led the marketing department to make more profit.
(B) He is a very independent leader.
(C) He holds a master's degree in management.
(D) The president of the company elected him.

弗蘭克斯頓先生為什麼會得到晉升？

(A) 他帶領行銷部門獲得更多利潤。
(B) 他是一位非常獨立的領導人。
(C) 他擁有管理學碩士學位。
(D) 公司經理推舉他。

---

58. What problem was mentioned?

(A) Their logistics system isn't big enough.
(B) They spent too much money at the fundraiser.
(C) The company's delivery speed is slow.
(D) Why their marketing campaign wasn't successful.

什麼問題被提出來？

(A) 他們的物流系統不夠大。
(B) 他們在募款活動上花了太多錢。
(C) 公司的送貨速度有點慢。
(D) 為什麼他們的行銷活動並未成功。

單字
associate manager 副經理　　vice president 副總經理　　enterprise 企業
thrilled 很高興，很興奮　　fundraiser 募款活動　　independent 獨立的
elect 推選

Questions 59 through 61 refer to the following conversation.

W: Now that our sales manager is planning to resign next month, we should try to find a person who is experienced in upper-level management.

M: A few days ago, we received a job application from Derek Robinson. He once worked for Fanhong International, and is adept at negotiating and resolving conflict between staff.

W: What about his work ethic and personality? Having strong leadership skills is a must.

M: He claims to be punctual, pro-active and have a charismatic spirit.

W: We could arrange an interview and put him on a probationary period for three months. If he demonstrates the right traits, we'll keep him.

59-61 題參考以下對話。

女：既然我們的業務經理計劃下個月辭職，我們應該設法找到一個有上層管理經驗的人。

男：幾天前，我們收到德瑞克・羅賓遜的求職申請。他曾在翻紅企業工作，擅長談判和解決員工之間的衝突。

女：他的職業道德和個性是如何呢？擁有優異的領導能力是必需的。

男：他聲稱自己是守時、積極主動的人，並且擁有個人魅力。

女：我們可以安排一次面試，讓他進入為期三個月的試用期。如果他表現出正確的特質，我們就留住他。

---

59. Where most likely is the conversation taking place?

(A) **The human resources management**
(B) The procurement department
(C) The research and development department
(D) The IT department

談話地點最有可能在哪裡？

(A) 人力資源管理部
(B) 採購部
(C) 研發部
(D) 資訊科技部門

---

60. What is true about Derek?

(A) He lacks leadership skills.
(B) His work ethic isn't up to scratch.
(C) **He is a pro-active worker.**
(D) He needs to work on his negotiation skills.

德瑞克的真實情況如何？

(A) 他缺乏領導能力。
(B) 他的職業道德並沒有達到標準。
(C) 他是一位積極主動的工作者。
(D) 他需要研究他的談判技巧。

---

61. What does the woman suggest they do?

(A) **Give Derek time to prove he is a suitable candidate.**
(B) Send Derek an email.
(C) Attend an on-the-job training course.
(D) Phone Derek tomorrow.

該女子建議他們做什麼？

(A) 讓德瑞克有時間證明他是一個合適的人選。
(B) 發電子郵件給德瑞克。
(C) 參加在職訓練課程。
(D) 明天打電話給德瑞克。

單字

upper 上面的	adept at 擅長於	negotiate 協商；談判
conflict 衝突	ethic 道德	punctual 準時的；守時的
pro-active 積極主動的	charismatic 有魅力的	spirit 精神
probationary 試用的	period 期間	demonstrate 表現，展現
trait 特點	lack 缺乏	

TEST 01
PART 3

Questions 62 through 64 refer to the following conversation.

M: Can you give us an overview of what you discussed at the business meeting on Tuesday?

W: Sure. First point, our manufacturing invested a total of $ 15,000 on upgrading the machinery on our production line. Second point, Mr. Brown suggested that we provide more value to our customers and more effectively increase our exposure to the outside world. And finally, Hilary Penn has been assigned the role of overseeing the sales promotion activity in July.

M: Ok, it seems like everything in our business is on track. Have we developed a strategic plan to expand our business into China?

W: That will obviously take time, because China is such a dynamic market. However, our CEO said that we should employ lateral thinking to overcome this challenging problem.

62-64 題參考以下對話。

男：你能概括一下你週二在商務會議上討論過的內容嗎？

女：好的。第一點，我們的製造部門在生產線上投入了 15,000 元來為機器升級。第二點，布朗先生建議我們為客戶提供更多價值，並更有效地增加我們對外界的曝光率。最後，希拉蕊·潘恩被任命負責監督七月份的促銷活動。

男：好的，我們的業務應該一切都在軌道上。請問我們是否制定了將業務擴展到中國的戰略計劃？

女：那顯然需要時間，因為中國是一個充滿活力的市場。然而，我們的 CEO 說我們應該採用水平思考來克服這個具有挑戰性的問題。

---

62. What are the speakers discussing?

(A) The details of an activity
(B) What was covered in a business meeting
(C) How to upgrade their machinery
(D) How much to invest in sales campaigns

說話者在討論什麼？

(A) 活動的細節
(B) 商務會議涉及的內容
(C) 如何升級他們的機器
(D) 投資銷售活動多少錢

---

63. According to the woman, how should they solve the problem of expanding to China?

(A) Look at the problem from a different angle
(B) Apply for a business license
(C) Make their business more dynamic
(D) Collaborate with the Chinese government in business

據女子所說，他們應該怎樣解決擴展到中國市場的問題？

(A) 從不同角度看問題
(B) 申請營業執照
(C) 使他們的業務更具活力
(D) 與中國政府合作開展業務

---

64. Who was given the role of supervising the activity in July?

(A) Mr. Brown
(B) The assistant manager of the sales department
(C) Hilary Penn
(D) The leader of the marketing department

誰被指派在七月份擔任監督活動的角色？

(A) 布朗先生
(B) 銷售部經理助理
(C) 希拉蕊·潘恩
(D) 行銷部門的領導者

單字
effectively 有效地　　assign 指派　　dynamic 充滿活力的
challenging 具有挑戰性的　　cover 涵蓋，包含　　angle 角度

Questions 65 through 67 refer to the following conversation and discount voucher.

M: Hello, ma'am. I'm looking for brakes. I looked around this aisle, but could only see car brakes. This store has Lyndall Gold brakes for motorcycles in stock, right?

W: Of course, sorry you couldn't find them. We just rearranged this aisle and moved the brakes to aisle seven. I'll take you there.

M: OK, great. Also, my wife gave me this discount coupon. I'm hoping to buy BikeMaster brakes for my Yamaha.

W: Sorry, but the first three brake models listed have already sold out today. It's a pity you didn't come three hours ago.

M: That's OK! I don't mind.

W: After making your selection, please be sure to present the voucher to the cashier.

Discount Voucher

The holder of this voucher is entitled to a discount of 30% on any of the following motorcycle brakes.

1. EBC
2. BikeMaster
3. SBS
4. Galfer

Expiry date: December 20, 2019

---

65. Where were the brakes moved to?

    (A) Aisle 3
    (B) Aisle 4
    (C) Aisle 6
    (D) Aisle 7

66. Look at the graphic. Which brand of brakes will the man purchase today?

    (A) Galfer
    (B) BikeMaster
    (C) SBS
    (D) EBC

TEST 01
PART 3

67. Where does the woman most likely work?　　該女子最有可能在哪裡工作？

(A) At an auto parts shop　　**(A)** 汽車零件商店
(B) At a paint store　　(B) 油漆店
(C) At a sports store　　(C) 體育用品店
(D) At a restaurant　　(D) 餐館

單字	brake 剎車（器）	aisle 走道，通道	rearrange 重新排列
	coupon 優惠券	present 出示；展示	

Questions 68 through 70 refer to the following conversation and price list.

M: Hello, Jeffrey Hews speaking, how may I help you?

W: Hi, Mr. Hews, it's Emily. I'm calling about my car. I assume that by now you have already finished doing the repairs to my alternator. When will it be ready to be collected?

M: Actually, we had to replace both your alternator and generator so we had one ordered in, but it won't arrive until the 21st of September. I'll have my secretary call our suppliers later on and find out if those spare parts have been sent out yet. It should only take about two days to carry out repairs on the car. If it isn't ready for collection in less than two weeks from now, we'll give you a 20% discount on the repair fee.

W: Okay, I'll call you at the end of next week.

M: Sure.

Albert's vehicle spare parts price list	
Alternator	$30
Generator	$25
Radiator	$20
Bumper	$27
Front and back door handles	$16.50

68. Where is the woman calling?

   (A) A motorbike repair store
   (B) A second-hand auto parts store
   (C) A car retailer
   (D) A mechanic shop

69. What is the man waiting for?

   (A) Spare parts for the woman's car
   (B) The products that the manager ordered
   (C) Tools to fix the car
   (D) A coupon

68-70 題參考以下對話和價格表。

男：您好，我是傑福瑞・休斯，很高興為您服務。

女：嗨，休斯先生，我是艾蜜麗。我要問我的車。我想現在你們已經修好了我的交流發電機。什麼時候可以取車？

男：事實上，我們必須更換你的交流發電機和發電機，我們已經訂了零件，但它要到9月21日才會到。我稍後會請我秘書打電話給供應商，看看這些零件是否已出貨。維修只需要兩天左右的時間。兩週內如果無法取車，我們將為您提供20%的折扣。

女：好的，我會在下週末打電話給你。

男：好的。

艾柏特汽車零件價格表	
交流發電機	$30
發電機	$25
散熱器	$20
保險桿	$27
前後門把手	$16.50

女子打電話去哪裡？

(A) 摩托車維修店
(B) 二手汽車零件商店
(C) 汽車零售商
(D) 汽車維修店

男子在等待什麼送到？

(A) 該女子之汽車的零件
(B) 經理訂購的產品
(C) 修理汽車的工具
(D) 優惠券

TEST 01 PART 3

70. Look at the graphic. How much does the woman have to pay?

(A) $30
(B) $25
(C) $16.50
(D) $55

請看圖表。該女子要支付多少錢？

(A) 30 美元
(B) 25 美元
(C) 16.50 美元
(D) 55 美元

| 單字 | assume 認為；假設　　alternator 交流發電機　　generator 發電機
secretary 秘書　　spare part 備用零件　　radiator 散熱器
bumper 保險桿　　front and back door handles 前後門把手
retailer 零售商 |

TEST 01
PART 4

Questions 71 through 73 refer to the following announcement.

Hello, Taichung residents. My name is Raphael Jones and I'm speaking on behalf of the International Alzheimer's Foundation. We urgently need your assistance this year in our battle to find a cure for Alzheimer's disease. Your donation of $100, $200 or $300 will be dedicated to scientific research conducted on this harmful disease. It could possibly help save one of your friends' or family members' life one day. Wouldn't you consider contributing some money to this charitable cause this year? We would greatly appreciate any amount, even as small as $5. To make a pledge to the IAF, please call 880-565-8426 between 8 a.m. and 8 p.m. (Pacific Time) or browse our website at www.iaf.org. If you'd rather mail us a contribution, please send a money order to IAF, 43 Riverside Lane Palm City, FL 34990. Thanks for your time.

71-73 題參考以下公告。

台中市民們您好！

我是拉斐爾・瓊斯，我為國際阿茲海默症基金會代言。今年我們亟需你們的幫助，以找出阿茲海默症的治療方法。你們贈的 100 美元、200 美元或 300 美元都將用於對這種有害疾病的科學研究。有天它也許有助於拯救你們朋友或家人的生命。你想過今年為這個慈善事業捐一點錢嗎？我們非常感謝您的任何金額，即使只有 5 美元。想捐款給 IAF，請在太平洋時間上午 8 點至晚上 8 點之間致電 880-565-8426，或瀏覽我們的網站 www.iaf.org。如果您比較喜歡郵寄捐款，請將匯票寄至 IAF：34990，佛羅里達州棕櫚市河畔巷 43 號。感謝你們撥出時間。

---

71. What is the purpose of this announcement?

(A) To cure breast cancer
(B) To solicit donations
(C) To obtain a free gift
(D) To assist friends or family members

這則公告的目的是什麼？

(A) 治療乳癌
(B) 募款
(C) 獲得免費禮物
(D) 協助朋友或家人

72. Who is the announcement for?

(A) Those who live in Taipei
(B) People living in Kaohsiung
(C) People residing in Taichung City
(D) Those who are suffering from an illness

這則公告的對象是什麼人？

(A) 住在台北的人
(B) 住在高雄的人
(C) 住在台中市的人
(D) 患有疾病的人

73. When is the best time for the listeners to call the IAF?

(A) Between 7 a.m. and 5 p.m. Central Time
(B) Between 8 a.m. and 9 p.m. Western Time
(C) Between 8 a.m. and 8 p.m. Pacific Time
(D) Between 8 a.m. and 5 p.m. Pacific Time

何時是打給 IAF 的最佳時間？

(A) 中部時間上午 7 點至下午 5 點
(B) 西部時間上午 8 點至晚上 9 點
(C) 太平洋時間上午 8 點至晚上 8 點
(D) 太平洋時間上午 8 點至下午 5 點

單字

urgently 緊急地	assistance 幫助	dedicate 專用於；投身於
scientific 科學的	conduct 進行，執行	disease 疾病
contribute 捐贈	charitable 慈善的	make a pledge to 捐款給
browse 瀏覽	would rather 寧願	solicit 徵求，請求

TEST 01
PART 4

Questions 74 to 76 refer to the following report.

This is meteorologist Harrison Fletcher in the CBS weather center. Now that summer's over, it's time to start preparing for cooler weather. As can be seen on this KOPS satellite image, a storm front is heading towards America's east coastline, and will bring torrential rain and gales tonight. Tomorrow afternoon, we should expect showers after clear skies in the morning. Temperatures will hit 35 degrees this afternoon and 37 tomorrow, so it is best to stay out of the sun. Taking a look at the weekday forecast, this high-pressure system coming in from the north will bring more rain on Thursday, interspersed with periods of partially clear skies. Highs from Thursday to Friday will climb toward 38, with lows possibly dropping to the mid 20's. Looking out over the western states, things look arid there, with little rain expected, and highs remaining steady in the mid-to-upper 30s for the next week.

74-76 題參考以下報告。

我是 CBS 氣象中心的氣象學家哈瑞森·弗萊徹。夏天已經結束了，應該開始為涼爽的天氣做準備了。從這張 KOPS 衛星圖像可以看出，風暴前沿正朝著美國東部海岸線前進，今晚將帶來暴雨和強風。明天下午，我們應該會在早上晴朗的天空之後看到陣雨。今天下午氣溫將達到 35 度，明天將達到 37 度，因此最好避開陽光。從工作日的預測來看，這個從北方進入的高壓系統將在週四帶來更多的降雨，其中穿插著部分晴朗的天空。週四至週五的高點將攀升至 38 度，低點可能跌至 25 度上下。眺望西部各州，情況看起來很乾旱，預計雨量很少，而下週的高溫將穩定持續在 35 度和以上。

74. Which direction is the storm front moving?

(A) Eastern coast of USA
(B) Southeast coast of USA
(C) Mexico's west coastline
(D) Mexico's north coastline

暴風雨移向哪裡？

(A) 美國東海岸
(B) 美國東南海岸
(C) 墨西哥西海岸
(D) 墨西哥北海岸

75. What does the speaker advise the audience to do?

(A) Look at a satellite photo
(B) Don't go out in the sun this afternoon
(C) Put on suntan lotion tomorrow
(D) Prepare for warmer weather

報告者建議聽眾做什麼？

(A) 看一張衛星照片
(B) 今天下午不要出去曬太陽
(C) 明天要擦防曬乳液
(D) 準備迎接溫暖的天氣

76. What will happen from Monday to Friday?

(A) Temperatures will hit 38 degrees.
(B) It will drizzle.
(C) It will gradually get colder.
(D) It will rain heavily for several days in the eastern part of America.

星期一到星期五會發生什麼事？

(A) 溫度將達到 38 度。
(B) 會下毛毛雨。
(C) 逐漸變冷。
(D) 美國東部將會下幾天大雨。

單字

meteorologist 氣象學者
torrential（雨）滂沱的
suntan lotion 防曬乳液
satellite 衛星
intersperse 點綴
drizzle 下毛毛雨
coastline 海岸線
drop 下降；掉落
gradually 逐漸

Questions 77 through 79 refer to the following radio broadcast.

This is Fiona Brassels with your 5 p.m. ICT traffic report. Well, for all those on the roads listening to this, you already know that traffic is quite chaotic everywhere. Vehicles crossing the bridge over the Hudson River on State Route 50 have come to a halt both northbound and southbound, and the traffic flow on the freeway running through Hudson valley is stop-and-go from Albany through to Yonkers. Highway 17 is slow through the city, then clears out until Overpass Road. What's worse is, a severe accident has caused traffic congestion on Georgetown Street downtown, and cars waiting to get onto the freeway will have to wait 15 minutes before traffic will start flowing smoothly again. This has been Fiona Brassels with your 5 p.m. ICT-AM traffic update. Our next traffic report will be just before 5:30 p.m.

77-79 題參考以下廣播。

我是菲歐娜・布拉索斯，陪你在下午五點鐘的 ICT 交通路況報導。嗯，對於所有在路上聽路況的人來說，你已經知道到處交通都很混亂。50 號州道上跨越哈德遜河的橋樑上的車輛南北向都停下來了，穿越哈德遜河谷的高速公路上的交通流量從奧爾巴尼一直到揚克斯都是走走停停。穿過城市的 17 號公路行駛很緩慢，直到高架道路才通暢。更糟糕的是，一起嚴重的事故導致喬治城街市區的交通壅塞，等待進入高速公路的汽車將需要等待 15 分鐘才能再順暢地行駛。這是菲歐娜・布拉索斯陪您在下午 5 點鐘的 ICT-AM 路況更新。我們的下一次路況報導將在下午 5:30 之前播出。

77. Who most likely are the listeners of the broadcast?

(A) Bus passengers
(B) Business executives
(C) Vehicle drivers
(D) Subway passengers

誰最有可能是這則路況報導的聽眾？

(A) 巴士乘客
(B) 企業高層
(C) 車輛駕駛員
(D) 地鐵乘客

78. What does the speaker say about traffic?

(A) Only one part of the city is having traffic congestion.
(B) An accident is obstructing the traffic downtown.
(C) It is clear on State Route 50.
(D) It is fast only on north-south roads.

報導者說交通怎麼了？

(A) 只有一部分城市有交通堵塞。
(B) 一起事故阻礙了市中心的交通。
(C) 50 號州道很順暢。
(D) 僅在南北向道路上是順暢的。

79. What is scheduled to happen at 5:30 p.m.?

(A) The roads will be cleared.
(B) A weather report will be broadcasted.
(C) A baseball game will be played.
(D) A traffic update will be aired.

下午 5:30 會發生什麼？

(A) 道路將會暢通
(B) 天氣預報
(C) 棒球比賽
(D) 路況更新報導

單字
- chaotic 一團亂
- overpass 高架道路
- obstruct 阻塞；堵塞
- freeway（免收費）高速公路
- accident 意外事故
- air 播報
- stop-and-go 走走停停
- congestion 擁擠；堵車

TEST 01
PART 4

Questions 80 through 82 refer to the following announcement.

The Mooloolaba Beach would like to notify residents of the Anzac Day parade that will be held next week. On April 25th, 8 a.m. to 12 p.m., a large parade in Mooloolaba, from River Esplanade to Burnett Street. Participants should gather at Foote Street and River Esplanade intersection ten minutes before the activity commences. After the parade is finished, all people are welcome to attend a lunch reception in the Mooloolaba Lifeguard Hall, where Anzac biscuits, pavlova, and other scrumptious treats will be served. From 8 a.m. to 2 p.m., the streets in close proximity to the parade location will be blocked off to vehicle traffic. Pedestrians will still have access to businesses and shops along the parade route. During the parade, traffic will be re-routed through Hancock Street. If you have any inquiries, you are welcome to phone the city manager's office at 41-690-412. The office is open from 8 a.m. to 6 p.m., Mondays through Fridays.

80-82 題參考以下公告。

穆魯拉巴沙灘通知居民將在下週舉行澳紐軍團日遊行。4 月 25 日早上 8 點到 12 點，在穆魯拉巴，有一個從 River Esplanade 公園到 Burnett 街的大型遊行。參與者應在活動開始前十分鐘在 Foote 街和 River Esplanade 公園交叉口集合。遊行結束後，歡迎所有人參加穆魯拉巴救生員廳的午餐招待會，屆時將供應澳紐軍團餅乾、帕芙洛娃蛋糕和其他美味佳餚。上午 8 點到下午 2 點，靠近遊行地點的街道將管制車輛通行。行人仍然可以沿著遊行路線進入公司行號和商店。在遊行期間，交通將改道漢考克街。如果您有任何疑問，歡迎致電 41-690-412 與市政經理辦公室聯繫。辦公室開放時間為週一至週五上午 8 點至下午 6 點。

---

80. What is the purpose of this announcement?

(A) To notify listeners of a surfing activity
(B) To invite people to attend a party at the town hall
(C) To warn people of bad traffic conditions
(D) To inform people of a parade activity

這份公告的目的是什麼？

(A) 通知聽眾衝浪活動
(B) 邀請人們參加市政廳的聚會
(C) 警告人們交通狀況不佳
(D) 告知人們遊行活動

---

81. What did the speaker mention about lunch?

(A) Only apple pies and strawberries will be served.
(B) Lunch will be served prior to the activity.
(C) People are invited to lunch at the Lifeguard Hall.
(D) Lunch will be followed by a documentary.

發言人提到了什麼關於午餐的內容？

(A) 只提供蘋果餡餅和草莓。
(B) 午餐將在活動開始前供應。
(C) 邀請人們在救生員廳吃午餐。
(D) 午餐之後將播放一部紀錄片。

---

82. When will cars have access to River Esplanade?

(A) At 12 noon
(B) At 3 p.m.
(C) At 2:30 p.m.
(D) At 2 p.m.

當地車輛何時可以開始進入 River Esplanade 公園？

(A) 中午 12 點
(B) 下午 3 點
(C) 下午 2:30
(D) 下午 2 點

單字

intersection 交叉口　　commence 開始　　lifeguard 救生員
pavlova 帕芙洛娃蛋糕　　scrumptious 美味的　　proximity 接近，靠近
documentary 紀錄片

Questions 83 through 85 refer to the following advertisement.

Valentine's Day is right around the corner—are you looking for the perfect gift to pamper your spouse or loved one? Look no further! Here at Velvet Box, you'll find that prices of diamonds, wedding bands, engagement rings, and exquisite jewelry are truly unbeatable. Plus, all items sold in our store come with a twelve-month money-back guarantee, so you'll find superb quality you can trust. Salespeople here aren't paid based on commission so you won't feel pressured to purchase any items you don't want, and you are certain to get honest answers to all of your questions. As of today, we are offering an 8 month no-interest option with a minimum monthly payment. Those who visit us within the next two days and mention that you heard this ad on 102.6 FM will receive a 10% discount on the total price of any item! Make this Valentine's day the most unforgettable day by shopping at Velvet Box.

83-85 題參考以下廣告。

情人節即將來臨──您是否正在尋找寵愛配偶或愛人的完美禮物？不要再猶豫了，因為在 Velvet Box，您會發現鑽石、結婚戒指、訂婚戒指和精美珠寶的價格確實無與倫比。此外，我們商店出售的所有商品都有十二個月的退款保證，因此您將找到值得信賴的卓越品質。這裡的銷售人員並非只能賺取佣金，因此您不會感到有壓力得購買任何您不想要的物品，並且您的所有問題都會得到誠實的回答。今天起，我們提供 8 個月的無息分期付款，每月付最低額。那些在接下來的兩天內造訪我們並提及在 102.6 FM 上聽到此廣告的人將享有任何商品總價格的九折折扣！在 Velvet Box 購物，讓這個情人節成為最難忘的一天。

83. Where mostly likely would you hear this advertisement?

(A) In a supermarket
(B) On TV
(C) On the radio
(D) At a jewelry store

你最有可能在哪裡聽到這段廣告？

(A) 在超市裡
(B) 在電視上
(C) 在廣播裡
(D) 在珠寶店

84. Who most likely is the speaker?

(A) An office manager
(B) A sales person
(C) A business owner
(D) A client

誰是說話者？

(A) 辦公室經理
(B) 銷售人員
(C) 企業主
(D) 客戶

85. Which offer was NOT mentioned that would make purchasing appealing?

(A) 10% discount
(B) A lifetime warranty
(C) Money-back guarantee within one year
(D) A no-interest option for 8 months

廣告未提到哪項會吸引人購買的優惠方案？

(A) 九折折扣
(B) 終身保固
(C) 一年內的退款保證
(D) 八個月的無息分期貸款

單字
pamper 寵愛；嬌慣
exquisite 精緻的，精美的
appealing 吸引人的
spouse 配偶
jewelry 珠寶；首飾
engagement 訂婚；約會
certain 確定的

TEST 01
PART 4

Questions 86 through 88 refer to the following broadcast.

Attention, all passengers for Eastern Air Flight 547. Flight 547 bound for New York scheduled to depart at 2:30 will be delayed due to a late connecting flight from Los Angeles. The new departure time is now scheduled for 4 p.m. Consequently, the new boarding time for premium class and business passengers is at 3:10. Economy passengers will be boarding at 3:20. The gates will close at 3:40, twenty minutes prior to departure time. While you are waiting, we sincerely invite all passengers to the ticket desk to collect a free voucher for a beverage and dessert at the Apron JetStream Cafe. We sincerely apologize for any inconvenience and thank you for choosing to fly with Eastern Air.

86-88 題參考以下廣播。

東方航空 547 號航班的所有乘客請注意。預定於 2:30 飛往紐約的 547 號航班將因洛杉磯接駁航班延誤而延後起飛，新的出發時間現在定於下午 4 點。因此，白金艙和商務艙乘客的新登機時間為 3:10。經濟艙乘客將於 3:20 登機，登機門將在起飛前 20 分鐘，也就是 3:40 關閉。在您等待的同時，我們誠摯邀請所有乘客到售票處領取 Apron JetStream 咖啡廳的飲料和甜點免費招待券。對於給您帶來不便，我們深表歉意，並感謝您選擇搭乘東方航空公司。

---

86. What is the broadcast about?

(A) A promotion for Apron JetStream Cafe
(B) Gate numbers for a departing flight
(C) Changing departure times
(D) The boarding time for a flight to Los Angeles

這則廣播是關於什麼？

(A) Apron JetStream 咖啡廳的促銷活動
(B) 離境航班的登機門號
(C) 改變起飛時間
(D) 飛往洛杉磯的航班的登機時間

---

87. What problem was mentioned?

(A) The New York flight won't depart on time.
(B) Passengers flying to Chicago will board after 3:15.
(C) All flights for the day are cancelled.
(D) The airport cafe will be closing early.

廣播提到了什麼問題？

(A) 飛往紐約的航班不會準時起飛。
(B) 飛往芝加哥的乘客將在 3:15 之後登機。
(C) 當天的所有航班均被取消。
(D) 機場咖啡館將提前關閉。

---

88. What was offered to the passengers?

(A) A discount on flights this year
(B) A voucher for an upgrade to business class
(C) A refund at the counter
(D) A ticket for free food and a drink

航空公司提供什麼給乘客？

(A) 今年的航班折扣
(B) 升級到商務艙的招待券
(C) 櫃檯退款
(D) 免費食物和飲料的兌換券

單字

connecting 接駁的，銜接的　　premium 優質的；高價的　　voucher 抵用券，招待券
sincerely 真誠地　　inconvenience 不便

Questions 89 through 91 refer to the following advertisement.

This is Fredrick Taylor, manager of Fredrick Motors. If you're thinking of purchasing a brand-new car, it's the right time! We have a broad selection of new vehicles, and owing to government incentives, prices are at an all-time low. Not only will you get a 15% discount on all the new vehicles, we'll also throw in receiving a whopping $1,000 rebate under the government's program that encourages locals to sell second hand cars for cash. We're on the 5th Avenue on the east side of Interstate 40 in Barstow. We are open 8 a.m. to 8 p.m. Sunday through Friday. Tell the staff that you were sent by Taylor, and we'll change your car's oil the first time for free!

89-91 題參考以下廣告。

我是飛得利汽車公司的經理弗雷德瑞克・泰勒。如果您想購買一輛全新的汽車，現在是時候了！我們有廣泛的新車選擇，並且由於政府的獎勵措施，價格處於歷史最低點。您不僅可以獲得所有新車 15% 的折扣，我們還將根據政府補助的高達 1,000 美元的減免額，鼓勵當地人出售二手車換取現金。我們位於巴斯托 40 號州際公路東側的第 5 大道。我們的營業時間為週日至週五上午 8 點至晚上 8 點。告訴工作人員您是泰勒叫來的，我們會免費更換您的車油一次！

89. Who most likely is the speaker?

(A) An auto parts salesman
(B) An automobile sales manager
(C) A government official
(D) A mechanic

說話者最可能是誰？

(A) 汽車零件銷售員
(B) 汽車銷售經理
(C) 政府官員
(D) 機修工

90. Why would customers be interested in going to this business?

(A) Car buyers can get over 10% off.
(B) It is the best auto parts shop in town.
(C) Customers can continuously buy cars at low prices.
(D) They repair customers' cars for free.

為什麼顧客會有興趣參與交易？

(A) 汽車購買人可以有 10% 以上的折扣。
(B) 這是鎮上最好的汽車零件商店。
(C) 客戶可持續以低價購買汽車。
(D) 他們免費為顧客修理汽車。

91. What free service does the company offer?

(A) A free first oil change
(B) Three years aftersales service
(C) Free replacement of used parts
(D) An engine stability test

該公司提供哪些免費服務？

(A) 首次換機油免費
(B) 三年的售後服務
(C) 免費更換舊零件
(D) 引擎穩定度試驗

單字	incentive 獎勵；誘因	whopping 特大的	rebate 減免額，部分退款
	continuously 持續地	replacement 更換	stability 穩定；穩定度

TEST 01
PART 4

Questions 92 through 94 refer to the following talk and speech agenda.

Good morning, ladies and gentlemen. First off, I would like to extend my gratitude to Professor Jack Georgeson for inviting me to deliver this commencement address. Before the degrees and academic awards are conferred on all graduate students, I'd like to personally express my appreciation to my guidance professor and fellow classmates, who gave me lots of assistance with my studies throughout the past year. When structuring this speech, I asked myself what important lessons I have learned throughout my time at Bale University. I wish to spend three minutes to expound on how to overcome failure. By the end of my talk, hopefully I will have persuaded you that courageously taking risks and persevering to the end is the fastest path to success as a student and worker.

92-94 題參考以下談話與演講議程。

早安，女士和先生們。首先，感謝傑克・喬治森教授邀請我發表這個畢業典禮演講。在我們開始為我們的研究生授予學位和學術獎之前，我想親自向我的指導教授和同學表示感謝，他們在過去的一年裡給予我的學業很多幫助。在構思這個演講時，我問自己在貝爾大學的期間學到了什麼重要的經驗教訓。我希望花三分鐘來闡述如何克服失敗。在我的演講結束時，希望我能說服你們相信，勇敢地冒險並堅持到最後是學生和工作者成功的最快途徑。

June 28th Short Speech Agenda		
Speaker	**Time**	**Topic**
Johnnie Harrison	5 minutes	The importance of finding a mentor
George Thompson	10 minutes	How my professor changed my life
Annie Johnson	3 minutes	Persevering towards success
Riana Zuckerburg	10 minutes	The best jobs to do after 2020

6/28 演講議程		
演講人	時間	主題
強尼・哈瑞森	5 分鐘	找到導師的重要性
喬治・湯普森	10 分鐘	我的教授如何改變我的一生
安妮・強生	3 分鐘	堅持直到成功
瑞安娜・祖克柏	10 分鐘	2020 年後的最佳工作

92. Who is delivering this talk?

(A) A prominent scholar
(B) A famous athlete
(C) A college professor
(D) A graduating student

誰在發表這段談話？

(A) 傑出學者
(B) 著名運動員
(C) 大學教授
(D) 即將畢業的學生

93. Look at the graphic. Which speaker is delivering a talk now?

(A) Johnnie Harrison
(B) Annie Johnson
(C) Riana Zuckerburg
(D) George Thompson

請看圖表。現在是哪位發言人在發表談話？

(A) 強尼・哈瑞森
(B) 安妮・強生
(C) 瑞安娜・祖克柏
(D) 喬治・湯普森

94. Where would you mostly likely hear this kind of talk?

(A) At a graduation ceremony
(B) At a presidential inauguration
(C) In a college lecture
(D) At a high school orientation activity

你最常在哪裡聽到這類談話？

(A) 在畢業典禮上
(B) 在總統就職典禮上
(C) 在大學講座
(D) 在高中新生訓練

單字	commencement 畢業典禮	academic 學術的	personally 親自
	courageously 勇敢地	ceremony 典禮	orientation 新生訓練，新人訓練

TEST 01
PART 4

Questions 95 through 97 refer to the following talk and tour schedule.

Welcome aboard! For the next 3 hours, I'll introduce the scenic spots around Brisbane City and describe how the city has developed into the most populous city in Queensland. To your right, you'll behold the City Botanic Gardens that was officially opened in the late 1800s. If you have time after this tour, I recommend taking a stroll along the trails around the garden. There is also a three-hundred-year old Catholic cathedral that is full of history. Next, on the opposite side of the Brisbane River, you can see Kangaroo Point Cliffs Park. It is a hot spot for avid abseilers and rock climbers. Since most of you would want to dine at the cathedral restaurant for more than twenty minutes, we might have to skip the second-to-last destination on our list.

95-97題參考以下談話和旅遊行程表。

歡迎上車！在接下來的三個小時內，我將介紹布里斯本市周圍的景點，並說明它如何發展成為昆士蘭州人口最多的城市。在您的右邊，您將看到十九世紀末正式開放的城市植物園；如果您在這次旅遊後有時間，我建議您沿著花園周圍的小徑漫步。其次，有一間具有三百年歷史的天主教大教堂。接下來，在布里斯本河的對面，您可以看到袋鼠角懸崖公園，這是熱衷的游繩者和攀岩者的熱門景點。由於大多數人都想在大教堂餐廳用餐超過二十分鐘，我們可能不得不跳過倒數第二個目的地。

Brisbane Tour List of Destinations August 15, 2020	
Scenic spot name	Time spent looking around
City Botanic Gardens	1 hour
Catholic cathedral	20 minutes
Kangaroo Point Cliffs Park	20 minutes
Southbank	40 minutes
Queensland Art Gallery	40 minutes

布里斯本旅遊目的地清單 2020/8/15	
景點	遊覽時間
城市植物園	1 小時
天主教大教堂	20 分鐘
袋鼠角懸崖公園	20 分鐘
南岸	40 分鐘
昆士蘭美術館	40 分鐘

95. What is the purpose of the talk?

(A) To educate tourists about the location of Brisbane
(B) To survey the terrain of the Botanic Gardens
(C) To familiarize travelers with the city's scenic spots
(D) To convince students to attend the university

這段談話的目的是什麼？

(A) 向遊客介紹布里斯本的所在位置
(B) 調查植物園的地形
(C) 讓遊客熟悉這個城市的景點
(D) 說服學生上大學

96. Look at the graphic. Which place might the tour group NOT have enough time to see today?

(A) The Catholic cathedral
(B) Kangaroo Point Cliffs Park
(C) Queensland Art Gallery
(D) Southbank

請看圖表。旅行團今天可能沒時間去看哪個地方？

(A) 天主教大教堂
(B) 袋鼠角懸崖公園
(C) 昆士蘭美術館
(D) 南岸

97. What will the people most likely do when the tour is finished?

(A) Eat lunch at a restaurant near the river
(B) Go abseiling
(C) Go back to their hotel rooms
(D) Take a relaxing walk around the City Botanic Gardens

旅遊結束後人們最有可能做什麼？

(A) 在河邊的一家餐館吃午餐
(B) 玩遊繩下降運動
(C) 回到他們的酒店房間
(D) 在城市植物園悠閒漫步

單字			
	populous 人口眾多的	stroll 閒逛；漫步	trail 小徑
	Catholic cathedral 天主教大教堂	opposite 對面的	abseiler 游繩者
	destination 目的地	abseil（登山運動的）繞繩下降	

TEST 01 PART 4

Questions 98 through 100 refer to the following speech and awards list.

On behalf of Fareast Biomarine, I'd like to show my deepest gratitude for bestowing this award upon us. Five years ago, we started to build our business from the ground up, and have been continuously fighting battles against cut-throat competition in our business sphere. Our company was established for the purpose of becoming the top biotech innovator in the field of krill-harvesting. We expend lots of time and effort on researching creative ways to enhance both human and planetary health. Our core business revolves around cultivating and harvesting krill, a small sea creature. We then convert this animal into a nutritional supplement that can substantially improve humans' overall well-being. Not only have we been successful in developing strategies that help us to expand to many countries around the world, we have achieved outstanding levels of annual sales and profit.

98-100題參考以下的演講和獎項列表。

我謹代表遠東海洋生技公司,對於獲頒這個獎致以最深切的謝意。五年前,我們開始建立業務,並一直與同領域的同業進行惡性競爭。我們公司的成立是為了成為磷蝦捕撈領域的頂級生物技術創新者。我們花費大量時間和精力研究創造性方法,以增強人類和地球的健康。我們的核心業務圍繞著培育和收穫磷蝦,一種小型海洋生物。然後我們將這種動物轉化為營養補充劑,可以顯著改善人類的整體健康狀況。我們不僅成功地制定了有助於我們擴展到全球許多國家的戰略,我們還達成了出色的年銷售額和利潤水平。

Name of award	Awarded to which kind of company
Digital Technology Award	Companies with strong application of digital technologies
Best Growth Strategy of the Year Award	Companies with strong international expansion and market creation
Award for Innovation	Highly profitable and innovative companies
Global Investment Award	Companies that manage subsidiary businesses outside of their original market

獎項名稱	獲獎公司種類
數位技術獎	公司擁有強大的數位技術應用
年度最佳成長策略獎	公司具有強大的國際擴張力和市場創造力
創新獎	高利潤和創新的公司
全球投資獎	在原有市場之外管理子公司業務的公司

98. What was the main purpose of establishing the company?

(A) **To become a highly-profitable and innovative company**
(B) To use advanced technology in their business
(C) To compete with other biotechnology companies
(D) To expand their business to all parts of the world

成立這家公司的主要目的是什麼?

(A) 成為一家高利潤和創新型公司
(B) 在業務中使用先進技術
(C) 與其他生物科技公司競爭
(D) 將業務擴展到世界各地

99. Look at the graphic. Which award is being conferred to Fareast Biomarine?

    (A) Digital Technology Award
    (B) Best Growth Strategy of the Year Award
    (C) Award for Innovation
    (D) Global Investment Award

請看圖表。遠東海洋生技公司正獲頒哪個獎項？

    (A) 數位技術獎
    (B) 年度最佳成長策略獎
    (C) 創新獎
    (D) 全球投資獎

---

100. What does the business focus on doing?

    (A) Developing nutritional products to fight cancer
    (B) Growing and harvesting a kind of small sea animal
    (C) Researching digital cellphone applications
    (D) Expanding to all parts of their domestic market

這家企業專注的重點是什麼？

    (A) 開發抗癌的營養產品
    (B) 養殖和收獲一種小型海洋動物
    (C) 研究數位手機應用
    (D) 擴展到國內市場的所有部分

單字

bestow 授予	cut-throat competition 惡性競爭	sphere 領域
krill-harvesting 磷蝦捕撈	cultivate 栽培	nutritional 營養的
substantially 可觀地；顯著地	achieve 達成	digital 數位的
innovation 創新	investment 投資	

145

TEST 01
PART 5

101. Our company is one of the most -------- and well-established travel agencies in this country.

(A) repute
(B) reputed
(C) reputably
(D) reputation

我們公司是國內最知名和最有聲譽的旅行社之一。

(A) 名譽；名聲
(B) 有聲望的；知名的
(C) 有聲望地
(D) 名譽；聲望

| 解析 | 與 and 後面 well-established（地位穩固／享有聲譽的）相呼應，故應選 (B) reputed（有聲望的；知名的），同樣為過去分詞形式。 |

單字	company 公司　　　　　　　　　　　well-established 地位穩固的；享有聲譽的
	agency 代辦機構；代理商

---

102. If you -------- for vacancies, services, or businesses in Taiwan, you have come to the right place.

(A) are looking
(B) were looking
(C) have been looked
(D) looked

如果您正在台灣尋找職缺、服務或業務，那麼您已經來到了正確的地方。

(A) 正在尋找（現在進行式）
(B) 正在尋找（過去進行式）
(C) 一直被尋找（現在完成式被動語態）
(D) 尋找（過去式）

| 解析 | 與後面 have come ~（現在完成式）之時態要配合，而 (B) 和 (D) 都是過去式，故錯誤；look for（尋找）為主動，故 (C) have been looked（被動）為錯誤。 |

| 單字 | vacancy 空缺　　　　　service 服務　　　　　business 業務 |

---

103. You may also sign in if you would like to edit your -------- in the future.

(A) advertised
(B) advertising
(C) advertisements
(D) advertise

如果您將來要編輯修改廣告，您也可以登入。

(A) 廣告（動詞過去式）
(B) 廣告（動詞現在分詞）
(C) 廣告（名詞複數）
(D) 廣告（動詞現在簡單式）

| 解析 | 因為 your ＋名詞，故該選 (C) advertisements（廣告）這個名詞。(B) advertising 是動詞的現在分詞，後面要有受詞，而 (A)、(D) 都是動詞，故皆不正確。 |

| 單字 | sign in 登入（＝ log in）　　　edit 編輯　　　　　in the future 將來 |

146

104. The iPhone 17 is expected -------- alongside the iPhone 17 Pro and Pro Max in September.

(A) to launch
(B) launching
(C) to have launched
(D) having launched

iPhone 17 預計在九月份與 iPhone 17 Pro 和 Pro Max 一起推出。

(A) 推出（不定詞）
(B) 推出（現在分詞）
(C) 已推出（現在完成式）
(D) 已推出（完成式分詞構句）

解析	因為 is expected（預計）後面 + to + V~（不定詞），而 (C) to have launched 為完成式，表示發生在 is expected 之前，這與事實矛盾，故 (C) 錯誤。

單字	alongside 一起　　　　　launch 推出，發行　　　　　September 九月

105. The General Manager has noticed that many staff members are currently not -------- to the dress code guidelines that were laid out in our firm's employee manual.

(A) adhering
(B) identifying
(C) knowing
(D) complying

總經理留意到許多員工最近不遵守公司員工手冊中的服裝規定細則。

(A) 遵守
(B) 辨別
(C) 了解
(D) 遵守

解析	依句意，雖然 (D) complying 是遵守的意思，但應該用 complying ＋ with，而空格後面接 to，故 (A) adhering ＋ to 為正確。

單字	General Manager 總經理　　dress code 服裝規定　　guideline 準則 lay out 書面規定　　employee manual 員工手冊

106. You will no longer have to suffer -------- eye fatigue when looking at screens.

(A) by
(B) on
(C) in
(D) from

你看螢幕時，將不再飽受眼睛疲勞。

(A) 藉由
(B) 在…上
(C) 在…內
(D) 來自…

解析	suffer（受苦）後面常用 from（來自）。

單字	no longer 不再　　　　have to 必須　　　　suffer from 受…之苦 fatigue 疲勞　　　　　screen 螢幕

TEST 01
PART 5

107. The new software, -------- was developed by our in-house team, has significantly improved our data processing speed.

(A) that
(B) which
(C) they
(D) it

這款新軟體，由我們的內部團隊開發，已顯著提升了我們的數據處理速度。

(A) 那個（關係代名詞）
(B) 那個／其（關係代名詞）
(C) 它們（第三人稱複數主格）
(D) 它（第三人稱單數主格）

解析 which 是引導非限制形容詞子句的正確關係代詞，與逗號分隔的結構相符。非限制形容詞子句提供補充資訊（「由內部團隊開發」），與主句（「提升數據處理速度」）無衝突，符合英語寫作慣例。其他選項 that、they、it 皆非連接詞，無法引導句中出現之兩個動詞 was 和 has，無法滿足句法要求。

單字
software 軟體　　develop 發展，開發　　significantly 顯著地
improve 改善　　data 資料，數據　　process 處理；辦理

---

108. -------- our online programs are not popular with prospective employees, they provide practical on-the-job knowledge.

(A) Consequently
(B) As
(C) Instead
(D) Although

雖然我們的線上方案不受可能的員工歡迎，但這些方案提供了實用的職場專業知識。

(A) 因此
(B) 因為
(C) 取而代之
(D) 雖然

解析 依全句意義，逗號前為 not popular（不受歡迎），逗號後為 provide practical...（提供了實用…），一個負，一個正，故 although（雖然）正確。

單字
online program 線上方案／計畫　　prospective 可能的；有希望的
expertise 專業知識

---

109. The store is giving an -------- discount on this product this week! Get 25% off when you check out with the designated payment company.

(A) addition
(B) additional
(C) additionally
(D) additions

這家商店本週提供購買這個產品的額外折扣！您與指定的付款公司結帳時，可獲得 25% 的折扣。

(A) 額外（名詞單數）
(B) 額外的（形容詞）
(C) 額外地（副詞）
(D) 額外（名詞複數）

解析 空格後是名詞，空格裡用形容詞 additional 較適合。

單字
additional 額外的　　check out 結帳　　designated 指定的
payment 付款

110. We have over 15 years of experience -------- with energy and power.

(A) deals
(B) dealing
(C) to deal
(D) dealt

在處理能源和電力方面,我們有超過 15 年的經驗。

(A) 處理(現在式)
(B) 處理(現在分詞)
(C) 處理(不定詞)
(D) 處理(過去分詞)

| 解析 | 因為前面已有動詞 have,故後面的動詞必須改為現在分詞 dealing(處理),表主動。若為被動,則用過去分詞 dealt。 |

| 單字 | experience 經驗　　deal with 處理　　energy 能源
power 電力 |

---

111. Initially designed to be power saving, the new power generating device is now -------- to be high-speed spinning with zero attrition.

(A) encoded
(B) examined
(C) improved
(D) included

最初設計只是為了節電,這項新的發電裝置現在已改善到可以高速旋轉,零磨損。

(A) 編碼
(B) 檢查
(C) 改善
(D) 包括

| 解析 | 依句意,此項設備現在已經……,因此選 (C) improved(改善)。 |

| 單字 | initially 原先　　generate 發電　　device 裝置;設備
spin 旋轉　　attrition 消耗;磨損 |

---

112. Taichung is filled with a -------- of great food from all corners of the globe.

(A) variety
(B) various
(C) variously
(D) vary

台中充滿了來自全球各地的各種美食。

(A) 種種;多樣化(名詞)
(B) 多樣的(形容詞)
(C) 多樣地(複詞)
(D) 差異;變化(動詞)

| 解析 | a 和 of 之間需為名詞,故 (A) variety(種種)正確。a variety of 意即「各式各樣的」。 |

| 單字 | is filled with 充滿　　corner 角落　　globe 地球,全球 |

TEST 01
PART 5

113. One of the premier -------- to enjoy both exotic and local cuisine is the Art Museum Parkway.

(A) stations
(B) senses
(C) sources
(D) spots

藝博館大道是可以同時享受異國與當地美食的首要景點之一。

(A) 車站
(B) 感官
(C) 來源
(D) 景點

解析 依據句子意義，以 (D) spots（景點）為正確。藝博館大道是地點，而不是感官（senses），也不是來源（sources）或車站（stations）。

單字 premier 首要的；最佳的　　exotic 外來的，異國的　　cuisine（餐館的）菜餚；美食
parkway 林蔭大道

114. Take a look -------- the recommendations inside the folding pages of the brochure, or listen to what the wait staff has to say.

(A) for
(B) into
(C) at
(D) through

看看小冊子摺頁內的建議，或者聽聽服務人員說什麼。

(A) 為了
(B) 進入
(C) 在…點
(D) 從頭到尾

解析 依據句子意義，take a look at（注意看），故 (C) 正確。look for（尋找）、look into（調查）、look through（看透）都不合句意。

單字 recommendation 建議　　folding pages 摺頁　　brochure 小冊子
staff 人員

115. The university is 25 miles south of central Sydney and -------- reached by car or public transport.

(A) greatly
(B) shortly
(C) rarely
(D) easily

這所大學位於雪梨市中心以南 25 英里處，可透過開車或大眾運輸系統輕鬆抵達。

(A) 很大
(B) 不久
(C) 很少
(D) 輕易

解析 依句意：這所大學可以很「容易地」（easily）到達，故答案為 (D)。

單字 university 大學　　reach 到達　　public 公共的，公眾的
transport 運輸

116. The on-the-job training offered by this teaching center is the skills, knowledge, and -------- needed to foster creative thinking.

(A) compliments
(B) complements
(C) competencies
(D) commodities

這個教學中心提供的在職訓練是教導培養創造性思維所需的技巧、知識和能力。

(A) 稱讚
(B) 補充
(C) 能力
(D) 商品

| 解析 | 依句意，培養……所需的技巧、知識和能力（competencies），故答案為 (C)。 |

| 單字 | on-the-job 在職的　　offer 提供　　foster 培養
creative 創意的　　competency 能力；技能 |

117. Employees learn in an environment -------- they will need to practice the knowledge and skills taught in the program.

(A) where
(B) which
(C) that
(D) what

員工們在一個必須練習課程中所教授的知識和技能的環境中學習。

(A) 在哪裡
(B) 哪個
(C) 哪個
(D) 什麼

| 解析 | 空格前面是先行詞 environment，空格裡原本可用 which，但後面結構完整，依句意，與先行詞間需有介系詞 in，而 in + which = where，因此答案為 (A) where。 |

| 單字 | employee 員工　　environment 環境　　practice 練習 |

118. Our safety -------- and accident rate have been improved. As a result, all drivers in our company are now certified to drive Hi-Los.

(A) positions
(B) standards
(C) requirements
(D) concerns

我們的安全標準和事故發生率已有所改善。所以我們公司的所有司機現在都通過認證，可以駕駛 Hi-Los。

(A) 職位
(B) 標準
(C) 要求
(D) 關心的事

| 解析 | 依據句子意義，(B) standards（標準）為正確，因為後面的 accident rate（事故率）與之呼應。 |

| 單字 | improve 改善　　as a result 結果　　certify 通過認證的，合格的 |

TEST 01
PART 5

119. The best employee to -------- a phone interview is the hiring manager.

(A) conduct
(B) consult
(C) console
(D) concern

最適合進行電話面試的職員就是招聘部經理。

(A) 進行
(B) 向…諮詢
(C) 安慰
(D) 牽涉到

解析 依據句子意義，(A) conduct（進行）為正確。

單字 interview 面試　　hiring 雇用；招聘

---

120. For over 25 years, Axiomtek -------- among the major manufacturing companies in the field of industrial computers and embedded systems.

(A) was
(B) had been
(C) has been
(D) is

這 25 年多來，Axiomtek 一直是工業電腦和嵌入式系統領域的主要製造公司。

(A) 是（過去式）
(B) 曾經是（過去完成式）
(C) 一直是（現在完成式）
(D) 是（現在式）

解析 因為 for over 25 years 是一段時間，在這段時間內一直如此，因此動詞時態該用現在完成式：(C) has been。

單字
major 主要的
company 公司
industrial computer 工業電腦
manufacturing 製造
field 領域
embedded system 嵌入式系統

---

121. Since its establishment, the company has -------- gained worldwide recognition for its innovative designs.

(A) incredibly
(B) successfully
(C) probably
(D) fortunately

自成立以來，該公司已經成功地獲得了創新設計的全球認可。

(A) 難以置信地
(B) 成功地
(C) 可能
(D) 幸運地

解析 依據句子意義，應是 has successfully gained（成功地獲得）才正確，後面 worldwide recognition（全球認可）及 innovative designs（創新設計）都與之呼應。

單字
establishment 創立；成立　　gain 獲得　　recognition 認可
innovative 創新的　　design 設計

152

122. As a valuable and reliable industrial manufacturer, this corporation is devoted to producing -------- solutions that support users in achieving success.

(A) on-the-job
(B) versus
(C) state-of-the-art
(D) diplomatic

作為一個有價值而且可靠的工業製造商，該公司致力於生產最先進的解決方案，以支援用戶取得成功。

(A) 在職的
(B) 對；比較
(C) 最先進的
(D) 外交的

| 解析 | 依據句子意義，(C) state-of-the-art（最先進的）就是正確答案。前面的 a valuable and reliable（有價值而且可靠的），以及後面的 achieving success（取得成功）都與之呼應。 |

單字	valuable 有價值的　　reliable 可靠的　　industrial 工業的；產業的
	manufacturer 製造商　　corporation 公司　　devoted 致力於
	solution 解決方法　　support 支持；支援　　achieve 達到

123. Our consulting company takes pride in what we do through our -------- to excellence.

(A) component
(B) composite
(C) condition
(D) commitment

我們的諮詢公司透過達成卓越的承諾，在所做的工作中感到自豪。

(A) 成分；零件
(B) 合成物
(C) 條件
(D) 承諾

| 解析 | 依據句子意義，(D) commitment（承諾）就是正確答案。前面出現 takes pride（自豪），後面出現 excellence（卓越），都與 (D) 呼應。 |

單字	consulting 諮詢　　pride 自豪；得意　　excellence 卓越

124. Our focus is on developing new products -------- the most advanced technologies and customer-based experiences.

(A) using
(B) to use
(C) uses
(D) used

我們的重點是使用最先進的技術和基於客戶的經驗來開發新產品。

(A) 使用（現在分詞）
(B) 使用（不定詞）
(C) 使用（現在式）
(D) 使用（過去分詞）

| 解析 | 前面已有動詞 is，故後面的動詞必須改為分詞形式的 using（使用），這是現在分詞，表主動；若為被動，則用過去分詞 used。 |

單字	focus 焦點；重點　　develop 發展；開發　　product 產品
	advanced 先進的　　technology 科技；技術　　customer-based 以顧客為本的
	experience 經驗

TEST 01 PART 5

125. The company provides an extensive line of industrial computers, -------- embedded eBOX & tBOX systems.

(A) includes
(B) including
(C) to include
(D) included

該公司提供廣泛的工業電腦系列，包括嵌入式 eBOX 和 tBOX 系統。

(A) 包括（現在式）
(B) 包括（現在分詞）
(C) 包括（不定詞）
(D) 包括（過去分詞）

解析	前面已有動詞 provides（提供），故後面的動詞必須改為分詞形式的 including（包括），這是現在分詞，表主動；若為被動，則用過去分詞 included。

單字	extensive 廣泛的　　　　line（產品）系列　　　　industrial 工業的 embedded 嵌入式

126. Our goal is to develop high-quality and cost--------- server appliance hardware platforms.

(A) effective
(B) deductive
(C) creative
(D) submissive

我們的目標是開發高品質和具有成本效益的伺服器設備硬體平台。

(A) 有效的
(B) 演繹的
(C) 有創造力的
(D) 順從的

解析	依據句子意義，(A) cost-effective（具有成本效益的）就是正確答案，前面出現的 develop high-quality...（開發高品質的…）與 (A) 呼應。

單字	goal 目標　　　　quality 品質　　　　server 伺服器 appliance 器具；設備　　hardware 硬體　　platform 平台

127. The free association techniques used in psychoanalysis empower the analyst with chances of knowing -------- is happening in the patients' unconsciousness.

(A) what
(B) it
(C) that
(D) which

精神分析中使用的自由聯想技術使分析人員有機會了解患者潛意識中發生的事情。

(A) 什麼（關係代名詞）
(B) 它（第三人稱單數主格）
(C) 那個（關係代名詞）
(D) 那個（關係代名詞）

解析	因為空格前後都缺少一個名詞，因此該用複合關係代名詞 what，此處 what 等於 the thing which。

單字	association 聯想　　　technique 技術；方法　　　psychoanalysis 精神分析 analyst 分析師　　　　unconsciousness 潛意識

128. The theory initiated by Jean Piaget is a -------- view on human cognitive development.

(A) contemporary
(B) revolutionary
(C) necessary
(D) compulsory

皮亞傑創始的理論是關於人類認知發展的革命性觀點。

(A) 當代的
(B) 革命性的
(C) 必要的
(D) 強制性的

解析 依照句意，此理論是一個「革命性的」（revolutionary）觀點，故答案為 (B) revolutionary。

單字
theory 理論　　initiate 創始　　cognitive 認知的
development 發展

---

129. For the deaf or hard-of-hearing, complete -------- to Microsoft products and customer services is available.

(A) process
(B) access
(C) recess
(D) excess

對於聾人或聽力障礙者來說，可以完整使用到 Microsoft 的產品和客戶服務。

(A) 過程
(B) 管道，使用機會
(C) 休會
(D) 超額

解析 依據句子意義，(B) access（使用機會）就是正確答案。前面出現 the deaf or hard-of-hearing（聾人或聽力障礙者），後面有 ...customer services is available（客戶服務可資運用），與 (B) 呼應。

單字
deaf 聾的　　hard-of-hearing 有聽力障礙的　　complete 完整的，完全的
customer service 客戶服務　　available 可取得的；可利用的

---

130. For those majoring in psychology, the position of personality assessment is -------- in the personnel department.

(A) appreciable
(B) considerable
(C) predictable
(D) available

對於那些主修心理學的人員來說，可以得到人事部門中的人格評估職位。

(A) 可觀的
(B) 相當多的
(C) 可預測的
(D) 可取得的

解析 依據句子意義，(D) available（可取得的）就是正確答案。前面出現的 majoring in psychology（主修心理學），以及 the position of personality assessment（人格評估的職位），與 (D) 呼應。

單字
major 主修科目　　psychology 心理學　　position 職位
personality 人格　　assessment 評估　　personnel 人事
department 部門

TEST 01
PART 6

Questions 131-134 refer to the following advertisement.

131-134 題參考以下廣告。

Join us for a spectacular trip to see waterfalls and cascades along the Kashez River. The first few miles are ---------- (131) flat, and the Kashez River is mostly out of sight. ---------- (132), there will be views of the surrounding mountains. After about 2 miles, the trail will begin to run alongside the Kashez River. ---------- (133). But then it will begin its 500-foot descent to Black Cascade. Along the descent, there are numerous waterfalls and cascades ---------- (134) the river makes its way to lower elevation.

讓我們一起去卡許茲河旅遊，觀賞它壯麗的大小瀑布。在開始幾英里時，還看不到卡許茲河，路程相對平坦，但是可以看到週遭山脈的景色。大約2英里後，小徑就開始緊鄰著卡許茲河。起初河流相對平靜，之後會開始500英尺的陡降坡直到黑水崖。當河流持續流向低海拔時，沿著陡降坡有許多大小瀑布。

131. (A) surprisingly
    (B) frequently
    (C) presumably
    (D) relatively

(A) 令人驚訝地
(B) 經常
(C) 可能
(D) 相對地

解析 依句意，前面有 The first few miles（最先幾英里），表示在進行相對性描述，故用 (D) relatively（相對地）較適當。

132. (A) Besides
    (B) However
    (C) Or else
    (D) Accordingly

(A) 此外
(B) 但是
(C) 否則
(D) 因此

解析 依句意，前面有 ...out of sight（看不到），後面出現 views（景觀），故用 (B) However（但是）比較適當。

133. **(A) At first, the river is relatively calm.**
    (B) People used to come here.
    (C) Most visitors like to be here.
    (D) It is a pleasant experience.

(A) 起初河流相對平靜。
(B) 以前人們通常來這裡。
(C) 大多數遊客喜歡在這裡。
(D) 這是一個愉快的經歷。

解析 依句意，後面有 But then it will begin... 表示前面應有 it 所代表的名詞，那就是 the river（此河），因此用 (A) At first, the river is relatively calm.（起初河流相對平靜）比較適當。

156

134. (A) so
    (B) thus
    (C) as
    (D) but

    (A) 所以
    (B) 於是
    (C) 當⋯時
    (D) 但是

    > **解析** 依句意，前面有 Along the descent, there are numerous waterfalls and cascades...（沿著陡降坡有許多大小瀑布），而後面出現 the river makes its way to lower elevation（河流流向低海拔），因此用 (C) as（當⋯時）較為適當。

單字			
join 加入	spectacular 壯觀的	cascade 小瀑布
flat 平坦的	surrounding 周圍的	mountain 山
trail 小徑	descent 下降	numerous 很多的
elevation 高度，海拔		

TEST 01 PART 6

Questions 135-138 refer to the following letter.

May 5
Blake Wood, General Manager
Linden Appliances
30 Botany Road

Dear Mrs. Wood,

I am here to draw your attention to an issue we have had with a recent order from yourselves (ref no.46MA38RT). Not only was the ---------- **135** a week later than agreed, but when we tried to use the spare parts, we found that 50% of them were ---------- **136** and basically useless.

I spoke to your customer service manager, Jane Brown, about this matter. I hoped that you would replace the damaged spare parts, but she informed me that the spare parts were intact when delivered to us. ---------- **137** .

I believe that I am entitled to an explanation as to why Jane Brown has not answered my email. ---------- **138** this issue is dealt with promptly, then unfortunately, we will be forced to take further action. Please inform me how you are going to resolve this issue with the least possible delay.

Sincerely,
Gary White
Sigma Production Director

135-138 題參考以下信件。

5月5日
布蕾克·伍德，總經理
林登家電
波坦尼路30號

親愛的伍德太太：

我在此提請你注意最近我們向貴公司訂購一批貨所產生的問題（參考字號46MA38RT）。這批貨不僅交貨延遲一週，我們嘗試使用備用零件時，更發現其中有50%是損壞的，基本上無法使用。

我和你的客戶服務經理珍·布朗談過這件事。我希望你們能更換損壞的備用零件，但是她告訴我，備用零件在交付給我們時是完好的。我上週發了電子郵件給她，但至今仍未收到回覆。

我相信我有權知道為什麼珍·布朗沒有回覆我的電子郵件。除非這個問題得到迅速處理，否則我們將不得不採取進一步的行動。請盡速通知我如何解決這個問題。

蓋瑞·懷特 謹啟
Sigma 生產總監

135. (A) delivered
(B) delivering
(C) delivery
(D) deliver

(A) 已交貨的
(B) 投遞中
(C) 送貨
(D) 運送

> **解析** 本題考詞類，因前面為 the，後面必須接名詞 delivery（送貨）。

158

136. **(A) damaged**
(B) devastated
(C) destroyed
(D) detained

(A) 受損
(B) 被摧毀
(C) 被毀滅
(D) 被拘留

> 解析　本題考單字的用法，貨品受損（damaged）為被動，因此前面有 were。damaged 並非「被毀滅」（destroyed），也不是「被拘留」（detained），更不是「被摧毀」（devastated）。

137. (A) I was pretty upset.
(B) I talked back to her to vent my anger.
(C) I felt angry and decided not to talk to her again.
(D) I emailed her last week, but still received no response.

(A) 我很不高興
(B) 我對她頂嘴，發洩我的憤怒。
(C) 我感到憤怒，決定不再和她說話。
(D) 我上週發了電子郵件給她，但至今仍未收到回覆。

> 解析　依句意，前一句是 but she informed me that the spare parts were intact when delivered to us.（但是她告訴我，備用零件在交付給我們時是完好的），而且下一句是 I believe that I am entitled to an explanation as to why Jane Brown has not answered my email.（我相信我有權知道為什麼珍·布朗沒有回覆我的電子郵件），故知 (D) 為正確答案。

138. (A) Otherwise
(B) Nevertheless
(C) Unless
(D) Therefore

(A) 否則
(B) 然而
(C) 除非
(D) 因此

> 解析　本題依句意，空格後面的主句是 ...we will be forced to take further action.（我們將不得不採取進一步的行動），表示前面的句意為：除非⋯，故知 (C) Unless 為正確答案。

單字		
attention 注意	issue 問題	recent 最近的
order 訂購	spare part 備用零件	basically 基本上
useless 無用的	replace 更換	inform 告知
intact 完好無損的	entitled 有權的	explanation 解釋
resolve 解決	promptly 立刻；迅速地	unfortunately 不幸地
forced 被迫	further 更進一步的	delay 拖延

TEST 01
PART 6

Questions 139-142 refer to the following letter.

139-142 題參考以下信件。

Dear Mr. Sage,

After our ----------- (139) on Monday, my business partners and I talked about the situation, and we concluded that we intend to buy your business, Twice Over. We are willing to pay your ----------- (140) purchase price of $75,000, which includes both the business and all the equipment necessary to operate it, as per our discussion.

----------- (141). We will ----------- (142) all the necessary paperwork. These documents will be signed and completed, and we will tender payment, as agreed.

Sincerely,
James Brown

親愛的賽吉先生：

在星期一的討論之後，我的合夥人和我討論了這個情況，我們得出結論，打算購買您的企業——Twice Over。根據我們的討論，我們願意支付您所要求的 75,000 美元的購買價格，其中包括企業本身與經營所需的設備。

我們希望在下星期一 10 月 5 日與您見面，以完成交易。我們將攜帶所有必要的文件，這些文件將被簽署並完成，我們將按照約定付款。

詹姆斯・布朗 謹啟

139.
(A) negotiation
(B) conversation
(C) promotion
(D) discussion

(A) 談判
(B) 談話
(C) 推廣
(D) 討論

> **解析** 本題考字詞用法，空格後面為 ...and I talked about the situation, and we concluded that...（…和我討論了這個情況，我們得出結論，…），故知 (D) discussion（討論）較為正確。

140.
(A) request
(B) requesting
(C) requested
(D) requests

(A) 要求（現在式）
(B) 要求（現在分詞）
(C) 所要求的（過去分詞）
(D) 要求（現在式第三人稱單數）

> **解析** 因為前面已有動詞 are willing to（願意），故後面的動詞必須改為過去分詞 requested（所要求的），表被動；若為主動，則用現在分詞 requesting。

160

141. **(A) We would like to meet with you next Monday, October 5, to finalize the sale.**
(B) We would like to call you next Monday, October 5, to inform you of the sale.
(C) Both parties will have to hire a lawyer.
(D) Both parties will have to resolve the conflict through legal procedures.

(A) 我們希望在下星期一 10 月 5 日與您見面，以完成交易。
(B) 我們想在下星期一 10 月 5 日打電話給您，通知您這項交易。
(C) 雙方必須聘請律師。
(D) 雙方必須透過法律程序解決衝突。

解析 空格後面有 we will carry all the necessary paperwork.（我們將攜帶所有必要的文件），故知前面句子為 (A) We would like to meet with you next Monday, October 5, to finalize the sale.（我們希望在下星期一 10 月 5 日與您見面，以完成交易。）

142. (A) fetch
(B) carry
(C) make
(D) switch

(A) 去取來
(B) 攜帶
(C) 製造
(D) 轉換

解析 由於文件（paperwork）是攜帶來的，因此答案為 (B) carry（攜帶）。

單字
partner 夥伴
intend 打算
operate 經營；營運
sign 簽字；簽名
payment 款項
situation 情況
purchase 購買
paperwork 文件
complete 完成
conclude 得出結論
equipment 設備
document 文件
tender 提交；付（款）

TEST 01
PART 6

Questions 143-146 refer to the following letter.

143-146 題參考以下信件。

Mr. Peter Frantz
108 Oxford Street
Glen Cove, MA 39452

Dear Mr. Frantz,

Thank you for your letter ----------- April 4, 2020. **143** In response to your request for more information about our company, I am ----------- with this letter **144** a brochure about our company. -----------. I will be **145** available to meet with you next week. Please call my secretary anytime to set up an appointment. -----------, if you have any questions, please feel **146** free to call me at 482-9278.

Sincerely,
Sophia Smith
Executive Manager

彼得‧法蘭茲先生
牛津街 108 號
格倫科夫市 MA 39452

親愛的法蘭茲先生：

感謝您 2020 年 4 月 4 日的來信。為了回應您想要有關我們公司的更多資訊，我在信中附上關於我們公司的小冊子，希望您覺得有幫助。下週我有空與您見面，請隨時致電我的秘書約好見面時間。在此期間，如果您有任何問題，請隨時致電 482-9278。

索菲亞‧史密斯 謹啟
執行長

---

143. (A) dates
 (B) dated
 (C) dating
 (D) date

(A) 日期
(B) 日期為
(C) 訂定日期
(D) 日期

> **解析** 因為前面已有動詞 thank（感謝），故後面的動詞必須改為過去分詞 dated（日期為），表被動（因為信中的日期是被動產生，被訂定的）；若為主動，則用現在分詞 dating。

---

144. **(A) enclosing**
 (B) enclosure
 (C) enclosed
 (D) enclose

(A) 附上
(B) （信的）附件
(C) 隨信附上的
(D) 附上

> **解析** 因為前面已有 be 動詞 am，故後面的動詞必須改為現在分詞 enclosing（附上），表主動（因為是「我」〔I〕主動附上）；若為被動，則用過去分詞 enclosed（若前面主詞為所附上之內容）。

162

145.
(A) You are expected to know more.
(B) I hope you find it helpful.
(C) It is assumed that you are knowledgeable.
(D) You will be well-informed.

(A) 你應該知道更多。
(B) 希望你覺得有幫助。
(C) 大家以為你見多識廣。
(D) 你會知情的。

解析 空格前面有：I am <u>enclosing</u> with this letter a brochure about our company.（我在信中附上關於我們公司的小冊子），故知後面的句子為 (B) I hope you find it helpful.（希望您覺得有幫助）。

146.
(A) Above all
(B) Up to the present
(C) After a while
(D) In the meantime

(A) 尤其是，最重要的是
(B) 直到現在
(C) 過了一會兒
(D) 在此期間

解析 依據上下文，空格前為 Please call my secretary anytime to set up an appointment.（請隨時致電我的秘書約好見面時間），而空格後面為 if you have any questions, please feel free to call me...（如果您有任何問題，請隨時致電…），故知 (D) In the meantime（在此期間）為正確答案。

單字

response 回應	request 要求	information 資訊
enclose 附上	brochure 小冊子	available 有空的
secretary 秘書	set up 安排	appointment 會面

TEST 01
PART 7

Questions 147 through 148 refer to the following letter.

Date: July 1, 2019

Petra Hamilton
48 Montague Rd, Sunnybank Hills,
Brisbane, QLD 4101

Notice of Intent to Vacate

Dear Petra Hamilton,

This letter comprises my written 30-day notice that I will be moving out of the flat that I am renting from you on July 31, 2019.

I am leaving because I got a new job in another part of the city. If you find any serious problems with the flat, please contact me as soon as possible.

Please be sure to advise me on when you will return my security deposit of $300, and also if you will be deducting any money for damages other than normal wear and tear.

You can reach me at 0979-055022 and 25 Shell Road, Morningside, Brisbane, QLD 4170 after July 15, 2019.

Sincerely,
Jesse Hilton

18 Dorchester St.,
Coopers Plains, Brisbane, QLD 4101

147-148 題參考以下信件。

日期：2019 年 7 月 1 日

佩特拉・漢米爾頓
Montague 路 48 號，Sunnybank Hills，
布里斯本，QLD 4101

有意搬出通知

親愛的佩特拉・漢米爾頓：

這封信是我寫的 30 日前通知，我將在 2019 年 7 月 31 日搬出您租給我的公寓。

我要搬走，是因為我在這個城市的另一個地方找到了一份新工作。如果您發現公寓有任何嚴重問題，請盡快與我聯繫。

請務必告知我，您何時可退還我的 300 美元保證金，以及您是否將扣除任何正常損耗以外的損失賠償金。

在 2019 年 7 月 15 日之後，您可以藉由以下方式跟我聯繫：0979-055022 和 Shell 路 25 號，Morningside，布里斯本，QLD 4170。

傑西・希爾頓 謹啟

Dorchester 街 18 號
Coopers Plains，布里斯本，QLD 4101

---

147. Why is Jesse Hilton moving?

(A) The location of the flat is too inconvenient.
(B) He found a new job.
(C) The rent is too expensive.
(D) The flat lacks basic amenities.

為什麼傑西・希爾頓要搬家？

(A) 公寓的位置太不方便了。
(B) 他找到了一份新工作。
(C) 租金太貴了。
(D) 公寓缺乏基本設施。

148. Where will Jesse Hilton be after July 15?

(A) In Sydney
(B) In America on a business trip
(C) In a different suburb of Brisbane
(D) In Coopers Plains

傑西・希爾頓 7 月 15 日之後將在哪裡？

(A) 在雪梨
(B) 在美國出差
(C) 在布里斯本的另一個郊區
(D) 在 Coopers Plains

單字
vacate 空出，騰出
advise 通知；（正式）告知
deduct 扣除
comprise 包含，包括；構成，組成
security deposit 保證金
wear and tear （一段時期後的）磨損，損耗

TEST 01
PART 7

Questions 149 through 150 refer to the following online chat discussion.

Oliver [15:33]:	Hi, Lily! I want to know how to make an international call to Jamaica. Is the country code 2?
Lily [15:34]:	Are you residing in the USA?
Oliver [15:35]:	Yes, in Indiana.
Lily [15:36]:	Well, the country code is actually 1. Next, you need to dial the area code 876.
Oliver [15:37]:	Ok. Got it. Then I just dial the person's local phone number, right?
Lily [15:39]:	Yes. Then you should be able to reach them.
Oliver [15:40]:	What if the line is blocked? Last time my friend called a country near Jamaica, they couldn't get through.
Lily [15:43]:	That is because most telephone service providers give people the option to block all international calls. That is why the call couldn't be made.

149-150 題參考以下線上聊天內容。

奧利佛 [15:33]：	嗨。莉莉！我想知道如何打國際電話到牙買加。國碼是 2 嗎？
莉莉 [15:34]：	你住在美國嗎？
奧利佛 [15:35]：	是的，在印第安納州。
莉莉 [15:36]：	好，國碼實際上是 1。接下來你需要撥打區域碼 876。
奧利佛 [15:37]：	好的，懂了。然後我就撥打這個人的本地電話號碼吧？
莉莉 [15:39]：	是的。然後你應該就可以聯繫到對方。
奧利佛 [15:40]：	如果電話線路被停用怎麼辦？上次我的朋友打電話給牙買加附近的一個國家時，他們無法接通。
莉莉 [15:43]：	那是因為大多數電話服務供應商都會讓使用者可以選擇停用所有國際電話。這就是無法打通的原因。

149. What information is Oliver asking Lily for?

(A) The contact details of a Jamaican enterprise
(B) The best time to ring their overseas buyer
(C) How to make a phone call to a different country
(D) A way to block international calls

奧利佛要求莉莉提供什麼資訊？

(A) 一間牙買加企業的詳細聯繫方式
(B) 撥電話給海外併購者的最佳時機
(C) 如何打電話至其他國家
(D) 阻止國際電話的方法

---

150. What is indicated about telephone service providers?

(A) They provide poor phone reception.
(B) They allow people to block calls from overseas.
(C) Their customer service quality is poor.
(D) They limit customers to making domestic calls.

聊天內容指出什麼關於電話服務供應商的事？

(A) 他們提供的電話收訊很差。
(B) 他們允許人們停用來自海外的電話。
(C) 他們的客戶服務品質很差。
(D) 他們限制客戶僅能撥打國內電話。

單字

reside 居住，定居　　　block 阻擋；封鎖　　　option 選擇

Questions 151 through 152 refer to the following advertisement.

Bobco Plumbers

A well-established company is seeking 4 energetic and experienced plumbers.

Hours: Monday to Friday, 8:30 a.m. to 6:00 p.m. plus overtime (evenings and weekends)

Contract: On-going

Pay: Negotiable

Job description: Bobco Plumbers is Melbourne's largest independent plumbing company. Due to expansion and an increase of Spanish speaking clients, we have vacancies for fully-qualified plumbers who are proficient in Spanish or at least can communicate at a conversational level.

Duties: Doing interpretation of blueprints and building specifications to completely map the positions of pipes, drainage systems etc. Also, installation of fixtures, fix water supply lines and systems for waste disposal. All applicants must be proactive and be able to provide excellent customer service.

151-152 題參考以下廣告。

巴布科水電公司

一家信譽卓著的公司正在尋找四名積極熱心且經驗豐富的水管工。

工作時間： 週一至週五，早上 8:30 至下午 6:00，另需加班（晚上和周末）

合　約： 進行中

薪　資： 面議

工作內容： 巴布科水電公司是墨爾本最大的民營水電管道公司。由於擴編及西語客戶的增加，我們正在徵求精通西班牙語或至少能夠溝通對話的合格水管工。

職　責： 對藍圖和建築規格進行解釋，以完成管道、排水系統等的位置圖。此外，得安裝固定設備，固定供水管線和廚餘處理系統。所有應徵者必須主動積極，並能夠提供優質的客戶服務。

151. What is true about the nature of the work advertised?

(A) Workers will have to repair broken windows.
(B) Workers will spend most time in the office.
(C) Workers will be required to install pipes.
(D) Workers will have to interpret statistical graphs.

廣告的工作內容何者為真？

(A) 工人必須修理破損的窗戶。
(B) 工人將大部分時間待在辦公室。
(C) 工人將被要求安裝管道。
(D) 工人必須解說統計圖表。

---

152. What special skills do applicants need to possess?

(A) Ability to construct buildings
(B) A good command of the Spanish language
(C) Be able to draw up blueprints for city buildings
(D) Be able to answer customer inquiries

應徵者需要具備什麼特殊技能？

(A) 建造建築物的能力
(B) 熟練西班牙語
(C) 能夠繪出城市建築物的藍圖
(D) 能夠回答客戶的詢問

單字			
negotiable 可協商的；面議	plumber 水管工人	vacancy 職缺，空缺
proficient 熟練的；精通的	blueprint 藍圖	specification 規格
drainage 排水系統	fixture（房屋內的）固定設備	waste disposal 廚餘處理機
proactive 主動的，積極的	(have) a command of 掌握，精通	

TEST 01
PART 7

Questions 153 through 154 refer to the following memorandum.

To:	All Staff <stafflist@freeway.com>
From:	supervisor@freeway.com
Date:	March 4
Subject:	March 12 closure

I have recently been advised that the electricity in this building will be cut off next Tuesday due to the fact that repairs will be conducted on the electrical system. This will make it very hard for us to get anything done, so everyone will be allowed to take a day off work. I hope that everyone can find a way to continue your responsibilities from home.

The team leaders who are in charge of doing South American market research need to email me any of their findings. I will need them Wednesday morning before the annual conference.

Regards,
Sally Willington

153-154 題參考以下備忘。

收件者：	全體員工 <stafflist@freeway.com>
寄件者：	supervisor@freeway.com
日　　期：	3月4日
主　　旨：	3月12日關閉

我最近接獲通知，由於將對電氣系統進行維修，這棟大樓將在下週二停電。這將使我們很難完成任何工作，因此每個人都可以休假一天。我希望每個人都能找到在家繼續工作的方式。

負責南美市場研究的團隊負責人得透過電子郵件向我發送他們的任何調查結果，必須在年會前的星期三早上給我。

莎莉・威靈頓 謹啟

153. Why will the office NOT be open on Tuesday?

(A) The general manager will be away on a business trip.
(B) All employees will attend the conference.
(C) There will be no electricity in the building.
(D) No one needs to work on market research.

為什麼辦公室週二不開放？

(A) 總經理將出差。
(B) 所有員工都將參加會議。
(C) 建築物內將停電。
(D) 沒有人必須從事市場研究。

---

154. What does Mrs. Willington tell the team leaders to do?

(A) Send her an email
(B) Have a meeting about conducting market research
(C) Avoid using electricity
(D) Contact an electrician

威靈頓太太告訴團隊負責人要做什麼？

(A) 寄一封電子郵件給她
(B) 召開會議討論市場調查的進行
(C) 避免用電
(D) 聯繫電工

單字　advise 通知；（正式）告知　　market research 市場調查　　conference 會議，大會

TEST 01
PART 7

Questions 155 through 157 refer to the following news article.

Publix Restaurant Chain Ownership up for Sale

On Friday, Forever International, a large organic health care chain store based in Utah, announced its plans to acquire the Publix restaurant chain. Henry Miller, the owner of the chain, had been considering holding a large auction so he could pass on ownership of the chain. As stated by people with inside information, Publix has officially decided to not change the restaurant's name as part of the deal. Mr. Miller built his business from the ground up 35 years ago subsequent to graduating from business school. It was only a matter of time before the business started to become highly profitable. After 4 years' time, he had already started restaurants in Saint George, Logan and Cedar City. Now it has expanded to over 40 locations nationwide.

155-157 題參考以下新聞。

Publix 連鎖餐廳所有權出售

週五，位於猶他州的大型有機保健連鎖店 Forever International 宣布收購 Publix 連鎖餐廳的計畫。連鎖餐廳的老闆亨利・米勒（Henry Miller）一直在考慮舉辦一場大型拍賣會，以便他可以轉移連鎖店的所有權。正如內部消息人士所說，Publix 已正式決定不變更餐廳的名稱，以此為交易條件的一部分。米勒先生三十五年前從商學院畢業後，白手起家。他的事業開始變得非常有利潤僅僅是遲早的事。經過四年的時間，他已經在聖喬治、洛根和雪松城開設了餐廳。現在分店已擴展到全國四十多個地點。

155. In the news article, the word "acquire" in line 2, is closest in meaning to

(A) obtain
(B) surrender
(C) release
(D) accept

新聞裡，第二行中的 acquire 意義最接近以下何者？

(A) 獲得
(B) 投降
(C) 發佈
(D) 接受

---

156. What is suggested about Mr. Miller?

(A) Publix has expanded to many parts of America.
(B) He started Publix over 40 years ago.
(C) He is skilled at negotiating.
(D) He majored in finance.

這裡暗示關於米勒先生的哪件事情？

(A) Publix 餐廳已經擴展到美國很多地點。
(B) 他在四十多年前創立了 Publix。
(C) 他擅長談判。
(D) 他主修金融。

---

157. What kind of a company is Forever International?

(A) A restaurant chain store
(B) A large organic chain store
(C) An international trade company
(D) A sole proprietorship

Forever International 是一家什麼樣的公司？

(A) 餐館連鎖店
(B) 大型有機連鎖店
(C) 國際貿易公司
(D) 獨資企業

單字
organic 有機的
ownership 所有權
auction 拍賣；拍賣會
subsequent (to) 隨後的，接著的
pass on 傳遞；轉移
profitable 有利潤的；有益的

TEST 01
PART 7

Questions 158 through 160 refer to the following email.

To:	f.andrews@chinatravel.net
From:	zhangwu@gmail.com
Date:	June 16
Subject:	India travel

Dear Mr. Andrews,

My name is Zhang-wu Yang, I'm an avid traveler and cyclist who is residing in Beijing City, China. While flipping through a local travel magazine, I came across chinatravel.net. Your site seems to be an all-inclusive resource for travel-themed articles and related news about China.

I'd like to bring your attention to an electronic guidebook that my company recently published. It introduces all of my best-loved traveling routes in Chengdu and contains a complete collection of maps, mile markers, and precise descriptions of scenic spots. I also noticed that you included a specific page which is devoted to cycling around China; could you please mention my travel guide on this website?

The title of my book is *Around China in Two Months*, and can be bought through www.aroundchinaintwomonths.com/BS4KX. I would be extremely grateful if you could share this with those who subscribe to your website and weekly emails.

Thanks so much,
Zhang-wu

158-160 題參考以下 email。

收件者：	f.andrews@chinatravel.net
寄件者：	zhangwu@gmail.com
日　期：	6月16日
主　旨：	印度之旅

親愛的安德魯斯先生：

我的名字是楊彰武，我是一個熱衷的旅行者和自行車騎士，住在中國北京市。翻閱當地旅遊雜誌時，我看到了你們的 chinatravel.net，這似乎是一個廣納旅遊主題文章和中國相關新聞的網站。

我想提請您注意我的公司最近出版的電子版旅遊指南，它介紹了我在成都最受歡迎的旅行路線，並包含完整的地圖、里程標記和景點的精確描述。我還注意到你們有一個專門報導在中國騎自行車的專頁；您能在這個網站上提一下我的旅遊指南嗎？

我的書的書名是《兩個月環遊中國》，可以透過網站 www.aroundchinaintwomonths.com/BS4KX 買到。如果您能與訂閱您的網站和每週電子郵件的人分享，我將非常感激。

非常感謝。

彰武

158. What is indicated about Mr. Yang?

(A) He lives in Chengdu City.
(B) He is a tour guide in China.
(C) **He is passionate about traveling.**
(D) He is in charge of a travel website.

文中提到楊先生的什麼資訊？

(A) 他住在成都市。
(B) 他在中國當導遊。
(C) 他熱衷於旅行。
(D) 他負責旅遊網站。

---

159. Why is Mr. Yang writing to Mr. Andrews?

(A) **To recommend his own travel guide**
(B) To do appraisal of a business article
(C) To recommend a tour of China
(D) To confirm the publication of his new story

為何楊先生要寫信給安德魯斯先生？

(A) 推薦自己的旅行指南
(B) 評估一篇商業文章
(C) 推薦中國之旅
(D) 確認他的新故事的發行

---

160. In the email, the word "all-inclusive" in paragraph 1, line 3, is closest in meaning to

(A) **comprehensive**
(B) absolute
(C) accurate
(D) finished

在電子郵件中，第一段第三行的 all-inclusive 意義最接近以下何者？

(A) 包羅廣泛的
(B) 絕對
(C) 準確
(D) 完成了

單字

avid 熱情的；熱衷的	all-inclusive 包含一切的	guidebook 旅行指南
mile marker 里程標記	precise 精確的；準確的	be devote to 致力於；專用於
subscribe 訂閱		

TEST 01
PART 7

Questions 161 through 163 refer to the following article.

Sharp Communication Skills Make Outstanding Business Leaders

Richard Branson, a highly successful billionaire and founder of the Virgin Group, attaches great value to developing strong communication skills. He once stated that "Being an adept communicator is the most important skill any entrepreneur or business leader can possess."

Mastering the art of communication is the key to having an advantage over your competition and to influencing others. One of the most important communication skills to cultivate is the ability to give a powerful presentation. Here are several ways to help you deliver an exceptional presentation so that you stand out from the crowd.

Research: The first step in preparing for a speech is to conduct in-depth research on your topic. When that is done, one should structure an outline and jot down the key facts to support the key message of your speech. Next, revise the content you will cover, rehearse your speech by repeating your content aloud more than three times. Doing strict preparation, as well as learning from each presentation, can help to not only improve your presentation skills, but also gain more confidence in your public speaking ability.

Focus: A speech that rambles isn't going to impress the audience because it will make the speaker seem to be unorganized and egotistic. Before writing the outline of your speech, make sure that you write down the key point of your speech in one sentence and then expand and develop the speech's structure and content from that key sentence. Only by aiming to satisfy the interests and needs of your listeners will you be able to keep them engaged while you are speaking.

Passion: Having a deep passion for the subject is contagious and helps you engage your audience while you are speaking. Leaders who show passion when delivering presentations come across as more charismatic and authentic. Studies have shown that those who convey information with sincerity are more persuasive and can exert a stronger influence over their audience.

To sum up, honing your communication skills by regularly practicing public speaking is the best way for you to transform into a powerful and influential leader in your company.

161-163 題參考以下文章。

敏銳的溝通技巧創造傑出的商業領袖

理查德・布蘭森是一位非常成功的億萬富翁,他是維珍集團的創始人,非常重視培養強效的溝通技巧。他說過:「成為一名熟練的溝通者是任何企業家或企業領導者可以擁有的最重要的技能。」掌握溝通的藝術是獲得競爭優勢並影響他人的關鍵。最重要的溝通技巧之一是培養發表強而有力之簡報的能力。以下幾種方法可以幫助您進行優異的簡報,讓您脫穎而出。

研究:首先,準備演講的第一步是對您的主題進行深入研究。完成後,應該構建一個大綱並快速記下關鍵事實,以支持您的講演的關鍵訊息。其次,請修改您的內容,並以大聲說出演講內容三次以上的方式演練演講。進行嚴格的準備,並從每次演說中不斷學習,這不僅有助於提升您的簡報技巧,也能獲得公開演講的自信心。

焦點:一個散漫的演講不會給觀眾留下深刻的印象,因為它會使演講者看起來沒有條理且過度主觀。在編寫演講大綱之前,請務必用一句話表達演講的重點,然後從該句子延伸並發展演講的結構與內容。只有您努力去滿足聽眾的興趣和需求,您才能在講話時吸引他們的注意。

激情:對於主題充滿熱情就會產生感染力,可以幫助您在演講時吸引觀眾。在發表演講時表現出激情的領導者更具魅力和真實性。研究顯示,那些以誠意傳達資訊的人更有說服力,可以對聽眾產生更強大的影響力。

總而言之,透過定期練習公開演講來磨練您的溝通技巧是讓您轉變為公司裡強而有力且有影響力的領導者的最佳方式。

161. According to the article, why is it important for businessmen to enhance their communication skills?

(A) They will have a better public image.
(B) It can help them to have the upper hand over their competitors.
(C) It can turn them into passionate people.
(D) They can become sincere people.

根據這篇文章,為什麼企業人士加強溝通技巧很重要?

(A) 他們將擁有更好的公眾形象。
(B) 可以幫助他們優於競爭對手。
(C) 可以使他們變成一個充滿熱情的人。
(D) 他們可以變成誠懇的人。

TEST 01
PART 7

162. The word "egotistic" in paragraph 4, line 2, is closest in meaning to

(A) **self-centered**
(B) modest
(C) reserved
(D) passionate

第四段第二行的 egotistic 意義最接近以下何者？

(A) 以自我為中心的
(B) 謙虛的
(C) 矜持的
(D) 熱情的

---

163. What is indicated about the way to appealing to one's audience?

(A) Delete filler words from your speech
(B) Digress from the subject you are covering
(C) Continuously revise the content you write
(D) **Be enthusiastic about the topic they talk about**

文中提到什麼吸引觀眾的方法？

(A) 刪除演講中的填充詞
(B) 偏離所涉及的主題
(C) 不斷修改編寫的內容
(D) 對談論的主題充滿熱情

單字

possess 擁有；具有
ramble 沒完沒了的亂扯
charismatic 有魅力的
exceptional 優異的；例外的
egotistic 自我中心的
authentic 真實的；可靠的
stand out 出眾，脫穎而出
contagious（想法）具有感染力的
hone 磨練；磨利

178

Questions 164 through 167 refer to the following online chat discussion.

Tommy: [4:13 p.m.]	Two weeks ago, we signed a contract with AVAPowerPC and they agreed to finish complete construction of our website by the 19th of September, 2019. However, on the 20th I gave them a call and was told that only one-third of the website was finished.
Stanley: [4:14 p.m.]	What does the contract stipulate in regards to what they have to finish for us?
Franklin: [4:16 p.m.]	It says that the visual design, site development, site-mapping and wireframing should be done. What about the content design?
Tommy: [4:18 p.m.]	We agreed to do half of the content design, because there are some complicated parts of content that only people with expertise can complete.
Stanley: [4:19 p.m.]	There is something else that you may have overlooked. In the prior written agreement, it states that Tommy has to give them our part of the information for them to type into the website's structure by the 15th of September, 2019.
Tommy: [4:21 p.m.]	Oh no. It completely slipped my mind. I was so tied up with other work in the office.
Stanley: [4:25 p.m.]	Well, I guess we know the reason now. Tommy failed to fulfill his obligation, which constitutes a breach of contract, so we can't really terminate the contract or seek monetary damages.
Franklin: [4:28 p.m.]	How long did they say it will take them to finish setting up the website and have it launched?
Tommy: [4:29 p.m.]	About another 10 days. We can extend the deadline for the company so they can finish what they agreed to do. But I will need to negotiate this with the team leader of this project, and see if we can reach a consensus on how to handle this problem.

TEST 01
PART 7

164-167 題參考以下線上聊天內容。

湯米： [4:13 p.m.]	兩週前，我們與 AVAPowerPC 簽訂了合約，他們同意在 2019 年 9 月 19 日前完成我們網站的完整建構。但是，我在 20 日打電話給他們時，他們說只完成了三分之一的網站。
史丹利： [4:14 p.m.]	合約內容規定他們必須為我們完成什麼？
富蘭克林： [4:16 p.m.]	合約說應該完成視覺設計、網站開發、網站地圖和框架架構。內容設計現在怎麼樣？
湯米： [4:18 p.m.]	我們同意做一半的內容設計，因為有一些複雜的內容部分只有具備專業知識的人才能完成。
史丹利： [4:19 p.m.]	還有一些你可能忽視的東西。在之前的書面協議中，明言湯米必須向他們提供我方的資訊，以便他們在 2019 年 9 月 15 日前輸入網站的結構。
湯米： [4:21 p.m.]	糟了，我完全忘掉了。我在辦公室裡忙翻了。
史丹利： [4:25 p.m.]	嗯，我想我們現在知道原因了。湯米未能履行義務而構成違約，因此我們無法真正終止合約或要求金錢賠償。
富蘭克林： [4:28 p.m.]	他們說要花多長時間才能完成網站設置並啟動它？
湯米： [4:29 p.m.]	大約再十天。我們可以延長公司的截止日期，以便他們能夠完成他們答應的事情。但我需要與該計畫的團隊負責人進行協商，看看我們是否能達成處理這個問題的共識。

164. What was Tommy supposed to give the website developing company?

(A) A copy of the contract
(B) A copy of the prior written agreement
(C) A detailed explanation of how to complete the website
(D) His company's complex information

湯米應該給網站開發公司什麼？

(A) 合約副本
(B) 事先書面協議的副本
(C) 如何完成網站的詳細說明
(D) 他的公司的複雜資訊

---

165. What is indicated about the work AVAPowerPC agreed to do?

(A) Build a website by the 20th of September, 2019
(B) Finish designing all of the content
(C) Do website development and visual design
(D) Type up the company's difficult content

這裡提及哪一項 AVAPowerPC 答應做的工作？

(A) 在 2019 年 9 月 20 日前建立一個網站
(B) 完成所有內容的設計
(C) 做網站開發和視覺設計
(D) 輸入公司的高難度內容

---

166. What will Tommy most likely do next?

(A) Negotiate the price of building a website
(B) Visit AVAPowerPC Company
(C) Finish the rest of the website himself
(D) Try to reach an agreement about the project's new deadline

湯米接下來最有可能做什麼？

(A) 協商建立網站的價格
(B) 造訪 AVAPowerPC 公司
(C) 自己完成網站的其餘部分
(D) 嘗試就計畫的新截止日期達成協議

---

167. At 4:21 p.m., what does Tommy mean when he writes "It completely slipped my mind"?

(A) He didn't take a clear look at the prior written agreement.
(B) He forgot to sign the contract.
(C) He forgot to give the website developers his company's information.
(D) He didn't finish typing up the information on time.

湯米在下午 4 點 21 分寫下 "It completely slipped my mind" 的意思為何？

(A) 他沒有仔細考慮事先的書面協議。
(B) 他忘了簽合約。
(C) 他忘了向網站開發者提供公司的資訊。
(D) 他沒有按時完成資訊的輸入。

單字

stipulate 規定；明確說明
terminate 終止
expertise 專業知識
consensus 共識
be tied up with 忙於⋯

TEST 01
PART 7

Questions 168 through 171 refer to the following news article.

At a press conference on May 22, Donald Alberta, president of National Association of Investors Corporation, announced that the construction of a massive LEGO World Theme Park in Okinawa, Japan will commence in one month's time. Mr. Alberta expressed his desire for this large-scale case to improve the regional economy and tourism industry by attracting many investors from Taiwan and Japan. -[1]-

With many getting wind of this project, there have been growing concerns from tourist guides and local people that constructing such an attraction will encroach on the surrounding areas. -[2]-

According to a survey, most citizens and business owners in the neighbouring areas view this as a positive sign. "The new theme park will be highly appealing to tourists. It will be beneficial for this area in the long term," said Lucas Smith, an Okinawa resident and hotel owner. -[3]-

This theme park will not only capture people's interest, but it will also be a great place for the masses to enjoy outdoor entertainment. -[4]- The research conducted by experts in tourism shows that the revenue generated by tourists who visit will not only be beneficial to the theme park founder, it will also greatly invigorate the local tourist industry.

The theme park will include an adventure submarine ride where people can search for treasure in a sunken LEGO shipwreck. There will be more than 1,500 real animals, including fish, stingrays and sharks that will swim around the tank while riders are exploring.

168-171 題參考以下新聞。

在5月22日的記者會上，全國投資者協會理事長唐納德・艾伯塔宣布，將在一個月內開始在日本沖繩建設一座龐大的樂高世界主題公園。艾伯塔先生表示，他希望透過這個大案吸引台灣和日本的許多投資者，來改善區域經濟和旅遊業。-[1]-

隨著許多人得知這個建案，導遊和當地人越來越關注建構這樣的景點將侵占周邊地區。-[2]- 根據意見調查，鄰近地區的大多數公民和企業主認為這是一個正面的徵象。「新主題公園將吸引遊客。從長遠來看，這對該地區是有益的」，身為沖繩居民的飯店老闆盧卡斯・史密斯這麼說。-[3]-

這座主題公園不僅可以吸引人們的目光，也是大眾享受戶外娛樂的好地方。-[4]- 旅遊專家進行的研究顯示，造訪遊客所產生的收入不僅有利於主題公園創辦人，也將大幅度活化當地的旅遊業。

主題公園的活動將包含搭乘潛水艇探險，人們可以在沉沒的樂高沉船中尋找寶藏。將會有超過1500種真正的動物，包括魚、刺魟和鯊魚，當乘客探索時，牠們會在人工水域裡游動。

168. What does the article discuss?

   (A) An investment project
   (B) Why Japan's tourism industry needs to be boosted
   (C) A rapid growth in the entertainment industry
   (D) Tourist attractions promoted by local magazines

   文章討論的是什麼？

   (A) 一個投資方案
   (B) 為什麼日本旅遊業必須加以振興
   (C) 娛樂業的快速成長
   (D) 當地雜誌推廣的旅遊景點

169. In which of the positions marked [1], [2], [3] and [4] does the following sentence best belong?
   "Nonetheless, the theme park will undoubtedly breathe life into the economy in neighboring areas."

   (A) [1]
   (B) [2]
   (C) [3]
   (D) [4]

   下面的句子最適合放在標示 [1]、[2]、[3] 和 [4] 的哪個位置？
   「不過，主題公園毫無疑問地將為周邊地區的經濟帶來生命力。」

   (A) [1]
   (B) [2]
   (C) [3]
   (D) [4]

170. What is true about the theme park?

   (A) It will be based in mainland Japan.
   (B) It will have over 2,000 kinds of animals.
   (C) You can take a submarine ride and hunt for treasure.
   (D) Construction will start in the middle of August.

   關於主題公園，何者為真？

   (A) 它將設在日本本土。
   (B) 它將有超過 2000 種動物。
   (C) 您可以乘坐潛水艇並尋找寶藏。
   (D) 施工將於八月中旬開始。

171. What is suggested about the influence of the theme park?

   (A) It will stimulate Okinawa's economic growth.
   (B) It will have a negative influence on surrounding hotels.
   (C) Many Chinese people will invest in the island's tourism industry.
   (D) People will gain more interest in LEGO.

   這裡暗示關於主題公園的什麼影響？

   (A) 它將刺激沖繩的經濟成長。
   (B) 它將對周邊飯店產生負面影響。
   (C) 許多中國人將投資島上的旅遊業。
   (D) 人們將對樂高產生更多興趣。

單字

get wind of (something) 得到…的風聲，得知（某事）
encroach on/upon (something) 侵犯；侵佔；蠶食
submarine 潛水艇
revenue（公司的）收入，收益，營收
invigorate 活化；使興盛

Questions 172 through 175 refer to the following announcement.

Company Budget Surplus

I'm pleased to announce that, for the first time in three years, our company has a modest budget surplus. -[1]- This was only made possible by each department's prudent spending throughout the last three quarters. Owing to the fact that our accountant has confirmed that this surplus is a sign of an increase in profits, we are planning to reinvest 30% of this money into our business to increase our productivity and lower the amount of taxes we have to pay. -[2]- These monies will be set aside for two purposes. Firstly, money from the budget surplus will be used to upgrade our office machines and invest in machinery that will bring in greater profit. Secondly, we will expand our production capacity by spending more money on employee training, opening another factory in Tanzi Industrial Zone, and increasing the use of marketing in our expansion.

-[3]- Department managers and division chiefs, please send me a memo and specify which items in your offices or department are taking a lot of wear and tear, and should be our first priority to upgrade or replace. Also include a detailed explanation of the particular products that absolutely need to be bought and how they will benefit you in your future work. It is important to note that we will lose any funds that aren't used up by the end of July this year.

-[4]- Further information on our plans for expansion and dates for employee training will be announced in one month from now.

General Manager
Taylor Wittham

172-175 題參考以下公告。

公司預算盈餘

我很高興地宣布，三年來我們公司首度有了不錯的預算盈餘。這是因為每個部門在過去三個季度謹慎支出才得以實現此一目標。-[1]- 由於我們的會計師確認這筆盈餘是利潤增加的跡象，我們正計劃將這筆資金的 30% 再投資於我們的業務，以提高生產力，並降低必須支付的稅額。-[2]- 這些資金將用於兩個目的。首先，來自預算盈餘的資金將用於升級我們的事務機器，並投資於能帶來更多利潤的機器。其次，我們將擴大產能，在員工訓練上投入更多資金，在潭子工業區開設另一座工廠，並在擴建中增加行銷預算。

-[3]- 部門經理和主任，請發一份備忘錄給我，說明你們辦公室或部門的哪些物品容易損耗，需要優先升級或更換，這包括絕對需要購買的特定產品的詳細說明，以及它們在您未來的工作中將如何使您受益。值得注意的是，我們今年七月底之前沒有用完的預算就無法再使用了。

-[4]- 有關我們的擴展計劃和員工訓練日期的更多訊息，將在一個月後公佈。

總經理
泰勒・威特姆

---

172. In which of the positions marked [1], [2], [3] and [4] does the following sentence best belong?
"Within a month's time, department managers and division chiefs will be notified of the precise amount that will be at their disposal."

(A) [1]
(B) [2]
(C) [3]
(D) [4]

下面的句子最適合放在標示 [1]、[2]、[3] 和 [4] 的哪個位置？
「在一個月的時間內，各部門的經理和主任將獲通知他們可以使用的確切金額。」

(A) [1]
(B) [2]
(C) [3]
(D) [4]

---

173. The word "capacity" in paragraph 1, line 9, is closest in meaning to

(A) size
(B) facility
(C) stability
(D) competency

第一段第九行的 capacity 意義最接近於以下何者？

(A) 規模
(B) 設施
(C) 穩定性
(D) 勝任；能力

TEST 01
PART 7

174. What will the company do in the near future?

(A) **Increase training sessions for employees**
(B) Open up a subsidiary in Nantun District
(C) Expand their business to Europe
(D) Establish a logistics company

該公司在不久的將來將做什麼？

(A) 增加員工訓練課程
(B) 在潭子區開設子公司
(C) 將業務擴展到歐洲
(D) 建立物流公司

---

175. Why do the department managers and division chiefs have to send the general manager a memo?

(A) **They have to state which items in their office need to be replaced.**
(B) They need to explain how cooperating with other departments is beneficial to their work.
(C) They have to notify their manager how to pay less tax.
(D) They have to inform their CEO how their budget surplus was spent.

為什麼各部門經理和主任必須給總經理一份備忘錄？

(A) 他們必須說明他們辦公室中的哪些物品需要更換。
(B) 他們需要解釋與其他部門合作是如何有利於他們的工作。
(C) 他們必須通知他們的經理如何減少繳稅。
(D) 他們必須通知他們的 CEO 他們的預算盈餘是如何花費的。

單字

modest 不太大的；不錯的	budget surplus 預算盈餘	productivity 生產力
capacity 產量；生產力	division chief 主任	memo 備忘錄
specify 詳述；具體說明		

Questions 176 through 180 refer to the following form and letter.

Hotel One, Noosa, Sunshine Coast

Thank you for choosing to stay at Hotel One. In a concerted effort to enhance the quality of customer service and make all guests feel a greater sense of belonging in our hotel, we are kindly asking your honest opinion on your experience during your stay. Please spend some time to fill out the survey and return it to the receptionist when you check out.

Date: July 15
Customer Name: Jacob Morrison
Phone number: (07) 5447 5440

The purpose of your visit at our hotel was ☐ Business ☐ Pleasure ☑ Both

	Excellent	Good	Average	Below Average	Poor
Friendliness of front desk staff	✓				
Room and bathroom cleanliness				✓	
Comfortable bed and furniture		✓			
Reasonable price of room		✓			
Heating and cooling within the room		✓			
Décor			✓		
Overall, how would you rate our staff's hospitality, courtesy, kindness and ability to handle all problems?			✓		
Your OVERALL EXPERIENCE as a guest			✓		

How likely would you choose to stay at this hotel again if you were to return to this area? 50:50
Would you recommend this hotel to someone else, if they needed to find a hotel in this area? No

■ Comments:

    I stayed in Hotel One for 3 nights. My first impression of this place was the customer service was super friendly. Not only were all three receptionists at the front desk competent, but they were also able to answer all of my questions and went out of their way to have my bags delivered to my room on the second floor. However, I experienced some problems on the second and third nights of my stay. At night time, I tried to turn on the hot water but after two minutes it was still cold, so I called room service workers to have someone fix it. Later on, a room service staff called and told me that my room wouldn't have hot water for the next two nights. Even though I was allowed to take a shower in another room, I felt this inconvenience made my stay a little uncomfortable. On the third evening, I expected to have my room cleaned up after I returned from sightseeing. However, when I got back, the beds weren't made and the floor was still a little dirty. Aren't the housemaids supposed to clean up the guests' rooms in the daytime while the guests aren't present? I need someone to explain why both of these things happened ASAP. Overall, I suggest that you upgrade the quality of your hotel's amenities and learn to handle emergencies in a way that won't have a negative influence on guests during their stay.

Jacob Morrison
55 Mackay St, Moore 4606
QLD, Australia

Dear Jacob,

I'm the head manager of Noosa's Hotel One. It has been brought to my attention that your recent visit to our hotel was not up to par. As you are aware, providing the highest level of hospitality and making our guests feel at home here is our number one priority. Hearing that some aspects of our hotel's service have fallen below that standard is certainly something we will address promptly.

Even though there is no excuse for what happened those two nights, I'd like to explain the reason behind those problems. There was a pipe break in the same section of the building that you were staying and we couldn't find a plumber until the third day of your stay. The problem was more serious than we thought and repairing the pipe took a lot longer than we anticipated. On top of that, what made matters worse is two of the housemaids who are in charge of cleaning called in sick on the morning of the third day of your stay and we couldn't find anyone to do their work.

I truly hope that you can forgive us for the inconvenience and trouble this may have caused you. As a gesture of good will, we request you to kindly accept a free stay of two nights at our hotel the next time you come here as compensation for what you experienced.

Sincerely,
Marvin Smith
30 Sunset Dr., Noosa, 4567
QLD, Australia

176-180 題參考以下表格與信件。

Hotel One，努沙，陽光海岸

感謝您選擇入住 Hotel One 飯店。我們致力於提升客戶服務品質，讓所有客人對飯店有更大的歸屬感，我們誠摯地詢問您在住宿期間的經驗。請花一些時間填寫調查表，並在結帳時將其交給服務人員。

日　　期：7/15
客戶姓名：雅各・莫里森
電話號碼：(07) 5447-5440

您住宿我們飯店的原因是：☐ 商務　☐ 休閒　☑ 兩者皆是

	優秀	好	普通	不佳	差
前台工作人員的親切感	✓				
房間和浴室的乾淨程度				✓	
舒適的床和家具		✓			
合理的房價		✓			
房間提供空調		✓			
裝潢			✓		
總體而言，您如何評價我們員工的熱情好客、禮貌、親切和處理所有問題的能力？			✓		
作為嘉賓的整體感受			✓		

如果您重訪這個地區，有多大可能選擇再次入住這家飯店？　　一半一半
如果某人需要在這個區域找到一家飯店，您會推薦這家飯店給他／她嗎？　　不會

■ 意見：

　　我在 Hotel One 住了三晚。我對這個地方的第一印象是客戶服務非常友善。前台的三位接待員不僅僅勝任，他們還能夠回答我的所有問題，並竭盡全力將我的行李送到二樓的房間。但是，我在住宿的第二天和第三天遇到了一點問題。晚上的時候，我打開熱水，但兩分鐘後仍然很冷，所以我打電話給客房服務人員找人修理它。後來，一位客房服務人員打電話告訴我，我的房間在接下來的兩個晚上不會有熱水。即使我被允許在另一個房間洗澡，我覺得這種不便使我住得有點不舒服。第三天晚上，我希望觀光回來後房間已打掃乾淨，但我回來時，床沒有鋪，地板還有點髒。客人不在時，服務員不是應該在白天清理客房嗎？我希望盡快有人解釋為什麼發生這兩種狀況。整體來說，我建議你們升級飯店的設備並學習緊急應變，這樣就不會讓對住宿客人產生負面影響。

TEST 01
PART 7

雅各‧莫里森
Mackay 街 55 號，Moore 4606
澳洲昆士蘭州

親愛的雅各：
我是努沙的 Hotel One 飯店的總經理。我注意到您最近住宿我們飯店的情況並不符合標準。如您所知，提供最高水準的款待和讓客人有賓至如歸的感覺是我們的首要任務。聽到我們飯店的服務在某些方面已經低於這個標準，我們肯定會及時解決這個問題。

即使那兩個晚上所發生的狀況沒有任何藉口，我想解釋那些問題背後的原因。在您住的同一個區域，建築物有一條水管破裂，但我們找不到水管工，直到您住宿的第三天才找到。問題比我們想像的更嚴重，修理管道的時間比我們預期的要長很多。此外更糟糕的是，兩位負責打掃的女傭第三天早上臨時請病假，而我們一時找不到可以代班的人。

我誠心希望您能原諒我們給您帶來的不便和麻煩。作為善意的表示，我們懇請您在下次來到我們飯店時享受兩晚免費住宿，以補償您所經歷的不便。

馬文‧史密斯 敬上
落日大道 30 號，努沙，4567
澳洲昆士蘭州

---

176. What was the result of the housemaids calling in sick on Mr. Morrison's last day at the hotel?

(A) **Mr. Morrison's room wasn't cleaned up before he came back.**
(B) No one could fix the pipes when there was no hot water.
(C) The manager had to take a long time looking for someone to do the work.
(D) The halls weren't cleaned up after Mr. Morrison returned.

莫里森先生住旅館的最後一天，女傭打電話請病假的後果是什麼？

(A) **莫里森先生回旅館前，他的房間沒有打掃過。**
(B) 沒有熱水時，沒人能夠修理管線。
(C) 經理必須花很長時間找人來做這項工作。
(D) 莫里森先生回來後，大廳沒人打掃。

177. What does Mr. Morrison indicate about his stay at the hotel?

    (A) The housemaid's cleaning skills are not up to scratch.
    (B) He is dissatisfied with the interior decoration.
    (C) The receptionists need to work on enhancing their customer service.
    (D) He feels the staff workers don't know how to deal with emergencies properly.

莫里森先生對他在飯店住宿的說法是什麼？

    (A) 女傭的清潔技術無法達到要求。
    (B) 他對室內裝潢不滿意。
    (C) 接待員需要努力提昇他們的客戶服務。
    (D) 他覺得員工無法適當處理緊急狀況。

178. In the letter, the word "gesture" in paragraph 3, line 2, is closest in meaning to

    (A) command
    (B) expression
    (C) bid
    (D) motion

在信中，第三段第二行的 gesture 意義最接近以下何者？

    (A) 命令
    (B) 表達
    (C) 出價
    (D) 動作

179. What was mentioned about the problems that occurred during the second and third night of Mr. Morrison's stay?

    (A) Mr. Morrison couldn't use any water because of an electricity problem.
    (B) Mr. Morrison's room was left untidy because the housemaids forgot to clean it up.
    (C) It took a long time to find a plumber and have the pipes fixed.
    (D) The housemaids did a lousy job of making his bed.

莫里森先生入住的第二晚和第三晚期間發生了什麼問題？

    (A) 由於電力問題，莫里森先生不能使用任何水。
    (B) 莫里森先生的房間不整潔，因為女傭們忘了清理。
    (C) 花了很長時間才找到水管工並修好管路。
    (D) 女傭鋪床鋪得很差。

180. How did Mr. Smith choose to compensate Mr. Morrison for the problems that he experienced?

    (A) Give him a voucher to use at a nearby hotel
    (B) Allow him to stay in Hotel One for two nights
    (C) Give him a refund on the last two nights of his stay
    (D) Give him a 3-night stay for free

史密斯先生如何補償莫里森先生所遇到的問題？

    (A) 給他一張在附近飯店使用的優惠券
    (B) 讓他免費在 Hotel One 住宿兩晚
    (C) 在他住宿的最後兩晚給他退款
    (D) 免費給他三晚住宿

單字

concerted effort 齊心協力
up to par 達到一般水準，達到標準
promptly 立刻
competent 勝任的；能幹的
hospitality 熱情好客；款待
anticipate 預期，預料
amenity 便利設施
address 處理；應付

TEST 01
PART 7

Questions 181 through 185 refer to the following receipt and letter.

Natman Hardware
Door Hardware Price List

568 Widget Street, Kingaroy, 4608

QLD, Australia

Email: jacobm.natman@gmail.com

Phone: 305-714-6120

👍 Top quality! Top Service!

Customer Order No. 568-479-280

Date: December 5, 2019

Client Name: Jacob Morrison

Client Address: 55 Mackay St, Moore 4606 QLD, Australia

Quantity	Description	Price per unit	Total cost of products
44	Door hinges	$6.30	$277.20
24	Door knobs	$8.50	$204.00
60	Door knockers	$5.00	$300.00
10	Mail slots	$4.50	$45.00
		Sales Tax (5%)	$41.31
		Total	$877.51

Note: Delivery fee is $10.

192

Jacob Morrison
55 Mackay St, Moore, 4606 QLD
Australia

December 6, 2019

Dear Mr. Morrison,

Not long after we sent out your order and receipt for the goods ordered on the 5th of December, you sent us an email and made the following complaint: "The items that we purchased last week were just delivered to my shop. After carefully looking everything over, I feel that there has been a real big screw-up. Firstly, there were 6 missing from the box and we received 5 hinges that were different from what we paid for. Also, there are 10 mail slots that seem to be broken. Finally, when the delivery man showed us the receipt, the total price of all 4 products was $10 more expensive than what we agreed on last week. If there has been a change in the price of products, shouldn't we be informed about it before you sent out the products?"

We examined the cause of your receiving the wrong amount of products and now understand why this happened. The person who was in charge of packing the boxes accidentally confused your order with another order. However, we are unsure who is responsible for the broken items. In two days, I'll send a worker to your company to retrieve the 5 door hinges and the broken parts. As I will be visiting a customer in close vicinity of your shop around 10 a.m. next Thursday, I'll deliver all the replacement items, including the items missing from your last order. In regards to the change of price, last time I mentioned that we will be charging $10 extra for the delivery fee. I hope that you accept our heartfelt apology for what happened. To make it up to you, we will give you free delivery for all items you order from us in the next two months as well as a 10% discount on the total price of the mail slots. I'll do everything in my power to ensure this doesn't happen again.

If you have any other enquiries, please don't hesitate to contact me.

Sincerely,
Jason Spears
General Manager, Natman Hardware

181-185 題參考以下收據和信件。

奈特門五金
門類五金價格清單

威傑特街 568 號, Kingaroy, 4608

澳洲昆士蘭州

電子信箱：jacobm.natman@gmail.com

電話：305-714-6120

👍 一流品質！一流服務！

顧客訂單號碼： 568-479-280
日　　　　期： 2019 年 12 月 5 日
客 戶 名 稱： 雅各・莫里森
客 戶 地 址： 馬凱街 55 號, Moore 4606, 澳洲昆士蘭州

數　量	名　稱	單　價	產品總價
44	門鉸鏈	$6.30	$277.20
24	門把手	$8.50	$204.00
60	門　環	$5.00	$300.00
10	郵件槽	$4.50	$45.00
	營業稅 (5%)		$41.31
	總　計		$877.51

備註：運費 10 美元。

雅各・莫里森
馬凱街 55 號，Moore 4606
澳洲昆士蘭州

2019 年 12 月 6 日

親愛的莫里森先生：

在我們送出您在 12 月 5 日訂購的商品和收據後不久，您發了一封電子郵件並提出以下申訴：「我們上週購買的商品剛剛送到我的商店。在仔細查看之後，我覺得真是搞得一團亂。首先，盒子裡少了 6 個，而且我們收到了 5 個錯的鉸鏈。此外，有 10 個郵件插槽似乎損壞了。最後，當送貨員向我們出示收據時，所有四種產品的總價格比我們上週訂的價格貴了 10 美元。如果產品價格發生變化，在送出產品之前我們不應該先獲得通知嗎？」

我們研究了您收到的商品數量錯誤的原因，現在明白了發生這種情況的原因。負責裝箱的人不小心將您的訂單與另一張訂單混淆了。但是，我們不確定誰該對受損的品項負責。我會在兩天內派一名員工到貴公司取回 5 個門鉸鏈和受損的品項。由於我將在下週四上午 10 點左右到您商店附近拜訪客戶，我將順便提供所有替換品項，包括您上次訂單中缺少的品項。關於價格的變化，上次我提到我們將額外收取 10 美元的運費。我希望您接受我們對所發生狀況的衷心道歉。為了補償你們的需求，我們將在接下來的兩個月內為您訂購的所有商品免費送貨，同時所有郵件插槽的總金額也將打九折。我將竭盡全力確保不再發生這種狀況。

如果您有任何其他疑問，請不要猶豫，盡可與我聯繫。

奈特門五金 總經理
傑森・斯皮爾斯 敬上

---

181. What is indicated about the door hinges?

(A) Over ten of them were broken.
(B) Some were damaged by the delivery man.
(C) The worker who packed the boxes sent Mr. Morrison the wrong order.
(D) Seven of the door hinges delivered were different from what Mr. Morrison ordered.

信中提到門鉸鏈有什麼狀況？

(A) 其中有十幾個受損。
(B) 有些被送貨員損壞了。
(C) 裝箱的員工裝錯了莫里森先生的訂貨。
(D) 交付的門鉸鏈中有七個與莫里森先生訂購的不同。

TEST 01
PART 7

182. In the letter, the word "retrieve" in paragraph 2, line 5, is closest in meaning to

(A) repair
(B) get back
(C) save
(D) find

182. 在信中，第二段第五行的 retrieve 意義最接近以下何者？

(A) 修理
(B) 取回
(C) 保存
(D) 找到

---

183. How much will Mr. Morrison have to pay for the mail slots?

(A) $45.00
(B) $40.00
(C) $44.50
(D) $40.50

183. 莫里森先生需要為郵件槽支付多少費用？

(A) $45.00
(B) $40.00
(C) $44.50
(D) $40.50

---

184. How many door hinges did Mr. Morrison receive on December 5?

(A) 50
(B) 44
(C) 40
(D) 38

184. 莫里森先生在 12 月 5 日收到幾個門鉸鏈？

(A) 50
(B) 44
(C) 40
(D) 38

---

185. How did Mr. Spears promise to compensate Mr. Morrison?

(A) Give him a 5% discount on all items for the next month
(B) Cover the cost of product delivery until March 2019
(C) Not charge him delivery fees for the next two months.
(D) Have the door hinges and mail slots delivered for only $5

185. 斯皮爾斯先生答應如何補償莫里森先生？

(A) 給他下個月所有品項 5% 的折扣。
(B) 承擔產品運送成本，直至 2020 年三月。
(C) 不收取下兩個月的運費。
(D) 門鉸鏈和郵件槽的運費只需 5 美元。

單字

retrieve 去取回
in close vicinity of 在附近
make it up to somebody 補償某人
compensate 賠償
receipt 收據
replacement items 更換原件

Questions 186 through 190 refer to the following schedule, email, and message.

Sygnio Inc.
Weekly Shift Schedule with Pay

Date Name	Mon 12/5	Tue 12/6	Wed 12/7	Thu 12/8	Fri 12/9	Sat 12/10	Sun 12/11	Hrs	Pay
Sarah Brighton	10 hrs	12 hrs	10 hrs	12 hrs	12 hrs	OFF	OFF	56	$1288
James Mitchell	10 hrs	12 hrs	10 hrs	8 hrs	10 hrs	OFF	OFF	50	$1150
Douglas Witton	OFF	OFF	12 hrs	12 hrs	10 hrs	12 hrs	11 hrs	57	$1172
Andrew Fitzgerald	12 hrs	OFF	12 hrs	OFF	9 hrs	OFF	OFF	33	$759

To:	masterchief.sygnio@gmail.com
From:	magnificent.sygnio@gmail.com
Subject:	Mistake in Shift Payment

Dear Mr. Harrison,

I just took a look at the schedule that was given to us. I think you made a mistake in calculating the amount of money I will be paid for last week's work. Let me explain and you can judge for yourself.

Firstly, last Tuesday morning I substituted for Douglas, because he took sick leave during the first two days of the week. That day, I worked a total of 10 hours. Secondly, I was originally going to take my personal leave on Tuesday. But when I was asked to come into work last Tuesday morning, I asked you if I could take Thursday off instead. Could you please adjust these details on the schedule and clarify the exact amount of money that I will be paid?

Thirdly, Sarah claims to have worked for 12 hours on Wednesday. If that is the case, and we get paid $23 dollars per hour during weekdays, she should be paid an extra $46 dollars for last week's work. Please confirm this.

Sincerely,
Andrew Fitzgerald

TEST 01
PART 7

Dear Andrew,

Thanks for your email. I checked out the number of hours that you and Sarah worked last week. My answer is as follows:

1. You were right about everything you said about your pay. You can rest assured we will pay you for the work done on Tuesday.

2. I recall what happened last Wednesday. I asked Sarah to stay in the factory and work a total of 13 hours. That means she'll get another 23 dollars on top of what you said in your last email.

If there are any more issues regarding the payment you feel you deserve and your reason is valid, I'm open to negotiation.

Mr. Harrison

186-190 題參考以下時間表、email 與訊息。

絲尼歐公司
每週班次時間表與工資

姓名＼日期	週一 12/5	週二 12/6	週三 12/7	週四 12/8	週五 12/9	週六 12/10	週日 12/11	小時數	工資
莎拉・布萊頓	10 小時	12 小時	10 小時	12 小時	12 小時	請假	請假	56	$1288
詹姆斯・米契爾	10 小時	12 小時	10 小時	8 小時	10 小時	請假	請假	50	$1150
道格拉斯・威頓	請假	請假	12 小時	12 小時	10 小時	12 小時	11 小時	57	$1172
安德魯・費茲傑羅	12 小時	請假	12 小時	請假	9 小時	請假	請假	33	$759

收件者：	masterchief.sygnio@gmail.com
寄件者：	magnificent.sygnio@gmail.com
主　旨：	排班工資錯誤

親愛的哈里森先生：

我剛剛看了一下發給我們的時間表。我認為您在計算我上週工作所應得工資時出錯了。讓我解釋一下，您可以自己判斷。

首先，上週二早上我幫道格拉斯代班，因為他在週一週二兩天請病假。那天我總共工作了 10 個小時。其次，我原本打算在週二休假。但是當我上週二早上被要求上班時，我問您是否可以改在週四休假。您能否按時間表調整這些細節，並清楚讓我知道我應得的工資？

其次，莎拉聲稱週三她工作了 12 個小時。如果是這樣的話，由於我們在工作日每小時的工資是 23 美元，她應該為上週的工作額外領取 46 美元。請確認一下。

安德魯・費茲傑羅 謹啟

親愛的安德魯：

謝謝您的電子郵件。我查看了您和莎拉上週工作的小時數。我的答覆如下：

1. 您說的關於工資的一切都是正確的。您可以放心，我們將支付您在週二上班的工資。

2. 我記得上週三發生的事情。我要求莎拉留在工廠工作了 13 個小時。這意味著，除了您在上一封電子郵件中所說的之外，她還可以再獲得 23 美元。

如果您覺得關於自己應得的工資有其他問題，並且您的理由是合理的，我願意再進行協調。

哈里森先生

TEST 01
PART 7

186. In the email, the word "clarify" in paragraph 2, line 5, is closest in meaning to

(A) make clear
(B) complicate
(C) adjust
(D) systematize

在電子郵件中，第二段第五行的 clarify 意義最接近以下何者？

(A) 說清楚
(B) 複雜化
(C) 調整
(D) 系統化

187. How many extra hours does the boss need to pay Andrew for his work?

(A) 8 hours
(B) 9 hours
(C) 10 hours
(D) 12 hours

老闆需要再付多少小時的工資給安德魯？

(A) 8 小時
(B) 9 小時
(C) 10 小時
(D) 12 小時

188. For what day of work will Sarah get paid an extra $69?

(A) Sunday
(B) Monday
(C) Tuesday
(D) Wednesday

莎拉的哪一個工作日將獲得額外的 69 美元？

(A) 星期天
(B) 星期一
(C) 星期二
(D) 星期三

189. Why did Andrew have to work on Tuesday?

(A) Douglas had to visit a wholesaler.
(B) James had to re-install the multi-media software in the IT department.
(C) Douglas came down with an illness.
(D) Sarah had to take personal leave on Tuesday.

安德魯為什麼必須在星期二工作？

(A) 道格拉斯不得不拜訪批發商。
(B) 詹姆斯不得不在 IT 部門重新安裝多媒體程式。
(C) 道格拉斯生病了。
(D) 莎拉必須在星期二請事假。

190. What is indicated about the hourly wages?

(A) All workers make $30 on weekends.
(B) Workers get paid on the 10th of every month.
(C) All workers are paid $23 per hour.
(D) Those who work overtime are compensated $30 per hour.

關於時薪，email 裡提到什麼？

(A) 所有員工週末都賺 30 美元。
(B) 員工在每個月的十日獲得工資。
(C) 所有員工每小時工資為 23 美元。
(D) 加班工作者每小時可獲補貼 30 美元。

單字

substitute 代替
take ... off（某天）請假／請（…天）假
come down with 患上，染上（尤指小病）
take sick leave 請病假
rest assured 請放心
take personal leave 請事假
valid 合理的；有根據的

Questions 191 through 195 refer to the following job advertisement, online chat discussion and text message.

Balthazar French Cuisine

WE ARE HIRING!

Position: Restaurant manager

Job responsibilities:
- Demonstrate accountability for all budgets
- Order supplies
- Ensure that the restaurant complies with licensing, hygiene and health, and safety legislation/guidelines
- Seasonally update and change the key dishes on menus
- Conduct staff recruitment, training and supervision
- Increase company sales and forecasting future company performance

Qualifications and Skills
- More than 4 years of QSR experience
- A thorough understanding of how restaurants are operated
- Ability to work efficiently in a stressful environment
- Ability to coach and motivate staff members
- Ability to effectively advertise a restaurant through the media
- Experience in handling company budgets
- Experience in increasing company performance based on future financial forecasts
- Experience in innovatively promoting restaurants at trade and community events
- No criminal record and a satisfactory health checkup

How to apply:

Send your resume to George Finley, HR manager: gfinleymobilerestaurant@gmail.com. For any inquiries about the job's details, please call George Hillster on 0956 476 367, or add my LINE: toronto777.

201

Terry Hudson: (10:30 a.m.)	Hello, Mr. Hillster. How are you? My name is Terry Hudson. I just emailed you my resume. I hope you have had time to look it over.
George Hillster: (10:32 a.m.)	Yes, I'm taking a look right now. So far, most of your previous experience as a restaurant manager shows that you are the person we are hoping to hire. However, owing to the fact that you didn't mention anything about how you facilitate restaurant promotion activities at local events, I need you to explain how you went about increasing your customer base with the application of correct advertisement strategies while you were the manager at Cookston Country Club.
Terry Hudson: (10:37 a.m.)	During my time at the restaurant, I looked at events that were happening in my local area, and tried my best to get involved. For example, at the end of the year our community held a semi-marathon. I sent some staff to the venue and distributed pamphlets that said we would offer a discount for people who provided evidence that they finished or participated in the race. This brought in about 30 people, most of whom have become regular customers.
George Hillster: (10:42 a.m.)	That sounds great.
Terry Hudson: (10:43 a.m.)	I wish to clarify one aspect of my experience. I have only worked in one restaurant that served Eastern cuisine. Will I still be qualified for the position without 4 years of QSR experience?
George Hillster: (10:46 a.m.)	This will depend on how good you are at training new employees, as this will help to upgrade customer service and decrease the staff turnover rate. Our head chef has one last question to ask you before we consider whether or not to take you on board. Please reply as promptly as possible. Her question is, "If you were hired as our manager, how would you go about staff training?"
Terry Hudson: (10:50 a.m.)	Could I reply in twenty minutes from now? I have to handle some personal matters that just came up.

Hi, Mr. Hillster,

My answer to your last question is as follows.

I would first give them an orientation so they understand our restaurant's culture, regulations and way of cooking. Second, I would assign supervisory roles to my experienced employees so that they can lead and train new and current staff in different departments. Next, I would hire external trainers to teach employees additional work skills so that the employees feel motivated and appreciated by the company. Finally, I would recognize two of the top employees of the month by giving them an award so that I can boost overall staff morale and improve their work productivity.

Terry Hudson:
(11:12 a.m.)

191-195 題參考以下招聘廣告與線上聊天討論內容。

Balthazar 法國料理

招聘中！

▌職　　位：餐廳經理

▌工作職責：
- ☑ 對所有預算負責任
- ☑ 訂購耗材
- ☑ 確保餐廳符合執照、衛生與健康，以及安全法規／條例
- ☑ 季節性更新和更換菜單上的主菜
- ☑ 執行員工招聘、訓練和監督
- ☑ 增加公司銷售額並預測未來的業績

▌資格和技能：
- ☑ 超過四年的 QSR 經驗
- ☑ 全面了解餐廳的營運方式
- ☑ 能夠在高壓環境中高效工作
- ☑ 能夠指導和激勵員工
- ☑ 能夠透過媒體有效地宣傳餐廳
- ☑ 具有處理公司預算的經驗
- ☑ 曾經根據未來財務預測提升公司的業績
- ☑ 曾經在貿易和社區活動中有創意地宣傳餐廳
- ☑ 沒有犯罪記錄，有令人滿意的健康檢查

▌如何申請：

將您的簡歷發送至人力資源經理喬治・芬利：gfinleymobilerestaurant@gmail.com。
有關工作細節的任何疑問，請電洽 0956-476367 喬治・希爾斯特，
或把我加入 Line，ID: toronto777。

泰瑞・哈德森： (10:30 a.m.)	哈囉，希爾斯特先生。您好嗎？我叫泰瑞・哈德森。我剛才把我的簡歷用 email 寄給您了。我希望您已經看了。
喬治・希爾斯特： (10:32 a.m.)	好的，我現在正在看。到目前為止，您之前作為餐廳經理的大部分經歷都顯示您是我們希望聘用的人。但是，由於您沒有提及有關如何在當地活動中促進餐廳宣傳活動的經歷，我需要您解釋在您擔任庫克斯頓鄉村俱樂部經理時如何透過應用正確的廣告策略來增加客戶群。
泰瑞・哈德森： (10:37 a.m.)	我在該餐廳任職期間會觀察當地發生的事件，並盡力參與其中。例如：在年底，我們的社區舉行了半程馬拉松比賽，我派了一些工作人員到現場並分發小冊子，說我們將會為那些能提供證明他們已經完成或參加比賽的人提供折扣。這帶來了大約三十人，其中大多數已成為常客。
喬治・希爾斯特： (10:42 a.m.)	這聽起來很不錯。
泰瑞・哈德森： (10:43 a.m.)	我想澄清一下我的經歷中的一點。我只在一家供應東方美食的餐廳工作過，如果沒有四年的 QSR 經驗，我還有資格獲得這個職位嗎？
喬治・希爾斯特： (10:46 a.m.)	這將取決於您在訓練新員工方面的表現，因為這有助於升級客戶服務並降低員工流動率。在我們考慮是否讓您加入我們之前，我們的主廚還有最後一個問題要問您，請盡快回覆。她的問題是：「如果您被聘為我們的經理，會如何進行員工訓練？」
泰瑞・哈德森： (10:50 a.m.)	我可以在二十分鐘後回覆嗎？我必須處理剛剛出現的一些個人問題。

TEST 01
PART 7

> 嗨，希爾斯特先生：
>
> 我對你最後一個問題的回答如下：
>
> 我會首先給他們做職前訓練，以便他們了解我們餐廳的文化、規章和烹飪方式。其次，我會指派監督職務給經驗豐富的員工，以便他們能夠領導和訓練不同部門的新員工和現任員工。接下來，我會聘請外部講師來教導員工額外的工作技能，以便員工感受到公司的激勵和重視。最後，我會透過給予獎勵來認可當月的兩位頂級員工，這樣我就可以提升員工的整體士氣，並提高他們的工作效率。

泰瑞‧哈德森 (11:12 a.m.)

191. In the text message, the word "morale" in the second line from bottom, is closest in meaning to

(A) reputation
(B) appearance
(C) personality
(D) confidence

在簡訊中，倒數第二行的 morale 意義最接近以下何者？

(A) 聲譽
(B) 外觀
(C) 個性
(D) 信心

192. Why would Mr. Hudson mostly likely be hired?

(A) He used to be a manager at a fast food restaurant.
(B) He is adept at training staff.
(C) His advertising methods are effective.
(D) He has the ability to handle stress.

為什麼哈德森先生可能獲得錄用？

(A) 他曾經是一家快餐店的經理。
(B) 他擅長訓練員工。
(C) 他的廣告方法很有效。
(D) 他有能力處理壓力。

193. How did Mr. Hudson demonstrate competence in advertising his restaurant?

(A) He took advantage of local events to bring in new customers.
(B) His new employee training included getting involved in restaurant marketing.
(C) He gave discounts to frequent customers.
(D) He gave awards to employees for bringing new guests to the restaurant.

哈德森先生如何展示宣傳餐廳的能力？

(A) 他利用當地活動吸引新客戶。
(B) 他的新員工訓練包括參與餐廳的行銷。
(C) 他給常客提供折扣。
(D) 他獎勵員工將新客人帶到餐廳。

194. What is true about the methods Mr. Hudson mentioned about employee training?

(A) He would have new employees learn how to cook from a manual.
(B) He would motivate staff members by awarding the most diligent workers.
(C) He would teach all employees how to run a restaurant.
(D) He would teach staff members how to handle stress.

哈德森先生提到的員工訓練方法何者為真？

(A) 他會讓新員工學習如何從手冊中烹飪。
(B) 他會透過獎勵最勤奮的員工來激勵員工。
(C) 他會教所有員工如何經營餐廳。
(D) 他會教會工作人員如何處理壓力。

195. Which of the following qualifications in Mr. Hudson's resume does he need to include more information to show that he is qualified for the position?

(A) Experience of innovatively promoting restaurants at trade and community events
(B) Ability to effectively advertise restaurant through the media
(C) Ability to work efficiently in a stressful environment
(D) Experience handling company budgets and increasing company performance based on future financial forecasts

哈德森先生簡歷中的哪一項資歷需要提供更多資訊以證明他有資格擔任該職位？

(A) 曾經在貿易和社區活動中有創意地宣傳餐廳
(B) 透過媒體有效地宣傳餐廳的能力
(C) 在壓力環境中高效工作的能力
(D) 根據未來的財務預測，處理公司預算和提升公司績效的經驗

單字			
	accountability 負有責任	comply with 遵守	legislation 法律；法規
	coach 訓練；指導	facilitate 促進；推動	pamphlet 小冊子
	staff turnover rate 員工流動率	orientation 職前訓練	regulation 規章；條例；法規
	morale 士氣	productivity 生產力；生產率	

TEST 01
PART 7

Questions 196 through 200 refer to the following form, letter, and email.

Name	Background and Expertise	
Dr. Fredrick Arkens	**Division**: Mental illnesses **Current job**: Chief of the Psychiatry Department at Jen-Ai Hospital, Taichung.	**Specializes in**: • Addiction treatment • Child and adolescent health issues • Pain management
Dr. Benjamin Brown	**Division**: Children's health **Current job**: Attending Pediatric Physician at Taichung Chengqing Hospital	**Specializes in**: • Children's cardiology • Children's infectious diseases • Cardiac rhythm disorders
Dr. Bob Taylor	**Division**: Woman's health and pregnancy **Current job**: Doctor at National Taiwan University, Faculty of Medicine, Affiliated Hospital	**Specializes in**: • Infertility • Maternal-Fetal Medicine • Nurse Midwifery
Dr. Robert Perks	**Division**: Orthopedics **Current job**: Chief of Orthopedic Surgery Department at China Medical University Hospital in Taichung City	**Specializes in**: • Shoulder and knee surgery • Foot and ankle surgery • Sports injuries
Dr. George Malcom	**Division**: Plastic and Reconstructive Surgery **Current job**: Attending Plastic and Reconstructive Surgeon at Taichung Lin Xin Hospital	**Specializes in**: • Breast surgery • Laser surgery • Skin cancer surgery

Gillard,

Thanks for offering to take my friends and I to see different doctors next week. Before we set out, I need to explain what health problems we are experiencing.

Three days ago, I injured myself while I was playing an intense game of volleyball with my friends and the tendons in the back of my left hamstring started to hurt. I am in dire need of finding the right doctor to help me recover.

Second, Isabella and her husband have made an appointment with a doctor in Taipei for next Tuesday because they need to ask some questions about how to use natural medicine and herbs to boost her fertility.

Next, Abigail has been suffering from trauma since last year and needs to get some drugs to help her fall asleep at night. She has been thinking of seeing Dr. Arkens, but she would like to know more about his background as a doctor before she makes her final choice.

Finally, Elijah's son was diagnosed with heart disease and was advised to return to see his doctor before the end of this month.

Thanks so much for your help.

Olivia Gilbert

To:	o.gilbert@yahoo.net
From:	gillard@gmail.com
Date:	July 26
Cc:	egrey@yahoo.net; abigail555@hotmail.com; isabella1988.fredricks@hotmail.com
Subject:	Next week's doctors visit

Dear Mrs. Gilbert,

I just got in touch with the Orthopedic Surgery at China Medical University, and found out some news which you will find surprising. As of last month, Dr. Perks relocated to Hong Kong and started practicing medicine in his own clinic there. I've found a more suitable doctor for you whose name is Nancy Sioux. She graduated from Stanford Medical School and completed her orthopedic residency at Lutheran St. John's Medical Center in Boston. She is a leading expert in the field of sports medicine in Taiwan and is highly proficient in healing sports-related injuries. I'll take you to her clinic near Taichung Veterans Hospital next Thursday.

Second, I did a thorough check into Dr. Arkens' medical background and found him to be a competent and experienced doctor. Not only does he prescribe natural medicine that can help alleviate the effects of anxiety and insomnia, but he also spends extra time counseling patients so that they gradually mentally recover and return to a normal life.

Please inform your three friends that I'll be going to Taipei next Tuesday, and the next day I'll have time to go to the hospitals in Taichung City.

Yours,
Gillard Allerton

TEST 01
PART 7

196-200 題參考以下表格、信件與 email。

姓　名	背景與專業	
菲德瑞克・阿肯斯醫師	科　　室：精神科 目前任職： 台中仁愛醫院 精神科主任	專門從事： • 戒癮精神病學 • 兒童和青少年精神病學 • 疼痛管理
班傑明・布朗醫師	科　　室：小兒科 目前任職： 台中澄清醫院 兒科主治醫師	專門從事： • 兒童心臟病學 • 兒童傳染病 • 心律不整
鮑伯・泰勒醫師	科　　室：婦產科 目前任職： 國立台灣大學醫學院 附設醫院醫師	專門從事： • 不孕症 • 母胎醫學 • 護理助產
羅伯特・伯克斯醫師	科　　室：骨科 目前任職： 台中市中國醫藥大學附設醫院 骨科外科主任	專門從事： • 肩部和膝部手術 • 足部和踝部手術 • 運動損傷
喬治・麥爾坎醫師	科　　室：整形及重建外科 目前任職： 台中林新醫院 整形重建外科主治醫師	專門從事： • 乳房手術 • 雷射手術 • 皮膚癌手術

吉拉德：

感謝您邀請我和我的朋友下週去見不同的醫生。在我們出發之前，我需要說明一下我們目前的健康問題。

三天前我和朋友進行激烈的排球比賽，我受傷了，左腿筋後部的肌腱開始疼痛。我亟需找到合適的醫生來幫助我復元。

其次，伊莎貝拉和她丈夫於下週二在台北與一位醫生有約，因為他們需要問一些關於如何使用天然藥物和藥草來提高生育能力的問題。

接下來，阿比蓋爾自去年以來一直很痛苦，需要一些藥物來幫助她在晚上入睡。她一直想看阿肯斯醫師，但在她做出最終選擇之前，她想更加了解阿肯斯醫師的醫學背景。

最後，以利亞的兒子被診斷出患有心臟病，受到建議在本月底前回去看醫生。

非常感謝您的幫助。

奧莉維亞・吉爾伯特

收件者：	o.gilbert@yahoo.net
寄件者：	gillard@gmail.com
日　期：	7 月 26 日
副　本：	egrey@yahoo.net; abigail555 @ hotmail.com; isabella1988.fredricks@hotmail.com
主　旨：	下週拜訪醫師

親愛的吉爾伯特太太：

我剛連絡了中國醫藥大學的骨科部，獲知一些您會感到驚訝的消息。就在上個月，他搬到了香港，開始在自己的診所行醫。我找到了一位更適合您的醫生，她的名字叫南希·蘇。她畢業於史丹佛醫學院，並在波士頓路德聖約翰醫療中心完成了她的骨科住院實習。她是台灣運動醫學領域的頂尖專家，在治療運動相關傷害方面非常精通。我下週四帶您去她靠近台中榮民總醫院的診所。

其次，我對阿肯斯醫師的醫學背景進行了徹底的了解，發現他是一位稱職且經驗豐富的醫生。他不僅開了可以幫助緩解焦慮和失眠影響的天然藥物，還花費額外的時間為患者提供諮詢，使他們在精神狀態方面逐漸康復，能夠恢復正常生活。

請告知您的三個朋友，我將在下週二去台北，第二天我將有時間去台中市的醫院。

吉拉德·阿勒頓 謹啟

---

196. What is true about the Dr. Robert Perks?

(A) He specializes in spine and shoulder surgery.
(B) He recently moved to Hong Kong to start up a new clinic.
(C) He will help Olivia with her tendon injury.
(D) He is experienced when it comes to elbow surgery.

關於羅伯特·伯克斯醫師，何者為真？

(A) 他專攻脊椎和肩膀手術。
(B) 他最近搬到香港開了一家新診所。
(C) 他將幫奧莉維亞看肌腱傷。
(D) 他在肘部手術方面經驗豐富。

197. Why is Dr. Arkens a suitable doctor for Abigail?

(A) He is able to reduce the effects of depression.
(B) He can help her overcome her addiction.
(C) He has experience helping young people with sleeping problems.
(D) He is able to counsel her so she can get over her trauma.

為什麼阿肯斯醫師是阿比蓋爾的合適醫生？

(A) 他能夠減少憂鬱症的影響。
(B) 他可以幫助她克服上癮。
(C) 他有幫助年輕人解決睡眠問題的經驗。
(D) 他能夠為她提供諮詢，以便她可以克服她的創傷。

TEST 01
PART 7

198. What is suggested about Dr. Sioux?

(A) **She can help Olivia with her tendon injury.**
(B) She graduated from Harvard Medical School.
(C) She did her internship at St. Luke's Medical Center in Seattle.
(D) She is adept at skull reconstruction.

Email 中暗示關於蘇醫師的什麼事？

(A) **她可以幫奧莉維亞解決肌腱傷。**
(B) 她畢業於哈佛醫學院。
(C) 她在西雅圖的聖盧克醫療中心實習。
(D) 她擅長頭骨重建。

199. In the email, the word "alleviate" in paragraph 2, line 3, is closest in meaning to

(A) **ease**
(B) agitate
(C) sustain
(D) assist

在 Email 中，第二段第三行的 alleviate 意義最接近以下何者？

(A) **減輕**
(B) 使焦慮
(C) 維持
(D) 協助

200. Which of the four people will be taken to hospitals in Taichung?

(A) Isabella, Elijah's son, and Abigail
(B) Isabella and Olivia
(C) Olivia and Elijah's son
(D) **Abigail, Elijah's son, and Olivia**

四個人中哪幾位將被帶到台中的醫院？

(A) 伊莎貝拉、以萊亞的兒子和阿比蓋爾
(B) 伊莎貝拉和奧莉維亞
(C) 奧莉維亞和以萊亞
(D) **阿比蓋爾、以萊亞的兒子和奧莉維亞**

單字		
psychiatry 精神病學	adolescent 青少年	cardiology 心臟病學
pediatric (US) / paediatric (UK) 小兒科的		infertility 不孕症
midwifery 助產；接生	orthopedics 骨科	reconstructive 重建的
tendon 肌腱	hamstring 膕腱，腿筋	residency（醫師）住院實習
alleviate 減輕；緩解	anxiety 焦慮，憂慮	insomnia 失眠（症）

TEST 02
中譯・單字

TEST 02
PART 1 05

1.
(A) A black car is leaving from the village.
(B) A vehicle is parked in front of the house.
(C) Small fences are around the house.
(D) The vehicle is parked beside the fence.

(A) 一輛黑色汽車從村莊離開。
(B) 一輛車停在房子前面。
(C) 房子周圍有小柵欄。
(D) 車輛停在圍欄旁邊。

| 單字 | village 鄉村，村莊 | vehicle 交通工具；車輛 |

2.
(A) The coffee shop is full of people.
(B) The counter is stacked with a lot of food.
(C) The customers are waiting in a line for the coffee.
(D) The coffee shop is running a promotion for the festival.

(A) 咖啡店裡擠滿了人。
(B) 櫃台堆放了很多食物。
(C) 顧客正在排隊等咖啡。
(D) 咖啡廳正在為這個節慶做促銷。

| 單字 | counter 櫃台　　stack 堆疊；堆放　　promotion 促進；提昇；促銷 |
| | festival 節慶；節日 |

3.
(A) The couple is looking at each other.
(B) The couple is toasting each other.
(C) The food on the table has been eaten up.
(D) The girl is wearing a long-sleeve dress.

(A) 這兩人正在看著對方。
(B) 這兩人正在相互敬酒。
(C) 桌上的食物被吃掉了。
(D) 女孩穿長袖洋裝。

| 單字 | toast 敬酒 | sleeve 袖子 |

214

4. 
(A) A man is starting his jet ski.
(B) The jet ski is overturning into the water.
(C) The rider is falling into the water from his jet ski.
(D) The jet ski is racing across the surface of the water.

(A) 這名男子正在發動他的水上摩托車。
(B) 水上摩托車正朝水中翻覆。
(C) 騎士正從水上摩托車上跌入水中。
(D) 水上摩托車正疾駛過水面。

單字	jet ski 水上摩托車　　　overturn 翻覆；打翻　　　race 快跑；疾駛
	surface 表面

5. 
(A) Water is being poured into the bamboo basket.
(B) The two people are soaking in the water.
(C) The child is holding a banana leaf over her head.
(D) The mother and child are enjoying a bath.

(A) 水正被倒入竹簍子中。
(B) 兩個人正泡在水中。
(C) 孩子正把香蕉的葉子舉在她頭上。
(D) 媽媽和孩子正在享受洗澡。

單字	bamboo 竹子　　　basket 籃子　　　soak 浸泡

6. 
(A) The sunlight is shining into the room.
(B) The lady is booking a window seat.
(C) The woman is approaching the window.
(D) The lady is writing something on a magazine.

(A) 陽光照射在房間裡。
(B) 女士正在預訂靠窗的座位。
(C) 女士正靠近窗戶。
(D) 女士正在雜誌上寫東西。

單字	approach 接近　　　magazine 雜誌

TEST 02
PART 2　06

7. Would you please stand behind the podium?
   (A) The audience can't see you.
   (B) I'm sitting down.
   (C) Why? I am not going to give a speech now.

   你能站在演講台後嗎？
   (A) 觀眾看不到你。
   (B) 我正在坐下。
   (C) 為何？我現在不打算演講。

   | 單字 | podium 講台　　audience 聽眾；觀眾 |

8. We grew a lot this fiscal year, didn't we?
   (A) I agree. We are improving.
   (B) The company is experiencing slow growth.
   (C) Financial problems are haunting their company.

   今年度我們財務成長很多，對吧？
   (A) 對呀！我們正在成長。
   (B) 公司成長趨緩。
   (C) 財務問題困擾著他們的公司。

   | 單字 | fiscal 財政的；財務的　　improve 改善　　haunt 糾纏；困擾 |

9. Didn't they account for the money we lost?
   (A) I'll hold you accountable.
   (B) They explained to us why we lost it.
   (C) I'm not responsible for financial matters.

   他們沒有說明我們賠的錢嗎？
   (A) 我會讓你負責。
   (B) 他們向我們解釋了為什麼賠錢。
   (C) 我不負責財務。

   | 單字 | account for 說明；對⋯做解釋　　accountable 負有責任的 |

10. The newly purchased machinery has a serious structural flaw.
    (A) Why don't we get it repaired?
    (B) The floor collapsed.
    (C) We bought some machines yesterday.

    新買的機器有嚴重的結構缺陷。
    (A) 為什麼我們不將它送修？
    (B) 地板塌陷。
    (C) 我們昨天買了一些機器。

    | 單字 | structural 結構上的　　flaw 缺陷；瑕疵　　collapse 倒塌；崩潰 |

11. Can you explain why there were so many objections to our business plan?
    (A) Most people said it was infeasible.
    (B) I objected to his idea.
    (C) We plan to build a company from scratch.

    你能說明一下為什麼我們的商業計劃有這麼多反對意見嗎？
    (A) 大多數人都說這是不可行的。
    (B) 我反對他的想法。
    (C) 我們打算從零開始，建立一個公司。

| 單字 | objection 反對；異議 | infeasible 不可行的 | build ... from scratch 從零開始建立 |

12. Was the decision to start a new factory unanimous?

    (A) Only one person didn't support it.
    (B) Everyone voted in favor of moving our office.
    (C) The new factory opened last February.

設立新工廠的決定是否獲得一致同意？

    (A) 只有一個人不支持它。
    (B) 每個人都投票贊成搬遷我們的辦公室。
    (C) 新工廠於去年 2 月開業。

| 單字 | unanimous 一致同意的 | vote in favor 投票贊成 | factory 工廠，製造廠 |

13. Will you make remittance or pay in cash?

    (A) I'll wire the money tonight.
    (B) I think he has remitted his money.
    (C) I'll check my bank account tomorrow.

你要匯款還是付現金？

    (A) 我今晚會匯款。
    (B) 我認為他已經匯款。
    (C) 我明天會檢查銀行戶頭。

| 單字 | make a remittance = remit money 匯款 | wire 匯（款） |

14. Shall we attach the trademark to our logo?

    (A) It's up to you.
    (B) The papers are in the attachment.
    (C) I attached a document to the letter.

我們是否應將商標附在我們的標誌上？

    (A) 這取決於你。
    (B) 論文在附件中。
    (C) 我在信中附上了一份文件。

| 單字 | trademark 商標　　logo 標識，標誌　　attachment 附件 |
| | attach 附加　　document 文件 |

15. We need to enroll in this training course, don't we?

    (A) Thanks for the reminder.
    (B) I took a walk earlier today.
    (C) In the commercial building.

我們要註冊這堂訓練課程，對吧？

    (A) 謝謝你的提醒。
    (B) 我今天早些時候散步了。
    (C) 在商業大樓。

| 單字 | enroll 登記；註冊 | reminder 提醒 | commercial 商業的 |

TEST 02 PART 2

16. You work as a mechanical engineer, don't you?

(A) We are figuring out the mechanics.
(B) Well, I have been promoted to manager.
(C) Engineers work on the third floor.

你是機械工程師，不是嗎？

(A) 我們正在弄清楚機制。
(B) 嗯，我晉升為經理了。
(C) 工程師在三樓工作。

> **單字** mechanical 機械的　　figure out 理解；想出；弄清楚　　promote 晉升

---

17. Hasn't the technician installed the software yet?

(A) I've been so busy.
(B) It won't be done until tomorrow.
(C) Yes, it was stolen yesterday.

技術人員還沒有安裝軟體嗎？

(A) 我一直很忙。
(B) 明天才會來安裝。
(C) 是的，昨天被偷了。

> **單字** technician 技術人員；技師　　install 安裝

---

18. Did inflation make your business profitable this year?

(A) Inflation has hit the market hard.
(B) Our goods are being sold at higher prices.
(C) Most businesses aren't flourishing.

通貨膨脹讓你的公司更有利潤嗎？

(A) 通貨膨脹已經衝擊市場。
(B) 我們的產品正以高價出售。
(C) 大部份的公司沒什麼利頭。

> **單字** inflation 通貨膨脹　　hit... hard …受到很大打擊　　flourish 興盛；繁榮

---

19. We're hoping to downsize next year.

(A) Is it because of the poor economy?
(B) Their workers are asking for compensation.
(C) This issue has many downsides.

我們明年想要縮編。

(A) 是因為景氣不好嗎？
(B) 他們的員工正在要求補償。
(C) 這個議題有很多缺點。

> **單字** downsize 縮編；裁員　　economy 經濟；經濟狀況　　compensation 補償
> downside 負面；缺點

---

20. What is the purpose of this fundraiser?

(A) Please raise your hands.
(B) We want to raise money to fight lung cancer.
(C) They raised funds for our launch.

這個募款活動的目的是什麼？

(A) 請舉起你的雙手。
(B) 我們募資用來預防肝癌。
(C) 他們募集資金讓我們上市。

218

| 單字 | fundraiser 募款活動 | raise 募集；舉起 | launch 發行；上市 |

21. When will she go on maternity leave?　　她什麼時候休產假？

(A) She's five months pregnant.　　(A) 她懷孕五個月了。
(B) She'll go on vacation to Hawaii soon.　　(B) 她很快就會去夏威夷度假。
(C) As of next Tuesday.　　**(C) 從下週二起。**

| 單字 | maternity 孕婦的；產婦的 | pregnant 懷孕的 | as of 從⋯起（= as from） |

22. Why is there such a shortage of staff here?　　為何這裡工作人員這麼短缺呢？

(A) We are having a shortage of capable staff.　　(A) 我們缺少有能力的員工。
(B) The staff members are all diligent.　　(B) 員工們都勤勉盡責。
(C) The interviewees haven't been up to standard.　　**(C) 接受面試的人都未符合標準。**

| 單字 | shortage 短缺 | diligent 勤奮的 | interviewee 接受面試的人 |

23. Why didn't you fix the problem when you had the chance?　　你為什麼有機會時不解決這個問題呢？

(A) I left my change on the table.　　(A) 我把我的零錢留在桌上。
(B) He is a fixture at all meetings.　　(B) 他是所有會議的固定班底。
(C) It was not my responsibility.　　**(C) 那不是我的責任。**

| 單字 | fixture 固定班底 |

24. Who will make the opening remarks at this meeting?　　誰會在這次會議上致開場辭？

(A) Harry will say something about finances.　　**(A) 亨利會說些財務方面的事。**
(B) That remark was unacceptable.　　(B) 那樣的言論是不能接受的。
(C) John kicked off the meeting.　　(C) 約翰啟始了會議。

| 單字 | remark 言論；評論 | kick off 啟始；開始 |

TEST 02
PART 2

25. Where do I freight these goods?   我該把這些貨物運去哪裡？

(A) The freight can be paid to Mr. Johnson.
(B) They will be shipped to L.A.
(C) They will be sent by air.

(A) 運費可以支付給強生先生。
(B) 它們將被運到洛杉磯。
(C) 它們將被空運。

單字	freight 運送；貨物；運費

26. Whose choice was it to spend the money on stocks?   誰選擇把錢花在股票上？

(A) Hillary chose to make that investment.
(B) There are no goods in stock.
(C) Anthony spent all his money.

(A) 希拉蕊選擇做出那樣的投資。
(B) 沒有庫存了。
(C) 安東尼花了他所有的錢。

27. How long have you worked in this field for?   你在這個領域工作多久了？

(A) About 15 years.
(B) I was an electrician before.
(C) I am in a new line of work now.

(A) 大約 15 年。
(B) 我以前是電工。
(C) 我剛換工作。

單字	field 領域 electrician 電工；電氣技師

28. Who was nominated to be the boss of the franchising store?   誰被提名做加盟店的店長？

(A) John wants to franchise a chain store.
(B) My boss is Harry.
(C) Bob was chosen.

(A) 約翰想授予一間連鎖店加盟權。
(B) 我的老闆是哈瑞。
(C) 鮑伯被選上了。

單字	nominate 提名 franchise 授予加盟權

29. Which person would like to be the chairperson for the meeting?   哪個人想做會議的主席？

(A) Can I give it a try?
(B) Jack is a good business leader.
(C) The chairperson has called in sick.

(A) 我可以試試嗎？
(B) 傑克是一位很好的企業領袖。
(C) 主席打電話來說病了。

單字	chairperson 主席

30. Who should I consult about the price of this appliance?

(A) The shop staff are busy now.
(B) It'll cost an arm and a leg.
(C) The store manager will answer your inquiries.

這台電器的價格應該問誰？

(A) 店員現在很忙。
(B) 這將所費不貲。
(C) 店經理將回答您的詢問。

單字	appliance 家用電器　　　inquiry 詢問

31. Who is the manager at this subsidiary?

(A) We offer no subsidy for your loss.
(B) I think his name is Bob.
(C) He's a great guy.

該子公司的經理是誰？

(A) 我們不為您的損失提供補貼。
(B) 我認為是鮑伯。
(C) 他是個不錯的人。

單字	subsidiary 子公司　　　subsidy 津貼；補貼

TEST 02
PART 3

Questions 32 through 34 refer to the following conversation.

M: Hi, I'd like to rent a compact car for the next five days. My wife and I will be driving around the island.
W: Well, all of the compact cars have been rented out. We only have an economy and a standard car available.
M: I'd prefer an economy car. How much will you charge for 5 days?
W: $100. I strongly encourage you to pay for the damage waiver for those five days. It will only cost $11 per day.
M: No problem.
W: Please note that there is a mileage limit on this car. If you drive more than 600 miles in the car, we will have to charge you an extra fee.
M: Ok. I'll pay the deposit now and pick up the car next Tuesday morning.

32-34 題參考以下對話。

男：嗨，我想在接下來的五天租一輛小型車。我和我的妻子將開車環島。
女：所有的小型車都已經出租了。我們只有經濟型和標準型轎車。
男：我比較喜歡經濟型轎車。五天你要收多少費用？
女：100 美元。我強烈建議您保這五天的損害豁免險，它每天只需 11 美元。
男：沒問題。
女：請注意，這輛車有里程限制。如果您開車超過 600 英里，我們將收取額外費用。
男：好的。我現在支付訂金，下週二早上取車。

32. What kind of car does the man want to rent?

(A) Compact
(B) Economy
(C) Standard
(D) Minivan

該男子想要租什麼樣的車？

(A) 小型車
(B) 經濟型
(C) 標準型
(D) 多功能休旅車

33. According to the woman, how much does the man have to pay for the damage waiver per day?

(A) $11
(B) $12
(C) $13
(D) $14

根據該女子的說法，該男子每天需要支付多少損害豁免保險費？

(A) 11 美元
(B) 12 美元
(C) 13 美元
(D) 14 美元

34. What fee did the man pay today?

(A) Damage waiver
(B) Personal accident insurance
(C) Supplemental liability insurance
(D) A deposit

該男子今天付了什麼費用？

(A) 損害豁免險
(B) 人身意外傷害保險
(C) 補充責任保險
(D) 訂金

單字
compact car 小型車　　encourage 鼓勵　　damage waiver 損害豁免
mileage 里程　　deposit 訂金；保證金

Questions 35 through 37 refer to the following conversation.

M: In recent years, our company's turnover rate has been increasing. We need to come up with a way to reverse this problem.

W1: I guess we could change the way we hire people. We should not just look for people with strong skills that match the position; we should ask them specific questions to find out how they would behave in certain situations.

W2: That's a great idea. Also, when we are giving interviews, we should show candidates around our company and tell them about specific traits of our workplace culture. If they couldn't fit in, they will go to a place that is more suitable for them.

W1: On top of that, we should make sure our employees are compensated well. This means paying them wages commensurate with their skills and experience.

M: Another thing is that we should give them praise and rewards for contributing to the company, that way they will feel appreciated and recognized.

35-37 題參考以下對話。

男： 近幾年，我們公司的員工流動率一直在增加。我們必需想出辦法來改變這個狀況。

女1： 我想我們可以改變僱用員工的方式。我們不應該僅僅找符合職位技能的人，我們應該向他們詢問具體的問題，以了解他們在某些情況下的行為模式。

女2： 這是一個好主意。此外，當我們進行面試時，我們應該讓應徵者參觀公司，並告訴他們我們職場文化的具體特點。如果他們無法適應，他們可以去更適合他們的地方。

女1： 此外，我們應該確保我們的員工得到很好的酬勞。這意味他們的技能和經驗越好，薪資就越好。

男： 另一件事是我們應該為員工的貢獻給予他們讚揚和獎賞，這樣他們就會覺得受到賞識和肯定。

---

35. What is the conversation about?

    (A) Ways to introduce a person's company.
    (B) The amount of salary managers should be paid.
    (C) How to help employees gain compensation.
    (D) How to decrease the turnover rate.

對話在講什麼？

(A) 介紹個人公司的方法
(B) 應支付經理的薪資金額
(C) 如何幫助員工獲得報酬
(D) 如何降低員工流動率

---

36. What do the speakers say about things to do in an interview?

    (A) Only focus on finding competent workers
    (B) Tell candidates about specific workplace culture
    (C) Offer high wages to attract skilled workers
    (D) Give the candidate a lot of praise

說話者提到面試中要做的事情是什麼？

(A) 只專注於找到稱職的員工
(B) 告訴應徵者具體的職場文化
(C) 提供高薪資以吸引技術員工
(D) 給應徵者很多讚美

TEST 02
PART 3

37. According to the man, how should their company show appreciation for workers?

(A) Reward them for their hard work
(B) Give them an award
(C) Give them longer holidays
(D) Give them more compensation leave

據男子的說法,他們公司應該如何表達對員工的賞識?

(A) 因為他們辛勤工作而給予獎賞
(B) 給他們一個獎品
(C) 給他們更長的假期
(D) 給他們更多的補休

單字			
	turnover rate 人員流動率	increase 增加	come up with 想出;提出
	candidate 候選人;應徵者	trait 特點,特徵	workplace culture 職場文化
	compensate 支付報酬	commensurate 相當的,相稱的	recognize 認可,肯定;承認

Questions 38 through 40 refer to the following conversation.

M 1: Good morning. One of our clients in Italy filed a complaint against us because they didn't receive the 15 batches of radiators that we sent out last month. They said that this was the second time that this has happened.

W: Ok. I remember that the same time last year, they informed us that we sent them some faulty spare parts and they tried to get a refund.

M 2: These problems can be avoided. We simply need to upgrade our quality control and double check our products before they are packed and sent.

M 1: If these issues aren't promptly dealt with, this will greatly affect our profitability. I think I need to have a meeting with the logistics and manufacturing department manager.

38-40 題參考以下對話。

男 1： 早安，我們在義大利的一位客戶向我們投訴，因為他們沒有收到我們上個月發出的 15 批散熱器。他們說這是第二次發生這種情況。

女： 好的。我記得在去年的同一時間，他們告訴我們，我們給他們發了一些有瑕疵的備用零件，他們那時想要退費。

男 2： 這些問題可以避免。我們只需要升級我們的品質控制，並在打包和運送前仔細檢查我們的產品。

男 1： 如果不及時處理這些問題，這將大大影響我們的獲利能力。我需要與物流、製造部門經理開個會。

---

38. What problem was mentioned?

(A) Their production line is producing faulty products.
(B) Their quality control manager wants to resign.
(C) One of their customers is buying from another factory.
(D) A client said they didn't receive products they ordered.

對話裡提到什麼問題？

(A) 他們的生產線正在生產瑕疵品。
(B) 他們的品管經理想要辭職。
(C) 他們有個客戶要去另一家工廠購買。
(D) 一位客戶說他們沒有收到訂購的產品。

---

39. How will the problem influence the company?

(A) They won't be able to mass-produce products again.
(B) They will make less profit.
(C) Their logistics department will lose money.
(D) They will lose customers in Spain.

這個問題會對公司產生什麼影響？

(A) 他們將無法再次大量生產產品。
(B) 他們的利潤會減少。
(C) 他們的物流部門會賠錢。
(D) 他們將流失西班牙的客戶。

---

40. What products were sent last month?

(A) Some radiators
(B) 40 motors
(C) 50 air conditioners
(D) 20 car fans

上個月發送了什麼產品？

(A) 一些散熱器
(B) 40 台馬達
(C) 50 台冷氣機
(D) 20 個車用風扇

單字

file 提出（投訴）；提起（訴訟）　　batch 一批　　radiator 散熱器
faulty 有瑕疵的　　refund 退費　　upgrade 升級
promptly 迅速地；立刻　　deal with 處理（dealt 為 deal 的過去式、過去分詞）
logistics 物流

TEST 02
PART 3

Questions 41 through 43 refer to the following conversation.

M: I visited the dentist yesterday, and they found two cavities. I had been suffering from slight tooth decay for the last two months. The nurses advised me to floss more often and to start brushing 3 times a day.

W: My father got periodontal disease when he was 45. It causes swelling and bleeding of the gums, which means the person's mouth has been infected with bacteria. Eventually, if your teeth become loose, they will have to be extracted.

M: How did your eye surgery go last week?

W: It went smoothly. I entered the operating theater at 4 p.m. and came out about 90 minutes later. My eyes are still recovering. The problem was, I woke up feeling a bit nauseous, so I had to take some medicine to feel better.

41-43 題參考以下對話。

男：我昨天去看了牙醫，他們發現了兩個蛀洞。過去兩個月我一直患有輕微的蛀牙。護士建議我要更常使用牙線，並開始每天刷牙 3 次。

女：我父親在 45 歲時得了牙周病。它導致牙齦腫脹和出血，這意味著人的口腔已經感染了細菌。最後，如果你的牙齒鬆動，就必須拔除它們。

男：上週你的眼科手術進行得如何？

女：很順利。我下午 4 點進入手術室，大約 90 分鐘後出來。我的眼睛還在復元中。問題是，我醒來時感覺有點噁心，所以我不得不服用一些藥物讓自己覺得好一點。

---

41. What are the speakers mainly discussing?

(A) Ways to exercise effectively
(B) What to do after an operation
(C) The best dentist to visit
(D) Dental health and eye surgery

說話的人主要討論什麼？

(A) 有效的運動方法
(B) 手術後該做什麼
(C) 最值得看的牙醫
(D) 牙齒保健和眼睛手術

---

42. What problem did the woman say her father had?

(A) He sprained his ankle.
(B) He felt nauseous.
(C) He suffered from periodontal disease.
(D) Ten of his teeth fell out.

女子說她父親有什麼問題？

(A) 他扭傷了腳踝。
(B) 他感到噁心。
(C) 他患有牙周病。
(D) 他的牙齒掉了 10 顆。

---

43. Where did the woman go last week?

(A) To an operating room
(B) To the gym
(C) To a rehabilitation center
(D) To her company's headquarters

女子上週去哪裡？

(A) 去手術室
(B) 去健身房
(C) 去復健中心
(D) 去她公司的總部

單字

cavity 洞；蛀牙的洞	suffer from 患…病；受…折磨	tooth decay 蛀牙
floss 用牙線清理牙齒	periodontal disease 牙周病	swell 腫脹
gum 牙齦	infect 感染	bacteria 細菌
extract 拔出；取出	surgery 手術	nauseous 噁心，想吐
sprain 扭傷	ankle 腳踝	rehabilitation 復健

Questions 44 through 46 refer to the following conversation.

W: Hello, I'm Helen Ryder. My company, Nova International, dispatched 30 batches of semiconductors to your store two weeks ago. Have you received them yet?

M: Sorry, we haven't. When were they due to arrive here?

W: I was told you would receive them in less than 12 days. But I assume that something happened during delivery.

M: Ok. I sure hope I can get my order as soon as possible. This is urgent.

W: I'm terribly sorry for the delay. When I find out what's wrong, I'll find a way to compensate for the money you spent on shipping the goods. I'll call you back in 15 minutes.

(Sound of phone ringing)

W: I just got in touch with the logistics company. They said that the plane with the freight you ordered left France three days late due to some serious technical difficulties that they had with their aircraft. They promise you'll receive the goods in 2 days' time.

44-46 題參考以下對話。

女：你好，我是海倫・萊德。兩週前，我的公司 Nova International 發了 30 批半導體產品到你們店裡。你收到了嗎？

男：對不起，我們沒收到。它們該在什麼時候送達這裡？

女：我被告知你會在 12 天內收到它們。我覺得應該是運送時出了狀況。

男：好的。我當然希望能盡快收到我訂的東西。那是急件。

女：對於延誤，我十二萬分抱歉。我弄清楚後，會想辦法來補償你們在運送貨物時所花的錢。我會在 15 分鐘後給你回電話。

（電話鈴響）

女：我剛剛與物流公司聯絡，他們說，由於他們的飛機發生嚴重的技術問題，載運你的訂貨的飛機晚了三天才飛離法國。他們承諾你會在兩天後收到貨品。

---

44. Why didn't the man receive the goods he ordered?

(A) **The airplane carrying his goods departed too late.**
(B) He didn't pay the shipping fees.
(C) The freight plane had an accident.
(D) The woman forgot to dispatch the goods.

為什麼男子沒有收到他訂的貨物？

(A) 運載貨物的飛機太晚出發。
(B) 他沒有支付運費。
(C) 貨機發生事故。
(D) 女子忘了發貨。

---

45. Who did the woman contact?

(A) A law firm
(B) An advertising company
(C) **A logistics company**
(D) A technology repair shop

女子聯絡過誰？

(A) 律師事務所
(B) 廣告公司
(C) 物流公司
(D) 科技設備維修店

---

46. When will the man receive his order of semiconductors?

(A) In 3 days' time
(B) In one week's time
(C) **2 days later**
(D) Tomorrow

男子何時會收到他的半導體訂貨？

(A) 3 天後
(B) 一週後
(C) 2 天後
(D) 明天

單字
dispatch 發送；派遣　　semiconductor 半導體　　urgent 緊急的
compensate 補償　　freight 貨物；貨運

TEST 02 PART 3

Questions 47 through 49 refer to the following conversation.

M: Now that we have tested our prototype 4-wheel drive jeep, we need to start preparing our press release. Does the CEO have a launch date in mind?

W1: I was told he hopes it can be in January 2020. Who will be responsible for writing it up?

W2: I will do that. I'll make sure it is concise and appealing to readers so that we can grab the public's attention.

M: In this aspect, it's vital that you make our press release as provocative as possible so that it stands out from the similar ones. Be sure to find an eye-opening aspect to our release, and strongly emphasize our main points.

W2: Also, we should consider sending other materials with our release. Since we are in contact with a news reporter already, we need to send him a short cover letter to remind him what we discussed before and stimulate his interest in our product launch.

47-49 題參考以下對話。

男： 現在我們已經測試了我們的原型4輪驅動吉普車，我們需要開始準備我們的新聞稿。執行長心中有想好哪天發行嗎？

女1： 他說希望可以在2020年1月。誰負責寫新聞稿呢？

女2： 我負責寫。我會確保它簡潔又具吸引力，這樣才能引起大眾的注意。

男： 在這方面，我們的新聞稿盡可能具有啟發性是很重要的，這樣它才能從同類新聞中脫穎而出。一定要找到令人大開眼界的觀點，並有力地強調我們的重點。

女2： 我們還應考慮在發佈時加上其他資料。因為我們已經跟一位新聞記者聯絡了，要再給他一份簡短的說明函，提醒他我們之前討論過的事情，並激起他對我們產品上市的興趣。

---

47. What is the conversation about?

(A) **How to get ready for a press release**
(B) The best way to test their prototype
(C) The specifications of their product
(D) How they should handle the reporter's interview

對話在聊什麼？

(A) **如何為新聞稿做好準備**
(B) 測試原型的最佳方法
(C) 其產品的規格
(D) 他們應該如何處理記者的採訪

---

48. What will be sent to the news reporter?

(A) **Their press release and a cover letter**
(B) A staff member's resume
(C) An article about how the product was tested
(D) Specific details about how the product was manufactured

什麼會發給新聞記者？

(A) **他們的新聞稿和說明函**
(B) 工作人員的簡歷
(C) 關於產品如何測試的文章
(D) 關於產品如何製造的具體細節

---

49. What product is going to be launched?

(A) A new sports car
(B) A smartphone
(C) A truck
(D) **A four-wheel drive jeep**

要推出什麼產品？

(A) 新跑車
(B) 智慧型手機
(C) 卡車
(D) **四輪驅動吉普車**

| 單字 | concise 簡潔的；簡明扼要的
stand out from... 從…脫穎而出
cover letter 附函；說明函 | appealing 有吸引力的
press release 新聞稿 | provocative 引發思考的；啟發性的
eye-opening 令人大開眼界的 |

TEST 02
PART 3

Questions 50 through 52 refer to the following conversation.

W: Work has been so stressful recently, and it has been like that for the past year. I feel like I might be on the verge of a nervous breakdown.

M: If you work so hard that you end up collapsing, it isn't worth it. Why don't you find some ways to alleviate your stress? I once experienced the same problem as you and my doctor suggested that I work out at the gym and enjoy the sauna three times a week.

W: Ok. I'll try to adjust my lifestyle and get some rest. However, I feel dizzy if I do exercise that is too intense.

M: Well, just do some power walking or jogging. Lift some lightweight dumbbells.

50-52 題參考以下對話。

女：最近工作壓力很大，過去一年就是這樣。我覺得我可能正處於精神崩潰的邊緣。

男：如果你努力工作以至於最終崩潰，那就不值得了。你為什麼不找出一些緩解壓力的方法？我曾經歷過和你一樣的問題，我的醫生建議我在健身房訓練，每週洗三次三溫暖。

女：好的，我會嘗試調整自己的生活方式並休息一下。但是如果我做太激烈的運動，我會感到頭暈目眩。

男：嗯，只需做一些健走或慢跑。舉一些輕啞鈴。

---

50. What problem does the woman mention?

(A) She is under a lot of pressure at work.
(B) She has a cavity.
(C) She was diagnosed with cancer.
(D) She had a nervous breakdown.

女士提到了什麼問題？

(A) 她的工作壓力很大。
(B) 她有一顆蛀牙。
(C) 她被診斷出患有癌症。
(D) 她精神崩潰了。

---

51. How does the man suggest the woman solve the problem?

(A) Go on a holiday
(B) Brush your teeth more than once a day
(C) Visit a clinic
(D) Decrease the stress in her life

男士建議女士如何解決問題？

(A) 去度假
(B) 每天刷牙一次以上
(C) 去診所
(D) 減輕她生活中的壓力

---

52. What does the man say about exercise?

(A) Working out can reduce stress levels.
(B) He lifts weights 4 times a week.
(C) Doing intense exercise is harmful.
(D) Jogging makes one's heart stronger.

男士對運動表示什麼看法？

(A) 運動可以減輕壓力。
(B) 他每週舉重四次。
(C) 進行劇烈運動是有害的。
(D) 慢跑使一個人的心臟更強壯。

單字 alleviate 減輕；緩解　　on the verge of 接近於…；瀕於…　　nervous breakdown 精神崩潰
dizzy 頭暈目眩

Questions 53 through 55 refer to the following conversation.

M: It turns out that our hardcover book was the bestselling book of 2019 on the topic of business management. Macmillan just contacted us and told us that they have sold 120,000 books! Great work!

W: That couldn't be better. Each book was sold for US $13. That means together we can make US $124,800 from royalties. Now that we have finished this project, we can start our next book. There is a high demand for colorful children's books in Korea. I think we should commence that project as soon as possible.

M: Sure. Have you heard any news about the paperback book *The Rich Mentality* that I published four months ago?

W: The publishing company called last week and said they only sold 90,000 copies.

M: Ok. Well that's better than nothing.

53 至 55 題參考以下對話。

男：事實證明，我們的精裝書是 2019 年企業管理主題的暢銷書。麥克米倫公司剛聯絡我們，並告訴我們他們已售出 12 萬本書！做得好！

女：太棒了。每本書的售價為 13 美元，這意味著我們一共有 124,800 美元的版稅收入。現在我們已經完成了這個案子，我們可以開始下一本書。韓國對彩色兒童書籍的需求很大，我想我們應該盡快開始這個案子。

男：當然。你有聽到我四個月前發表的平裝書《致富心法》的消息嗎？

女：出版公司上週打電話說他們只賣了 9 萬本。

男：喔！那總比沒有好。

53. What was mentioned about the book that was published in 2019?

(A) It was written on logistics administration.
(B) The title of the book was *Stockholders*.
(C) Over 100,000 copies were sold.
(D) The price of one book is US $10.

關於 2019 年出版的這本書，他們提到了什麼？

(A) 它是寫物流管理的。
(B) 這本書的書名是《股東》。
(C) 銷售超過 10 萬本。
(D) 一本書的價格是 10 美元。

54. What is true about the next book they will write?

(A) It will be sold in Japan.
(B) It will be a colorful book about vintage cars.
(C) It will be a book for children.
(D) The title will be *Colors of the Rainbow*.

關於他們要寫的下一本書，何者為真？

(A) 它將在日本銷售。
(B) 這將是一本關於老爺車的彩色書籍。
(C) 這本書將是一本兒童書。
(D) 書名將是《彩虹的顏色》。

55. When was the book *The Rich Mentality* published?

(A) Last month
(B) In January
(C) In July
(D) Four months ago

《致富心法》這本書在什麼時候出版？

(A) 上個月
(B) 一月
(C) 七月
(D) 四個月前

單字	hardcover 精裝的；精裝書	royalty 版稅	commence 開始進行
	paperback 平裝	publish 出版；發表	

TEST 02 PART 3

Questions 56 through 58 refer to the following conversation.

M: My friends were involved in a serious accident. Their car collided with a BMW. Their car was a total write-off and they had to spend two days in hospital. They are still recovering from the after-effects of the accident. They are hoping to make an insurance claim.

W1: My vehicle also got damaged last week. It was hit by a tree that fell over in a storm. I am also planning to contact my insurance company.

W2: What insurance do you have?

W1: Collision insurance.

W2: Well, I doubt that you will get compensation money. This kind of insurance usually covers a collision with another vehicle or an object. Damage caused to your vehicle that is not related to driving, such as natural disasters or theft, aren't included.

56-58 題參考以下對話。

男： 我朋友捲入一場嚴重的事故。他們的汽車與一輛 BMW 相撞，他們的車完全報廢了，還在醫院住了兩天。他們還在事故後遺症的恢復期。他們希望可以申請保險理賠。

女1：上週我的車也受損了，它在暴風雨中被倒下的樹壓到了。我也打算聯絡我的保險公司。

女2：你保了什麼險？

女1：碰撞險。

女2：呃！我猜你申請不到理賠。這種保險通常理賠汽車相撞或撞到其他物體，與車輛駕駛無關的損害，例如自然災害或竊盜，是不包括在內的。

---

56. What was mentioned about the people who had an accident?

(A) They hit a tree.
(B) Their car was fixable after the accident.
(C) They haven't fully recovered.
(D) They paid around about $34,000 for their car.

關於發生事故的人，對話裡提到什麼？

(A) 他們撞到了一棵樹。
(B) 事故發生後，他們的車可以修復。
(C) 他們還沒完全康復。
(D) 他們的車買價大約 34,000 美元。

---

57. What happened to the woman's car?

(A) It was damaged by vandals.
(B) It got hit by a falling tree.
(C) It was destroyed in an earthquake.
(D) It was hit by a truck.

女子的車怎麼了？

(A) 被破壞者破壞了。
(B) 它被倒下的樹擊中了。
(C) 它在地震時遭毀壞。
(D) 被卡車撞到。

---

58. Why won't the woman be compensated for her car's damage?

(A) Her car was stolen.
(B) She hasn't paid her premium for the past two months.
(C) She didn't buy insurance.
(D) The damages were a result of a natural disaster.

為什麼女子的車不會得到理賠？

(A) 她的車被偷了。
(B) 她上兩個月的保險費還沒有付清。
(C) 她沒有買保險。
(D) 車子損壞是因為自然災害。

單字
collide 相撞，碰撞　　write-off 報廢的車輛　　after-effects 後遺症
insurance claim 保險理賠　　collision 相撞，碰撞　　premium 保險費

Questions 59 through 61 refer to the following conversation.

M: Check out this painting! I bought it at an auction in France last Saturday. It cost me $12,000.

W: Quite impressive. I also went to an auction last weekend. Hot rods and sports cars were being sold there. I made a bid for a Ford Model A, but didn't end up taking it home.

M: How much did the highest bidder pay for it?

W: Around $500,000. After attending this activity, I've learnt how I can strengthen my skills in this area. I have discovered that it's important to wait until the afternoon before I start bidding seriously. This is because most bidders usually spend all of their money and energy before the afternoon, I'll have less competition to win the bid.

M: It's also necessary to stay calm when you find the items you want to acquire. Don't let others know what you intend to buy, or they will compete to obtain the same item.

59-61 題參考以下對話。

男：看看這幅畫！我上週六在法國的一場拍賣會上買了它。它花了我 12,000 美元。

女：有看頭。我上週末也去了一場拍賣會，改裝車和跑車正在那裡銷售。我下標一輛福特 A 型車，但最終沒能把車帶回家。

男：最高出價者支付多少錢？

女：大約 500,000 美元。參加這項活動後，我學會了如何加強在這方面的技巧。我發現在我開始認真投標之前要等到下午是非常重要的。這是因為大多數競標者通常會在下午之前花掉他們所有的錢和精力，這樣我的競爭者會較少。

男：當你找到想要獲得的物品時，也必須保持冷靜。不要讓別人知道你打算購買什麼，否則他們將競爭獲取相同的物品。

---

59. How much was the Ford Model A bought for?

(A) About $555,000
(B) Around $600,000
(C) Roughly half a million dollars
(D) Under $400,000

福特 A 型車的購買車價是多少？

(A) 大約 555,000 美元
(B) 大約 600,000 美元
(C) 大約五十萬美元
(D) 低於 400,000 美元

---

60. Where did the man purchase the painting?

(A) At an art store in Paris
(B) At an auction in France
(C) At a shop in Germany
(D) At a sale in Vienna

該男子在哪裡買到這幅畫？

(A) 在巴黎的一家美術用品店
(B) 在法國的一場拍賣會
(C) 在德國的一家商店
(D) 在維也納的特賣會

---

61. According to the man, what should bidders NOT do?

(A) Start serious bidding in the morning
(B) Tell others the exact items you plan to buy
(C) Spend all of your energy before noon
(D) Spend most of your money after lunchtime

據男子說，投標人不應做什麼？

(A) 早上開始認真投標
(B) 告訴其他人打算購買的確切商品
(C) 中午之前消耗所有精力
(D) 午餐後花完大部分錢

單字

auction 拍賣；拍賣會　　　bid 出價；投標　　　acquire 取得；獲得；購得

TEST 02 PART 3

Questions 62 through 64 refer to the following conversation and movie showtimes.

W: Would you like to go and catch that movie during the night show tomorrow night? I read some reviews on the movie and found out that the film is based on the novel that was written six years ago.

M: I don't know if I really like thrillers. Plus, judging from the coming attraction that was played last week, it seems like a violent movie with a lot of crime.

W: OK, how about watching the 7:15 movie?

M: Seems to be OK. I'm curious about the main character who I heard is a retired intelligence agent. I want to know more about his rather mysterious past and how he exacts justice for innocent people in dangerous circumstances.

W: Great. I'll book two tickets for us online.

M: Hmm. See you tomorrow around 7:00.

| Beastland Cinema ||||
| Weekly Showtimes: Sunday, July 21st to Saturday, July 27th ||||
Title	Genre	Evening Show	Night Show
The Calling	Crime/ Thriller	7:00	9:40
Interstellar	Adventure	7:10	9:15
Edge of Tomorrow	Action	7:20	9:25
The Equalizer	Action	7:15	9:30

62. Why doesn't the man want to watch the thriller movie?

(A) Its movie trailer seems boring.
(B) It has too much violence.
(C) He just wants to read the novel.
(D) He only is interested in comedy movies.

63. Look at the graphic. What is the name of the movie that the man wants to watch?

(A) *The Calling*
(B) *Interstellar*
(C) *Edge of Tomorrow*
(D) *The Equalizer*

64. What is the 7:15 movie about?

(A) **A man who stands up for innocent people**
(B) A movie about crime
(C) A dramatic movie that was based on a novel
(D) A crime movie with lots of killing

七點十五分的電影,內容是關於什麼?

(A) **一個捍衛無辜人民的男子**
(B) 一部關於犯罪的電影
(C) 一部根據小說的精采電影
(D) 一部有很多殺戮的犯罪電影

單字
review 評論
intelligence agent 情報人員
circumstance 情況;環境
thriller 驚悚片
mysterious 神秘的
trailer 預告片
coming attraction(電影)預告片
exact justice for 為(某人)伸張正義

TEST 02
PART 3

Questions 65 through 67 refer to the following conversation and price list.

M: Maxine, have you found time to ask the Wordpress Inc. when our company's new website will finish construction?

W: Yes, I brought this up in a meeting we had two days ago. They are still in the process of testing the site now. The manager promised that it will go live in exactly one week from now. They also sent me a price list and mentioned that they will only charge us for creating the actual website content because we are their most loyal customers.

M: Great news! Did you get a chance to see if you are satisfied with the results?

W: Yes, I had a peek. Overall, they did a fine job on the overall design, and made it super user-friendly. However, there are still a few problems they need to work on before it is finished.

65-67 題參考以下對話和價格表。

男：瑪克莘，你有找時間向 Wordpress 公司詢問我們公司的新網站何時完工嗎？

女：是的，我在兩天前的一次會議上提出了這個問題。他們現在還在測試網站。經理承諾，它從現在起一週後上線。他們還發了一張價格表給我，並提到他們只會向我們收取創建實際網站內容的費用，因為我們是他們最忠實的客戶。

男：好消息！你有趁機看看結果令你滿意嗎？

女：是的，我看了一眼。總體而言，他們在整體設計方面做得很好，並且對使用者來說非常容易使用。但是，在完成之前還有一些問題需要解決。

Market Australia Website, Wordpress Inc.	
Website construction fees	
1. Design & Building	$200
2. Content Creation	$280
3. Training	$20
4. Future Maintenance	$50

Market Australia 網站 Wordpress 公司	
網站建構費	
1. 設計和建構	200 美元
2. 內容創建	280 美元
3. 訓練如何使用	20 美元
4. 未來維護	50 美元

65. What is said about the Wordpress Inc.?

(A) They are getting behind on their work.
(B) They have just completed a website.
(C) They provide customers with user friendly platforms.
(D) They don't know how to fix their company's computers.

關於 Wordpress Inc. 這間公司，下述何者正確？

(A) 他們的工作進度落後。
(B) 他們剛剛完成了一個網站。
(C) 他們為客戶提供用戶容易使用的平台。
(D) 他們不知道如何修理公司的電腦。

66. What is being tested now?

(A) The company's website
(B) The company's laptops
(C) The iPads used by the company staff
(D) The company's telephone system

現在正在測試什麼？

(A) 該公司的網站
(B) 該公司的筆記型電腦
(C) 該公司員工使用的 iPad
(D) 該公司的電話系統

67. Look at the graphic. How much does the company have to pay Wordpress Inc. for their services?

(A) $280
(B) $200
(C) $50
(D) $20

請看收據。該公司需要向 Wordpress 公司支付多少費用？

(A) 280 美元
(B) 200 美元
(C) 50 美元
(D) 20 美元

單字

loyal 忠誠的；忠實的   user-friendly 容易使用的

TEST 02
PART 3

Questions 68 through 70 refer to the following conversation and list.

M: My boss just informed me that some of our customers called in and filed a complaint against us recently.

W: Yes, it's a pity. Actually, I just got off the phone with one of them.

M: What exactly did she complain about?

W: She was frustrated with our service. Our driver picked her up right on time, but unfortunately got caught in heavy traffic when they were driving to the airport. She was minutes away from missing her flight overseas.

M: Oh, we should closely examine the roadwork where they ran into the traffic jam. Maybe that slowed down their drive that day.

W: I agree. We have loads of more issues to deal with. Take a look at this list of comments. We'll have to deal with them later on.

68-70 題參考以下對話與清單。

男：我的老闆剛剛通知我，我們的一些客戶最近打電話對我們提出投訴。

女：是啊，很遺憾。其實我剛講完一通投訴電話。

男：她究竟抱怨什麼？

女：她對我們的服務感到失望。我們的司機準時去接她，但不幸的是，在開車去機場的途中遇到塞車。她差點沒搭上國外航班。

男：哦，我們應該仔細確認他們遇到交通堵塞的路段的道路施工，也許施工阻礙了他們的速度。

女：我同意。我們還有很多問題要處理。看看這張意見清單。我們等一下就必須處理它們。

Name	Problem mentioned
Rita Williams	Dirty floor
Britney Spears	The company app isn't working
Carol Duncan	Didn't arrive at destination on time
Vanessa Aiko	Didn't receive a discount

名字	提出的問題
瑞塔・威廉斯	地板髒
布瑞妮・史比爾斯	公司的應用程式無效
卡蘿・鄧肯	未準時抵達目的地
凡妮莎・艾可	未獲得折扣

68. Where do the speakers most likely work?

(A) At a taxi company
(B) At a train station
(C) At a law firm
(D) At a trade company

說話的人最有可能在哪裡工作？

(A) 在計程車公司
(B) 在火車站
(C) 在律師事務所
(D) 在一家貿易公司

69. Look at the graphic. Which customer are the speakers talking about?

(A) Rita Williams
(B) Britney Spears
(C) Carol Duncan
(D) Vanessa Aiko

請看圖表。說話的人在談論哪個客戶？

(A) 瑞塔・威廉斯
(B) 布瑞妮・史比爾
(C) 卡蘿・鄧肯
(D) 凡妮莎・艾可

70. What will the speakers do next?

    (A) Review their list of customer complaints
    (B) Fill up on petrol
    (C) Rearrange their staff schedules
    (D) Organize a program to train drivers

說話的人接下來會做什麼？

(A) 檢視他們的客訴清單
(B) 加滿汽油
(C) 重新安排他們的員工時間表
(D) 安排一個訓練司機的計劃

單字　file a complaint 提出投訴　　minutes away from 差一點　　roadwork 道路施工

TEST 02
PART 4

Questions 71 through 73 refer to the following telephone message.

Hi Joy, this is Rudy. Firstly, I tried getting a hold of Alex, but I discovered that his number was disconnected. Maybe I wrote down the wrong number. When you have time, please check if this number is correct: 0979-066-022. Then please call and leave a message for him saying I can't come to the conference. Thanks. Also, I reached Mr. Vaughn, and he said he'll order five boxes of our new auto parts. You can charge them to the company. Lastly, we'll need to meet early next week to talk about the Gerber project. This morning I'll be out of the office, but I'll be in my office from 2 p.m. to 5:30 p.m. If you need to get in touch, call my cell: 0970-424-568. Please tell me, which days are best to meet up? And I'd appreciate it if you could get me Alex's number. Thanks Joy. Talk soon.

71-73 題參考以下電話留言。

嗨嬌伊，我是魯迪。首先，我試著聯絡亞歷克斯，但我發現他的電話不通。也許是我寫錯了號碼。如果你有時間，請檢查這個號碼是否正確：0979-066-022，然後請打電話給他，留言說我不能參加會議。謝謝。此外，我聯絡到沃恩先生，他說他將訂購五箱我們的新汽車零件。你可以記在公司的帳上。最後，我們需要在下週初會面討論葛伯的案子。今天早上我不在辦公室，但我下午 2 點到 5 點 30 分會在辦公室。如果妳需要聯繫，請打手機給我：0970-424-568。請告訴我，哪幾天會面最好？如果妳能給我亞歷克斯的電話號碼，我會很感激的。謝謝，嬌伊。一會兒再聊。

71. What problem did Rudy mention?
    - (A) He can't contact Alex.
    - (B) Alex ordered the wrong amount of auto parts.
    - (C) He will be late for the conference.
    - (D) The deal with Gerber fell through.

魯迪提到了什麼問題？
- (A) 他無法聯絡到亞歷克斯。
- (B) 亞歷克斯訂錯汽車零件的數量了。
- (C) 他出席會議將遲到。
- (D) 與葛伯的交易失敗了。

72. What is Joy most likely to do next?
    - (A) Check if Alex's number is correct
    - (B) Meet with Rudy to discuss the Gerber project
    - (C) Visit Rudy's office
    - (D) Go to the conference

嬌伊下一步最可能做什麼？
- (A) 檢查亞歷克斯的電話號碼是否正確
- (B) 與魯迪會面討論葛伯的案子
- (C) 造訪魯迪的辦公室
- (D) 去參加會議

73. What did the speaker mention about Mr. Vaughn?
    - (A) He'll be ordering some auto parts.
    - (B) He is charging Rudy's company with plagiarism.
    - (C) He's too busy to attend the annual conference.
    - (D) He is the manager of a subsidiary company.

說話的人提到了沃恩先生的什麼事？
- (A) 他將訂購一些汽車零件。
- (B) 他在告魯迪的公司剽竊。
- (C) 他太忙了，無法參加年會。
- (D) 他是一家子公司的經理。

單字 get (a) hold of ... 跟某人聯絡　　disconnected（電話）打不通　　auto part 汽車零件

Questions 74 through 76 refer to the following book review.

Are you struggling to get your unruly child under control? Do you often lose your temper when your rowdy teenager talks back and misbehaves? You may have questioned whether you should resort to harshly punishing your children or be more lenient on them. You may be at a loss as to how to handle this situation, and have desperately asked a friend for advice. Berry Gale offers a straightforward guide for parents with children that drive them crazy. It is a book that psychologists and many parents have proven to be effective. *Save Me from My Teenager's Grasp!* is a popular step-by-step guide to family education that you have been looking for.

74-76 題參考以下書評。

你是否正在努力讓你不規矩的孩子得到控制？當粗魯的少年孩子回嘴和行為失序時，你經常發脾氣嗎？你可能質疑過，你是否應該對孩子採取嚴厲的懲罰或對他們更加寬容。你可能會對如何處理這種情況感到茫然，並拼命地向朋友徵求意見。貝芮・蓋爾為被孩子激怒的父母提供了一個簡單的指南——一本心理學家和許多父母親證明有效的書。《讓我遠離青少年的掌控！》是你一直在尋找的獲得大眾認可的家庭教育逐步指南。

74. What kind of parents would be eager to buy this book?

   (A) Parents with disobedient children and teenagers
   (B) Parents with newborn babies
   (C) Parents with children who perform poorly on tests
   (D) Elderly parents

什麼樣的父母會渴望購買這本書？

   (A) 有不聽話的孩子和青少年的父母
   (B) 有新生嬰兒的父母
   (C) 在考試中表現不佳的孩子的父母
   (D) 年邁的父母

75. What have other people mentioned about this book?

   (A) It is helpful for understanding how to reward children.
   (B) They wish they had bought it before they had children.
   (C) It offers effective advice.
   (D) It was relatively easy to understand.

其他人提及這本書的什麼？

   (A) 了解如何獎勵孩子是有幫助的。
   (B) 他們希望在生孩子之前就買了它。
   (C) 它提供有效的建議。
   (D) 它相當容易理解。

76. What kind of book is being advertised?

   (A) A history book
   (B) A fitness book
   (C) A biography
   (D) A parenting guide

這篇評論在宣傳什麼樣的書？

   (A) 歷史書
   (B) 健身書
   (C) 傳記
   (D) 教養指南

單字

unruly 不守規矩的；難管教的
misbehave 行為不端
lenient 寬容的，寬大的，從輕的
psychologist 心理學家
rowdy 粗魯的；吵鬧的
resort to (sth) 訴諸；採取
straightforward 簡單的；易懂的
talk back 回嘴，頂嘴
harshly 嚴厲地
guide 指南；手冊

TEST 02
PART 4

Questions 77 through 79 refer to the following broadcast.

Donald Trump, highly experienced real estate investor and expert, has recently stated on a live interview on TV that "there will be an upswing in India's real estate market. India's incumbent president, Ram Nath Kovind, has done a fine job of uniting the country and leading it towards prosperity." Trump plans to make investments in the countries luxury developments and infrastructure because he has predicted that India's market is going to thrive. During the last six months, he has been planning to buy apartments and a tower in Delhi. Thanks to President Kovind's contributions to the nation, "the price of property per square meter in comparison with other cities is relatively low."

77. What is the broadcast about?

   (A) Donald Trump signing a deal with India
   (B) American entrepreneurs investing in Indian restaurants
   (C) How India has become so prosperous
   (D) Why Donald Trump plans to buy Indian property

78. What is suggested about India's economic situation?

   (A) The current president is helping India to flourish.
   (B) India's stock market is getting stronger.
   (C) Growing real estate prices are not appealing to investors.
   (D) India is thriving mainly because of American investment.

79. According to the broadcast, why is investment in Delhi attractive to Donald Trump?

   (A) The price of property is lower compared to America.
   (B) Investment in the city's apartments is quite cheap.
   (C) He wants to buy a tower in Mumbai.
   (D) The president promised to give him a discount on Delhi property.

單字

real estate 不動產，房地產
incumbent 現任的
thrive 興旺，繁榮

investor 投資者
prosperity 繁榮
in comparison with 與⋯相比

upswing 上揚；好轉
infrastructure 基礎建設

TEST 02 PART 4

Questions 80 through 82 refer to the following news report.

Good evening, welcome to our 6 p.m. NBS international news. My name is Dyllan Velvet. First up today, a correspondent that works at CBN News is suing liberal media figures for defamation. Aaron Philidor, the stepbrother of a Democratic National Committee staffer, Seth Dickson, who was killed in 2015, is pressing charges against liberal media figures and the *Toronto Times* for publishing theories about how Seth died. In a lawsuit filed Monday, Aaron attempted to prove that both Mr. Ray Butowsky, an influential financial advisor who was invited to speak on Fox Commercial Network, and Michael Couch, a liberal online critic, dishonestly and repeatedly made public statements about Aaron Philidor being a criminal. The lawsuit declared that the *Toronto Times,* a liberal newspaper, offered Mr. Couch and Mr. Butowsky a platform to publish groundless statements.

80. What is this news report about?

(A) Mr. Philidor being charged for defaming an online critic.
(B) Aaron Philidor filing a lawsuit against people for slandering his stepbrother.
(C) The story of a financial advisor winning a lawsuit.
(D) How to avoid getting into trouble with the law.

81. What is suggested about Ray Butowsky's conduct?

(A) His business practices are unethical.
(B) He is a man of great integrity.
(C) He said things to ruin a journalist's reputation.
(D) The comments he makes on live TV are too objective.

82. What charges were made against the *Toronto Times*?

(A) They spread theories on the media about nature of Seth Dickson's death.
(B) They offered Aaron Philidor a platform to lie about others.
(C) They called Dyllan Velvet a criminal.
(D) They made a dishonest deal with NBS News.

| 單字 | correspondent 通訊員，記者
staffer 職員，員工
theory 理論；推測，猜測
advisor 顧問
slander 詆毀；誹謗 | sue 控告；對…提起訴訟
press charges against (someone) 對（某人）提起訴訟
lawsuit 訴訟
critic 評論家
statement 聲明，言論 | defamation 誹謗
influential 有影響力的
groundless 沒有根據的 |

TEST 02 PART 4

Questions 83 through 85 refer to the following advertisement.

Loupe-Chaufourier, Inc. is one of the finest European art dealers in Austria. Located at 74 Rosenstrasse, Wolfsohl. Loupe-Chaufourier specializes in collecting and displaying a spectacular array of historical European paintings and antiques, chiefly from France and Germany. We open our gallery to the public from Monday to Friday, though it is advised that you make an appointment in advance due to our erratic business schedule.

Loupe-Chaufourier, Inc. was established in 1988 by two French ardent artists, Denis Loupe and Claude Chaufourier who passionately endeavored to collect all forms of European artwork. Now, these two men have been recorded in European art history as the most successful names in the field of art preservation.

83-85 題參考以下廣告。

魯普－喬福瑞耶公司是奧地利最優異的歐洲藝術品經銷商之一。位於佛爾福梭的玫瑰街 74 號，魯普－喬福瑞耶公司專門收集和展示一系列壯觀的、歷史悠久的歐洲畫作和古董，主要來自法國和德國。我們從週一到週五向公眾開放我們的畫廊，但建議您提前預約，因為我們的商務行程變化太大。

魯普－喬福瑞耶公司成立於 1988 年，由兩位熱情的法國藝術家丹尼・魯普和克勞德・喬福瑞耶創立，他們熱情地致力於收集所有形式的歐洲藝術品。現在，這兩個人已經留名於歐洲藝術史，成為藝術品保存領域最成功的名字。

83. What kind of work does Loupe-Chaufourier specialize in?

(A) Art collection and preservation
(B) Leading art enthusiasts through art museums
(C) International business
(D) Tours of Austria

魯普－喬福瑞耶公司專精於什麼樣的工作？

(A) 藝術品收藏和保存
(B) 透過藝術博物館引導藝術愛好者
(C) 國際商務
(D) 奧地利之旅

84. Why does the ad suggest customers make appointments in advance?

(A) Denis Loupe and Claude Chaufourier's business schedule is hard to predict.
(B) Denis Loupe and Claude Chaufourier are usually out of Austria.
(C) They are often called away on business trips to France.
(D) It is difficult to make an appointment with them for the weekends.

為什麼這則廣告建議客戶提前預約？

(A) 丹尼・魯普和克勞德・喬福瑞耶的商務行程很難預測。
(B) 丹尼・魯普和克勞德・喬福瑞耶通常不在奧地利。
(C) 他們經常出差到法國。
(D) 週末的大部分時間都很難與他們預約。

85. What kind of items are mostly likely displayed in Denis Loupe and Claude Chaufourier's business?

(A) Books that describe the history of France.
(B) Maps of Germany
(C) A wide variety of art from many parts of Europe
(D) Antiques from South America

丹尼・魯普和克勞德・喬福瑞耶的業務中最常展示哪些項目？

(A) 描述法國歷史的書籍
(B) 德國地圖
(C) 來自歐洲許多地方的各種藝術品
(D) 來自南美洲的古物

| 單字 | dealer 經銷商
array 一系列；一大批
erratic 難以預測的；多變的
preservation 保護，維護；保存 | specialize in 專攻；專門從事
antique 古物；古董
ardent 熱情的；熱心的 | spectacular 壯觀的；令人驚歎的
chiefly 主要
endeavor to 致力於；努力 |

TEST 02
PART 4

Questions 86 through 88 refer to the following telephone message.

Hi Ryan, it's Candice Sterling. I just received your voice message. So, are you bound for San Francisco? It's a pity you forgot those documents; I'll look for them around the office and drop them by your house before 10 p.m. tonight. You also mentioned that your car is being repaired and no one will be available to give you a lift to the airport. You always insist on leaving for the airport three hours prior to take off, but I think it is advisable if you leave five hours earlier, in case you encounter an unforeseen problem before you check in at the airport. How about I pick you up at 6 a.m. tomorrow? In any case, return my call so we can decide on a suitable departure time.

86-88 題參考以下電話留言。

嗨萊恩，我是坎蒂絲・史特林。我剛收到你的語音留言。所以你要去舊金山？很遺憾你忘記了這些文件，我會在辦公室找到它們，然後在今晚 10 點之前順便把它們送到你家。你還提到你的汽車正在維修，而且沒有人可以載你到機場。你總是堅持在起飛前三個小時出發去機場，但我建議你提前五個小時出發，以免你在機場辦理登機手續之前遇到意料之外的問題，這是明智的。我明天早上 6 點去接你如何？不管怎樣，請回我的電話，以便我們決定合適的出發時間。

86. Why will the speaker visit Ryan at 10 p.m.?

    (A) To give her documents she forgot to bring
    (B) They have to discuss an important project
    (C) They need to pack their luggage into the car
    (D) To show her a business proposal

為什麼說話的人將在晚上 10 點拜訪萊恩？

(A) 拿給他忘記帶的文件
(B) 他們必須討論一個重要的專案
(C) 他們需要在車裡把行李打包
(D) 向她出示商業計劃書

87. Why does the speaker want Ryan to leave at an earlier time?

    (A) She has to attend a conference meeting at 8 a.m.
    (B) She has to collect her motorbike from the mechanic shop.
    (C) She was informed that the airport changed the departure time.
    (D) She hopes that Ryan doesn't arrive at the airport too late.

為什麼說話的人要萊恩提前出發？

(A) 她必須在上午 8 點參加會議。
(B) 她必須去修理廠取她的摩托車。
(C) 她獲通知機場改變了出發時間。
(D) 她希望萊恩不會太晚到達機場。

88. Where most likely will the speaker take Ryan?

    (A) To a repair shop
    (B) To a cafeteria
    (C) To an airport
    (D) To a bus stop

說話的人最有可能帶萊恩去哪裡？

(A) 去修車廠
(B) 去自助餐廳
(C) 去機場
(D) 去公車站

單字　adviseable 明智的　　unforeseen 意料之外的　　departure 出發

Questions 89 through 91 refer to the following voice mail.

Thank you for calling Harriston Law Firm. We are closed today because we are relocating to the fifth floor of the commercial building on 592 Lodgeville Road, Minneapolis. We will be reopening our business in three days' time at our new location, and our new business hours will be 9 a.m. to 6 p.m. However, if you need to consult our tax attorney, he will be on the fourth floor of the same building starting tomorrow. Our legal team that specializes in civil law will be on the fifth floor. Please note that we will station a receptionist on both the fourth and fifth floor as of next Wednesday morning. So if you happen to have made an appointment with one of our tax attorneys, please remember to take an elevator to the fourth floor. Please press the pound key to leave a message for us. Thank you.

89-91 題參考以下語音留言。

感謝您致電哈瑞斯頓律師事務所。我們今天休息，因為我們即將搬到明尼阿波利斯市洛奇維爾路 592 號商業大樓的五樓。我們將在三天後在新地點重新開張，我們的新營業時間是上午 9 點到下午 6 點。但是，如果您需要諮詢我們的稅務律師，他從明天開始就會在同一棟樓的四樓。我們專門從事民法的法律團隊將在五樓工作。請注意，我們將在下週三上午在四樓和五樓安排接待員。因此，如果您碰巧與我們的一位稅務律師預約，請記得乘電梯到四樓。請按 # 字鍵給我們留言。謝謝。

---

89. Why isn't the Harriston Law Firm open today?

(A) Its office is being refurbished.
(B) It is relocating to another building.
(C) The business went bankrupt.
(D) It is vacation time.

為什麼哈瑞斯頓律師事務所今天沒開？

(A) 它的辦公室正在翻修。
(B) 它正搬遷到另一棟樓。
(C) 公司破產了。
(D) 這是休假時間。

---

90. What does the speaker mention will happen tomorrow?

(A) They will take on a new receptionist.
(B) They will offer some legal services on different floors.
(C) The organization will shorten its business hours.
(D) All attorneys will help with moving.

說話的人提到明天會發生什麼？

(A) 他們將雇用一位新的接待員。
(B) 他們將在不同樓層提供一些法律服務。
(C) 該機構將縮短其營業時間。
(D) 所有律師都會幫忙搬家。

---

91. According to the speaker, how long do clients have to wait before the business starts operating again?

(A) 2 days
(B) 1 day
(C) 1 week
(D) 3 days

根據說話者的說法，客戶需要等多久該事務所才能開始營業？

(A) 2 天
(B) 1 天
(C) 1 週
(D) 3 天

單字

law firm 法律事務所	relocate 搬遷	commercial 商業的
attorney 律師	civil law 民法	receptionist 接待員
pound key # 字鍵	refurbish 翻修	

TEST 02
PART 4

Questions 92 through 94 refer to the following excerpt from a meeting.

Thank you for attending this month's meeting at such short notice. Let's go over our first item on the agenda, the upcoming 2019 Annual General Meeting. The CEO of Wickim Inc. has just confirmed that he will be sending most of our company's shareholders to attend this conference. It is vital that we send at least five of our board members to this event, so we can have the opportunity to gain valuable insights into our mother company's growth throughout the past fiscal year, and be able to participate in the election of new board members. Please take a close look at this chart. On the 3rd of December, we booked the tickets for one treasurer, one secretary, five executives, and twenty-five shareholders. However, something came up recently, and the secretary won't be able to make it. Mary, since you are in charge of ordering the tickets, could you please contact the ticket seller and cancel the ticket? Thank you.

92-94 題參考以下會議摘要。

謝謝你們參加臨時通知的本月會議。讓我們仔細看議程中的第一個項目──即將召開的 2019 年度大會。維京姆公司的執行長剛剛確認他將派出我們公司大部分的股東參加此次會議。至關重要的是，我們至少派出五名董事會成員參加此次活動，這樣我們就有機會獲得有關母公司上一會計年度成長的寶貴見解，並能夠參與選舉新董事。請仔細查看此圖表。我們在 12 月 3 日為一位財務主管、一位秘書、五位高階主管和二十五位股東預訂了票。然而，最近出現了一些問題，秘書將無法成行。瑪麗，既然妳負責訂票，可以聯繫售票員並取消票嗎？謝謝。

---

92. What is the purpose of the 2019 meeting?

(A) To learn more about their subsidiary's growth
(B) To gain insights into investment opportunities
(C) To broaden their knowledge of accounting
(D) To understand how much their mother company has grown

2019 年會議的目的是什麼？

(A) 了解有關其子公司成長的更多訊息
(B) 深入了解投資機會
(C) 拓展會計知識
(D) 了解他們母公司的成長程度

---

93. What was Mary asked to do?

(A) Order another ticket for a shareholder
(B) Cancel the secretary's ticket
(C) Write the meeting minutes
(D) Hold a meeting with the treasurer

瑪麗被要求做什麼？

(A) 為股東訂購另一張票
(B) 取消秘書的票
(C) 寫會議記錄
(D) 與財務主管召開會議

---

94. What is TRUE about the upcoming conference?

(A) Many shareholders from the company will attend the event.
(B) Board members will be in charge of electing a new vice manager.
(C) The vice president of the company will not attend.
(D) The treasurer won't be able to come.

即將舉行的會議何者為真？

(A) 公司的許多股東將參加此次活動。
(B) 董事會成員將負責選舉新的副經理。
(C) 公司副總經理不會參加。
(D) 財務主管無法前來。

單字

shareholder 股東
fiscal year 會計年度
secretary 秘書
board member 董事
election 選舉
executive 高階主管
insight 洞察力；深刻見解
treasurer 財務主管

TEST 02 — PART 4

Questions 95 through 97 refer to the following excerpt from a meeting and agenda.

Ok, let's kick off the meeting. Please take a look at the meeting agenda I just placed in front of you. It's evident that I made some updates from the one I sent you two days ago. Yesterday morning, Sonic Electronix, which produces heaters and toasters, informed us that the shipment they originally planned to send today won't arrive until May 21. That will be our first item to cover. Jackie has agreed to go over how this delay will have a negative effect on our stores' sales, and we will look into the possibility of moving our winter heater sale to a later date. Please note that this discussion might occupy most of our meeting time. I really doubt we'll have the time to review the reopening of our office in Tainan. If we don't, that item will be included in next week's agenda. Ok—it's your turn, Jackie.

Meeting Agenda (updated on 1st of May)	
Presenter	**Topic**
Jackie Klein	Delay in delivery of products
Zhang Wu-Qin	Expansion of subsidiaries into China
Jessie Mollick	Printing of new brochure
Jimmy Stratham	New office location

95. Where most likely does the speaker work?

(A) At a thermal power plant
(B) At a department store
(C) At a trading company
(D) At an appliance retailer

96. What problem was mentioned?

(A) There was a delay in the delivery of some goods.
(B) Two dates on the schedule aren't correct.
(C) Expansion to China is not possible.
(D) They can't obtain a permit to do business overseas.

252

97. Look at the graphic. Which presenter might NOT have a chance to present during the meeting?

(A) Zhang Wu-Qin
(B) Jimmy Stratham
(C) Jackie Klein
(D) Jessie Mollick

請看圖表。哪位報告者可能沒有機會在該次會議期間提出報告？

(A) 張武欽
(B) 吉米・史特拉森
(C) 潔姬・克萊恩
(D) 潔西・莫里克

單字	update 新資訊；更新	heater 電暖器；暖氣機；暖爐	toaster 烤麵包機
	sale 特價活動	appliance 工具；（尤指）家用電器	

TEST 02
PART 4

Questions 98 through 100 refer to the following telephone message and product order form.

Hi, this is Johnathon Hilston. This message is for Andrew Parker. I apologise for missing your phone call. I was out of the office on business. I'm contacting you in regards to the five items I purchased there last Friday. When I made the order last week, I gave you the wrong address for my home. Please note that my correct home address is 24 Harrison Avenue, Coopers Plains, Brisbane. My family and I won't be at home on Tuesday the 12th. Could you have the sofa delivered to my house exactly one week later than the originally arranged date? As I haven't paid for the furniture yet, I'll remit the money for all products this afternoon before 5p.m. Please confirm that you have received my payment before you have the items delivered.

98-100 題參考以下電話留言及產品訂購表。

嗨，我是強納森・希爾斯頓。這是留給安德魯・派克的訊息。我很抱歉錯過了您的電話，那時我因忙於業務而不在辦公室。我聯絡您是因為我上週五在那裡購買了五件物品。很抱歉我上週訂購時給錯住家地址了，請留意我家的地址是哈瑞森大道 24 號，Coopers Plains，布里斯本。我和我的家人在 12 日星期二時不在家。您可否安排在原先日期晚一週時將沙發送到我家？由於我還沒有支付這些家具的費用，我會在今天下午 5 點之前匯入所有物品的費用。在運送物品之前，請確認您已收到我的付款。

Product order form Date: Friday, December 8		
Name of product	**Product price**	**Delivery Date**
Large royal sofa	$300	December 12
King-sized bed	$370	December 12
Queen-sized bed	$230	December 22
Pantry	$55	December 24
Stacking cabinet	$50	December 25

產品訂單表格 日期：12 月 8 日（五）		
品名	價格	運送日期
皇家大沙發	$300	12 月 12 日
特大號床	$370	12 月 12 日
大號床	$230	12 月 22 日
食品儲存櫃	$55	12 月 24 日
組合櫃	$50	12 月 25 日

98. What is the telephone message about?

 (A) Changing a delivery date
 (B) Adjusting the date of a convention
 (C) Why Mr. Parker should get a promotion
 (D) The arrangement of a staff recruitment program

電話留言在講什麼？

 (A) 改變交貨日期
 (B) 調整會議日期
 (C) 為什麼派克先生應該獲得升遷
 (D) 安排員工招聘方案

99. Look at the graphic. When will the mentioned items be delivered to Mr. Hilston's home?

 (A) December 12
 (B) December 22
 (C) December 19
 (D) December 14

請看圖表。提到的物品將在哪個日期運送給希爾斯頓先生？

 (A) 12 月 12 日
 (B) 12 月 22 日
 (C) 12 月 19 日
 (D) 12 月 14 日

100. What did Mr. Hilston say he will do today?　希爾斯頓先生說他今天會做什麼？
    (A) Pay the store a short visit
    (B) Call the furniture store back
    (C) **Transfer money to the furniture store's account**
    (D) Pick up the items he ordered

    (A) 到該店拜訪一下
    (B) 回電話給家具行
    (C) **轉帳到家具行的帳戶**
    (D) 拿他訂購的物品

單字　remit 匯（款）　　　deliver 運送；遞送

TEST 02
PART 5

101. The annual Conference on International Cooperation -------- next month.

(A) will hold
(B) are held
(C) is held
(D) will be held

國際合作年度會議將在下個月舉行。

(A) 將舉行（現在未來式）
(B) 被舉行（被動語態，動詞複數）
(C) 被舉行（被動語態，動詞單數）
(D) 將被舉行（未來式被動語態）

解析 本題考動詞時態和語態。後面出現 next month（下個月），因此該用未來式：will + V~；因主詞為 conference（會議），故用被動語態 will be held（將被舉行）。

單字 annual 每年的　　conference（大型）會議　　international 國際的
cooperation 合作

---

102. If you have any questions or concerns, please do not hesitate to -------- us at 380-9048 and ask for Jane Lee.

(A) touch
(B) debrief
(C) welcome
(D) contact

如果您有任何問題或疑慮，請隨時與我們聯絡，請撥 380-9048，並向 Jane Lee 詢問。

(A) 觸摸
(B) 聽取回報
(C) 歡迎
(D) 聯絡

解析 本題考單字用法。與人聯絡可以用 get in touch with = contact，故應該用 (D) contact。

單字 hesitate 有疑慮、猶豫　　debrief 聽取、匯報

---

103. Due to the recent floods, all public parks will be closed -------- further notice.

(A) until
(B) during
(C) before
(D) unless

由於近期發生水災，所有公園將關閉，直至另行通知。

(A) 直到
(B) 在…期間
(C) 在…之前
(D) 除非

解析 本題考介系詞文法。根據句子意義：「所有公園將關閉，直至另行通知」，因此用 (A) until（直到）。

單字 due to 由於　　recent 最近的　　flood 洪水
further 更進一步的　　notice 通知

104. Come and see our new apartment -------- from 2 to 5 bedrooms.

(A) ranged
(B) ranges
(C) range
(D) ranging

進來看看我們有二到五間臥室的新公寓。

(A) 範圍從…（過去式）
(B) 範圍從…（現在式第三人稱單數）
(C) 範圍從…（現在式）
(D) 範圍從…（現在分詞）

| 解析 | 本題考分詞用法。前面已有動詞 come and see（來看看），故後面動詞必須改為 ranging（範圍從…），現在分詞表主動，因 range 無被動用法。 |

| 單字 | apartment 公寓　　　　　range 在…範圍內　　　　　bedroom 臥室 |

---

105. All our flats have -------- carpeting, modern kitchen appliances, and spacious bedrooms.

(A) face-to-face
(B) room-to-room
(C) wall-to-wall
(D) door-to-door

我們所有的公寓都有鋪滿整個地板的地毯、現代廚房電器和寬敞的臥室。

(A) 面對面的
(B) 房間到房間的
(C) 鋪滿整個地板的
(D) 挨家挨戶的

| 解析 | 根據句子意義，「鋪滿整個地板的地毯」才合乎邏輯，故 (C) wall-to-wall 正確。若用 room-to-room，則反而房間沒有地毯，其他依此類推。 |

| 單字 | flat 公寓　　　　　carpet 鋪地毯　　　　　appliance 家用電器
spacious 寬敞的 |

---

106. Mr. Jacob -------- a great asset to our company over the years and we will miss him.

(A) was
(B) has been
(C) used to be
(D) will be

雅各先生多年來一直是我們公司的一大資產，我們會懷念他。

(A) 是（過去式）
(B) 一直是（現在完成式）
(C) 曾經是
(D) 將是（未來式）

| 解析 | 本題考動詞時態。後面出現 over the years（好幾年），為時間段落，故用現在完成式 (B) has been。 |

| 單字 | asset 資產　　　　　miss 想念；懷念 |

TEST 02
PART 5

107. It is my pleasure to -------- you with information about Kent University's business management program.

(A) inform
(B) offer
(C) support
(D) provide

我很榮幸向您提供有關肯特大學企業管理課程的資訊。

(A) 通知
(B) 提供
(C) 支持
(D) 提供

| 解析 | 本題考單字用法。提供某人某事物：provide + someone with something，因此該用 (D) provide。(A) inform 後面要用 of，(B) offer 後面不用介系詞，句中有 with，故不可用 offer。 |

| 單字 | pleasure 榮幸；樂趣　　business management 企業管理　　program 課程；計畫 |

108. The sixteen courses required for the business management -------- take two years to complete.

(A) diploma
(B) certificate
(C) degree
(D) level

企業管理學位要求的十六門課程需要兩年時間才能完成。

(A) 文憑
(B) 證書
(C) 學位
(D) 級別

| 解析 | 本題考單字用法。有學位證書的稱為 degree（學位），只有（高中、國中、小學）畢業證書的稱為 diploma（文憑），只修某些科目的則稱為 certificate（證書）。故本題應該用 (C) degree（學位）。 |

| 單字 | course 課程　　require 要求；規定　　complete 完成 |

109. Please feel free to contact me with any questions -------- the business management program.

(A) concerning
(B) concernment
(C) concerned
(D) concerns

有關企業管理課程的任何問題，請隨時與我聯絡。

(A) 關於（現在分詞）
(B) 有關之事（名詞）
(C) 有關的；關心的（形容詞）
(D) 重要的事；關心的事（名詞）

| 解析 | 本題考分詞文法。前面已有動詞 please feel free（請自在不拘），故後面動詞須改為現在分詞 concerning（關於…），表主動，因為 concerning 後面直接加名詞 the business...。 |

| 單字 | contact 聯絡　　concerning 關於 |

110. Cruise Direct is a leading online cruise travel company dedicated to -------- its customers with access to great deals on cruise vacations.

(A) providing
(B) provide
(C) provided
(D) provision

Cruise Direct 是一家頂尖的遊輪旅行線上公司，致力於提供客戶獲得遊輪度假的優惠。

(A) 提供（動名詞）
(B) 提供（動詞現在式）
(C) 提供（動詞過去式）
(D) 供應（名詞）

| 解析 | 本題考動名詞文法。空格前面 dedicated to（致力於）的 to 為介系詞，故後面應使用 V-ing 動名詞。 |

| 單字 | leading 領先的；頂尖的　　online 線上的　　　　　　　　cruise 巡航；巡遊 |
| | customer 顧客；客戶　　　access 管道；機會；有權使用　vacation 假期 |

---

111. We work with the industry's leading suppliers, and that gives us -------- to special rates.

(A) access
(B) exit
(C) pavement
(D) road

我們與業界頂尖的供應商合作，讓我們獲得特別費率。

(A) 管道
(B) 出口
(C) 人行道
(D) 道路

| 解析 | 本題考單字用法。access（管道／途徑）泛指一切可行的途徑或方法，exit 指具體的出口（入口為 entry），pavement 意指人行道（英式英語），road 指一般的道路；故本題應該用 (A) access（管道）。 |

| 單字 | industry 工業；產業　　　supplier 供應商　　　　　　special 特別 |
| | rate 費用；費率 |

---

112. Our company is so confident -------- we're willing to back up all the deals on our site with a price guarantee!

(A) as
(B) that
(C) when
(D) but

我們是如此自信，以致於願意用保證價格來為我們網站上所有的交易背書！

(A) 跟…一樣
(B) 以致於
(C) 何時
(D) 但是

| 解析 | 本題考文法。so...that... 意指「如此…以致於」，故本題應該選 (B) that。 |

單字	confident 有自信的　　　　back up 支持　　　　　　　deal 交易
	price 價格　　　　　　　　guarantee 保證
	back up something = to prove something is true 證明；支持

TEST 02
PART 5

113. When it's time to make your reservation, our cutting- -------- booking engine gives you live pricing and availability.

(A) piece
(B) section
(C) margin
(D) edge

您要預訂時，我們最先進的預訂引擎可為您提供實時定價和便利使用。

(A) 一件
(B) 部分
(C) 邊緣；保證金
(D) 邊緣

解析 本題考複合詞。cutting-edge 意指「最先進的」，故本題應該選 (D) edge（邊緣）。此外，常用複合詞包括 marginal effect（邊際效應），master-piece/masterpiece（傑作）。

單字
reservation 預訂；保留　　cutting-edge 最先進的　　booking 預訂
live pricing 實時定價　　availability 可利用；方便使用

---

114. -------- you ever need the advice of an expert, our service staff are available via phone and LiveChat.

(A) Would
(B) Could
(C) Should
(D) Must

如果您需要專家的建議，我們的服務人員可透過電話和 LiveChat 進行。

(A) 就會
(B) 可以
(C) 萬一
(D) 必須

解析 本題考假設語氣。If + S + should（萬一）+ V~ 可以代換為：Should S + V~，將 should 移到前面成為倒裝句，故 (C) Should 為正確答案。

單字
advice 忠告；建議　　expert 專家　　staff 員工；全體職員
via 透過，藉由

---

115. It would be helpful if you would -------- this authorization so the vendors will recognize me as your agent.

(A) confirm
(B) console
(C) concern
(D) conduct

如果您確認此授權，那就很有幫助，如此一來供應商將認可我做為您的代理商。

(A) 確認
(B) 安慰
(C) 關注
(D) 進行

解析 本題考單字用法。confirm（確認）可泛指對一切事務的確定，console（安慰）意指安撫他人的哀傷，concern 意指關心，conduct 意指進行。故本題應該選 (A) confirm（確認）。

單字
authorization 授權　　vendor 供應商　　recognize 承認；認可
agent 代理商

116. If you would, please sign this document, save a copy, and return the -------- to me at your convenience.

(A) draft
(B) copy
(C) original
(D) replicate

如果你願意，請簽署本文件，保存一份副本，並在方便的時候將原稿還給我。

(A) 草稿
(B) 副本
(C) 原稿
(D) 複製品

解析 本題考單字用法。(A) draft 是草稿，還有待修正；copy 是副本，由原稿拷貝成的；replicate 與 copy 同義。故本題應該選 (C) original（原稿）。

單字
sign 簽字　　　　　　　　document 文件　　　　　　　save 保存
copy 副本；影印本　　　　convenience 方便

---

117. As an attorney and a long-time friend of your parents, I am -------- that you would turn to me for legal counsel.

(A) pleasing
(B) pleased
(C) pleasant
(D) pleasure

作為您父母的律師和長期朋友，我很高興您會找我做法律諮詢。

(A) 取悅（現在分詞）
(B) 感到高興（被動式；形容詞）
(C) 愉悅（形容詞）
(D) 愉悅（名詞）

解析 本題考情緒動詞。「感到喜悅」要用被動語態：I am pleased.（我很高興），但如果 please 表示主動取悅，其分詞形式要用現在分詞 pleasing，如 She is good at pleasing everybody.（她善於取悅每個人）。

單字
attorney 律師　　　　　　legal 法律的　　　　　　　counsel 建議；忠告

---

118. I -------- such rude treatment for several weeks from one of your tellers that I refuse to tolerate it any longer.

(A) have experienced
(B) experienced
(C) had experienced
(D) am experiencing

幾個星期以來，我在一個櫃員那裡經歷了這麼粗魯的對待，我再也忍不住了。

(A) 已經經歷過（現在完成式）
(B) 經歷（過去簡單式）
(C) 以前經歷過（過去完成式）
(D) 正在經歷（現在進行式）

解析 本題考動詞時態。for several weeks（好幾個禮拜）是一段時間，動詞該用現在完成式，故 (A) have experienced（已經經歷過）為正確答案。

單字
experience 經歷；體驗　　　rude 粗魯的　　　　　　treatment 對待
teller 出納員　　　　　　　refuse 拒絕　　　　　　tolerate 容忍

TEST 02 PART 5

119. I am writing a letter in the hope of -------- a position as a laboratory assistant during next year's field-work in International Valley.

(A) securing
(B) requiring
(C) demanding
(D) struggling

我正在寫應徵信，希望在明年國際谷的田野調查期間獲得實驗室助理職位。

(A) 獲得
(B) 要求
(C) 要求
(D) 奮鬥

解析 本題考片語。securing a position（獲得一個職位），比 requiring（要求）、demanding（要求）及 struggling（奮鬥）符合句意，故本題應該選 (A) securing（獲得）。

---

120. I am sorry that I will be unable to -------- a time to meet with you next Thursday to discuss your career plans.

(A) estimate
(B) predict
(C) schedule
(D) obtain

對不起，我下週四無法排定時間與你見面，討論你的職業生涯計畫。

(A) 估計
(B) 預測
(C) 排定
(D) 獲得

解析 本題考單字用法。依句意，(C) schedule (a time)（排定時間）比其他答案 (A) estimate（估計）、(B) predict（預測）及 (D) obtain（獲得）都恰當，故本題應該選 (C) schedule（排定）。

單字
schedule 排定　　career 生涯；職業

---

121. During our last meeting, we came to some -------- decisions about working together.

(A) primary
(B) preliminary
(C) preparatory
(D) perfunctory

在上次會議期間，我們達成了關於共同合作的初步決定。

(A) 主要的
(B) 初步的
(C) 預備的
(D) 敷衍的

解析 本題考單字用法。依句意，(B) preliminary（初步的）比其他答案 (A) primary（主要的）、(C) preparatory（預備的）與 (D) perfunctory（敷衍的）更恰當，故本題應該選 (B)。

單字
preliminary 初步的　　decision 決定

122. As --------, I have enclosed a copy of our most recent catalog, complete with price guides.

(A) promising
(B) promise
(C) promised
(D) promises

根據承諾，我附上一份我們最新的目錄，包含價格指南。

(A) 承諾（現在分詞）
(B) 承諾（現在簡單式）
(C) 承諾（過去分詞）
(D) 承諾（現在式第三人稱單數）

| 解析 | 本題考分詞片語。As promised（依據我所承諾），是 As it is promised 的省略形式，形成分詞構句。 |

| 單字 | enclosed 隨信附上　　recent 最近的　　catalog 目錄
complete 完整的　　guide 指南 |

123. -------- I understand the need to restructure our department, I disagree with the plan to lay off nearly half of my staff.

(A) Whether
(B) While
(C) When
(D) Where

雖然我知道有必要重組我們的部門，但我不同意將我的員工裁減近一半的計畫。

(A) 是否
(B) 雖然
(C) 何時
(D) 哪裡

| 解析 | 本題考連接詞。空格後是 I understand the need...（我了解…），逗點後是 I disagree...（我不同意…），故知 (B) while（雖然）為正確答案。 |

| 單字 | restructure 重組；改組　　department 部門　　disagree 不同意
lay off 解雇　　staff 員工 |

124. We have read your -------- plans to improve our tax deductible investment procedures and are very interested in your proposal.

(A) innovate
(B) innovative
(C) innovation
(D) innovating

我們已經看到您改善我們的免稅投資程序的創新計畫，並對您的建議非常感興趣。

(A) 創新（動詞）
(B) 創新的（形容詞）
(C) 創新（名詞）
(D) 創新（動名詞）

| 解析 | 本題考詞類。因為空格後面是名詞，故空格裡要用形容詞 innovative（創新的）。 |

| 單字 | innovative 創新的　　improve 改善　　tax deductible 應稅所得減免
investment 投資　　procedure 程序 |

TEST 02
PART 5

125. If you can comply -------- our work requirements, please call me to discuss the legal implications of your proposal.

(A) by
(B) to
(C) with
(D) for

如果您能配合我們的工作需求，請來電以便討論提案所涉及的法律問題。

(A) 藉由
(B) 到／向
(C) 與／隨
(D) 為了

解析 本題考動詞片語。comply + with 是「遵守」的意思，如果是 conform + to ~，則是「遵從」的意思。

單字
requirement 要求；規定
proposal 提案
legal 法律的
implication 可能的影響（或後果）；牽涉

---

126. Those who pay within 30 days receive a 3% discount. We encourage you to take -------- of this money-saving opportunity.

(A) advance
(B) advantage
(C) advice
(D) advent

在 30 天內付款的人將享有 3% 的折扣。我們鼓勵您利用這個省錢的機會。

(A) 進步
(B) 好處
(C) 建議
(D) 出現

解析 本題考動詞片語。依句意，應該用 take advantage of（利用）。此外，make use of 和 avail oneself of 也是「利用」的意思。

單字
discount 折扣　　encourage 鼓勵　　advantage 好處；利益
opportunity 機會

---

127. Customers -------- pay the $21 monthly service fee before the first-of-the-month due date pay only $20!

(A) who
(B) whoever
(C) what
(D) whatever

在第一個月到期日之前支付 21 美元每月服務費的客戶只需支付 20 美元！

(A) 那些（客戶）
(B) 任何（客戶）
(C) 什麼
(D) 任何（東西）

解析 本題考關係代名詞。空格前面的先行詞 customers（客戶）為人，後面缺主詞，故 (A) who 為正確答案。注意：whoever 用在無先行詞時。

單字
customer 顧客；客戶　　monthly 每月的　　service fee 服務費
due date 到期日

128.

The reason I'm making you this offer is -------- you into the habit of ordering your computer supplies from us.

(A) getting
(B) gets
(C) to get
(D) got

我給您這個特價的原因是讓您習慣從我們這裡訂購電腦耗材。

(A) 讓…（現在分詞）
(B) 讓…（現在式第三人稱單數）
(C) 讓…（不定詞）
(D) 讓…（過去簡單式）

| 解析 | 本題考不定詞。凡尚未發生的行為，用 to + V~，本句 The reason... is to + V~ 意指「…的理由是去…」，故 (C) to get 是正確答案。 |

| 單字 | reason 原因；理由　　offer 特價　　order 訂購
supplies 補給品 |

129.

We hope they are as satisfying to you to operate as they were for us to manufacture. They are second to -------- in dependability.

(A) all
(B) none
(C) both
(D) neither

我們希望他們在營運方面讓你們滿意，如同他們在製造方面讓我們滿意一樣。他們在可靠性方面是首屈一指的。

(A) 所有
(B) 毫無
(C) 兩者
(D) 兩者都不

| 解析 | 本題考片語。second to none 的直接白話解釋是「僅次於無一物」，意即「首屈一指」，故答案為 (B) none。 |

| 單字 | satisfying 令人滿意的　　operate 營運；經營　　manufacture 製造
dependability 可靠性 |

130.

With much reluctance, I wish to inform you of my -------- as personnel director, effective as soon as arrangements can be made to hire a new director.

(A) responsibility
(B) reduction
(C) resignation
(D) replacement

我很遺憾通知你，我要辭去人事主任之職，一旦安排僱用新主任，就可以生效。

(A) 責任
(B) 減少，降低
(C) 辭職
(D) 替代

| 解析 | 本題考單字用法。依句意，由前面的 With much reluctance（不情願）…inform（通知）可知，(C) resignation（辭職）最為適當。 |

| 單字 | reluctance 不情願　　inform 通知　　personnel 人事
director 主任　　effective 有效的；生效的　　arrangement 安排
hire 僱用 |

TEST 02
PART 6

Questions 131-134 refer to the following email.

From: Gary <gary@oxfordu.edu>
To: Andrew@erols.com
Subject: Hotel Reservations for Conference
Date: Sunday, July 27, 2019, 21:38:01
MAIL-Priority: High

Dear Mr. Andrew Rice,

I just received your letter today and have tried to fax the hotel ----__131__---- form down to you at 515-418-7749, but that number does not answer. ----__132__----. I presumed the 27th was your deadline but not the hotel's. Please do sign me up for the meeting on the 28th and 29th. I shall be flying with Eastern Air (flight #2333), ----__133__---- Dallas at 8:00 p.m. and arriving at DC National at 9:35 p.m. I can arrange ----__134__---- a doctoral student at the City University to pick me up and take me to the hotel.

Looking forward to seeing you.

Prof. Gary Johnson
Texas Tech University

131-134 題參考以下 email。

寄件者：Gary <gary@oxfordu.edu>
收件者：Andrew@erols.com
主旨：會議的飯店預訂
日期：2019/7/27 星期日 21:38:01
優先級：高

親愛的安德魯・賴斯先生：

我今天剛剛收到您的信，並試著傳真給您飯店預訂表，但 515-418-7749 這個號碼沒有回應。我今晚和明天早上會再試一試。我猜 27 日是您的截止日，而不是飯店的。請代我登記 28 日和 29 日的會議。我將搭乘東方航空班機（航班 2333），晚上 8 點離開達拉斯，並於晚上 9 時 35 分抵達 DC 國際機場。我可以安排在城市大學的博士生接我，帶我去飯店。

很期待見到您。

蓋瑞・強生教授
德克薩斯理工大學

---

131. (A) conservation
   (B) reservation
   (C) preservation
   (D) subservience

(A) 保護
(B) 預訂
(C) 保存
(D) 唯命是從

> **解析** 本題考不同單字用法。傳真飯店訂房表單（fax the hotel reservation form）與訂旅館較有關係，故 (B) reservation 正確。

132. (A) I felt exhausted after the whole thing.
   (B) It happened sometimes in similar cases.
   (C) It is a matter of time and effort.
   (D) I'll try later tonight and tomorrow morning.

(A) 在整件事之後，我感到疲憊不堪。
(B) 它有時在類似的情況中發生。
(C) 這是一個時間和努力的問題。
(D) 我今晚和明天早上會再試一試。

266

解析	本題考克漏句子。空格前面是：...but that number does not answer.（…但這個號碼沒有回應），故知後面的句子應為 (D) I'll try later tonight and tomorrow morning.（我今晚和明天早上會再試一試。）

133. (A) to leave
     (B) left
     (C) leaving
     (D) and left

     (A) 離開（不定詞）
     (B) 離開（過去式）
     (C) 離開（現在分詞）
     (D) 離開（動詞過去式）

解析	本題考分詞。因為前面已有動詞 shall be flying，且後面有 and + arriving，故空格裡的動詞要用現在分詞 leaving（離開），表主動。

134. **(A) for**
     (B) by
     (C) with
     (D) to

     (A) 關於
     (B) 藉由
     (C) 與
     (D) 到／去

解析	本題考介系詞。表達「安排某人做某事」的英語句型是：arrange for sb to do sth，故 (A) for 正確。

單字	fax 傳真　　　　　　　　　reservation 預訂　　　　　　deadline 最後期限
	sign up 登錄　　　　　　　arrange 安排　　　　　　　doctoral student 博士生
	pick sb up 接（某人）

TEST 02
PART 6

Questions 135-138 refer to the following business letter.

135-138 題參考以下商務書信。

Dodge White
Customer Service Manager
Sage Digital Camera Corp.
300 Park Avenue, LA, California

Dear Mr. White,

On December 4, I bought a digital camera, with the product number RT-0756 from one of your shops ------- (135) Botany Road. Unfortunately, your product has not performed well, which is quite disappointing. To ------- (136) the problem, I would appreciate if I can have an exchange for a new one. -------（137). I look forward to your reply, and will wait ------- (138) December 14 before I seek help from the consumer protection agency. Please contact me at the below address or by telephone at 0938-388388.

Sincerely,
Peter Johnson
56 Disgruntled Street,
LA, California

道奇‧懷特
客服部經理
賽奇數位相機公司
加州，洛杉磯，公園大道 300 號

親愛的懷特先生：

我 12 月 4 日在您波塔尼路的一家分店買了一台數位相機，產品編號為 RT-0756。很糟的是，你們的產品操作不良，這令我感到很失望。為了解決這個問題，如果可以換新的，我會很感激。這裡附上我的購買憑單的副本，我希望 12 月 14 日前收到您的回覆，否則我將尋求消費者保護機構的協助。請透過以下地址或電話 0938-388388 與我聯繫。

彼得‧強生 謹啟
加州，洛杉磯，迪斯格倫透街 56 號

---

135. (A) for
(B) at
(C) on
(D) in

(A) 為了
(B) 在…點
(C) 在…上
(D) 在…內

> **解析** 本題考介系詞。on + 街道名稱，in + 大都市，at + 門牌號碼，故 (C) on 為正確答案。

---

136. (A) resolve
(B) demand
(C) conceive
(D) exile

(A) 解決
(B) 要求
(C) 想像；想出
(D) 放逐

> **解析** 本題考單字用法。因空格後是 the problem（問題），顯然 resolve the problem（解決問題）才合理，故 (A) 為正確答案。

137. (A) We don't have to get this over with ASAP.
(B) I may have mishandled the product.
(C) Enclosed is a letter of complaint.
(D) Enclosed are copies of my purchase receipt.

(A) 我們不必盡快解決這個問題。
(B) 我可能草率地處理了這個產品。
(C) 這裡附上投訴信。
(D) 這裡附上我的購買憑單的副本。

解析	本題考克漏句子。空格前面是：I would appreciate if I can have an exchange for a new one.（…如果可以換新的，我會很感激），故知後面這一句應為 (D) Enclosed are copies of my purchase receipt.（這裡附上我的購買憑單的副本）。

138. (A) while
(B) until
(C) despite
(D) during

(A) 當…的時候
(B) 直到
(C) 儘管
(D) 在…期間

解析	本題考連接詞。空格後面有 ... before I seek help from the consumer protection agency.（在我尋求消費者保護機構的協助之前），可知 (B) until（直到）正確。

單字	digital camera 數位相機　unfortunately 不幸地　perform 運作；表現 disappointing 令人感到失望的　appreciate 感謝　exchange 更換 look forward to 期待　consumer 消費者　protection 保護 agency 機構　contact 聯絡

TEST 02
PART 6

Questions 139-142 refer to the following business letter.

139-142 題參考以下商業書信。

Paul Snider
R & D Department
Prime Human Resource Organization
200 Oxford Road
Atlanta, Georgia, USA

Dear Mr. Snider,

I am writing to ask you to ---------- an addition to your marketing team. Your organization has been in the news as a leader in the industry. I am an ---------- of new ideas, an excellent communicator with buyers, and have a demonstrated history of marketing success.

---------- .

---------- is my resume for your review and consideration. I would like to use my talents to market your quality line of technical products. If you prefer, you may reach me in the evenings at (777) 666-3333.

Thank you for your time. I look forward to meeting you.

Sincerely,
John Linden

保羅‧斯奈德
研發科
首要人力資源組織
牛津路 200 號
亞特蘭大市，喬治亞州，美國

親愛的斯奈德先生：

我寫信請您考慮增加您行銷團隊的成員。根據新聞報導，您的企業已經成為該產業的領頭羊。我是具有新觀念的創新者，一個優秀的買家溝通者，並且具有市場行銷成功的經歷。我相信我會很適合您的組織。

這裡附上我的簡歷，供您審查和考量。我想利用我的天賦來行銷您的優質科技產品系列。如果您願意，晚上可以打（777）666-3333 找我。

感謝您看我的信。我期待著與您見面。

約翰‧林登 謹啟

---

139. (A) consider
(B) recommend
(C) decide
(D) promote

(A) 考慮
(B) 推薦
(C) 決定
(D) 提倡

解析 本題考單字用法。因全篇文字是自我推薦，故知 (A) consider（考慮）增加團隊成員為正確答案。

270

140. (A) creator
(B) negotiator
(C) producer
(D) innovator

(A) 創造者
(B) 談判代表
(C) 製造商
(D) 創新者

| 解析 | 本題考單字用法。因為空格後面有 ...new ideas（新觀念），故知 (D) innovator（創新者）為正確。 |

141. (A) I know it is high time that I applied for the position.
(B) I have confidence that I can be a good leader.
(C) I believe I would be a good fit in your organization.
(D) I strongly recommend myself to be one of the members.

(A) 我知道現在是申請職位的時候了。
(B) 我有自信我可以成為一個很好的領導者。
(C) 我相信我會很適合您的組織。
(D) 我強烈推薦自己成為其中一員。

| 解析 | 本題考克漏句子。空格前面是 ...have a demonstrated history of marketing success.（…具有市場行銷成功的經歷），故知後面這一句應為 (C) I believe I would be a good fit in your organization.（我相信我會很適合您的組織）。 |

142. (A) Enclosed
(B) Enclosing
(C) Encloses
(D) Enclose

(A) 附上（過去分詞）
(B) 附上（現在分詞）
(C) 附上（現在式第三人稱單數）
(D) 附上（現在簡單式）

| 解析 | 本題考分詞。因為空格後面已有動詞 is，故前面之動詞要用過去分詞 enclosed（附上），表被動，指後面的 resume（履歷表）被附上去。 |

| 單字 | addition 增加物；添加物
industry 產業
communicator 溝通者
review 審查
consideration 考慮
reach 聯絡到 | marketing 行銷
innovator 創新者
demonstrate 證明；示範
It's high time(that) 是…的時候／時機了
resume 履歷表 | quality 優質的
organization 組織；機構
excellent 優秀的
enclose 隨信附上
talent 天賦
technical 技術的；科技的 |

TEST 02
PART 6

Questions 143-146 refer to the following business letter.

July 10, 2019
Frank Zatinski
656 Gilmour St., Apt. 908
Chicago, IL 60611

Dear Frank,

We regret to inform you that your employment at Epson Systems Inc. will be ----143---- as of Tuesday July 31, 2019.

I would like to make it absolutely clear that in no way does your termination reflect that the company is in any way unhappy with your work performance over the past 18 months. ----144----. The company will give you one week's extra pay for each month you worked beyond 12 months. In your case, this will amount to 6 weeks of severance pay.

I am confident that you will be able to find another position in the ----145---- near future. If you would like, I would be pleased to write a ----146---- letter for you.

Sincerely,
Ted Bohr
Unit Manager

143-146 題參考以下商業書信。

2019 年 7 月 10 日
法蘭克・扎廷斯基
吉爾莫街 656 號，908 號公寓
芝加哥市，伊利諾州，60611

親愛的法蘭克：

很遺憾通知您，您在 Epson Systems 公司的工作將於 2019 年 7 月 31 日星期二終止。

我想明確表示，您的職位終止絕不表示公司在過去 18 個月內對您的工作表現不滿意。事實上，您是我們最具有績效的員工之一。您工作超過 12 個月後的每個月，公司將給您一週的額外工資。您的情況，會有六週的資遣費。

我相信您將能夠在不久的將來找到另一個職位。如果您願意，我會很樂意為您寫一封推薦信。

泰德・玻爾 謹啟
單位經理

---

143. (A) termination
  (B) terminated
  (C) terminates
  (D) terminate

(A) 終止（名詞）
(B) 終止（過去分詞）
(C) 終止（現在式第三人稱單數）
(D) 終止（現在簡單式）

> **解析** 本題考動詞用法。因為前面已有 be 動詞 will be，故後面的動詞要用過去分詞 terminated（終止），表被動。

272

144. (A) However, we are experiencing serious financial difficulties.
(B) In fact, you have been one of our most productive employees.
(C) No doubt, other employees will feel at a loss.
(D) In any event, we are going to miss you.

(A) 但是,我們處於嚴重的財務困境。
(B) 事實上,您是我們最具有績效的員工之一。
(C) 毫無疑問,其他員工會感到不知所措。
(D) 無論如何,我們會想念你。

> **解析** 本題考克漏句子。空格前面是 ...in no way does your termination reflect that the company is in any way unhappy with your work performance over the past 18 months.(…絕不表示公司在過去 18 個月內對您的工作表現不滿意),故知後面這一句應為 (B) In fact, you have been one of our most productive employees.(事實上,您是我們最具有績效的員工之一)。

145. **(A) relatively**
(B) shortly
(C) urgently
(D) absolutely

(A) 相對地;相當
(B) 不久
(C) 緊急地
(D) 絕對地

> **解析** 本題考單字的用法。因空格後面是 near future(不久的將來),故知 (A) relatively(相對地;相當)為正確答案。

146. (A) recommended
(B) recommending
(C) recommendation
(D) recommend

(A) 推薦(動詞過去式)
(B) 推薦(動名詞)
(C) 推薦(名詞)
(D) 推薦(動詞現在簡單式)

> **解析** 本題考複合詞。recommendation letter(推薦信)是名詞+名詞組合而成的複合詞,前面的名詞當形容詞用。

單字

regret 感到遺憾	inform 通知	employment 工作;職業
terminate 終止	absolutely 絕對地;完全地	reflect 反映;表達
performance 表現	amount 總計(達)	severance 遣散;解僱
pay 工資	confident 有信心的	position 工作職位
pleased 開心的;樂意的	recommendation letter 推薦信	

TEST 02
PART 7

Questions 147 to 148 refer to the following online chat discussion.

Tyler: (2:32 p.m.)	I just called Sonicson Computer Shop and asked him how to fix my computer. He tried his best, but he didn't solve the problem because of his lack of experience.
Sophia: (2:35 p.m.)	What problem are you experiencing?
Tyler: (2:36 p.m.)	I believe it is a disk drive failure. I bought this computer 3 years ago and the warranty expired a year ago.
Sophia: (2:39 p.m.)	Has your fan been moving too slowly?
Tyler: (2:41 p.m.)	No. I've been hearing lots of clicking sounds and noise coming from the system hardware.
Sophia: (2:45 p.m.)	Well, based on experience, improper ventilation may be the problem. I suggest that you put thermal paste between the heat sink and the CPU to cool it down and make it run smoother. If you experience further problems, have your computer's fans repaired.

147-148 題參考以下線上聊天討論內容。

泰勒： (2:32 p.m.)	我剛剛打電話給 Sonicson 電腦商店，問他如何修理我的電腦。他盡了最大努力，但他因為缺乏經驗而無法解決問題。
蘇菲亞： (2:35 p.m.)	你遇到了什麼問題？
泰勒： (2:36 p.m.)	我認為這是磁碟機故障的問題。我 3 年前買了這台電腦，保固在一年前到期了。
蘇菲亞： (2:39 p.m.)	你的風扇轉得太慢嗎？
泰勒： (2:41 p.m.)	不，我聽到很多來自系統硬體的咔噠聲和噪音。
蘇菲亞： (2:45 p.m.)	嗯，根據經驗，通風不良可能是問題所在。我建議你在散熱器和 CPU 之間塗一些散熱膏，讓它冷卻下來，讓它運作得更順暢。如果你遇到其他問題，請修復電腦的風扇。

147. What problem has Tyler been having with his computer?

(A) His computer was infected with a virus.
(B) His computer freezes sometimes.
(C) His computer has been making clicking sounds.
(D) His computer can't be turned on.

泰勒的電腦有什麼問題？

(A) 他的電腦感染病毒了。
(B) 他的電腦有時會當機。
(C) 他的電腦一直發出咔噠聲。
(D) 他的電腦無法開機。

---

148. What did Sophia advise Tyler to do?

(A) Take his computer to Sonicson
(B) Shut the computer down when it makes sounds
(C) Run the latest version of an anti-virus program
(D) Use thermal paste to help the computer cool down

蘇菲亞建議泰勒怎麼做？

(A) 把他的電腦帶去 Sonicson
(B) 發出聲音時關掉電腦
(C) 執行最新版本的防病毒軟體
(D) 用散熱膏幫電腦降溫

單字			
disk drive 磁碟機		warranty 保固	expire 到期
ventilation 通風；通風系統		thermal paste 散熱膏	heat sink 散熱座，散熱器

Questions 149 to 150 refer to the following invitation.

Dear Mr. Charles Brown,

In recognition of your longstanding contribution to the marketing profession and the care you have demonstrated in your charity work done in our community, the city of Trenton is proud to invite you to attend our 36th annual humanitarian ball & entrepreneur dinner. We are also honored to bestow the Hartman Johnston Memorial Plaque upon you to show recognition for your exceptional achievement as a businessman and commitment to the welfare of those in society.

April 22, 2020
Lord Gibson Hall
973 Drummond Street, Trenton

4:30 p.m.-10 p.m.
(Dinner time: 6-8 p.m. Award ceremony: 8 p.m.)

149-150 題參考以下邀請函。

查爾斯・布朗先生：

為了表彰您對行銷業界的長期貢獻，以及您在我們社區裡所做的慈善工作中展現的關懷，特倫頓市很榮幸邀請您參加我們的第 36 屆年度人道主義舞會和企業家晚宴。我們也很榮幸授予您哈特曼・強生紀念匾額，以表彰您作為企業家的傑出成就和對社會福利的熱情支持。

2020/4/22
吉布森勳爵廳
特倫頓市卓蒙德街 973 號

下午 4:30 ～晚上 10:00
（晚宴時間：下午 6 ～ 8 點。頒獎典禮：晚上 8 點。）

149. Why is Mr. Brown being invited to attend this event?

(A) He is a member of the city council.
(B) He is the manager of a charity organization.
(C) He is delivering a speech.
(D) He is receiving an award.

為什麼布朗先生受邀參加這個活動？

(A) 他是市議會的成員。
(B) 他是慈善機構的經理。
(C) 他正在發表演講。
(D) 他將接受頒獎。

---

150. What is indicated about the kind of work Mr. Brown does?

(A) He does charity work.
(B) He owns a large international enterprise.
(C) He works at a job agency.
(D) He is a public speaker.

關於布朗先生做的工作，文中提到什麼？

(A) 他做慈善工作。
(B) 他擁有一家大型國際企業。
(C) 他在一家工作仲介公司工作。
(D) 他是公眾演說家。

單字			
recognition 表彰；表揚	long-standing 長期的	profession 專門職業；業界
charity 慈善事業	humanitarian 人道主義的；人道主義者
entrepreneur 企業家	bestow 頒發；授予	plaque 匾額，牌匾
exceptional 優異的；傑出的	commitment 支持，擁護；熱情	welfare 福利

TEST 02
PART 7

Questions 151 to 152 refer to the following form.

Name: George Freeman
Department: Sales
Period: From Nov. 4 to Nov. 6, and from Dec. 16 to Dec. 19
Per Mile Reimbursement: 0.32
Total Reimbursement Due: $1198.00

Date	Description of events	Airfare	Lodging	Ground Transportation
Nov. 4	Traveling from New York to Boston for Sales 3.0 conference	$350.00	$150.00	$45.00
Dec. 16	Flying from New York to Tokyo for 10x Growth Conference	$434.00	$165.00	$54.00

Note: Due to financial problems our company is having, we won't be able to reimburse you until the beginning of March 2020. Sorry for the inconvenience.

151-152 題參考以下表格。

姓名：喬治・費里曼
部門：業務
時間：11 月 4 日至 11 月 6 日，以及 12 月 16 日至 12 月 19 日
每英里補貼：0.32 美元
補貼總額：1198.00 美元

日期	活動	機票	住宿	接送機／交通
11 月 4 日	從紐約至波士頓參加 Sales 3.0 會議	$350.00	$150.00	$45.00
12 月 16 日	從紐約飛往東京進行 10 倍成長會議	$434.00	$165.00	$54.00

注意：由於公司遇到財務問題，我們要到 2020 年 3 月初才能把費用支付給您。很抱歉給您帶來不便。

151. What is implied in the form?

(A) Mr. Freeman works in the HR department.
(B) Mr. Freeman will be reimbursed in December 2020.
(C) Mr. Freeman has to travel a lot for his job.
(D) Mr. Freeman is a sales manager.

表格內容暗示什麼？

(A) 費里曼先生在人力資源部門工作。
(B) 費里曼先生將於 2020 年 12 月獲得補貼。
(C) 費里曼先生的工作必須經常旅行。
(D) 費里曼先生是業務部經理。

---

152. Why can't Mr. Freeman receive his reimbursement straight away?

(A) The accountant made a mistake when calculating the money.
(B) The company is struggling financially.
(C) He won't be back at the company until next year.
(D) He didn't submit his air tickets to the accountant.

為什麼費里曼先生不能馬上收到他的補貼？

(A) 會計師在計算費用時犯了一個錯誤。
(B) 公司在財務上有困難。
(C) 他明年之前不會回到公司。
(D) 他沒有向會計師提交機票。

單字

reimbursement 核銷；償還；補償

lodging 住宿處

Questions 153 to 154 refer to the following notice.

Apartment for Rent

This small luxury flat is on a quaint street and situated in the heart of downtown Taichung city, close to the art museum. The landlord has spent thousands of dollars finely furnishing it. It has a large and bright bedroom with a queen-sized bed, and a side kitchen that's equipped with all necessary amenities. The apartment comes with a Wi-Fi internet connection. What makes this place special is the 10 square meter terrace where tenants can relax and admire the peaceful surrounding scenery. This home is within walking distance to public transportation.

Apartment Features:

Bedroom: 1
Area: 45 m²
Monthly price of rent: $10,000
Includes: 1 double bed, 1 table, 2 chairs, washing machine, refrigerator, Wi-Fi connection
Security deposit: 2 months rent

153-154 題參考以下啟事。

公寓出租

這間豪華的小公寓位於一條古色古香的街道上，坐落在台中市中心，靠近藝術博物館。房東花了數千美元精心裝修它。寬敞明亮的臥室配有一張大號雙人床，旁邊的廚房配有所有必要的設施。公寓有裝無線網路。這裡的特別之處是有 10 平方公尺的露天平台，你可以放鬆身心，欣賞周圍寧靜的風景。這個家在步行距離內就有大眾運輸系統站點。

特　點：

臥　　室：1
面　　積：45 平方公尺
每月租金：10,000 元
包　　含：1 張雙人床、1 張桌子、2 張椅子、洗衣機、冰箱、Wi-Fi
保 證 金：2 個月租金

153. What is indicated about the apartment?

(A) It doesn't come with a chair.
(B) Tenants are able to relax on the terrace.
(C) It is far from a bus stop.
(D) It is situated on the outskirts of Taichung.

有關這間公寓，文中提到什麼？

(A) 它沒有椅子。
(B) 房客可以在露台上放鬆身心。
(C) 它離公車站很遠。
(D) 它位於台中市郊區。

---

154. Which kind of people would want to rent this apartment?

(A) Couples with 3 children
(B) Young couples that have no children
(C) People who usually drive to work
(D) Those who like going shopping

哪種人會租這間公寓？

(A) 有 3 個孩子的夫婦
(B) 年輕的沒有孩子的夫婦
(C) 通常開車上班的人
(D) 喜歡去購物的人

單字

quaint 奇特有趣的；古色古香的
equip 裝備；配備
landlord 房東
amenity 便利設施
furnish 為…配備家具
tenant 房客

TEST 02
PART 7

Questions 155 to 157 refer to the following advertisement.

Join us for our 30th Anniversary Party!
Sunday, November 11, 4 p.m. to 11 p.m.

Featuring: Live Entertainment, Food & Drink, Specials & Giveaways
Meet old Friends and Make new ones!
8896 Burmingham Ave
www.scottishpub.com

Note: Those who attend will receive a voucher (as below). If you bring a friend who is on a first visit, we will give both you and your friend two vouchers.

~Voucher~

Buy one of the following beers and get the second one for half price:
Sheepshaggers Gold, Santa's Swallie, Simmer Dim, Double Espresso, Ladeout, Kilt Lifter IPA, Seven Giraffes, Skull Splitter, Dead Pony Club

Present this voucher when you visit us.

Expiration date: 26th of November, 2019

- This voucher is only for two drinks, then it will become invalid.

155-157 題參考以下廣告。

加入我們的30週年派對吧！
11/11 星期日，下午4點至11點

特色：現場娛樂、食品和飲料、特價品和贈品

認識老朋友，結交新朋友！
伯明罕大道8896號
www.scottishpub.com

注意：參加者將獲得一張優惠券（如下所示）。如果你帶第一次來的朋友，我們會給你和你的朋友共兩張優惠券。

~優惠券~

購買下列啤酒，第二瓶半價：
Sheepshaggers Gold, Santa's Swallie, Simmer Dim, Double Espresso, Ladeout, Kilt Lifter IPA, Seven Giraffes, Skull Splitter, Dead Pony Club

入場時出示此優惠券。
截止日期：2019年11月26日
※ 此優惠券限購買兩瓶飲品，之後失效。

155. What activity is being advertised?

(A) A restaurant opening party
(B) An anniversary party
(C) A clearance sale
(D) A beer drinking competition

這則廣告在宣傳什麼活動？

(A) 餐廳開幕派對
(B) 週年紀念派對
(C) 清倉拍賣
(D) 喝啤酒比賽

---

156. What will people be able to do at the activity?

(A) Watch pole dancing
(B) Eat Irish food
(C) Enjoy entertainment
(D) Join in a dancing competition

在這項活動中，人們能夠做什麼？

(A) 觀看鋼管舞
(B) 吃愛爾蘭食物
(C) 享受娛樂節目
(D) 參加舞蹈比賽

---

157. What is true about the voucher?

(A) It will be given to those who come to the activity.
(B) Those who bring a friend will only receive one.
(C) It expires three weeks after the activity.
(D) It can be used to get more than two drinks for free.

關於優惠券何者為真？

(A) 它將贈送給參加活動的人。
(B) 帶朋友的人只會收到一張。
(C) 活動結束後三週到期。
(D) 它可以用來獲得二杯以上飲料免費。

| 單字 | voucher 優惠券 | giveaway（給顧客的）贈品 | invalid 無效的，作廢的 |

TEST 02
PART 7

Question 158 to 160 refer to the following letter.

Craig Hilston
147 Brady Road,
Grantville, PA, 19973.

Optigma Enterprises Ltd.
Date: April 25
Subject: General Manager Resignation Letter

Dear Mr. Hilston,

Throughout my 7 years of employment at this esteemed organization, I've mastered the skills of managing, team leading and conflict management. After contributing much to the growth of this company, I've earned great appreciation, enjoyed a fine reputation, and developed my potential as a business manager to the fullest.

It is with mixed feelings that I'm announcing my resignation as I'm searching for a better position at Royal Kingdom Enterprises Ltd. During my tenure, I've not only strived to direct, manage and oversee the functioning of all employees and staff to the best of my ability, but I've also developed a special friendship with all members and I'll always miss their presence.

With this resignation, I wish Optigma Enterprises Ltd. a bright and profitable future in all their business endeavors. I kindly request that you approve my resignation and contact me at 5793-3682 to confirm my successful application.

Sincerely,
Jacob Turner
General Manager
Optigma Enterprises Limited

158-160 參考以下信件。

克雷格・希爾斯頓
布雷迪街 147 號，
賓州格蘭特維爾，19973

Optigma 企業有限公司
日期：4 月 25 日
主題：總經理辭職信

親愛的希爾斯頓先生：

在這個有口皆碑的機構工作 7 年的過程中，我精通了管理、團隊領導和衝突管理的技能。在為這家公司的成長做出很大貢獻之後，我獲得了很高的評價，享有聲譽，並且充分發揮了我作為業務經理的潛力。

我夾雜著去與留的情緒，在此宣布辭職；因為我正在皇家王國企業有限公司尋求更好的工作。在我任職期間，我不僅努力指導、管理和監督所有員工和職員的運作，我還與所有成員建立了特殊的友誼，我將永遠懷念他們。

在我辭職的同時，我希望 Optigma 企業有限公司在他們所有的商業奮鬥中都有一個光明和豐饒的未來。我懇請您批准我的辭呈，並撥電話 5793-3682 與我聯絡，以確認我的離職。

雅各・特納 敬上
總經理
Optigma 企業有限公司

TEST 02
PART 7

158. What is implied about what he gained during his time at the organization?

(A) Stronger team management skills
(B) Ability to supervise and manage staff in the HR department
(C) Stronger negotiation skills
(D) Ability to resolve conflicts between enterprises

他說他在該機構期間獲得了什麼？

(A) 更強的團隊管理技能
(B) 監督和管理人力資源部門員工的能力
(C) 更強的談判技巧
(D) 解決企業之間衝突的能力

159. Why is Jacob resigning from his position at Optigma Enterprises Limited?

(A) They won't give him a promotion.
(B) There are too many disputes between staff members.
(C) He wants to find a more suitable position at another company.
(D) He doesn't feel competent enough to handle the work.

為什麼雅各辭去 Optigma 企業有限公司的職務？

(A) 他們不會給他晉升。
(B) 工作人員之間的爭議太多。
(C) 他想在另一家公司找到更合適的職位。
(D) 他覺得自己沒有足夠的能力來應付這項工作。

160. The word "tenure" in paragraph 2, line 2, is closest in meaning to

(A) reign
(B) ownership
(C) time in office
(D) residence

第二段第二行的 tenure 意思最接近以下何者？

(A)（君主）統治時期
(B) 所有權
(C) 任期
(D) 官邸

單字			
enterprise 企業；公司	resignation 辭職；辭呈	esteemed 受人尊敬的
tenure 任期	oversee 監督	endeavor 努力；盡力

Questions 161 to 163 refer to the following invitation.

Dear esteemed staff and colleagues,

As we approach the end of the fiscal year, I would like to take this opportunity to show my appreciation for all the effort you have put into increasing our annual turnover during the last fiscal year. -[1]-

I would like to extend an invitation to all of you to attend our special event our general manager has arranged to reward you for your hard work. It will be held on Saturday, the 15th of June. -[2]- We have arranged a special trip to a winery in Cleveland, where we will enjoy a long, extravagant lunch in a restaurant overlooking a picturesque scenic spot. After enjoying lunch, we will have the chance to taste fruity red wine fresh from the vineyard, and then take a tour of the local scenic spots. I can guarantee it will be an unforgettable day. -[3]-

Activity details are as follows:

Activity Venue: Versailles Valley Vineyards
Meeting place prior to the activity: The front of our company's office
Meeting time prior to the activity: 7:30 a.m.
Time to return to the office: 6 p.m.

Would all who are interested in joining us on this special occasion please send an email to me at winston.brighton@gmail.com? -[4]- The last day to confirm your attendance is the 5th of June, 2019.

Yours truly,

Winston Brighton
Vice General Manager
Sequel Enterprises

TEST 02
PART 7

161-163 題參考以下邀請函。

親愛而可敬的員工和同事們：

在我們接近會計年度結束時，我想藉此機會，對你們在上一會計年度為增加年營業額所付出的所有努力表示感激。-[1]-

我想邀請大家參加我們總經理已經安排好的獎勵大家的特別活動。它將於 6 月 15 日星期六舉行。-[2]- 我們安排了一次特別的旅遊，去克里夫蘭的一個釀酒廠，在那裡我們將在一個俯瞰風景如畫景點的餐廳享受悠長而奢華的午餐。享用午餐後，我們將有機會品嚐剛釀好的新鮮果味紅葡萄酒，然後參觀當地的景點。我可以保證那肯定是難忘的一天。-[3]-

活動詳情如下：

活動地點：凡爾賽谷葡萄園
集合地點：我們公司的辦公室前
集合時間：上午 7:30
回辦公室的時間：下午 6 點

如果有興趣參加這個盛會，請發送電子郵件至 winston.brighton@gmail.com。-[4]- 確認您要參加的最後日期是 2019 年 6 月 5 日。

溫斯頓‧布萊頓 敬上
副總經理
希閎企業

161. In which of the position marked [1], [2], [3], and [4] does the following sentence best belong?

"We have had our share of ups and downs, and despite the great amount of pressure, you all performed extremely well."

(A) [1]
(B) [2]
(C) [3]
(D) [4]

下面的句子最適合放在標示 [1]、[2]、[3] 和 [4] 的哪個位置？

「我們共同經歷了很多盛衰起伏，儘管面臨巨大的壓力，你們都表現得非常好。」

(A) [1]
(B) [2]
(C) [3]
(D) [4]

---

162. The word "extravagant" in paragraph 2, line 4, is closest in meaning to

(A) normal
(B) moderate
(C) costly
(D) ridiculous

第二段第四行的 extravagant 意義最接近以下何者？

(A) 正常的
(B) 適度的
(C) 昂貴的
(D) 荒謬的

---

163. What is true about the trip the workers will go on?

(A) They will pay a lot of money for the bus ride.
(B) They will enjoy white wine.
(C) They will be able to take in impressive scenery.
(D) All workers were invited by the secretary.

關於員工要去的旅遊，何者為真？

(A) 他們將為搭乘巴士付很多錢。
(B) 他們將享用白葡萄酒。
(C) 他們將能夠欣賞到難以忘懷的美景。
(D) 秘書邀請所有員工。

單字
fiscal year 財政年度，會計年度
turnover（某一時期內的）營業額
picturesque 美麗如畫的
ups and downs 盛衰起伏
extravagant 奢侈的，奢華的

TEST 02
PART 7

Questions 164 to 167 refer to the following text message chain.

Timothy [6:13 a.m.]
In the last five weeks, I've been experiencing lots of problems with my landlord. My apartment is old and I asked the landlord to inspect which things need to be repaired. He refused to do so. Also, last week I tripped over a crack in my front pathway and fractured my wrist.

Bradley [6:14 p.m.]
That's terrible. Did you let him know what happened?

Timothy [6:16 p.m.]
Yes, I did. I talked this over with my landlord, and he didn't seem to care. He even said that since I was paying so little rent, I should repair the house and pathway myself.

Bradley [6:18 p.m.]
That's ridiculous. I think you should seek arbitration and file a personal injury claim so you can be compensated.

Timothy [6:19 p.m.]
I'm planning on doing that. But with my landlord's strong personality, it'll be a waste of time trying to reconcile our differences.

Bradley [6:21 p.m.]
I guess you could consider litigation, even though it will be a lengthy and costly process.

Timothy [6:25 p.m.]
Litigating can cost a person a lot of money, and I don't want to spend so much right now. However, I'm certain this is serious and I doubt arbitrators can make sure that justice is done.

Bradley [6:28 p.m.]
I understand. I have been through something similar to you a while ago. After my company's landlord negligently caused a workplace accident, I hired a lawyer who was an expert in commercial and civil law to handle this situation. With his expertise, he helped my company to win the case.

Timothy [6:31 p.m.]
Well, you must know what you are talking about.

290

164-167 題參考以下一連串的簡訊。

提摩西 [6:13 a.m.]
在過去的五週裡，我和房東一直有很多問題。我的公寓老舊，我要求房東檢查哪些物件需要修理。他拒絕了。另外，上週我被門前小路上的裂縫絆倒，手腕骨折了。

布萊德利 [6:14 p.m.]
那太糟了。你有沒有讓他知道發生了什麼？

提摩西 [6:16 p.m.]
有，我告訴他了。我和我的房東談了這件事，但他似乎並不關心。他甚至說，既然我付這麼少租金，我應該自己修理房子和小路。

布萊德利 [6:18 p.m.]
這太荒謬了。我認為你應該尋求仲裁並提出人身傷害索賠，以便獲得賠償。

提摩西 [6:19 p.m.]
我打算這樣做。但由於我的房東個性很強，試圖調解我們的分歧很浪費時間。

布萊德利 [6:21 p.m.]
我想你可以考慮訴訟，即使這將是一個漫長而花費很高的過程。

提摩西 [6:25 p.m.]
訴訟可能會花費很多錢，而且我現在不想花這麼多錢。但是，我確定事態嚴重，我懷疑仲裁人能否確保正義得到伸張。

布萊德利 [6:28 p.m.]
我明白。我不久前經歷過與你類似的事情。在我公司的房東因疏忽而造成工傷事故後，我聘請了一名律師，他是商事法和民法專家，由他處理這種情況。憑藉他的專業知識，他幫我的公司贏得了此案。

提摩西 [6:31 p.m.]
好吧，你說的有道理。

TEST 02
PART 7

164. What was suggested about the landlord?

(A) He takes good care of his property.
(B) He wants to take his tenant to court.
(C) He likes to spend money on repairs.
(D) He was negligent and doesn't want to compensate his tenant.

這裡暗示關於房東的哪件事？

(A) 他把他的房地產照顧得很好。
(B) 他想把他的房客告上法庭。
(C) 他喜歡花錢修理。
(D) 他怠忽職責並且不想賠償他的房客。

165. What is Bradley's opinion of litigation?

(A) It is costly and ineffective.
(B) Lawyers won't be able to solve his problem.
(C) It will save him more time than arbitration.
(D) It can ensure that justice is done for Timothy.

布萊德利對打官司的看法是什麼？

(A) 成本高且效率低。
(B) 律師無法解決他的問題。
(C) 與仲裁相比，可為他節省更多時間。
(D) 可以確保為提摩西伸張正義。

166. What did Bradley mention about the incident in his workplace?

(A) His landlord refused to fix the leaking ceiling.
(B) An accident happened.
(C) A death at his workplace led to litigation.
(D) His landlord can't be reasoned with.

布萊德利提到關於工作場所的什麼事？

(A) 他的房東拒絕修復漏水的天花板。
(B) 發生了一起事故。
(C) 他工作場所的死亡事件導致訴訟。
(D) 他的房東不講道理。

167. At 6:31 p.m., what does Timothy mean when he writes "Well, you must know what you are talking about."?

(A) He decided to take the case to a lawyer.
(B) Bradley is adamant that only arbitration will not work.
(C) Bradley knows lots of about civil law.
(D) Bradley has a good knowledge of commercial leases.

提摩西在下午 6 點 31 分時寫下 "Well, you must know what you are talking about." 的意圖為何？

(A) 他決定把此案交給律師。
(B) 布萊德利堅持認為僅是仲裁的話不會有效。
(C) 布萊德利很了解民法。
(D) 布萊德利很懂商業租約。

單字	landlord 房東	compensate 賠償	litigation 訴訟
	arbitration 仲裁	arbitrator 仲裁人	expertise 專業知識

Questions 168 to 171 refer to the following autobiography.

Autobiography

My name is Lucas Trump. I was born in Australia and raised in America, so I have dual citizenship. When I was in the second year of university, I successfully applied for a scholarship and was an exchange student in National Tokyo University for one year. During this year, I spent my spare time teaching English as a tutor on a part-time basis. After I graduated with a master's degree in English Language Instruction, I decided to stay in Japan and teach children and adults English.

I have a deep passion for teaching English, and it's this passion that drives me to continuously find ways to upgrade my teaching skills and excel as a language teacher. Currently, I am an English teacher at Amami Senior High School. I have wide experience in speaking, reading, writing and listening instruction, as well as helping students prepare for exams like TOEFL and IELTS. I have taught in high schools for more than one year, in university for one year as a part-time teacher, and in adult English cram schools for over 4 years. I have also taught junior high school students and young children English.

My father is an entrepreneur who runs a mechanic business, my mother is a housewife, my older brother is a general practitioner and a part-time lecturer in university. My older sister is an accountant and lives with her husband in North America, my younger brother is still pursuing his studies, my wife is Japanese who is very frugal and works hard to make our domestic life happy. My future goal is to further upgrade my language teaching skills and knowledge of well-rounded education so that I can help other Japanese students greatly improve their English. At the same time, I hope that I can strive towards becoming a high-level manager and educator, and give full play to my professional skills while working and growing in my career.

I sincerely hope that I will have an opportunity to work in cooperation with your company. It would be a great honor to use my teaching skills and methods to help English learners in your school, and be an example of excellence in English teaching.

168-171 題參考以下自傳。

自 傳

我的名字是盧卡斯・川普，我在澳洲出生，在美國長大，所以我有雙重國籍。當我在大學的第二年，我成功申請到獎學金，並在國立東京大學做了一年的交換生。在這一年裡，我利用業餘時間以兼職的方式當家教教英語。我以英語語言教學碩士畢業後，決定留在日本，教孩子和成人英語。

我對英語教學充滿熱情，正是這種熱情促使我不斷尋找提升教學技巧並成為優異語言教師的方法。目前，我是奮美高中的英語教師。我在口說、閱讀、寫作和聽力教學方面擁有豐富的經驗，並幫助學生準備托福和雅思等考試。我在高中教了一年多，在大學兼任教了一年，在成人英語補習班教了四年多。我也教過初中生和幼兒英語。

我的父親是一名經營機械業務的企業家，我的母親是家庭主婦，我的哥哥是家醫科醫師，也是大學的兼任講師。我的姐姐是一名會計師，和她的丈夫一起住在北美，我的弟弟仍在求學，我的妻子是非常節儉的日本人，努力使我們的家庭生活幸福。我未來的目標是進一步提升我的語言教學技能和通才教育的知識，這樣我就可以幫助其他日本學生大幅提升他們的英語程度。與此同時，我希望我能夠努力成為一名高階經理和教育工作者，並在工作和職涯成長的同時充分發揮我的專業技能。

我真誠地希望我有機會與貴公司合作。能夠用我的教學技巧和方法幫助你們學校裡學英語的學生，並成為英語教學的卓越典範，我將感到非常榮幸。

168. What is Mr. Trump's main goal as an English teacher?

(A) To teach children's English in the future
(B) To teach students how to pass the TOEFL exam
(C) To work in high-level management
(D) To do teacher training

川普先生做英語教師的主要目標是什麼？

(A) 將來教兒童英語
(B) 教學生如何通過托福考試
(C) 從事高階管理工作
(D) 做教師培訓

---

169. The word "excel" in paragraph 2, line 2, is closest in meaning to

(A) to conquer
(B) to be inferior
(C) to be proficient
(D) to overcome

第二段第二行的 excel 意義最接近以下何者？

(A) 征服
(B) 低一等
(C) 精通
(D) 克服

---

170. What kind of teaching experience does Mr. Trump have?

(A) He has experience teaching junior high school students.
(B) He has worked in adult language instruction for over 6 years.
(C) He has taught as a full-time English lecturer.
(D) He was a full-time English tutor.

川普先生有什麼樣的教學經歷？

(A) 他有教國中學生的經驗。
(B) 他已從事成人語言教學超過 6 年。
(C) 他曾擔任全職英語講師。
(D) 他是一名全職英語家教。

---

171. What is true about Mr. Trump's family?

(A) All of his family members are in Australia.
(B) His father works as a family doctor.
(C) His older brother is an accountant.
(D) His spouse is from Japan.

關於川普先生的家人何者為真？

(A) 他的所有家庭成員都在澳洲。
(B) 他的父親是一名家庭醫師。
(C) 他的哥哥是一名會計師。
(D) 他的配偶來自日本。

單字
dual citizenship 雙重國籍
frugal 節儉的
general practitioner 家醫科醫師
well-rounded 全面的；多方面的

TEST 02
PART 7

Questions 172 to 175 refer to the following letter.

Bidbest Inc.
13 Whicter Road,
Gillman QLD, Australia
www.bidbest.co.au

March 24
Michael Murray
Teys F & B Corporation
1420 Alice Boulevard
Tokyo, Japan

Dear Mr. Murray,

I would like to take this opportunity to introduce my company to you. Bidbest Inc. has been recognized as one of the most prominent and pioneering food and beverage distributors in Queensland, Australia. -[1]- We have developed over 60 business units and we specialize in wholesaling food service, fresh produce, beer, and meat. We offer customers an extensive range of fresh produce, which is from 400-600 lines depending on the season. We have a splendid array of all prime, sub-prime and portion control cuts such as pork, veal, beef, lamb, game and poultry. -[2]- In addition, our company is also a market leader when it comes to distributing frozen seafood, cleaning products, and packaging materials. -[3]-

Our comprehensive product range, exceptional service, and user-friendly order facilities enable us to service a wide variety of customers. Some of our customers include pubs and clubs, hotels, restaurants, pizza shops, hospitals, offices, retirement villages, and prisons.

I became aware of your expertise in exportation and business expansion overseas from a brochure that was mailed to my office. -[4]- Please find enclosed this letter a detailed explanation of how my company plans to export to Japan. When I am not tied up with work, which will be in the next week or two, I'll take some time to visit you so we can discuss this in detail. Please advise me of a suitable time to visit you and take a look at my business plan.

I look forward to hearing from you.

Best regards,
Beckham White,
President, Bidbest Inc.

172-175 題參考以下信件。

Bidbest 公司
惠克特路 13 號
澳洲昆士蘭州吉爾曼區
www.bidbest.co.au

3 月 24 日
麥可・莫瑞
Teys F & B 公司
日本東京愛麗絲大道 1420 號

親愛的莫瑞先生：

我想藉此機會向您介紹我的公司。我們 Bidbest 公司已獲公認為澳洲昆士蘭州最著名和最具開創性的食品和飲料經銷商之一。-[1]- 我們已經發展出 60 多個營業單位，我們專門從事批發餐飲服務、新鮮農產品、啤酒和肉類。我們為客戶提供種類繁多的新鮮產品，按照季節有 400 至 600 種之多。我們有一系列上好的極佳、特選和切割分裝的肉品，如豬肉、小牛肉、牛肉、羊肉、野味和家禽肉。-[2]- 此外，我們公司在經銷冷凍海鮮、清潔產品和包裝材料方面也是市場領導者。-[3]-

我們全面的產品系列、卓越的服務和用戶方便使用的訂購功能使我們能夠為廣泛的客戶提供服務。我們的客戶包括酒吧和俱樂部、旅館、餐館、比薩餅店、醫院、辦公室、退休村和監獄。

收到郵寄給我辦公室的小冊子後，我了解了您在出口海外和業務拓展方面的專業知識。-[4]- 隨函附上資料，其中詳細說明我的公司計劃如何出口日本。如果我有空，可能在下週或下兩週，我會花一些時間去拜訪您，這樣我們就可以詳細討論了。請告訴我適合拜訪您的時間並看看我的商業計劃書。

我期待著您的回音。

祝好
貝克漢・懷特
總經理
Bidbest 公司

TEST 02
PART 7

172. What is the purpose of this letter?

(A) To introduce the way Bidbest does international business
(B) To propose a joint venture with an exportation company
(C) To introduce the correct ways to choose meat
(D) To make an inquiry about how to expand their business overseas

這封信的目的是什麼？

(A) 介紹 Bidbest 展開國際業務的方式
(B) 與出口公司建立合資企業
(C) 介紹選擇肉類的正確方法
(D) 詢問如何拓展海外業務

---

173. The word "array" in paragraph 1, line 5, is closest in meaning to

(A) display
(B) adornment
(C) package
(D) settlement

第一段第五行的 array 意義最接近以下何者？

(A) 大批；系列
(B) 裝飾品
(C) 包裹
(D) 結算

---

174. In which of the position marked [1], [2], [3], and [4] does the following sentence best belong?
"As we are seeking to expand to Japan, I'm hoping to know the steps that I should take to develop the Japanese market."

(A) [1]
(B) [2]
(C) [3]
(D) [4]

下面的句子最適合放在標示 [1]、[2]、[3] 和 [4] 的哪個位置？

「在我們尋求擴展到日本的時候，我希望知道我應該採取哪些措施來發展日本市場。」

(A) [1]
(B) [2]
(C) [3]
(D) [4]

---

175. What does Mr. White plan to do in the near future?

(A) Write up a business proposal for Mr. Murray
(B) Start distributing products to retirement villages
(C) Talk about his plan to export with Mr. Murray
(D) Send an email to a business consultation company

懷特先生計劃在不久的將來做些什麼？

(A) 幫莫瑞先生寫一份商業企劃書
(B) 開始向退休村經銷產品
(C) 與莫瑞先生談談他的出口計劃
(D) 發一封電子郵件給商業諮詢公司

單字　prominent 著名的；重要的　　pioneering 開創性的　　distributor 經銷商
　　　specialize in 專攻；專門從事　wholesale 批發　　　　facility 設施；功能

Questions 176 to 180 refer to the following message and announcement.

Hi Fred,

Recently, I have been thinking that we need to implement some strategies that will both motivate all employees to work to their full potential and also recognize their contributions to the company. The best way to do this is to start an employee reward program so we can overtly reward four of the most earnest and productive workers each month of the year. This will not only encourage all employees to engage in healthy competition, it will certainly increase workers' performance. We can consider using cash prizes, but the rewards shouldn't be only confined to monetary compensation. We could also use other forms of incentives, such as free company parking for a month, a day off work, or coupon to a local spa.

Please write up a list of the most efficient and diligent workers in your department, and give them awards according to the following categories:

Name of Award	Achievement of Employee
Most Innovative Employee	Contribution and execution of creative ideas to enhance product development.
Outstanding Salesman of the Month	Increasing number of loyal clients and reaching or surpassing a sales target set by the sales department manager.
Excellence in Customer Service	Offering clients top-notch service that leads to clients' referral of other customers to our company and a dramatic increase in sales.
Best Team Player	Showing integrity in one's work ethics, being a cooperative and hardworking team player, and promptly fulfilling the tasks assigned by one's team leader.

I have already announced to all department heads that this program will start at the beginning of next month. You'll be in charge of organizing the awards from now on.

Yours,
Jimmy Abbot
CEO of Hummingbird International

Employee of the Month
Oliver Addington
1st of February, 2019

On behalf of Hummingbird International, I would like to extend our warmest congratulations to Oliver Addington, who has been the most efficient and productive worker in November. A recent graduate from the Weber State University, Utah, Oliver joined us in 2016 and immediately mastered the skills of leading a sales team and handling customer inquiries and complaints. During the course of the last five months, he has spent many hours of his personal time sharpening his sales skills by attending self-development seminars.

Oliver went through many months of arduous effort in order to complete the tasks that were assigned him. In the month of January this year, he single-handedly managed to generate in excess of $25,000 from selling vacuum cleaners, which surpasses the record that Kyle Dylan set at the end of last quarter by $7,000. He always shows a passion for excellence in customer service and this increased our frequent customer base by 10%. Most of these customers stated that they came to our store because our products were recommended by their friends. This accomplishment is not only quite exceptional, it also proves that anything is possible with persistence and hard work.

To show our appreciation for his dedication to our company's goals, our company is paying for Oliver's 6-day trip to the Bahamas for Christmas this year. This young man is an example to all of what dedication and passion for your work can do. All employees here have the potential to achieve exactly what Mr. Addington has done by earnestly completing the assigned tasks.

We congratulate Oliver for his great achievements and sincerely hope he keeps up the good work.

Fred Gardner
Sales Manager

176-180 題參考以下訊息與公告。

嗨，福瑞德：

最近，我一直在考慮我們需要執行一些策略，這些策略既可以激勵所有員工充分發揮潛力，也可以表揚他們對公司的貢獻。實現這一目標的最佳方式是啟動員工獎勵計劃，以便我們可以在一年中的每個月公開獎勵四位最認真和最具成效的員工。這不僅可以鼓勵所有員工參與良性競爭，也一定能提高員工的績效。我們可以考慮使用現金獎勵，但獎勵不應僅限於金錢報酬。我們也可以使用其他形式的獎勵措施：例如免費在公司停車一個月、休假一天或當地水療中心的優惠卷。

請列出您所在部門中效率最高、最勤奮的員工名單，並根據以下類別給予獎勵：

獎項名稱	員工的成就
最佳創意員工獎	貢獻並執行創意，以加強產品開發。
本月傑出推銷員獎	忠誠客戶數量增加，達到或超過銷售部門經理設定的銷售目標。
卓越客戶服務獎	為客戶提供一流的服務，使客戶將其他客戶轉介到我們公司，銷售額大幅增加。
最佳團隊精神獎	在一個人的工作倫理中表現出誠信，成為一個配合度高且勤奮的團隊合作成員，並迅速完成其團隊領導者分配的任務。

我已經向所有部門主管宣布，這個計劃將在下個月初開始實施。從現在開始，你將負責籌備獎項。

吉米・艾博特
蜂鳥國際公司執行長

TEST 02 PART 7

本月最佳員工
奧利佛・愛丁頓
2019 年 2 月 1 日

我謹代表蜂鳥國際公司向奧利佛・愛丁頓表示最熱烈的祝賀，他是 11 月份最有效率和最具成效的工作伙伴。不久前畢業於猶他州韋伯州立大學的奧利佛於 2016 年加入我們，並立即掌握了領導銷售團隊和處理客戶諮詢與投訴的技能。在過去的五個月中，他花了很多個人時間，透過參加自我發展研討會來提升他的銷售技巧。

奧利佛經歷了好幾個月的艱辛努力，以完成分配給他的任務。在今年 1 月份，他憑藉銷售真空吸塵器一手創造了超過 25,000 美元的銷售額，比凱爾・狄倫在上一季末設定的銷售額超出 7,000 美元。在客戶服務方面，他總是表現出卓越的熱情，這使我們的常客群增加了 10%。大多數客戶表示，他們來到我們的商店是因為我們的產品是他們的朋友推薦的。此一成就不僅非常優異，而且證明藉由堅持不懈與努力，任何成就都是可能的。

為了感謝他對公司目標的努力奉獻，我們公司打算支付奧利佛今年聖誕節 6 天巴哈馬之旅的費用。這位年輕人就是所有人的榜樣，他對工作有如此的奉獻和熱情。透過認真完成分配到的任務，這裡的所有員工都有潛力達成像愛丁頓先生的成就。

我們祝賀奧利佛取得了非凡成就，並衷心希望他能繼續保持優異的表現。

福瑞德・加德納
銷售經理

---

176. According to the two passages, which awards will Mr. Addington receive?

(A) Most Innovative Employee; Best Team Player
(B) Outstanding Salesman of the Month; Excellence in Customer Service
(C) Excellence in Customer Service; Most Innovative Employee
(D) Most Innovative Employee; Outstanding Salesman of the Month

根據這兩篇文字內容，愛丁頓先生將獲得哪些獎項？

(A) 最佳創意員工獎、最佳團隊精神獎
(B) 本月傑出推銷員獎、卓越客戶服務獎
(C) 卓越客戶服務獎、最佳創意員工獎
(D) 最佳創意員工獎、本月傑出推銷員獎

177. What is indicated about Mr. Addington's performance at work?

(A) He demonstrates integrity and completes tasks best by cooperating with others.
(B) He greatly increased the company's customer base.
(C) His passion for manufacturing increased his sales amount.
(D) He exceeded the highest sales record by $5000.

178. What is true about the company's employee reward program?

(A) The best employees are only rewarded with money.
(B) Staff members are encouraged after they come up with creative ways to enhance customer service.
(C) Rewarding employees' hard work encourages friendly competition.
(D) Those who are adept at customer service usually get the best reward.

179. In the message, the word "overtly" in paragraph 1, line 4, is closest in meaning to

(A) sharply
(B) undoubtedly
(C) publicly
(D) precisely

180. What is true about the way that Mr. Addington was recognized?

(A) His company paid for his trip to Hawaii.
(B) The company wrote a letter of appreciation to him for his hard work.
(C) His company gave him 5 days off work.
(D) His department manager publicly recognized him for his diligence in completing his work.

TEST 02 PART 7

單字			
	implement 實施；執行	overtly 公開地	confine 局限
	incentive 獎勵；誘因	innovative 創新的；革新的	execution 執行；履行
	surpass 超過	top-notch 第一流的	integrity 正直；誠實；誠信
	sharpen 改善；提升	arduous 艱辛的；艱鉅的；費力的	customer base 客戶群
	earnestly 認真地		

Questions 181 to 185 refer to the following advertisement and letter.

Hiring: Highly competent manager assistant.

Job description: Woolworths is searching for a talented worker to take on the position of manager assistant.

Job requirements: The person must have good interpersonal communication skills, as well as be very efficient in dealing with very stressful situations. It is essential that applicants hold a bachelor's degree in business management or marketing, as they will be more qualified to hold this position.

Job description: The person's responsibilities will include assisting the general manager of Woolworths with paperwork as well as advertising and marketing Woolworths in the local district.

Salary: Negotiable. Based on the person's experience in business.

Starting date: Within the next 30 to 50 days.

January 13, 2019

Dear Brett Scoffield,

I am writing to apply for the position of manager assistant that was published in the *Greenwich Newspaper* last Monday. I have attached my resume to this letter and hope that you consider me for this position.

To summarize my resume, I would have to say that I fit most of the characteristics needed to apply for this job. I worked as the assistant for the chief operating officer in a computer company during the past five years. I am proficient in processing information with Word, Office and handling complicated tasks at the same time. I am a conscientious worker and have carried out many tasks that involve interpersonal communication in my last job. I also have lots of experience in business planning and coordination. I believe that this experience in business gives me a competitive advantage over other applicants and makes me more qualified to hold the position of manager assistant.

I have a question regarding my qualification for this job. I don't hold a bachelor's degree in business management or have lots of experience in marketing. However, I do have a business certification. Do you still see me as qualified to take on this position? I am willing to put the effort into getting a higher degree and learning the skills required to do this job well.

Thanks,
Andrew Lackley

TEST 02 PART 7

181-185 題參考以下廣告和信件。

招　　聘：高度勝任的經理助理

工作描述：伍爾沃斯公司正在尋找一名有才能的人員擔任經理助理。

工作要求：該人員必須具備良好的人際溝通技巧，並且能夠非常有效率地處理高壓力情境。申請者必須持有企業管理或市場行銷學士學位，因為他們更有資格擔任這個職位。

工作內容：該人員的職責包括協助伍爾沃斯公司的總經理進行文書工作，並在當地為伍爾沃斯公司做廣告和行銷。

薪　　水：面議。根據該人員的商務經歷。

開始日期：未來 30 到 50 天內。

2019 年 1 月 13 日

親愛的布瑞特・史考菲爾：

我正寫信申請上週一你們在《格林威治報》上刊登的經理助理的職位。我已經在這封信中附上了我的簡歷，並希望您把我列入這個職位的考慮人選。

總結我的簡歷，我不得不說，我符合這項工作所需的大部分特點。過去五年，我擔任電腦公司營運長的助理。我善於用 Word、Office 處理資訊，同時處理複雜的任務。我是一名認真負責的員工，在我上一份工作中執行了許多有關人際溝通的工作。我在商業計畫和協調方面也有很多經驗。我相信這種商業經驗使我比其他申請者更具有競爭優勢，使我更有資格擔任經理助理的職位。

我對這份工作的資格有疑問。我沒有取得企業管理學士學位，也沒有很多的行銷經歷，但是我確實擁有商業認證的證書。您還認為我有資格擔任這個職位嗎？我願意努力獲得更高的學位，並學習做好這項工作所需的技能。

謝謝
安德魯・拉克利

181. What is the purpose of the advertisement?

(A) To hire a suitable marketing expert for their company
(B) To find a manager assistant
(C) To find a suitable sales assistant
(D) To hire a clerk

這則廣告的目的是什麼?

(A) 為他們的公司聘請合適的行銷專家
(B) 找一位經理助理
(C) 尋找合適的銷售助理
(D) 僱用一名職員

---

182. According to the advertisement, what type of work will the successful applicant do?

(A) Give presentations on the business he works at
(B) Represent the company at large events
(C) Plan business trips for the general manager
(D) Do lots of marketing and advertisement for Woolworths

根據廣告,應徵成功者將要做什麼類型的工作?

(A) 報告他從事的業務
(B) 在大型活動中代表公司
(C) 幫總經理規劃商務行程
(D) 為伍爾沃斯公司做大量的行銷和廣告

---

183. What makes Mr. Lackley qualified for this position?

(A) He is a good communicator and very diligent.
(B) He holds a bachelor's degree in business administration.
(C) He's experienced in marketing and advertising.
(D) He's a good public speaker.

是什麼使得拉克利先生能夠勝任這個職位?

(A) 他是一位很好的溝通者,而且很勤奮。
(B) 他持有企業管理學士學位。
(C) 他在行銷和廣告方面經驗豐富。
(D) 他是一個很好的公眾演講者。

---

184. According to the letter, what is true about Andrew's work experience?

(A) He was in charge of designing advertisements.
(B) He worked as a C-level executive.
(C) He is skillful when it comes to using computers.
(D) He worked hard at marketing his manager's products.

根據信件,安德魯的工作經歷何者正確?

(A) 他負責設計廣告。
(B) 他曾擔任高階主管。
(C) 在使用電腦方面他很熟練。
(D) 他努力推銷經理的產品。

---

185. In the letter, the word "coordination" in paragraph 2, line 6, is closest in meaning to

(A) grouping
(B) sorting
(C) organization
(D) sizing

在信件中,第二段第六行的 coordination 意義最接近以下何者?

(A) 分組
(B) 分類
(C) 安排(協調)
(D) 按尺寸製作

307

TEST 02 PART 7

單字

competent 能勝任的	talented 有才能的	interpersonal 人際的
efficient 效率高的	deal with 處理	situation 情境
essential 絕對必要的	marketing 行銷	responsibility 職責;責任
district 地區	attach 附加,附上	summarize 總結;概述
characteristic 特徵;特性;特點	previously 以前	proficient 精通的
process 處理	conscientious 認真負責的	carry out 執行
competitive 競爭的	advantage 優勢;利益	applicant 申請人;求職者
qualification 資格;資歷	certification 證書	

Questions 186 to 190 refer to the following autobiography and emails.

Dear Mr. Stratsfield,

My name is Andrew Johnson. In reference to your job advertisement in the *China Times*, I'm writing to apply for the position of HR manager in your company. I have attached my resume. Below is a copy of my autobiography for your reference. Please contact me in regard to my application as soon as possible.

Andrew Johnson

> **Autobiography**
>
> I was born in America and grew up in Australia. My major in university was human resource management. When I was in the third year of university, I worked as the assistant of a human resource coordinator and learnt the skills of workforce planning and supervision. After I graduated with my bachelor's degree in international business, I decided to continue working in the same company, and was eventually promoted to manager at the HR department. I am very experienced in both managing and supervising staff, and inspiring workers to perform their best in the company.
>
> I am a responsible and earnest worker and have a deep passion for excellence in business. I make sure that I complete each task with particular attention to detail. I always find ways to upgrade my work skills and deepen my knowledge of how to run a business successfully. At the beginning of next year, I will obtain a dual master's degree in human resources and business management. Upon graduation, I hope to use my professional knowledge to help other people reach their potential in the workplace.
>
> It would be a great honor to use my management skills and methods to contribute to your company and be a great example in workplace management.

TEST 02
PART 7

To:	ajohnson.highmanagement@gmail.com
From:	stratsfieldnumber1@gmail.com
Subject:	Job application
Date:	June 25, 2019

Dear Mr. Johnson,

Thank you for your application and autobiography. My boss and I looked over your resume, and have to clarify some details about the nature of the job we are advertising. If you fit the requirements, then you will most likely be hired.

Firstly, my boss requires applicants to have 5 years of experience managing large teams of more than 40 staff members. Do you have this kind of experience? Secondly, we need applicants to have effective negotiation skills and experience handling conflict between staff. How much experience do you have in negotiation?

Please answer these questions and I will get back to you on the result of your application.

Sincerely,
John Stratsfield

To:	stratsfieldnumber1@gmail.com
From:	johnson.highmanagement@gmail.com
Subject:	Re: Job application
Date:	June 26, 2019

Dear Mr. Stratsfield,

Thank you for your letter. To answer your first question, I was the manager of a company with over 55 staff for a period of 6 years. During my time there, I resolved lots of disputes. I also evaluated staff performance, and offered training and consultations to improve the efficiency of staff work habits. With the support and guidance of my general manager, I handled issues related to salary, work benefits, and managed conflict between staff members.

Hope to hear from you soon.

Andrew Johnson

186-190 題參考以下自傳和電子郵件。

親愛的史特拉斯菲爾德先生：

我叫安德魯・強生。我在《中國時報》看到貴公司的人事廣告，我寫信應徵貴公司的人力資源經理職位。我附上了我的簡歷。以下是我的自傳，供您參考。請盡快與我聯繫。

安德魯・強生

自傳

我出生在美國，在澳洲長大。我的大學主修是人力資源管理。大三的時候，我擔任人力資源協調員的助理，學習了勞動力規劃和監督的技能。拿到國際商業學士學位後，我決定繼續在同一家公司工作，最後晉升為人力資源部門的經理。我在管理、監督員工和鼓舞員工於公司中表現出色這些方面非常有經驗。

我是一個負責任和認真的工作者，對商業上的卓越表現具有極大的熱情。我確保完成每項任務，並且特別注意細節。我總能找到提升工作技能的方法，並加深我對如何成功經營企業的了解。明年初，我將獲得人力資源和企業管理雙碩士學位。一畢業後，我希望用我的專業知識幫助其他人充分發揮他們在工作場所的潛能。

能夠用我的管理技能和方法為貴公司做出貢獻，並成為職場管理的卓越典範，將是我的榮幸。

收件者：	ajohnson.highmanagement@gmail.com
寄件者：	stratsfieldnumber1@gmail.com
主　旨：	工作應徵
日　期：	2019 年 6 月 25 日

親愛的強生先生：

感謝你的應徵和自傳。我和我的老闆瀏覽了您的簡歷，並且要澄清一些關於我們所廣告之工作性質的細節。如果您符合要求，那麼您最有可能獲得僱用。

首先，我的老闆要求應徵者有五年以上管理超過四十位員工團隊的經驗。您有這樣的經歷嗎？其次，我們需要應徵者擁有有效的談判技巧和處理員工之間衝突的經驗。您在談判方面有多少經驗？

請回答這些問題，我會回覆您的應徵結果。

約翰・史特拉斯菲爾德 謹啟

TEST 02
PART 7

收件者：	stratsfieldnumber1@gmail.com
寄件者：	ajohnson.highmanagement@gmail.com
主　旨：	Re: 工作應徵
日　期：	2019 年 6 月 26 日

親愛的史特拉斯菲爾德先生：

感謝您的來信。先回答您的第一個問題，我以前是一間公司的經理，有超過五十五名員工，為期六年。我在那裡時處理了很多糾紛。我也評估員工的工作表現，並提供培訓和諮詢，以提升員工工作習慣的效率。在總經理的支持和指導下，我處理過有關工作人員的薪資、工作福利等問題，並且解決了員工之間的衝突。

希望早日收到您的訊息。

安德魯・強生

---

186. What is the purpose of the email written by John Stratsfield?

(A) To inform Andrew that they can't hire him
(B) To clear up some issues regarding Andrew's work experience
(C) To inform Andrew that he is qualified for the position
(D) To arrange a time for an interview

約翰・史特拉斯菲爾德寫 email 的目的是什麼？

(A) 通知安德魯他們不能僱用他
(B) 澄清有關安德魯工作經驗的一些問題
(C) 通知安德魯他有資格擔任這個職位
(D) 安排面試時間

187. In the second email, the word "dispute" in line 3 is closest in meaning to

(A) conflict
(B) trouble
(C) problem
(D) confusion

在第二封電子郵件中，第三行的 dispute 意義最接近以下何者？

(A) 衝突
(B) 麻煩
(C) 問題
(D) 困惑

188. What is said about Andrew's communication skills?

(A) He is good at negotiating with other workers.
(B) He isn't a good communicator.
(C) He is experienced at negotiating the price of products.
(D) He lacks the skills to deal with disputes in the workplace.

這裡提到關於安德魯溝通技巧的哪件事？

(A) 他擅長與其他工作人員談判。
(B) 他不是一個好的溝通者。
(C) 他在產品價格方面的談判經驗豐富。
(D) 他缺乏處理職場紛爭的技能。

312

189. What skills does Andrew have that shows he's qualified for the position?

   (A) He excels in handling conflict, negotiating and inspiring workers to perform their best.
   (B) He has experience training workers from different organizations.
   (C) He has good time management skills.
   (D) He's a highly efficient worker.

安德魯有什麼技能顯示出他有資格擔任這個職位？

   (A) 他擅長處理衝突、談判和激勵員工。
   (B) 他有訓練來自不同組織員工的經驗。
   (C) 他有很好的時間管理能力。
   (D) 他是一名高效率的工作者。

190. What is stated about Andrew's knowledge of team management?

   (A) He is still learning the basics of managing staff.
   (B) He knows nothing about how to manage staff.
   (C) He already holds a degree in business management.
   (D) He has experience in leading large teams of workers, and was the manager of the HR department.

這裡指出安德魯了解團隊管理的哪件事？

   (A) 他仍在學習管理員工的基本知識。
   (B) 他對如何管理員工一無所知。
   (C) 他已經擁有企業管理學位。
   (D) 他具有管理大型員工團隊的經驗，曾擔任人力資源部門的經理。

單字

autobiography 自傳	assistant 助理	workforce 勞動力；全體員工
graduate 畢業	promote 晉升	supervise 監督
earnest 認真的	excellence 卓越	assign 分派，指派
particular 特別的	deepen 加深	dual master's degree 雙碩士學位
potential 潛能；潛力	resume 履歷（原為 résumé）	requirement 要求；必要條件
negotiation 談判；協商	resolve 解決	dispute 爭論；糾紛
evaluate 評價；評估	consultation 諮商；諮詢	improve 改善；提升
efficiency 效率	guidance 指導	

Questions 191 to 195 refer to the following online advertisement and emails.

Star Artefacts Galore

The finest collection of superstar collection items in USA!

Our store has a vast collection of highly sought-after items that were previously owned by American superstars. They are available for avid collectors and buyers to purchase.

Some of the items we have collected include many of Elvis Presley's belongings, such as his pink Cadillac, jumpsuit, bongos, the very Aloha shirt that he wore in his Hawaiian concerts, and a total of two hundred artefacts that have been moved from Graceland, Tennessee for preservation and sale. We also have items such as Michael Jackson's vest, as well as the white gloves and shoes that he wore at his Beat It concerts in the 1980s, and many more.

Our manager is also willing to pay 120% of the retail price to anyone who is in possession of collectable items once owned by a famous American superstar.

For more information, please visit us and decide what you'd like to purchase.

Price List for Products On Sale

Please click on the links below to view some of the artefacts that we are currently selling.

- Cars: Open for negotiation
- Instruments: $400
- Records, Tapes: $20
- Apparel: $50
- Music and songbooks that were signed by superstars: $70 to $90
- Accessories (rings, earrings, bracelets, etc): $25 to $35

For further information, please contact the store manager, Bob Stallard, at bstallard@sagalore.com.

Date:	January 21
From:	Sophia Calverta <scalverta@kmail.com>
To:	Star Artefacts Galore <sagalore@sagalore.com>
Subject:	Elvis Presley Guitar

Dear Mr. Stallard,

My father owns a beautiful Gibson J200 acoustic guitar that was owned by Elvis in the 1960s. I recently came across your website and thought that your shop might be interested in purchasing it.

The guitar was bought by Elvis in the early 1960s and was used for about half a decade in many of his concerts. My father purchased the guitar from an auction in Memphis for US$200 several years after Elvis passed away, and my father would like to sell it to a shop that cherishes such a valuable and historical item.

Please inform me of your purchasing procedures and how you would like to pay for the guitar.

Thank you,
Sophia Calverta

Date:	January 23
From:	Bob Stallard <bstallard@sagalore.com>
To:	Sophia Calverta <scalverta@kmail.com>
Subject:	Re: Elvis Presley Guitar

Dear Ms. Calverta,

Thank you for your email. I did some research into the guitar that you mentioned, and found that it is extremely rare and valuable. Upon examining the guitar, we should be able to buy it for $45 higher than what your father bought it for. Do you think that is fair?

In regard to method of payment, I think you should visit us in person and show us the guitar. We can pay you in cash after ensuring that it's in good condition.

Drop us a line and let us know when you plan to visit us.

Hope to see you soon.

Bob Stallard
Manager, Star Artefacts Galore

191-195 題參考以下線上廣告和電子郵件。

明星文物寶庫

（美國超級巨星收藏品最佳大集合！）

本店擁有大量十分搶手的品項，這些品項以前由美國超級巨星所擁有，可供渴望的收藏家和買家購買。

我們收集的品項包括許多貓王的個人物品，比如他的粉紅色凱迪拉克、連身褲、邦戈鼓、他在夏威夷音樂會上穿的阿羅哈襯衫，以及從田納西州雅園運過來的 200 件文物供保存和銷售。我們還有其他物品，比如麥可·傑克森的背心，以及他在 1980 年代的 Beat It 演唱會上穿戴的白色手套與鞋子等等。

我們經理也願意支付 120% 的零售價給任何擁有美國巨星曾擁有之可收藏物品的人。

欲了解更多訊息，請造訪我們並決定您想購買什麼。

銷售產品價目表
請點擊以下連結，查看我們當前銷售的一些文物。

- 汽車：開放議價
- 樂器：400 美元
- 唱片、錄音帶：20 美元
- 服裝：50 美元
- 有超級巨星簽名的唱片和樂譜：70-90 美元
- 配件（戒指、耳環、手鐲等）：25-35 美元

如需更多資訊，請聯繫店長鮑伯·斯塔拉爾，
bstallard@sagalore.com。

日　期：	1月21日
寄件者：	蘇菲亞・卡爾維達 <scalverta@kmail.com>
收件者：	明星文物寶庫 <sagalore@sagalore.com>
主　旨：	貓王吉他

親愛的史代勒先生：

我父親擁有一把漂亮的 Gibson J200 木吉他，在 1960 年代由貓王擁有。我最近偶然發現您的網站，認為您的店可能有興趣收購它。

這把吉他在 1960 年代初被貓王買下，在他的許多音樂會中使用了大概五年之久。我父親在貓王去世幾年後，在孟菲斯中的一場拍賣會上以 200 美元買了這把吉他，我父親想把它賣給一家珍視這種寶貴歷史文物的商店。

請告訴我你們的收購程序，以及您想如何支付這把吉他的價格。

謝謝
蘇菲亞・卡爾維達

日　期：	1月23日
寄件者：	鮑伯・斯塔拉爾 <bstallard@sagalore.com>
收件者：	蘇菲亞・卡爾維達 <scalverta@kmail.com>
主　旨：	Re：貓王吉他

親愛的卡爾維達小姐：

謝謝您的來信。我對您提到的吉他進行了一些研究，發現它非常罕見且非常珍貴。在我們檢查過吉他的品質後，應該可以提出比你父親當初購買時高出 45 美元的價格。您認為這樣合理嗎？

關於付款方式，我想您應該親自到我們這裡來，給我們看這把吉他。確定狀況良好後，我們可以用現金支付。

請寫信給我們，讓我們知道您打算何時造訪我們。

希望很快能見到您。

鮑伯・史代勒
經理
明星文物寶庫

TEST 02
PART 7

191. What is NOT true about Star Artefacts Galore?

(A) It has a large variety of American superstars' previously owned valuables.
(B) The shop is seeking to expand the range of items it sells.
(C) It only has two highly sought-after items that belonged to Michael Jackson.
(D) The store sells songbooks with superstars' signatures for a very high price.

關於明星文物寶庫，哪項不是真的？

(A) 它擁有各種美國超級巨星以前擁有的貴重物品。
(B) 該店正在尋求擴大其銷售品項種類的範圍。
(C) 它只有兩樣屬於麥可‧傑克森的搶手物品。
(D) 該店以昂貴的價格銷售超級巨星簽名的樂譜。

192. How much will Ms. Calverta sell her item to Mr. Stallard for?

(A) $250
(B) $245
(C) $240
(D) $230

卡爾維達小姐會以多少錢把她的東西賣給史代勒先生？

(A) $250
(B) $245
(C) $240
(D) $230

193. What is suggested about Ms. Calverta?

(A) Her father attended Elvis' concert in Hawaii.
(B) She owned an electric guitar used by Elvis.
(C) She has an acoustic guitar that Elvis played for several years.
(D) She bought Elvis' Cadillac at an auction in Memphis.

這裡暗示關於卡爾維達小姐的什麼事？

(A) 她的父親在夏威夷參加了貓王的音樂會。
(B) 她擁有貓王使用的電吉他。
(C) 她有一把貓王彈了好幾年的木吉他。
(D) 她在孟菲斯的一次拍賣會上買了貓王的凱迪拉克。

194. What is indicated about Star Artefacts Galore?

(A) It sells clothes that were worn by superstars.
(B) Most of the items they sell used to belong to Elvis Presley.
(C) The store buys any valuable items despite the quality.
(D) They pay for valuable items by wiring money to the customers.

這裡指出關於明星文物寶庫的什麼事？

(A) 它出售超級巨星穿過的衣服。
(B) 他們銷售的物品大部份是貓王過去擁有的東西。
(C) 店家購買任何有價值的物品，不論其品質。
(D) 他們透過匯款來支付有價值的物品。

195. What is the purpose of Ms. Calverta's email?

(A) To enquire about the price of a CD being sold by the store
(B) To understand how she can cooperate with the store in selling artefacts
(C) To make an inquiry into the quality of Michael Jackson's vest
(D) To see if the store is willing to buy a rare acoustic guitar

卡爾維達小姐發 email 的目的是什麼？

(A) 詢問該店裡一片 CD 的銷售價格
(B) 了解如何與他們合作銷售文物
(C) 詢問麥可・傑克森背心的品質
(D) 看看該店是否願意購買一把稀有的木吉他

單字			
	galore 豐富的；大量的	jumpsuit 連身褲	bongos 邦戈鼓
	preservation 保存；保護	be in possession of 擁有	apparel 服裝
	accessory 配件	bracelet 手鐲	acoustic guitar 木吉他
	cherish 珍愛；珍視	historical 歷史上的	in regard to 關於
	ensure 確保；確定	drop ... a line 寫短信／打電話給某人	

Questions 196 to 200 refer to the following notice, email, and article.

Attention Everyone!
Journalist Interview This Monday Afternoon

We have exciting news for all staff—*The Courier-Mail* will be doing a special report on our restaurant in an article that discusses the best restaurants to visit in Central Brisbane! The manager of the company has already contacted me and arranged for the reporters to come and interview the staff on Monday, 12th of December, at 12 p.m. Subsequent to the interview, photographers will also be there to take photos of our restaurant. The session will be between 40 minutes and 1 hour.

As this will be a great chance to increase our profits and exposure to the local community, I hope that all staff can place value on this meeting. All employees in our restaurant will be included.

Since we opened in July last year, the amount of frequent customers has almost doubled, so we all should be proud of being recognized by the media.

To:	Joseph Bates <jbates@trang.net>
From:	Jessica Robertson <jrobertson@couriermail.com>
Date:	Wednesday, 7th December
Subject:	Monday Interview Appointment

Dear Mr. Bates,

Last week we arranged to have an interview and photography session next Monday at 12:00 p.m. Owing to the fact that our work schedule will be busy that day, could we possibly change the time to 12:20 p.m.? Please make sure to confirm this time with your staff and let me know by tomorrow morning. As discussed last time, the interview and photo shoot will be at your restaurant, and we will ask you questions about the cuisine and beverages you sell, the history of your restaurant and how you have grown since the restaurant was established. Following this, we will take some photos of your waiters working and interacting with the customers.

Please contact me if you have any questions. Looking forward to seeing you all on Monday!

The Courier-Mail Photography Group

Stylish Aussie Restaurant

by Darren Allaway

When you dine out at Trang's Restaurant on any day of the week for lunch or dinner, you'll receive not only a warm welcome, and experience warm customer service, but also be able to enjoy exquisite local Australian food that will bring water to your mouth.

Established more than one year ago, the restaurant has grown into one of the most bustling and profitable restaurants on the West End. The menu features scrumptious kangaroo pie, organic salads, one-of-a-kind cranberry ice cream, and other delicious local Aussie food. The head chef, Andy Watson, comments, "We only choose native ingredients that can transform average Australian food into gourmet cuisine. We use the freshest ingredients from the countryside, including native herbs, berries, and spices to produce a truly Australian taste. We also offer a wide variety of wines to drink with your meals."

On a recent Monday afternoon, James Peters, a visitor from Ireland, was enjoying the food there. He stated, "This is truly the freshest and most unique tasting food I have ever tried in Australia. They sure put their heart into making fine gourmet dishes."

Trang's Restaurant is located on 143 Eagle Street, Eagle Street Pier, Brisbane, and is open seven days a week, from 11:00 a.m. – 9:00 p.m. The interior is decorated with Australian aboriginal art, and pictures of local scenery and wildlife. The staff are super hospitable and the delicious food can be bought at a reasonable price. Reservations are only needed for big events like parties.

TEST 02
PART 7

196-200 題參考以下通知、電子郵件和文章。

大家注意！
星期一下午有記者採訪

我們有令人興奮的消息發布給所有員工，《信使郵報》將在一篇文章中對我們的餐廳做特別報導，討論布里斯本市中心最好的餐館！公司經理已經和我聯繫，安排記者於 12 月 12 日星期一中午 12 點前來採訪工作人員。採訪之後，攝影師也將在那裡為我們的餐廳拍照。活動期間大約有 40 分鐘到 1 個小時。

因為這將是增加我們的利潤和在當地社區曝光率的大好機會，所以我希望全體員工都能重視這次集會。我們餐廳的所有員工都要出席。

自去年 7 月份開業以來，常客數量幾乎翻了一倍，大家都應該以得到媒體的認可為榮。

收件者：	約瑟夫・貝茲 <jbates@trang.net>
寄件者：	傑西卡・羅伯森 <jrobertson@couriermail.com>
日　　期：	12 月 7 日星期三
主　　旨：	週一採訪之約

親愛的貝茲先生：

上週我們安排了下週一中午 12:00 進行採訪和攝影。由於我們當天的工作時程將會很忙碌，是否可能將時間改為中午 12:20？請務必跟您的工作人員確認這個時間，並於明天早上通知我。正如上次討論的那樣，採訪和拍照會在您的餐廳內進行，我們會問您有關你們銷售的菜餚和飲料、餐廳的歷史，以及自餐廳開業以來你們的成長情況。在此之後，我們會拍攝你們的服務生工作時，以及與顧客互動時的照片。

如果您有任何疑問，請與我聯絡。

期待週一見到你們！

《信使郵報》攝影組

時尚的澳洲餐廳

文：戴倫・艾樂威（作家）

當您在一週中任何一天的午餐或晚餐時間在 Trang 餐廳用餐時，您都會受到親切的歡迎和熱情的顧客服務，並且能夠享受精緻的澳洲當地食物，這將讓你垂涎三尺。

一年多前成立的這家餐廳已經發展成為西區最繁華、最賺錢的餐廳之一。菜單特色是美味袋鼠派、有機沙拉、獨一無二的蔓越莓冰淇淋和其他美味的澳洲當地食品。主廚安迪・華生評論說：「我們只選擇能夠將一般澳洲食物轉化為珍饈的當地食材。我們使用來自農村的最新鮮食材，包含本地香草、漿果和香辛料相結合，產生真正的澳洲風味。我們還提供各式各樣的美酒伴你用餐。」

在最近的一個週一下午，來自愛爾蘭的訪客詹姆士・彼得斯正在那裡享用美食。他表示：「這是我在澳洲嚐過的最新鮮、最獨特的美味食物，他們肯定全心投入打造美食。」

Trang 餐廳位於布里斯本鷹街碼頭的鷹街 143 號，每週七天都營業，從上午 11:00 至下午 9:00。室內裝飾著澳洲的原住民藝術品，以及當地風景與野生動物的照片。工作人員非常殷勤，而且美味的食物價格合理。只有像派對這樣的大型活動才需要預訂。

---

196. In the article, the word "exquisite" in paragraph 1, line 3, is closest in meaning to

(A) delicate
(B) meticulous
(C) flawed
(D) unrefined

文章中，第一段第三行的 exquisite 意義最接近以下何者？

(A) 精緻的
(B) 一絲不苟的
(C) 有缺陷的
(D) 未精製的；未精煉的

197. What is indicated about the interview?

(A) The chefs will be asked secrets about how they make the food so delicious.
(B) Mr. Bates will be asked questions about what food and drinks he sells.
(C) The manager will talk about the history of Australian cuisine in Brisbane.
(D) Photographs will be taken of the chefs interacting with diners.

這裡指出關於採訪的什麼內容？

(A) 廚師將被問及他們如何讓食物如此美味的秘訣。
(B) 貝茲先生將被問及他銷售什麼食品和飲料。
(C) 經理將在布里斯本談論澳洲美食的歷史。
(D) 廚師與用餐者互動會被拍成照片。

198. What time will the photo shoot finish?

(A) Around 12:00 p.m.
(B) About 10:20 a.m.
(C) Before 1:30 p.m.
(D) About 12:50 a.m.

照片拍攝將在什麼時候結束？

(A) 中午 12:00 左右
(B) 大約上午 10:20
(C) 下午 1:30 前
(D) 上午 12:50 左右

TEST 02
PART 7

199. What is NOT true about Trang's Restaurant?

(A) It is open from 11:00 a.m. to 9:00 p.m.
(B) Its interior decoration includes native American paintings and local scenery.
(C) It's located on Eagle Street in Brisbane.
(D) It serves a large variety of wines to enjoy while eating.

關於 Trang 餐廳，哪項是錯的？

(A) 從早上11:00開始營業到晚上9點。
(B) 室內裝飾包括美國原住民的繪畫和當地的風景。
(C) 它位於布里斯本的鷹街。
(D) 在用餐時可以品嚐到各式各樣的葡萄酒。

200. What does James Peters mention about the restaurant's cuisine?

(A) It is impressive how fresh and unique the food tastes.
(B) He read an introduction to the food in a magazine.
(C) He thought the price of food wasn't reasonable.
(D) He wants to visit the restaurant again.

關於該餐廳的美食，詹姆士・彼得斯提到什麼？

(A) 令人印象深刻的是，食物吃起來多麼新鮮與獨特。
(B) 他在雜誌上看到了食物的介紹。
(C) 他認為食物的價格不合理。
(D) 他想再度造訪該餐廳。

單字

journalist 新聞記者
exposure 曝光；宣傳
photo shoot 照片拍攝
cranberry 蔓越莓
ingredient 成分；原料；食材
herb 香草，藥草
hospitable 好客的；熱情招待的
subsequent 隨後的
community 社區
cuisine 菜肴
Aussie 澳洲的
gourmet 美食家；美味的
decorate 裝飾
session 活動期間
frequent 經常的，慣常的
scrumptious 美味的
native 當地特有的
countryside 鄉村
aboriginal 最早就有的；原始的

TEST 01 解答表

LISTENING SECTION

	題號	答案		題號	答案
PART 1	1	(B)		51	(A)
	2	(C)		52	(B)
	3	(D)		53	(D)
	4	(D)		54	(C)
	5	(B)		55	(A)
	6	(C)		56	(B)
PART 2	7	(A)		57	(A)
	8	(A)		58	(C)
	9	(B)		59	(A)
	10	(B)		60	(C)
	11	(B)		61	(A)
	12	(A)		62	(B)
	13	(A)		63	(A)
	14	(A)		64	(C)
	15	(B)		65	(D)
	16	(A)		66	(A)
	17	(A)		67	(A)
	18	(B)		68	(D)
	19	(B)		69	(A)
	20	(A)		70	(D)
	21	(A)	PART 4	71	(B)
	22	(C)		72	(C)
	23	(A)		73	(C)
	24	(A)		74	(A)
	25	(A)		75	(B)
	26	(A)		76	(A)
	27	(B)		77	(C)
	28	(C)		78	(B)
	29	(C)		79	(D)
	30	(A)		80	(D)
	31	(B)		81	(C)
PART 3	32	(A)		82	(D)
	33	(A)		83	(C)
	34	(A)		84	(C)
	35	(D)		85	(B)
	36	(A)		86	(C)
	37	(A)		87	(A)
	38	(B)		88	(D)
	39	(D)		89	(B)
	40	(A)		90	(A)
	41	(B)		91	(A)
	42	(A)		92	(D)
	43	(B)		93	(B)
	44	(B)		94	(A)
	45	(D)		95	(C)
	46	(A)		96	(D)
	47	(A)		97	(D)
	48	(B)		98	(A)
	49	(B)		99	(C)
	50	(B)		100	(B)

READING SECTION

	題號	答案		題號	答案
PART 5	101	(B)		151	(C)
	102	(A)		152	(B)
	103	(C)		153	(C)
	104	(A)		154	(A)
	105	(A)		155	(A)
	106	(D)		156	(A)
	107	(B)		157	(B)
	108	(D)		158	(C)
	109	(B)		159	(A)
	110	(B)		160	(A)
	111	(C)		161	(B)
	112	(A)		162	(A)
	113	(D)		163	(D)
	114	(C)		164	(D)
	115	(D)		165	(C)
	116	(C)		166	(D)
	117	(A)		167	(C)
	118	(B)		168	(A)
	119	(A)		169	(B)
	120	(C)		170	(C)
	121	(B)		171	(A)
	122	(C)		172	(C)
	123	(D)		173	(A)
	124	(A)		174	(A)
	125	(B)		175	(A)
	126	(A)		176	(A)
	127	(A)		177	(D)
	128	(B)		178	(B)
	129	(B)		179	(C)
	130	(D)		180	(B)
PART 6	131	(D)		181	(C)
	132	(B)		182	(B)
	133	(A)		183	(D)
	134	(C)		184	(D)
	135	(C)		185	(C)
	136	(A)		186	(A)
	137	(D)		187	(C)
	138	(C)		188	(D)
	139	(D)		189	(C)
	140	(C)		190	(C)
	141	(A)		191	(D)
	142	(B)		192	(B)
	143	(B)		193	(A)
	144	(A)		194	(B)
	145	(B)		195	(A)
	146	(D)		196	(B)
PART 7	147	(B)		197	(D)
	148	(C)		198	(A)
	149	(C)		199	(A)
	150	(B)		200	(D)

TEST 02 解答表

LISTENING SECTION

	題號	答案		題號	答案
PART 1	1	(D)		51	(D)
	2	(B)		52	(A)
	3	(A)		53	(C)
	4	(D)		54	(C)
	5	(B)		55	(D)
	6	(A)		56	(C)
PART 2	7	(C)		57	(B)
	8	(A)		58	(D)
	9	(B)		59	(C)
	10	(A)		60	(B)
	11	(A)		61	(B)
	12	(A)		62	(B)
	13	(A)		63	(D)
	14	(A)		64	(A)
	15	(A)		65	(C)
	16	(B)		66	(A)
	17	(B)		67	(A)
	18	(B)		68	(A)
	19	(A)		69	(C)
	20	(B)		70	(A)
	21	(C)	PART 4	71	(A)
	22	(C)		72	(A)
	23	(C)		73	(A)
	24	(A)		74	(A)
	25	(B)		75	(C)
	26	(A)		76	(D)
	27	(A)		77	(D)
	28	(C)		78	(A)
	29	(A)		79	(B)
	30	(C)		80	(B)
	31	(B)		81	(C)
PART 3	32	(A)		82	(A)
	33	(A)		83	(A)
	34	(D)		84	(A)
	35	(D)		85	(C)
	36	(B)		86	(A)
	37	(A)		87	(D)
	38	(D)		88	(C)
	39	(B)		89	(B)
	40	(A)		90	(B)
	41	(D)		91	(D)
	42	(C)		92	(D)
	43	(A)		93	(B)
	44	(A)		94	(A)
	45	(C)		95	(D)
	46	(C)		96	(A)
	47	(A)		97	(B)
	48	(A)		98	(A)
	49	(D)		99	(C)
	50	(A)		100	(C)

READING SECTION

	題號	答案		題號	答案
PART 5	101	(D)		151	(C)
	102	(D)		152	(B)
	103	(A)		153	(B)
	104	(D)		154	(B)
	105	(C)		155	(B)
	106	(B)		156	(C)
	107	(D)		157	(A)
	108	(C)		158	(A)
	109	(A)		159	(C)
	110	(A)		160	(C)
	111	(A)		161	(A)
	112	(B)		162	(C)
	113	(D)		163	(C)
	114	(C)		164	(D)
	115	(A)		165	(D)
	116	(C)		166	(B)
	117	(B)		167	(A)
	118	(A)		168	(C)
	119	(A)		169	(C)
	120	(C)		170	(A)
	121	(B)		171	(D)
	122	(C)		172	(D)
	123	(B)		173	(A)
	124	(B)		174	(D)
	125	(C)		175	(C)
	126	(B)		176	(B)
	127	(A)		177	(B)
	128	(C)		178	(C)
	129	(B)		179	(C)
	130	(C)		180	(D)
PART 6	131	(B)		181	(B)
	132	(D)		182	(D)
	133	(C)		183	(A)
	134	(A)		184	(C)
	135	(C)		185	(C)
	136	(A)		186	(B)
	137	(D)		187	(A)
	138	(B)		188	(A)
	139	(A)		189	(A)
	140	(D)		190	(D)
	141	(C)		191	(C)
	142	(A)		192	(B)
	143	(B)		193	(C)
	144	(B)		194	(A)
	145	(A)		195	(D)
	146	(C)		196	(A)
PART 7	147	(C)		197	(B)
	148	(D)		198	(C)
	149	(D)		199	(B)
	150	(A)		200	(A)

分數預測表

聽力測驗 原始分數	預測分數	閱讀測驗 原始分數	預測分數
96-100	485-495	96-100	455-495
91-95	445-495	91-95	410-490
86-90	400-475	86-90	380-455
81-85	360-450	81-85	350-430
76-80	330-420	76-80	315-405
71-75	300-385	71-75	290-380
66-70	265-355	66-70	260-355
61-65	235-330	61-65	235-325
56-60	210-305	56-60	205-300
51-55	185-275	51-55	175-270
46-50	165-250	46-50	155-235
41-45	140-225	41-45	125-205
36-40	115-195	36-40	105-170
31-35	95-165	31-35	85-140
26-30	80-135	26-30	65-115
21-25	65-110	21-25	55-90
16-20	35-90	16-20	45-75
11-15	10-70	11-15	30-55
6-10	5-60	6-10	10-45
1-5	5-50	1-5	5-30
0	5-35	0	5-15

換算方式

1. 確認聽力及閱讀測驗的原始分數（答對一題為一分）
2. 找出對應的預測分數範圍
3. 將聽力及閱讀測驗的預測分數範圍加總後即為預測總分範圍

範例

聽力測驗分數 63，預測分數範圍為 235-330

閱讀測驗分數 72，預測分數範圍為 290-380

加總後，預測總分範圍為 525-710 之間

TEST 01 模擬測驗 答案卡

TEST 02 模擬測驗 答案卡